Table Of Con

CW01499796

Last Executions Aroun~ ~~~~~~ ~~~ Ireland
(1800-1964)

1) William Brown (1856) – Last Public Execution at Leicester
2) David Jennings (1941) – Last Execution at Dorchester
3) Sarah Thomas (1849) – Last Public Execution at Bristol
4) Robert Smith (1868) – Last Public Execution in SCOTLAND
5) Mary Timney (1862) – Last Public Execution of a Woman in SCOTLAND
6) Thomas Rawcliffe (1910) – Last Execution at Lancaster
7) Oliver Butler (1952) – Last Execution at Oxford
8) Edward Palmer (1903) – Last Execution at Devizes

9) Henry Carey & William Pickett (1859) – Last Public Execution at Lincoln

10) Francis Hynes (1882) – Last Execution at Limerick – IRELAND

11) William Charlton (1862) - Last Public Execution at Carlisle

12) William Haywood (1903) – Last Execution at Hereford

13) Joseph le Brun (1875) – Last Public Execution in the British Isles

14) William Slack (1907) – Last Execution at Derby

15)/16) Edwin Preedy and Charles Fooks (1863) – Last Public Execution at Dorchester

17) William Hampton (1909) – Last Execution at Bodmin

18) Philip Murray (1923) – Last Execution at Calton, Edinburgh – SCOTLAND

19) Djang Djing Sung (1919) – Last Execution at Worcester

20) *William Stevens (1864) – Last Public Execution at Aylesbury*

21) *James Kirk & Patrick McCooey (1852) – Last Execution at Dundalk, IRELAND*

22) *Frederick Southgate (1924) – Last Execution at Ipswich*

23) *John Eayrs (1914) – Last Execution at Northampton*

24) *John Ducker (1863) – Last Public Execution at Ipswich*

25) *William Collier (1866) – Last Public Execution at Stafford*

26) *George Reynolds (1928) – Last Execution at Duke Street, Glasgow, SCOTLAND*

27) *Thomas Keeley (1902) – Last Execution at Galway, IRELAND*

28) *John Logue (1866) – Last Public Execution in IRELAND*

29) *John Tapner (1854) – Last Execution on Guernsey*

Cover - Peter Allen & Gwynne Evans

Case 1
"The Hanging
Of
Peppermint Billy"

~The Toll-Gate Horror ~

William BROWN (33)
Murders
Of
Edward (79) and James Woodcock (10)

[1856]

"Ah! It's a nice place ain't it!" I should like to lie under the trees!" -
The night before his execution, Peppermint Billy, was shown his
grave by the prison authorities, hoping that he would make a final
confession ….

***Diabolically fiendish double murder of an old man and
his 10-year-old grandson, at a remote toll-gate near the
Leicestershire town of Melton Mowbray, in the Summer
of 1856, in the dead of the night ….***

By the Summer of

1856, **E**dward Woodcock, was 79-years-old: up until the late
1840s, he had spent his whole life in and around Leicester, and the
town of Melton Mowbray, working as a farm labourer: Eventually,
he was too old to do manual work, and he moved to the small village
of Thorpe Arnold on the main Leicester to Grantham Road, situated
on the top of a hill just 1/2 a mile or so to the north-east of the town
of Melton, where he was employed at the local toll-gate, where he
lived in *Toll Bar Gate House* …. The job was ideal as his own son's
family also lived in the village – indeed just a few hundred yards
away …. Although the job could involve anti-social hours – the gate
had to be opened whenever someone came to it, regardless of the
time – Mr Woodcock enjoyed his job as it gave him all the time to
see his family …. Now a widow, he also enjoyed his own company;
however, he was often accompanied by his 'assistant' - his **10-year-
old grandson James** …. Initially, James would spend the days at the
toll-gate, but the family felt what with Mr Woodcock's advanced age,
it might be a good idea, for the grandson to stay the odd night with
his grand-dad too …. However, young James didn't want to stay ….
each night, when he'd said he would stay, right at the last moment,
he would run home – *Toll Bar Gate House* was just too isolated and
eerie …. Then on the night of **Wednesday, June 18th, 1856**, James
said he would definitely stay – Mr Woodcock thought he would bolt
when it became dark; but this time he didn't ….

Once there, young James, became quiet excited that some midnight stranger would raise the familiar sound of 'Gate' …. And indeed such a shout did come – although it was at about two-thirty am **(Thursday, June 19th)** …. it was a voice that Mr Woodcock recognised – the same man had come through two days earlier …. In his night-shirt, the old man opened his front-door and waited for the standard penny payment …. But Mr Woodcock received something far more than that – he was shot through the rib with fire from a pistol – the shot shattered his rib and went through his right lung: a shot heard by a number of local villagers …. despite his injuries, Mr Woodcock, was able to grapple with his assailant - a youngish man in his early thirties …. the two men fell backwards into the house, where the attacker launched into a savage assault with a knife repeatedly stabbing the toll-keeper in the chest and throat: he was stabbed nearly a dozen times …. Eventually, the armed and much younger man overcame, Mr Woodcock, who was left dying on the floor …. During the assault, the attacker realised that the old man was not alone in his house …. Young James had remained in his room frightened half to death under the bed-clothes; but the house was quite small, and so the assailant must have heard the young boy moving around …. The young man quickly found James Woodcock – what he did next was to make the case headline news throughout the country …. he seized the little boy – stabbed him in the groin, ripped open his stomach with his knife; and then to make absolutely sure he had killed him …. he slit his throat …. Then silence once again descended on the toll-gate ….

At 3.40 am the routine of the village began – it was beginning to become light – and the local milkman-cum-baker, Alfred Routen, came to the gate on his horse-and-cart …. Like everyone else he called out – there was no reply – this was most unusual, as Mr Woodcock was usually most reliable – Mr Routen called out again …. nothing …. With the gate closed, and with other people wanting to come through soon too, the milkman went in search of the toll-keeper …. Mr Routen pushed at the front door, and very quickly saw the corpse of Edward Woodcock …. He had no reason to think that the grandson was in the house, and so quickly left and ran into the village to raise the alarm at the village police-station, where he roused the local bobby, Constable John Clayton …. Along with the officer, a group of local men made their way to the toll-gate, where they quickly found the corpse of the little boy .... By mid-morning, Superintendent William Condon, had arrived from Leicester to take charge of the case – he was completely au fait with the toll-gate as he was from Melton Mowbray himself, and his family still lived in the town .... What struck the officer and the town was the violence used .... although robbery may have been the motive, nothing was stolen, and by the mid 1850's toll-gates were going out of fashion, as local authorities began financing and looking after the road network themselves: two sixpences were found in Mr Woodcock's pockets; and a watch was found at the head of the little boy's bed .... and, indeed, why kill the little boy ? Superintendent Condon believed Mr Woodcock knew his killer ....

By lunch-time in Melton, a number of locals had approached the police – they believed they knew who might be responsible – indeed, it was a man that Superintendent Condon also knew of .... it was a man in his early thirties, who everyone in Melton called ***Peppermint Billy***: **33-year-old William Brown,** a tall and slim man – nominally a farm labourer – he had just returned to the area and, most of the time, he didn't seem to work ..... He was so named as his dad made peppermint sweets: He was known to the police, as in January 1843, he had been given a 10-year sentence in Leicester for theft – he had stolen a number of spoons: but was also a 'habitual criminal': he had many convictions for theft and was also a suspected arsonist .... he had been transported to Tasmania in the following April – he had served his sentence, and had stayed on in the colony before returning to Melton Mowbray in May .... Locals had seen Brown in and around Melton and Thorpe, and one witness said that Brown had told him that Mr Woodcock had refused to fetch him a glass of water; whilst another had asked whether the old man lived *alone* .... One of the witnesses said the man kept blinking – and as well as the name *Peppermint*, Brown was also known as *Blinking Billy* .... This was enough for the police, and a manhunt began in earnest ....

William Brown had headed north .... by two pm, he had arrived in Nottingham: here he boarded the train for Leeds .... The next day he was in Wetherby, by which time the whole of Britain was aware of the terrible events in Melton .... With the information that Brown had boarded the train for Leeds, the police forces in Yorkshire were issued with a description and line-drawing of the suspect, which by the standards of the day, was extremely detailed [*See Picture*] …. However having fled to Yorkshire, William Brown, then did his best to court detection …. on the following Sunday, he went into a Methodist Chapel in Wetherby, and caused a disturbance – he refused to remove his hat, and refused to sit down …. after disrupting the service, he followed the congregation into a local pub, where he carried on his performance …. He became such a nuisance, that the landlord of the pub, James Mason, began asking the trouble-maker some questions …. He clearly wasn't from Wetherby or Yorkshire – he seemed to have a strange mixture of an accent …. As soon as Brown began speaking, Mr Mason, was suspicious of him …. the man also looked incredibly like the line-drawing of Brown, that was in all the papers that weekend, including the *Leeds Mercury* …. Mr Mason could see that the murders had taken place in Leicestershire, and he thought that the man sounded a bit like he had come from that area …. The landlord discretely had the police called …. William Brown seemed completely oblivious to what was happening – he may, by now, also have been under the influence of drink …. he calmly drank up and left the pub …. as he did so, one of the local officers, Constable William Eccles, arrived ….

William Brown left the pub and wandered off for a few hundred yards – then he stopped, and began talking to some local children …. When he saw Constable Eccles approaching, he didn't realise he was going to be arrested, although when told about why he was being detained, he claimed to be 'William Parker' from Bedford – a servant who had never left England: he said he had slept rough in Nottingham the night before, and that the clothes he had been wearing, he had bought off a tramp for a shilling …. The next day he was put on the train to Melton with a large detachment of police …. When the train pulled into the town's railway-station a large mob awaited William Brown – the overwhelming number of policemen were able to keep the crowds at bay – all they could do was boo and hiss and shake their fists ….

On Monday, July 14th, William Brown, appeared at the Leicester Assizes before the Lord Chief Justice, Sir John Jervis, in a day-

long trial .... Brown smirked as he pleaded 'not guilty' - he had told fellow prisoners and prison-officers, that he would be acquitted - how could it possibly be proved that he was the killer ...?

In the toll-gate house, the police found two important items – one was a fired pistol: it was a large bore weapon .... the other, was what was called a 'tobacco stopper' - an instrument for pressing down the tobacco in a pipe .... the police felt it could be shown that the pistol was the murder weapon – it fired two-ounce balls .... the one fired at Mr Woodcock was found near the body, and was the correct ball size .... A gun-expert said the pistol was very rare in England, and was far more common in the Colonies .... the guns were made here, but were often used in places like Australia as horse-pistols; often used by bush-rangers .... the 'tobacco stopper' was far more common and a local watch-maker in Melton, said he had seen Brown pull one out amongst some loose change, whilst in his shop, three days before the murders .... It was vital to show that Brown was in possession of this murder weapon .... the gun; indeed, the knife had never been found ....

After Brown had returned home, he paid a visit to a brother – John .... There was bad blood between them, as they had both fancied the same girl – Anne, who had eventually married John, when Brown was sent to Tasmania .... As soon as Brown saw Anne again, John, thought they were having an affair .... For several days Brown and Anne disappeared and gossip was rife in their home village of Scalford some 4 miles to the north of Melton .... When they did return to the village, Brown, brandished and threatened his brother with a pistol, which Brown explained was of a rare type not seen in England: John also claimed that Brown had threatened him with a large knife .... In court, John Brown, said that the pistol found in the toll-house, looked the same as the one he had seen .... But given the relatively primitive state of forensic evidence, including, of course, the inability to use finger-prints, it could not be definitively proved, it was the same gun .... furthermore, no other witnesses had ever seen Brown with a gun, including Anne .... Despite using a knife on two victims, including cutting the throat of the little boy, there was no blood on any of Brown's clothing, when he was *arrested* .... However, the police believed they could show that Brown, had changed his clothes …. On June 21st, in a ditch some three miles on the road to the nearby village of Hose, was found: a black silk handkerchief, a striped waist-coat, a shirt, corduroy trousers and a black hat …. they were all cut, torn and wet, as if an attempt had been made to clean them …. crucially in the lining of the trousers were bloodstains …. John Brown told police that he had lent the trousers to his brother; Anne said the shirt was her husband's …. Furthermore, witnesses said that Brown had been making inquiries about Mr Woodcock, and the toll-gate, and they all described his clothes, as those that had been found in the ditch …. However, when arrested, Brown, had been wearing dark blue trousers and a straw-hat; clothes he had been seen in before the murders wearing in Leicester – the inference being that he must have taken these clothes with him on the night of the murder, presumably hiding them away from the toll-house in the ditch, to change afterwards ….

It seems Brown was right in thinking that he would be acquitted – during Sir John's final submission to the jury, he said that the pistol, and the tobacco stopper could not conclusively be linked to the accused …. it could be proved that Brown had been *near* the toll-house – indeed, he must have known about it, and he probably knew Mr Woodcock by sight, and probably from the past too …. as to motive, Sir John, asked the jury, would a refusal of water lead to such a crime …? But do guilty men leave their villages and make for Leeds? As to the gun - it was so uncommon, surely it was inconceivable, that John Brown, could make-up its description, unless he had actually seen it …. ? But then, the judge had said, that the evidence of the clothing was clear: *it was damming evidence against the prisoner* …. The jury did not even leave their box – they found William Brown guilty of murder …. Sir John said, given the nature of the crime, there could be no question of mercy, in his opinion …. before he was sentenced to hang, William Brown, said he was as 'innocent as a child' ….

William Brown's execution was set for just 11 days time – **Friday, July 25th, outside Leicester Prison at eight am** …. Although Brown paid no attention to the official religious help offered, it was noted that eventually he did pray *privately* …. However, what disturbed the authorities was that he continued to maintain his complete innocence …. To force the issue, Brown – on the day before the hanging – was shown his grave …! All he said was: "Ah! It's a nice place ain't it!" I should like to lie under the trees!" Some of Brown's relatives, including his dad, came to visit him in the death-cell; and he asked that his father should come and see him 'turned off' …. The next day, Mr Brown, did indeed gain himself a perfect view of the execution – in front of the local pub, the *Turk's Head* , which looked across to the prison - he was there four hours before the execution, drinking beer, and engaging in conversation with many people …. Having slept well and eaten a full English breakfast, William Brown, had also told the authorities, that he intended to address the crowds – estimated to be some 25,000 – for at least an hour …! The Prison-Governor told Brown he could speak for a few minutes, but that he could say, whatever he liked …. Out of such a vast crowd, William Brown, recognised his dad, by the white handkerchief that he was waving …. On the drop, whilst Brown, did bow to the crowd, his courage failed him, and he could not speak …. This silence was the sign for the **hangman, William Calcraft**, to step forward …. however, Brown, did not die immediately – he 'died hard': his body could be seen struggling at the end of the rope for several minutes …. However his dad shouted out: "Well done Billy. Tha's died a brick."

There had been a concerted attempt by the *Society of Friends* – or as they are better known – the *Quakers*, to save William Brown from the gallows …. Apart from their unconditional opposition to the death penalty per se, they believed that Brown was insane …. Apart from being known as '*Peppermint*' and '*Blinking*', he was also called '*Silly Billy*' in his village and around …. Furthermore, since he had been tried, it was now revealed that Brown's original 10-year sentence in Tasmania, had actually been reduced to one of six; and all them had been served in the *New Norfolk Lunatic Asylum* in Hobart, under the care of a Dr John Meyer …. Quite by chance, the doctor, was now on leave in England …. However, despite this, the **Home Secretary, Sir George Grey**, declined to see him on the grounds that the defence of insanity had not been raised at the trial, and furthermore, he had been examined by the Prison Medical Officer in Leicester Prison, and deemed to be sane …. Brown himself said that he was sent to the asylum, as the Prison-Governor in Hobart, did not like the fact that his daughter, appeared to like Brown – Brown claimed they were in love …. Brown said in Hobart, he was allowed out of the asylum to preach and was a Methodist …. He said he would rather be executed than returned to Australia under a life-sentence, which would mean around 20-years confinement ….

It was in the death-cell, that the motive for the murder of Mr Woodcock came out …. whilst on the boat back to England, Brown, swore revenge on the witnesses, who had given evidence against him in 1843 …. He said he would either use a pistol or knife …. However, Mr Woodcock, was not one of the witnesses …. and Brown knew this – the motive was …. robbery …. Brown now admitted, that whilst he did not take any of the toll money, he did take some money off Mr Woodcock ….

The last execution at Leicester Prison was in 1953 ….

Case 2
"A Question of Malice"

David Jennings
(1941)
Murder
of
Albert Farley

In 1941 a young soldier, drunk and heartbroken that his girlfriend had left him, broke into the NAAFI canteen in Dorchester to rob the safe. He failed, fled, but turned when he heard someone. He fired his rifle and an elderly man died. At his trial the concept of intent came under intense scrutiny. What did the young man intend when he fired the rifle – Was it murder, manslaughter or an accident?

Albert Farley (65) was a married man who also owned a grocer's shop in the Grove in the county town of Dorset, Dorchester. He was very much part of Dorchester life, having been the secretary of a local skittles club and was well known for his charity work, as well as serving in the trenches in the Great War. In 1941 he had just opened his own shop having worked for a clothes factory for the last 20 years. If that wasn't enough he was also doing his war duty at the local NAAFI stores as a fire-watcher in Princess Street.

Such was Mr Farley's love of working that he broadened out his work at the NAAFI stores to become the caretaker. On the night of **January 26th, 1941** he finished his job at the NAAFI's canteen at about ten-thirty p.m. to begin his fire-watching duty.

For the next hour or so the girls in the canteen cleaned up and the last of of them, Mrs Warren, left at just after 11.30. Albert Farley was in his usual good spirits and said he would see Mrs Warren tomorrow night. Tragically the two were never to see each other again.

Although **David Jennings** was a man who was also doing his duty, there the similarity with Albert Farley ended. Jennings had joined the army in December 1938 at 17. He was just 20 years old and on the night of the January 26th, 1941 in contrast to Mr Farley he had spent the evening drinking in the local pubs. That night Miller drank a lot and was later to be described as "merry" at just after 10.30 p.m.

Jennings was regarded by his army mates as a good soldier and heavy drinking was not seen as that unusual - and in this case Jennings was deliberately trying to get drunk, because his girlfriend had just left him. However his friends were surprised when he left their hut taking a rifle and ammunition. At first the other soldiers thought Jennings was going to play a foolish prank. However when Jennings tried to leave his hut one soldier tried to stop him, only to be threatened. As Jennings slammed the door behind him he said his was going "to make a break".

The barracks in Dorchester were only a short distance from the NAAFI canteen, which included a social club, and shortly before midnight the owner of a garage, Mr Jesse Broughton, heard several short thuds, which woke him up. Mr Broughton thought it was an army vehicle that had backfired, and they were repeated a few seconds later. Several minutes later David Jennings returned to his hut, his face bleeding profusely.

Now quite sober from shock, Jennings, blurted out that he tried to break into the NAAFI canteen and thought he had shot and killed a man. The police were called immediately and Jennings taken to

Dorchester police station by Sergeant Lill. At the NAAFI canteen the police with Corporal Leith gained entry into the canteen easily, although once inside they fell over a body in the darkness.

They found that Mr Farley had been shot by the entrance and that robbery did appear to be the motive. Mrs Warren said that about two pounds had been in the canteen cash-box when she left, but the police only found two shillings. Plus the in the social-club office, the safe had been dented by bullets.

The dramatic events had quickly cleared Jennings' head and he explained to the police that he fired the rifle ten times in all. He said, firstly he had fired six shots to break the lock on the canteen door. Then once inside he said he had shot three more times at the canteen safe. Jennings then said he heard someone approach and started to run away along Princes Street. He sensed someone appearing out of the canteen in the half-light and turned and fired instinctively. He explained the cuts on his face by saying one of his shots in the canteen office had caused metal to fly of the safe and which had cut his face.

Mr Farley had been killed instantaneously. The old man had been hit by a shot just under his heart: the bullet was from a .303 service rifle. Although Jennings told the police that he wasn't sure if he had shot Mr Farley, Private Joe Riley, a soldier at the hut, said Jennings told him: " I have broken into the NAAFI and I have shot a civvy bloke. " Furthermore Corporal Leith told the police of Jennings' indifference when he said that Jennings had told him: " If I go to prison, it will come in handy for cigarettes for me."

On examining the NAAFI canteen the police soon realised that Jennings attempt at breaking into the safe had been somewhat wild, since one of his shots had cut through a gas pipe. Also Jennings had made so much noise that it was unlikely that he would have got away with any money even if he had broken into the safe, because he had woken up the street. With an air of despair he told the police: " To tell you the truth, I'm broke, I'm short of money."

David Jennings had worked as a farm labourer and miner before he joined up at 17. He was from Warrington in Cheshire and on the night of January 26th he had was trying to drown his sorrows having received a letter from his girlfriend that she no longer wanted to see him. He said that at the *George Hotel* he had drunk five whiskey and beers mixed before going on to the *Antelope* and *Ship* before returning to the *Antelope*. He said he had tried to sober up at a milk bar with a pie and a cup of tea.

Jennings said that back at the hut he decided to rob the NAAFI canteen but that he no real idea why he put his running shoes on, and he denied it was so that he couldn't be heard running away. He said he went to where the arms were kept and took a clip of ammunition. Jennings seemed genuinely unconcerned about his fate and was struck dumb when he was charged with murder. He protested that he had no intention of killing Albert Farley and had only shot at the old man when he sensed he was there. Nevertheless on February 20th, 1941 the town's magistrates committed him for trial at the county assizes, which since Dorchester was a county town, would be held in the town. At the beginning of June David Jennings, who had turned 21, appeared before **Mr Justice Charles.**

The crux of the case for the prosecution was the fact that Jennings had committed murder because he intended to fire the gun, and this was embodied in his statement to the police. However of course Jennings used the meaning of intent in quite a different sense to the legal definition of the word.

For the Crown **Mr John Scott-Henderson, K.C.,** questioned Jennings in the box about his statement. Jennings admitted he had returned to the barracks and changed into a pair of soft running shoes, although he denied this was to approach the canteen without being heard, and was simply because he was fed up of wearing his heavy army boots. Jennings explained that he knew the NAAFI canteen well as he often went there and because it was so small he knew the location of the safe and the small cash-box.

Mr Scott-Henderson said that to prove murder the Crown had only to show that Jennings had fired the intentionally at Mr Farley or fired the gun intentionally to further his aim of robbing the canteen safe. Mr Scott-Henderson said it was irrelevant that Jennings may have genuinely wished no harm to come to Mr Farley. He said the fundamental was whether Jennings had pulled the trigger other than by a complete accident. Turning to the jury he said that first nine shots were clearly deliberate and intentional to further the robbery, so what was different about tenth that killed Mr Farley- surely Jennings couldn't claim it was a pure accident?

Jennings told the court that he was in a highly disturbed state when he broke into canteen and he said he fired at Mr Farley when he saw a shaft of moonlight. However Jennings admitted to the judge that he knew someone was there because he had heard a shout.

Naturally in such cases where a man's life depended on an interpretation of words, much was made of Jennings reaction when he returned to the barracks. Corporal Leith and Private Riley told the court that Jennings had said he had shot a man: Jennings told the court he had shot at a man, but implied it had not been intentionally.

For the defence **Mr John Trapnell, KC**, said that it would be perverse to suggest that the jury bring in a verdict less than manslaughter, but he said that Jennings was not guilty of murder because he lack the intent to murder. Mr Trapnell explained that in his opinion Jennings' mind was so clouded with drink that he could not legally form the specific intent to commit murder. He suggested to the jury that Jennings may have gone to the canteen quite determined to commit robbery, once there his efforts were somewhat bizarre. After all who had ever heard of an attempt at safe breaking by firing a rifle at it?

In his finally speech to the jury Mr Trapnell concluded: "Is it not more likely that this stupid half-drunken young soldier merely fired widely to frighten and scare?" Jennings' counsel then made play of the fact that Jennings had been evacuated from Dunkirk and that he joined the army nearly a year before the conflict had begun, such was his devotion to his country. However this last statement bought a rebuke from the judge, who said he was tired of hearing it used to excuse criminal behaviour.

Mr Scott-Henderson, in his closing speech, naturally dismissed Mr Trapnell's argument of drunkenness being a defence to this charge. He reminded the jury that when Jennings had returned to his hut he had said that the victim had "come for him", which rather suggested that Jennings had shot him to prevent himself from being caught and that was a clear cut case of murder.

In his summing up Mr Justice Charles said that regardless from where Jennings had fired the rifle - and Jennings had told the police he had done so from the hip, since he had no intention of killing - it was still murder if the trigger had been pulled on purpose and not by accident.

Mr Charles continued that the jury could not convict Jennings on the evidence of the soldiers at the hut alone, but they could use this evidence in conjunction with all the other evidence, namely the fact that Mr Farley had been shot dead.

On the question of drink, the judge said it was his duty to tell the jury that it was no defence at all to any criminal charge, except where the amount of alcohol effected the mind and therefore the mental state of the accused. Since Jennings had not pleaded insanity it was no defence. Furthermore in this case Jennings appeared to have made the intent to commit robbery and apart from his failure to open the safe had done everything else to further the robbery.

The judge concluded that the only hope of manslaughter verdict for Jennings was if he had shot at the shaft of light not knowing anyone was there: However his own signed statement suggested he knew someone was there and he probably knew it was someone who might try and apprehend him. In his final words he severely rebuked the military authorities for allowing a drunken young man out of his hut and out of the barracks with a rifle and ammunition.

On **June 3rd, 1941** the jury, which included two women, retired for just over two hours, before returning to court. There were gasps in the court, not because they had found Jennings guilty of murder - that much was expected - but that they added *no* recommendation to mercy. During the war juries were apt at being very sympathetic to servicemen, even those who had committed quite dreadful crimes.

As the black cap was placed on Mr Justice Charles' head, Jennings screamed out: " I did not intend to kill that man." Nevertheless the judge said he fully concurred with the jury's verdict and ordered that Jennings be hanged y the neck until he was dead.

On July 7th, the appeal court in London heard Jennings' appeal but quickly ruled that the verdict was quite correct and Jennings was returned to Dorchester Prison to await the hangmen on **July 24th, 1941**.

It had been 28 years since and execution at Dorchester Prison. In 1913 Walter Burton had been hanged for the murder of his mistress in the Dorset village of Gussage St Michael.

There was no execution chamber at Dorchester Prison, so Jennings had to be walked from his death-cell into the courtyard and to the execution shed in one corner. Here he was handed over to the hangmen, Thomas Pierrepoint and Alex Riley, who once they had control, hanged him within 30 seconds. Such was the antiquated system at Dorchester that it proved to be the last execution there.

Although it was Britain's lowest part of the war a massive petition had been organised to save Jennings. It had started in Warrington and had been supported by the army and the West Dorset MP Captain Simon Wingfield-Digby, but it proved to be of no avail. The Home Office took the view that those who were prepared to use firearms to further a robbery must take the consequences, if someone was killed in the course of the robbery. Harsh as it seems they felt society was better protected if Jennings was hanged.

Case 3
"The Mysterious Affair Of The Dog That Didn't Bark"

~The Trenchard Street Murder~

Sarah THOMAS (19)
[1849]
Murder
Of
Miss Elizabeth Jeffries (61)

"You must have thought we were killing each other" - Part of the apology for the sounds that had woken the neighbours during the night – it was blamed on the cat …!

Terrible murder of an old lady in her Bristol city-centre home in the Spring of 1849 – she was beaten to death

with a large stone – she was a woman known to bully a succession of young female servants – her latest being a teenager from the city – had this latest one finally snapped, or was the murder premeditated, in order to burgle the old lady …?

Notes:

1) ST age is variously given between 17 and 21; however both the Home Office and the Trial Assize Record have her as 19 yo ….

It was shortly after five am on the morning of **Saturday, March 3rd, 1849**, when Mrs Isabella Fry was suddenly woken by a number of screams as she slept at her home in Bristol …. moments later her lodger, Mrs Anne Ham, also heard the screams – they were piercing and terrifying …. they had come from the house next door – **number 6, Trenchard Street in Bristol city-centre, in an area that at the time, was known as St Augustine's** …. They were both sure the screams had come from the bedroom of the house's owner, **Miss Elizabeth Jeffries (61)** …. Mrs Ham banged on the wall with her walking-stick, and suddenly the noise stopped: the two ladies wandered what to do next, but that was it – there were no more sounds …. Soon anyway, Bristol city-centre would be alive for business …. the women thought no more of the strange sounds, that they heard just a few hours prior, and anyway, such things were not all that uncommon in the city-centre ….

At around seven am, Mrs Jeffries' latest young servant, **Miss Sarah Thomas (19)**, knocked on Mrs Fry's door …. It was answered by Mrs Ham, who hadn't actually seen the girl before, as old Mrs Jeffries went through so many servant-girls, that it was difficult to keep track of all of them …. If she hadn't come, then the two women would have probably forgotten about the noise during the night: Miss Thomas said she had come to apologise – she said it was the cat, who had suddenly jumped onto Mrs Jeffries' bed: it had frightened the old lady 'half to death'; the girl then added: "You must have thought we were killing each other" .... she was joking .... *of course* .... Reminded of the disturbance, Mrs Ham, said that wasn't the sound of a cat, and then asked if everything was all right .... She, like everyone else in Trenchard Street, knew how difficult Mrs Jeffries could be, adding, that she had heard the servant-girl crying in the back-yard earlier in the evening .... Mrs Ham said she thought the noise was the old lady trying to pull the girl out of bed to start her daily chores .... Sarah said, no that wasn't what had been happening; but then confided in Mrs Ham, that her employer was 'such a good for nothing woman' .... Mrs Ham thought that'll be another one going soon ....

Apart from her latest servant, people rarely visited Mrs Jeffries, and her only apparent living relative - a brother – avoided her like the plague .... However, she did have one close friend – a Mrs Susan Miller – who visited her almost daily, and was due back later in the day .... When Mrs Miller came back, she was surprised to see no-one at home, and the house was locked up, as if the occupants had gone away .... Mrs Miller was quite concerned about her old friend, and began asking the neighbours, if they had seen anything untoward .... no-one thought anything was really amiss. However, one neighbour, who lived directly across the street, said she had seen the servant girl, and a young man leaving the property .... and with a bundle, having come in and out of the house, with a number of items .... As Mrs Miller asked further questions, she was told that the pair had gone into a sweet-shop in nearby Maudlin Lane, and in here was the bundle .... it had been left by the young man and the servant, to be collected later that day ....

Meanwhile, Sarah Thomas, turned up at her parents two-miles to the north in Horfield, now a suburb of Bristol .... She arrived there with some luggage – they assumed she'd left her latest job – they asked no questions .... she went back into the city-centre, and returned at 9.30 pm with the bundle from the sweet-shop .... her parents again asked no questions .... Exhausted, Sarah went to bed – the next day she went through the bundle – it was full of money, jewellery and silver-wear .... still Sarah's parents – George and Ann – asked no questions …. They must have had some idea, she was up to no good – Sarah frequently left her job; and often turned up with goods, presumably stolen, from her latest employer …. Despite her age, Sarah Thomas, was, in effect, a 'professional criminal' ….

Meanwhile, back in the city-centre, Mrs Miller, and some other neighbours in Trenchard Street made contact with Miss Jeffries' brother, Henry, to say that no-one had seen his sister since Friday …. The brother came to the property late on **Wednesday [March 7th]** and immediately called the police – they found his sister's body in her bed …. but something other than nature had been involved …. the old lady's face and head were covered in blood, and her pillow was saturated in blood …. The whole house had been ransacked …. Mr Jeffries was a retired surgeon, and it was obvious to him, and the police-officers, that Elizabeth Jeffries, had been murdered …. By the bed was the apparent murder weapon – it was a large stone weighing four pounds, which was used as a doorstop in the kitchen: it was covered in blood, and had human hairs attached to it: they were grey like that of the victim …. In the outside-toilet in the back-yard, was the body of her dog – strangely no-one had heard it bark during the night; and it had a distinct dislike of strangers …. Soon afterwards a post-mortem was carried by a surgeon, Mr Ralph Bernard, who quickly concluded, that Mrs Jeffries, had been beaten to death with the stone …. She had been struck three viscous blows to the left side of her face; one on the top of her head; and one on the right side of her face; her face was cut and bruised all over, and her left hand was bruised too …. Mrs Jeffries' position in the bed suggested, she had been struck whilst asleep; and then the attack had continued, as she had tried to get out of bed; and she had used her left hand to defend herself …. when Mr Bernard placed the stone into the wounds on the face, it fitted perfectly ….

Sarah Thomas and the young man were the 'obvious' suspects …. no-one seemed to have any idea, who the man was, but the police quickly found out where the servant's parents lived, and soon arrived in Horfield …. It seems that the Thomas family were all also criminals by vocation …. Mrs Thomas denied that their daughter was in: the police pushed passed her …. they searched the small cottage, eventually finding Sarah hiding under the stairs in the coalhole: she was half-naked …. The cottage also turned out to be an Aladdin's cave of stolen goods – there was money, jewellery, foreign coins, and directly linked to the murder case – a gold chain and four shirts each marked with the initial 'E.J.' on it …. the reason why Sarah was hiding, *half-naked*, soon became clear – some of her hidden clothes and, in particular, her petticoat were *bloodstained* …. Taken back to the city-centre, Thomas, was stripped-searched, and hidden and pushed down one of her stockings were …. five silver tea-spoons …. The spoons were engraved with the letters 'E.J.' ….

Despite her age, Sarah Thomas, seemed a hardened criminal to the officers – she told them that she could help the police with their case – she said the killer was none other than …. Mrs Jeffries' brother …. The police clearly didn't believe her …. so she made a second statement …. she said that early on Saturday morning, a previous servant turned up at the house, asking to see Mrs Jeffries …. She said, in fact, she wasn't *asking* to see the old lady … she was *demanding* …. Sarah then told a shocking tale …. this servant said that Mrs Jeffries hadn't furnished her with references to allow her to obtain a new job …. so she marched up to the old lady's bedroom, even though she was still in bed, picked up the heavy stone on the way, and threatened her with it …. Thomas said there was nothing she could do to stop this previous servant …. soon afterwards, when she went up to see her mistress, she found she had been horribly murdered …. Sarah then admitted that she was party to the burglary – the killer said she should rob the house, flee, and the other servant-girl would lock up afterwards …. Thomas promised not to say anything about the murder …. and who was this other girl, asked the officers – Maria was her first name; her surname was either Lewis or Williams …. like so many people in Bristol, she came from a Welsh background, that's all Sarah Thomas knew …. Mrs Miller said, there had been so many young women, who had worked for Mrs Jeffries, that the only recent one, she could remember, was called 'Rebecca' ….

Bristol, like the other big cities at this time, had a well organised system of work agencies – the supply of domestic servants was big business; and so the police began visiting each agency – called 'intelligence offices' - in the city, to see if they could give details if any of them, had supplied the workers to Mrs Jeffries …. Most had heard of the old lady – and indeed her reputation – but none had any details of young women, who had gone to her house …. However, from Mrs Miller, the police were able to trace the last known girl to work in Trenchard Street – it was Lucy Chard (16) …. She had lasted only just over a month with Mrs Jeffries …. Miss Chard was not in good health, and blamed the old lady's 'unkind treatment' for a relapse …. she said, that the old lady was quite security conscious – she checked all the windows and doors at night – the front and back door was always locked, and she slept with the keys in her bedroom, close by her pillow …. If this was the case, how did Sarah let in 'Maria' on Saturday morning …? Surely if she had gone for the keys in the bedroom, it would have woken the old lady up …? However, Lucy Chard, told officers she had left Mrs Jeffries' employment in the third week of January – and Sarah Thomas joined on February 5th – so who did the old lady employ for the missing two weeks or so …? Some of the agencies certainly had records of young women going for interviews at Trenchard Street, but none were actually employed ….

A local girl, 9-year-old Mary Ann Sullivan, told the police a strange and curious tale …. her uncle, John Collins, was blind and lived on benefits …. but to supplement his income, he played the fiddle in the local city-centre pubs …. As Mr Collins was blind, little Mary Anne, would lead him around the pubs and then back home …. the little girl knew Sarah Thomas quite well …. she said that for at least a month before the murder, the servant girl had been going out with a soldier – a rifleman …. She said on Friday evening, she and her uncle had been in the *Flitch of Bacon* pub, which backed onto Mrs Jeffries' place, when she saw a man called Matthew Lyons, who she knew – he was drinking with two riflemen – one of whom was Sarah's boyfriend …. The little girl said she had overheard the three men plotting the robbery, and if necessary, the murder of Mrs Jeffries …. According to Mary Ann, later that night at around midnight, she watched the three men climb over the 20-foot wall, into the back-yard of 6, Trenchard Street …. Incredibly, she claimed to have followed them, and to have seen Lyons – she said that although the men climbed over a wall – she had gone through a door that was in the wall and it was *open* – strike the old lady on the head with a stone, whilst one of the soldiers hit the victim on the side of the head with a blow from his sword …. she then said that she saw them leave – Lyons killing the dog, when it began to look as if it was about to start growling ….

The police were somewhat sceptical of the story …. surely the men would have tried the door first, before scaling the wall …? The landlady of the pub said although she did not know the little girl well, she had heard that her family were a 'bad lot', and the little girl, was 'not quite in her senses' …. And, of course, she knew or was friend's with *Sarah Thomas* …. However, the police had found the keys to Mrs Jeffries' house in a groove of a front window-sill of the pub on the same day the body was discovered …. could the men have left them there having escaped by the side of the pub, or had someone planted them after the murder …? It seemed the latter, as although the windows were protected by shutters at night, it seemed unlikely they would have remained unnoticed until the *Wednesday*; and indeed they were found at closing-time on Wednesday night, and so after the discovery of the corpse …. But Mary Ann stuck to her story – she was threatened with imprisonment for perjury – but nevertheless signed a statement …. When told about the little girl's statement, Sarah Thomas, burst out laughing ….

The authorities completely disregarded Mary Anne Sullivan's evidence, deeming it 'wholly unworthy of credit' …. the police were sure that Sarah Thomas *alone* committed the murder, and then involved her boyfriend or male acquaintance, and family, in the moving and hiding of the stolen goods …. It was a view taken by the coroner's jury, who after **a four-day hearing on March 15th** found a case against Sarah Thomas; and she was committed for trial at the **Gloucester Assizes on Tuesday, April 3rd**. When she heard this, she broke down crying into her handkerchief …. she partially collapsed, and was carried out of the hearing in the arms of several policemen …. Outside, a large menacing crowd had gathered to boo and hiss the teenager – any talk of any mistreatment by Elizabeth Jeffries was far outweighed by what appeared to be the premeditated murder of an old lady killed whilst asleep, in order to carry out a burglary …. An equally large presence of police, safely saw Sarah

Thomas into the waiting carriage, and the journey to Gloucester Prison ....

Appearing before **the judge, Baron Thomas Platt**, Sarah Thomas listened as a number of witnesses came forward to say the victim often ill-treated her servants, and sometimes this included violence .... Mrs Ham said she had heard the old lady call the accused a 'dirty hussy' .... she would often shout out, that the girl was working too slowly, or not doing her job properly etc .... Lucy Chard and other servants said that they were threatened with a beating, and that in order to get value for money, Mrs Jeffries, would wake her servant at five am .... This time was crucial – the defence now admitted that Sarah Thomas had killed the victim, but they suggested that the robbery was an afterthought – they said that the prisoner had killed having been woken and abused and threatened with violence .... and yet, the victim had been killed in her bed, and with a weapon taken from the *kitchen* .... the defence said that having woken Thomas, Mrs Jeffries returned to her bed (she wasn't wearing her full night-clothes) – greatly distressed, Thomas had gone downstairs to start her work, when she saw the stone – unable to control herself, she went back upstairs .... it was pointed out, that there were several other potential weapons in the house, that would have been far more effective for premeditated murder – an axe, a poker, a hammer, many knives .... and yet, the young servant, picked up a stone - it was almost the choice of a child .... she was about to start a hard day's work in the kitchen, when she saw the doorstop – a large stone .... Mrs Ham and Mrs Fry said that they believed the screams were that of *Sarah Thomas* not Mrs Jeffries .... The defence pleaded for a verdict of manslaughter on the grounds of provocation .... If guilty of murder, then Sarah Thomas' life 'would be sacrificed', the jurymen were told .... During the defence's final speech, the prisoner constantly wept ....

The judge, in his final charge, paid tribute to the defence's 'strong, eloquent and pathetic appeal'; but he told the jury, only the facts were of importance .... The jury were out for 30 minutes – during this absence, and with Sarah Thomas still in the dock, the judge heard a case of horse-stealing - there was a good deal of laughter in this very short trial – and it was noted, that the young prisoner, awaiting to hear her fate, joined in heartily …. the jury filed back – theirs was a verdict of guilty of …. murder, but with a recommendation to mercy, on account of Sarah Thomas' age …. As she was told she would be 'hanged by the neck', the young woman buried her head in her hands, and cried out: "Oh, I cannot stand that!" The judge said he would forward the jury's recommendation in his report to the Home Office – but he cautioned Thomas not to put any hope in it at all – the judge said he completely disagreed with it …. Crying and screaming, the now condemned, said she would not leave the dock, until the judge had spared her life, which theoretically, he had the power to do, in *exceptional* cases[1], which this was not …. Sarah Thomas refused to move, and had to be taken away by two prison-officers …. Her screams could be heard long after she had been removed from the court-room ….

The **Home Secretary, Sir George Grey**, saw no reason to spare Sarah Thomas, and her execution was set for **Friday, April 20th, outside Bristol Prison at 10.00 am** …. He had received, amongst many petitions for mercy, one signed by 3,500 women from Bristol. Thomas was guarded 24 hours a day by four female prison-officers …. at around midnight, she ate a hearty meal of mutton chop …. Sarah Thomas did not sleep that night, and had no breakfast …. At seven, the prison chaplain arrived; and for the first time since her arrest, she decided to listen to him …. At 9.30 am, the Prison-Governor spoke to Thomas, saying he hoped she would walk to the gallows with dignity, and give him and his staff no problems …. There was a problem, however – childlike, Thomas, stamped her feet, and said she would not go …. The governor could not calm her down, and requested six prison-officers to accompany her to the entrance to the drop …. it was decided to move Sarah Thomas now, and in harrowing scenes, it took all six men to drag and carry her to the edge of the scaffold …. She seemed eventually to calm down, but faltered, as she saw the open sky and the drop: she was held here until just before ten – she then required two prison-officers to walk her to the trap-door …. By now, her screaming was most distressing, and was affecting the crowd. As **William Calcraft, the hangman,**

1   Such as when a young child or pregnant woman was convicted of murder – this power was taken away from the judges in 1861 ….

who was being helped by George Smith, put the rope around her neck, Thomas, shouted out: "The Lord have Mercy upon me! I hope my mother and none of my family are present." The lever was pulled and Sarah Thomas (19) died immediately: the crowd, estimated to be around 30,000, fell silent ….

Having been executed, the authorities released a confession …. Sarah Thomas said that two days before the murder, Mrs Jeffries, had attempted to hit her, and had then locked her in the kitchen all night …. when allowed out, she said she intended to hit the old lady, but didn't …. She said that on some nights, she slept in the same room as Mrs Jeffries, and did so on the night of the crime …. she said when she awoke, she decided to go downstairs, and fetch the stone from the kitchen, and to hit her mistress …. she said the victim was asleep when hit – three times …. she said between the second and third blows, Mrs Jeffries, said 'Christ God!' Thomas, then robbed the house, killed the dog and left …. she said no-one else was involved …. she said there was no boyfriend helping with the bundle at the sweet-shop: she had paid a complete stranger 8d to help her …. she re-iterated that *anger* and not robbery had motivated her …. With some of the money she had stolen, she took a cab back to her parents with the stolen items ….

The police were praised for their organising of the crowd at the execution – the *Times* lamented that many were smoking, swearing and joking, until the young woman appeared on the drop …. there was some crushing, but strong barriers had been erected, and they did their job …. **Sarah Thomas was the last person hanged in public in Bristol …. The prison had opened in 1820, but had been virtually destroyed during the famous *Bristol Riots* in 1831 …. it was not finally re-built until 1872, and a decade later, it was declared unfit for prisoners, and was closed, being replaced by a new prison at …. Horfield …. The last execution at the old prison was 1880; and at Horfield in 1963** ….

English Heritage have designated the survived prison entrance wall and gateway and the south-east perimeter wall as a Grade II listed building. It is now the centre-piece of a redevelopment project in this area of Bristol city-centre ….

The last execution at Bristol Prison was in 1963 ….

Case 4
"The Cummertrees Beast"
And The
Terrible Murder
Of
Little Thomasina"

~The Fatal Errand To Annan~

Robert SMITH (19)
[1868]
Murder
Of
Thomasina Scott (9)

"Robert Smith. My address is Dumfries County Prison. Write soon, Dear Jane and let me know how you are now ...." Letter written to a woman, whom Smith had shot in the head, then tried to strangle her;

then to cut her throat, to strangle her again; and had then put her head in a vice-like bar in a chair to rape her, until he was interrupted by a knock at the door ....

It is hard to imagine a worse murder case than this one, in the late Winter of 1868 in Dumfries-shire – a little girl, aged 9, sent on an errand from her village was raped, strangled including being hanged from a tree, by a young man, who also stole her money .... The killer was quickly caught, and his resulting execution, was the last to be held in public in Scotland (just two weeks before the equivalent one in England) .... The Scottish authorities did their best to make the execution as private as possible – the Home Office in London had said it must be held in public[2] - and in the end, only 300-400 people, actually witnessed it ....

Notes:

The *Illustrated Police News* **picture is inaccurate on the attempted murder of Mr C. - this was inside ....**

John Scott was a shoemaker and grocer, who lived at *Burnside Cottage* in the Dumfries-shire village of Cummertrees, which lies some four miles to the west of the town of Annan .... He lived with his wife, Dinah, and their ten children, including, a **daughter Thomasina (9)**, who was a well-developed child for her age[3], and was delegated the jobs of going into Annan with messages and buying small items for their shop, and was duly sent to the town on **Saturday, February 1st, 1868,** on such an errand .... On this day, she had also a pair of clogs that were to be repaired .... Thomasina was to be given 10s, but was actually given 1d less .... This was put in a purse, and she was also given a basket for the shoes .... At around 10.45 am, she left their home .... Generally, the little girl would run and walk, but she had been given enough money to catch the train back from Annan,

---

2   There was no separate Scottish Office until 1885 ....
3   The first reports of the case described the victim as being 'fourteen' ....

should the weather change later on …. Allowing for conversations in Annan, at the latest, Thomasina should be back in Cummertrees by three pm: if she caught the train, it would be just after 4.10 pm, when it came into the village …. when it came to tea-time between five and six, Dinah Scott, was beside herself …. something was not right …. Mrs Scott and the rest of the village were also greatly concerned, as they heard that a villager, and near-neighbour to the Scotts - Jane Crichton - who lived at *Longfords Cottage*, had suffered some kind of life-threatening injury …. Another daughter was sent to walk along the road towards Annan and then Mrs Scott followed …. neither of them could find Thomasina …. However, the other child had run into Annan, and discovered that the little girl, had not delivered the message or taken in the shoes …. she seemed not to have reached Annan ….

Back in Cummertrees, Mrs Scott, now found out that Mrs Crichton had been shot in the head from a pistol, her throat cut with a knife; then she had been forced to the ground and was partially strangled – she was still alive and was able to give a description of her attacker: fortunately for Jane Crichton her attacker had not loaded the gun correctly …. When Mrs Scott said that her daughter had disappeared, the whole village came out to look for her …. Meanwhile, the police came from Annan, and were amazed to find that Mrs Crichton was able to tell them a lot about her attacker – she and her husband, Robert, knew him reasonably well …. She said he was **19-year-old Robert Smith**, a farm labourer and handyman, who had been in the property on the day before and a few weeks prior …. At this time, he had been white-washing a number of local properties …. On Friday, Smith, had come in the morning – Mrs Crichton was alone with him – and he stayed until it became dark …. However, he did no work and Mrs Crichton wondered if her husband had sent him – he said nothing and just 'hung' about …. but that was all …. When the darkness started to fall, Smith told Mrs Crichton, that he was off to Annan …. Although he had done nothing or said anything sinister, Jane Crichton, was deeply suspicious of him …. During the day, at various points, Mrs Crichton, couldn't see Smith, and then he came and knocked on her door saying, that he had seen one of her sons, and that the boy had told Smith, that Mrs Crichton's mum was ill at *Longfords Farmhouse*, and that she should go to her at once …. She didn't go – she didn't believe Smith and thought he had an ulterior motive, whatever that might be …. Later, she found out her mother was, indeed, not ill at all …. Then on Saturday morning, he turned up at ten am again …. This time he only stayed about an hour – this was partly because the weather was quite bad – it was stormy and very cold and constantly threatening heavy rain …. Just after he left, Thomasina, passed *Longfords Cottage* and popped in for a few words …. It was now raining heavily, and the little girl needed shelter, as did another local, David Johnstone …. Then, who should come back, but …. Robert Smith: he needed shelter too, and Mrs Crichton didn't like to refuse him entry into the cottage …. Smith was there as Thomasina explained why she was going into town ….

The rain soon stopped and Thomasina Scott was the first to leave …. Smith said he too was going to Annan and would walk with the little girl, and the pair left together …. It was now a few minutes past 12 o'clock …. Despite her unease about Smith, the day before, Mrs Crichton, had no qualms about Smith going with Thomasina …. At some point between three and four pm, Robert Smith, came back to *Longfords Cottage* …. Thomasina wasn't with him, but, again, Mrs Crichton attached no importance to this …. indeed, she might have thought it strange, if they had have come back together …. Mrs Crichton was on her hands and knees washing the kitchen-floor, and Smith walked up to the fire-place …. He said nothing and in an almost familiar way, warmed himself against the lit fire …. At various points, Jane Crichton, had her head away from Smith and his right-hand, when suddenly …. she felt a terrible searing pain in her head – Smith had shot her …. Briefly stunned, Mrs Crichton, tore off her work hat, looked up at Smith, who pushed her down onto the floor and started to strangle her …. In Smith's left hand was a knife, and he started to cut at the right-side of the woman's throat …. Incredibly, Mrs Crichton was able to seize the knife …. then, it became clear, why Smith had *apparently* attacked the woman – he grabbed Mrs Crichton around the waist and began dragging her into the bedroom, where he forced her to the ground …. Smith then pushed Jane Crichton's head into a chair, so the bars of it acted like a vice, and she could not move her head, and then he began trying to strangle her again with his hands …. Smith did not have time to rape the victim, as there was a knock at the front-door, and Smith stood up like a bolt …. Smith left – there were two boys at the door – and in the meantime – with great difficulty and pain - Mrs Crichton manoeuvred her head out of the chair – she ran to the front-door and past Smith screaming for help once outside …. Mrs Crichton ran towards the farmhouse, passing Mr Johnstone on the way ….

Jane Crichton said the 'white-washer Smith' had been 'abusing' her …. there was blood pouring from her head and throat …. Mr Johnstone helped the victim towards the farmhouse, where her husband would be, as well as her mum; and as they did so, they saw a young man running away across the fields towards the railway-line, and as he did so, he was wiping his hands across his clothes …. The man was dressed in black, just as Smith had been, when he had walked towards Annan with Thomasina Scott – a number of locals saw them on the road – no-one could recall the little girl in the town; but at 2.00 pm, Smith went into an ironmongers in Annan, and bought a pistol for 2s 6d and some powder, shot and caps …. One of the boys, who had knocked on the cottage-door, said that they could hear sounds inside, and it reminded them of the sounds of a parrot screeching …. when they knocked a bit louder, the noises stopped …. When Smith opened the door, the boys could see that he was covered in blood, particularly on his hands and face …. They could see Mrs Crichton had a knife in her hand …. Smith fled, and was seen minutes later by a railway-worker washing his face and hands in a stream by the line …. he then dried himself with a handkerchief ….

While all this was all happening, the search for Thomasina Scott went on …. The Scotts went to the Crichton cottage – to their horror, they were told their daughter had been there with …. *Robert Smith* and that the pair had then left for Annan …. eventually Thomasina was found – a young man in the village, John Gillepsie, an apprentice blacksmith was searching in a wood - *Croftheads Plantation* on *Howe's Farm* just to the north of the road between Cummertrees and Annan – it was between ten and eleven pm, when by torchlight and lantern …. they saw a body, which was lying on its back …. the feet were resting in a hollow and were clearly apart and the underwear and underclothes had been pushed up over the waist: it was clearly the body of Thomasina Scott – although she had left home in a hat – she was bear-headed and her hair was all over the place, and her hat was found nearby[4] .... by her left-side was a basket .... Mr Gillespie pulled her clothes back into position .... under the body another searcher, John Graham, found a white handled-knife, whilst a purse was also by her side .... Thomasina had also been strangled (both manually and with a cord) and the post-mortem revealed, she had been raped before death: the cord marks around her neck also suggested something truly terrible – there had been an attempt to hang her from a nearby tree, on which were the corresponding marks .... The doctors told the police that Thomasina had been 'outraged with great violence', which had, itself, contributed to her death .... the body was brought back to *Burnside Cottage* between eleven and midnight .... the body was left untouched, until the police could examine it, next morning – the purse was empty ....

During January, Robert Smith, had been lodging in Dumfries .... He left on the thirtieth with a small amount of money saying he was travelling the 15 miles eastwards to Annan .... The day after the murder, a large number of officers – some armed – descended on his lodgings in Dumfries and arrested Smith; his clothes bloodstained; and in his room were a pair of boots, the prints of which, matched exactly those at the murder-scene .... Two days later, Smith appeared before a hearing, in front of a Sheriff – David Hope – where he confessed .... he said he originally came from the village of Annandale some 15 miles to the north of Annan .... He was unmarried and had been living rough in the countryside around the town .... He said en route to Annan, it looked like it might rain again, and Smith persuaded the victim to go into the wood for shelter .... He agreed he had raped the little girl first, then strangled her with a cord – shown the knife, he said it was the one that he had used .... he said he had cut the money out of her purse; he made no mention of trying to hang the victim from the tree first, however .... On returning to Cummertrees with the pistol, he said that he had intended to kill Mrs Crichton .... Somewhat bizarrely, he said he did this, as he thought if he pleaded guilty to the murder of the *woman*,

---

4   *Oban Times, and Argyllshire Advertiser - Saturday 25 April 1868* – says Mrs Scott was shown the hat in court and said it belonged to her daughter ....

he would 'avoid the consequences of what he had done to the girl Scott'; although, as we shall see, in a letter to Jane Crichton, the motive appeared to be robbery and the fact, she had seen him with the victim …. He said he threw the pistol into the stream, where he had cleaned himself, and from where it was retrieved ….

Robert Smith appeared at **Dumfries High Court on Tuesday, April 21st, 1868,** before the **Lord Justice-Clerk, George Patton - Lord Glenalmond, and Charles Neaves - Lord Neaves, in a trial that lasted just 4 ½ hours** …. Aside from murder, the prisoner was charged with the rape of the little girl, and the attempted murder of Mrs Crichton …. although the death penalty for the latter two crimes had been abolished in England & Wales and Ireland in 1861, rape remained a capital offence in Scotland until 1887[5]; and incredibly, attempted murder was still, *in theory*, punishable by death in Scotland until 1957[6] …. Robert Smith attempted to plead guilty to all three offences, but was informed by the judges, that no such plea could be accepted by a Scottish court in *capital* cases …. Smith's defence then, said, that when the trial began their defence to the charge of murder was one of manslaughter on the grounds of diminished responsibility, and they would offer no defence to the other two charges ….

Having heard the evidence for the Crown: the defence called no-one; in his summing up, the Lord Justice-Clerk, said there was no suggestion that Robert Smith was in any way mentally ill: the **jury were out for just five minutes, and the verdict was 15-0 for murder** …. the judge then told Smith, there would be no hope of mercy, and that he would be **hanged outside Dumfries Gaol on Tuesday, May 12th** ….

Before the trial, Robert Smith, had written to Jane Crichton: given what he had done to her, it seems quite extraordinary, the way he wrote it ….

---

5   The last execution for rape in Scotland was in 1835 in Dundee.
6   The last execution for attempted murder in Scotland was in 1834 in Glasgow.

"Dear Jane Crichton, I write you a few lines to let you know that I am well at present, hoping this will find you and all your family enjoying the good health, thank God for it. Dear Jane, I was a great blackguard when I could have taken away the young girl's life so most wickedly and then to come and boldly to your house again and then to fire a pistol at you and then to seize you by the throat for to choke you and then to take my knife and to try and cut your throat. If the Lord had not been merciful to you and saved your life — if it had been the other way round — it would have been a most horrible case for me to have done. But I thank God that he was merciful to do so to you. Dear Jane, you and your friends may be mad at me for it, but you can tell them all that it is against me that I would let any of them do anything to me now after I have seen it, for the Lord's hand is mightier than the Devil's, for the Lord saved your life that day, but I heard you were getting better for I hope that when you receive this you will be all better and going about again the same as usual. Dear Jane, I had many a thought of taking away your life. I wanted to rob your house and I did not know how to do it until that day the young girl came in. I thought if I had a pistol I could soon have taken your life away. I thought it was a good job when I got the ten shillings from the young girl and got the pistol. I thought it was all right for I thought that the shot would have ended your days too, and then, there would not have been any could have informed the police bout me and I would have got clear from the hands of men in the meantime. But the Lord proved merciful to me and you. But the young girl is resting in the grave and I will be there to soon and I well deserve it and something far worse. Dear Jane, the Lord was great to save your life, the Devil is great but thanks be to God for he is greater than the Devil. Dear Jane, I have no more to say at present. Give my kind love to all the neighbours, to your son John and all the men and tell them that I will not see none of them on Earth but I trust in God that I will see you and yours and them in heaven. Robert Smith. My address is Dumfries County Prison. Write soon, Dear Jane and let me know how you are now."

Indeed, the letter being so coherent, seemed to suggest that Smith was anything but insane – and in fairness to him, the Crown did not call it in evidence …. In the death-cell, Smith, said he did not want or indeed did he expect any mercy …. No petition was started for

Smith and no-one in Scotland thought the Home Office in England would do anything but refuse a reprieve …. A petition was, however, sent to the **Home Secretary, Gathorne Hardy,** pleading for the execution not to be carried out in public …. as we know, the law to abolish public executions was almost on the statute books, but it was to be another two weeks **(Friday, May 29ᵗʰ) until Royal Assent made it actual law**[7] …. this was two weeks prior, and the law was the law ….

And, as we shall find out, May 12ᵗʰ, was intended to be the date of the execution of Michael Barrett in London – this date was postponed (and again on May 19ᵗʰ) due to the complexities of the case …. William Calcraft had been hired for the twelfth at Newgate, but once postponed, there was no time for him to reach Dumfries – Barrett was respited on Sunday evening (May 10ᵗʰ) …. So the Dumfries authorities turned to **Thomas Askern,** the so-called 'Hangman of York' and a fee of 20 Guineas …. he arrived in the town at five pm on Monday evening …. Officials feared the Yorkshireman wasn't coming and stations en route from York were telegraphed – fortunately at 3.30 pm, he was seen at Carlisle – Askern also pointed out that, for religious reasons, he did not travel on Sundays …. At Dumfries Railway-Station the hangman was met by two prison-officers – he, as he said he would have, had a waterproof coat over his arms …. by now a large crowd had reached the station hoping to see the executioner …. Given the nature of Robert Smith's crime, no-one booed or hissed the hangman, as they often did in Scotland ….

The lawmakers in England may have stopped the execution being in private, but the Scottish authorities tried their best to get around this – they built the gallows *inside the prison*, so that on Tuesday morning, only the barest minimum could be seen; this satisfying the law that it was in *public* …. The gallows – built during the week – was constructed next to the death-cell – the door would literally open up onto the scaffold …. Again, unlike in England, here there was no beam – instead an iron-bar was attached to a wall and the noose

---

7   The Capital Punishment Amendment Act 1868 (31 & 32 Vict. c.24) received Royal Assent on *29 May 1868*

attached to that …. It was just a yard long …. it looked literally like a yard-arm ….

Smith appeared to take in his religious 'advice' - so much so, that he slept *unguarded* in the death-cell …. He was woken at six am on the Tuesday morning …. The night, like the day of the murder, had been rainy and very cold – consequently, only about 300-400 people gathered outside the prison to see Smith die …. a few sang hymns; some preached – a common occurrence at executions in Scotland …. At 7.30 am, the execution officials entered the prison – in Scotland it was the local magistrates who organized everything …. At the same time, Askern, put the noose up – it was noted, that the hangman, was wearing a pure white outfit …. At 7.57 am, the executioner went into the death-cell for the condemned – Smith was calm and resigned …. he said he hoped he was going to a 'better world' …. As Smith stepped onto the gallows, a group of young girls in the crowd screamed …. Smith just smiled pleasantly at them …. Smith said nothing on the drop …. he looked around …. it was now it was realised that Askern had made a mistake …. The noose was not around Smith's neck properly – it had to be taken off, placed back on, and re-adjusted …. This done, Askern, shook hands with Smith, and went quickly to the lever – he pulled it …. Askern ran back inside, but it was then obvious, he had made another mistake – Smith's body shook for nearly four minutes – he had died in agony by strangulation – the knot had not been in the correct place …. Obviously, the way the gallows had been built, meant that no-one outside, could see this …. The crowd – described as very orderly by the police – then went on their way ….

Robert Smith's body was left for the customary one hour, and as it was being taken down, a man from Carlisle arrived – named Rushfirth – he asked that he might take a death-mask of Smith …. There being no good reason to oppose his request, the mask was taken and shown to the public – Smith appeared a pleasant looking 'country' boy – indeed, as we know, he could also read and write: it was noted, however, that he was 'illegitimate'; and both his parents died when he was young, and he was brought up by an Uncle, the only person to visit him in prison …. At the age of eight, he began working in a lime quarry …. Smith never stayed in one job very long, and there were suspicions, that he was a thief – eventually, no-one in and around Annan, would employ him on a regular basis ….

The previous execution at Dumfries - on April 29th, 1862 - was that of Mary Reid (27), who was also the last woman hanged in public in Scotland; and the previous execution to that, in the town, had been in 1826 …. The original prison was completed in 1807. It was replaced in 1851 by a larger structure, and was demolished in 1885 ….

Case 5
"The Last Woman Executed In Public In Scotland"

~What Really Happened At Carsphad Farm~

Mary TIMNEY (27)
[1862]
MURDER
Of
Ann Hannah (37[8])

"You must tell us. We cannot let you away till you answer this question." - The judge to a little girl not quite ten …. her answer would help send her mother to the gallows ….

---

8   c.1825 Ancestry ….

"I declare it was my own mother, Margaret Corson, who murdered Ann Hannah" …. A third statement to the police …..

"Mother, put on the kettle and have a cup of tea before you go." What Mary Timney said after she claimed her mum had told her she was the real killer ….

'The time of all of us in this world is short, with most of us it is uncertain, but it is necessarily short in your case. Your days are numbered.' - What the trial judge told Mary Timney ….

That Ann Hannah was brutally done to death in her remote cottage in south-west Scotland in early 1862 is beyond doubt; but what really happened is open to doubt …. rarely in Scotland it lead to the execution of a woman – just 27-years-old – outside Dumfries Prison - in what was to become the <u>last public execution in Scotland of a female</u> …. It was also an interesting social case – one of the petitions for a reprieve was on the grounds that as women could not vote, should they be held responsible in law for their actions ….?

<u>M</u>ary Timney (27),

was described in the language of the day in 1862, as 'slimly made and by no means repulsive' …. but she had a temper and lived a volatile life with her Irish husband Francis, described as a 'road-surface man' and their children in a small two-roomed cottage at a place called ***Carsphad Farm* a few miles to the north of New**

Galloway in the tiny village of Kells on Glenkins Road, and twenty-five-miles to the west of Dumfries in the old county of Kirkcudbrightshire[9] …. The Timneys' next door neighbours – they were 50 yards apart - were the Hannahs, who owned the Timneys' cottage – there were two brothers William and Lockhart and their sister **Ann (37)** …. Their next nearest neighbours were about a ¼ of a mile away …. The Hannahs had lived there for many years – the Timneys had been there about 2 ½ years …. One villager who had known the Hannahs all her life was Agnes McLellan, who lived ½ a mile away, and on January 9th, 1862, Ann Hannah, her close friend, whose mum had recently died, asked her to keep an eye on her brothers, as she would be away until **Monday [January 13th, 1862]** …. On that day one of Mary Timney's daughters – Susan - came to Agnes - and asked whether she would bake a cake for her mother as she was a bit poorly ….. This was at noon and Agnes made her way to the Timneys at about one passing en route the Hannahs …. What she saw next would stay with Agnes McLellan for the rest of her life ….

As she past the Hannahs she noticed the front-door slightly opened – pushing it back a bit she saw Ann Hannah lying facedown on the floor in a pool of blood in the doorway to the kitchen …. She called out thinking there had been a terrible accident – Ann must have fallen and struck her head …. Agnes ran to the nearest house to raise the alarm …. Other villagers returned with her to the farm …. One, Robert Coats, turned Ann over – the face wounds were horrendous …. But she was still alive and she was lifted into bed, carried through other large pools of blood …. Over the next eight hours or so, twice Ann said 'Oh dear' and **then died at 9.30 pm** …. By the body on the floor, was a butcher's knife, dripping in blood, but there was no apparent wound to Ann's neck …. A poker was on the floor – it had very little blood on it[10] - but it had pieces of hair attached to it – the same colour as Ann Hannah's – it was next to the body ….. The small cottage was awash with blood splatterings but nothing was

---

9   Now Dumfries & Galloway ….
10   One report says there was blood on the poker – Dr MacLagan said he couldn't find any on it ….

in disorder – it *appeared* that nothing had been taken or looked for
…. It appeared that Ann had been interrupted whilst doing her
clothes-washing …. Moments after Agnes and the villagers had
arrived …. Mary Timney came in too …. Apparently in great shock
– like everyone else – she said: "Dear me, Nanny[11], I think the like o'
this never happened here afore!" …. Timney said she would stay
along with everyone else …. She then offered to fetch the local
doctor …. Meanwhile the Hannah brothers came in, William first
followed later by Lockhart ….

Eventually, Dr Andrew Jackson, arrived …. It was 2.30 pm and he
determined that Ann Hannah had been attacked with blows from a
poker shaped from an iron-bar and a wooden mallet – her whole face
had been smashed to bits …. her face was unrecognisable – her skull
fractured – two of her ribs broken, and her arms discoloured with the
strokes …. in all there were ten distinctive blows – all from heavy
objects, although the wounds on the face were more like cut-wounds
- those on the head from blows – the knife could have been used –
Ann Hannah could not have fallen and caused so many and so many
different types of wounds …. The murder must have taken place a
few hours before as some of the blood had dried …. The neighbours
asked Mary Timney if she or her children had heard anything – she
said 'no' which they all found somewhat surprising …. Her reply
was that she did not feel well and had been in bed since her husband
left for work in the morning ….

William and Lockhart Hannah had left for work at 8.40 am …. They
were working about 2 ½ miles away …. They were there when they
received a message to come to their cottage immediately …. At
some point William asked Mary Timney to go home as she had
brought a small child that was crying …. He told the police that
morning he had lent her husband 2s 6d …. Francis Timney said he
was broke and wanted to give his wife some money for their home
…. He said Mrs Timney was in the habit of borrowing things from
their family - tea, sugar &c , and she also sent the children to borrow.

---

11 Agnes was also called Nan ….

Just recently Ann had refused to lend anything to Mary Timney ....
And they also had words about her carrying away wood from the
Hannahs' farm – this was about four or five weeks before. This
appeared to be the first time that the two families had quarrelled ....
A few days before the murder Ann had told William, that she had
seen Mrs Timney with a stone in her hand approaching their farm ....
William said he had seen Mary Timney at about eight am at her pig-
house - William had not spoken to her for a month and did not speak
to her that morning, he told officers .... As they all gathered around
Ann, William, was suspicious of Mary Timney .... when she left he
searched the house and found some money of his own untouched in
a chest in a room .... *But some tea and sugar was missing* .... He
said that on this Monday, Ann, would not have had any money to
lend. He added that the knife was used for killing pigs ....

A police-officer in New Galloway, Constable John Robson, went
from the Hannahs' cottage to see Mary Timney – she was in bed,
although fully clothed - he said he saw several spots of blood on her
clothes .... But by the bed was a night-dress, the wrist of it was wet,
apparently with fresh blood .... A child's night dress was also stained
with spots, and was a little wet with water and had holes cut in it ....
Constable Robson then looked in the loft .... it was very dark .... but
there was nothing untoward *apparently* – but there was a green
tartan dress wrapped in amongst other clothes, as the officer quickly
glanced – it appeared not to have blood on it – it did appear wet at
the front - there were, however, three areas of fresh blood on a
petticoat in the bundle .... It was distinctly wet with blood at the
bottom .... Behind a bed, the officer found a woman's cap and a
handkerchief. Both were wet, as if they had been newly washed.
Then Constable Robson found .... a mallet. It was behind the food
barrel, on the left side of the fireplace, in a dark crevice[12]. It was
very wet with what he assumed was water; it too must have been
washed, he thought. The officer put it back – initially he did not
think it important .... The officer did find, and think it important,
several pieces of cake - they were at the bottom of a pile of clothes –
clearly hidden .... At ten pm, Constable Robson, arrested Mary
Timney on suspicion of murder .... He later returned to the house

12 It was also 6.00 pm so would have been dark ....

finding 7s 7d in a glove, but it did not belong to the Hannahs' – but, again hidden, he found some tea and sugar wrapped in a piece of cloth …. On the fifteenth, the police came and took away the mallet …. In full light it appeared the wetness had been blood and they could also see hairs on it ….

Agnes Sproat, a farmer's daughter and teaching-assistant said she had passed the Hannahs' door at 9.35 am with two school-children and spoke to Ann …. She then passed the Timneys' place putting her head around the door having seen the children playing and their mum inside …. Susan Timney told the police that her mother had then gone to the Hannahs' cottage after this ….
They also claimed that she had said that she saw her mum return – *with blood on her dress – the green tartan dress ….*

Mary Timney appeared at Dumfries High Court on Tuesday, April 8th, before the judge Lord George Deas and a packed courtroom – the case had caused a sensation throughout Dumfries & Galloway …. She stood in the dock with an expression 'being vacant and insensate, rather than cool or self possessed' …. Then as the trial proceeded and her barrister spoke, 'tears occasionally trickled down her visage' …. She was even more upset when her daughter Susan[13] was put in the witness-box, where she contradicted what she had told the police – she kept saying that her mum had not gone to the house straight after Agnes Sprout had passed by …. nine times in all she said 'no' until finally and dramatically Lord Deas said : "You must tell us. We cannot let you away till you answer this question." The little girl, after a pause at length, said …. 'Yes' …. Susan Timney, was not however forced to tell the court about the blood on her mother's dress ….

Another local policeman, Constable James Richardson, said on the Thursday before the murder, Mary Timney had asked to borrow 6d,

---

13 Born early 1852 ….

which he refused …. Other villagers said she had asked for either money or tea in the days before the crime ….

Apart from the weapons used in the murder, a number of other articles were taken to Edinburgh to be forensically examined by a Dr David MacLagan and he finally reported on February 25th …. He confirmed it was, indeed, blood on the mallet – and the hairs were long, fine and brown, as Ann Hannah had …. He did say that other stains of blood found in the Timney cottage were either quite old or what he thought to be menstrual blood …. some stains were vegetable juice …. On Mary Timney's dress – the green tartan one, he found blood, as we know …. this was in the chest area and seven inches square …. it had soaked through the material …. it had stained into the lining …. there was more staining on the right elbow and sleeve; and on the wrist …. there was much staining on the left sleeve …. Some of the blood he thought menstrual blood, but it could not account for all of it …. there was a vast amount of blood on the dress …. He pointedly added, that no blood stains were seen on the back of the dress. There was also a large amount of blood on a petticoat …. it looked as if the article had been wrung out to almost dry out the blood …. A bed-gown showed blood staining that corresponded to the tartan dress as if they had been placed next to each other …. Dr MacLagan said that whilst there was no direct test for human blood, animal blood was detectable under a micro-scope …. and what he had observed wasn't the latter ….

Mary Timney's defence consisted of three statements to the authorities – the day after the crime, three days later and on February 4th …. She began by saying that at Christmas time Ann Hannah had called her a thief for taking fire-wood, also saying she had stolen some turnips …. Mrs Timney claimed that after that, she had not spoken to the victim or been in her house until she saw her dying in the cottage …. she claimed the tea and sugar wrapped in a piece of cloth had been bought by her eldest girl at William Smith's, a grocer in nearby St John's Town Dalry, on the previous Saturday night – something Mr Smith said was not true …. she said some of the blood in the cottage was from her being unwell …. On January 17th she said she had never seen the mallet before …. Then on February 4th she made the most shocking and dramatic statement …. It began: "I am desirous of making a statement relative to the charge against me, and which I have kept to myself for the last three weeks, and suffered for another …. I declare it was my own mother, Margaret Corson, who murdered Ann Hannah …. there were gasps in court …. She claimed her mum came to her cottage, changed, and put on her own *green tartan dress* …. She said her mother looked out of the door and said she could see Ann Hannah …. then she said: "Mary, I have a mind before I leave this world to give Ann Hannah her licks …." saying that any problems between Mary and her husband were the fault of Ann Hannah's …. In about ten minutes Mrs Timney said her mother returned covered in blood, and she said: "Preserve me! mother, has Ann Hannah killed you?" She said: "No, Mary, but I think I have near killed her." She claimed her mum then took the green tartan dress off and some other items of clothing she had swapped at her daughter's …. Mary Timney said her mother wanted to leave immediately, but Mary Timney said she said: "Mother, put on the kettle and have a cup of tea before you go." …. A string of family members told the court this was all complete lies – Mary Corson had been at home at the time of the murder in St John's Town of Dalry ….

The prosecutor then addressed the jury. After a few words upon the duty they had to perform, he said: "In a quiet district of a quiet country a deed had been perpetrated which had made their ears to tingle." He would not say robbery was the motive as to why Mary Timney went to her neighbour's cottage …. He said it was possible that the accused thought Ann Hannah had been spreading gossip about her and her husband …. The defence began by telling the jury that they should disregard Mary Timney's third statement – it was plainly false …. He said it was the product of the pressure Mrs Timney was under …. He said she was in a 'state of feeling and desperation, amounting almost to weakness of mind, that she did not know what she was doing when she made the third declaration.' He suggested that some terrible struggle may have flared up rendering Mary Timney's offence not murder but manslaughter …. If Mary Timney were indeed in the cottage …. had someone else killed Ann

Hannah, they asked …? Lord Deas' summing-up took just 50 minutes …. He made it clear he thought Mary Timney guilty of murder …. **The jury were out for just 30 minutes – they unanimously – 15-0 under Scottish law – found the prisoner guilty of murder** …. **The trial had lasted just 10 hours** …. Mary Timney appeared expressionless …. When told to stand to hear sentence of death she asked the judge for mercy …. Lord Deas said he believed the motive was one of deep anger towards Ann Hannah for her not lending Mary Timney any more money or foodstuff and for the accusations of theft …. *The judge said that she had taken the mallet clearly with the intention of causing the victim serious harm* …. Mary Timney, in tears, said: "My Lord, it never was me, it never was me." But the judge replied 'The time of all of us in this world is short, with most of us it is uncertain, but it is necessarily short in your case. Your days are numbered.' Lord Deas asked Mary Timney to repent …. **He then ordered her to be hanged outside Dumfries Prison on Tuesday, April 29th, 1862, at eight am** …. 'and by the hands of the common executioner, be hanged by the neck upon a gibbet till you be dead …. which is pronounced of doom' …. Mrs Timney screamed out 'Oh my weans' …. Continuing to scream Mary Timney was forced from the dock – many in the court crying …. For several days in the death-cell she remained prostrate and motionless on her bed …. but eventually she began to listen to the prison-chaplain ….

And eventually Mary Timney confessed …. To the authorities she gave 'minute details' of the crime …. She claimed that she and her husband had lived quite happily for eight years before moving to Kells …. then she said Ann Hannah …. 'acquired a great influence over her husband, which caused great differences between them, and originated in her mind a jealousy of the deceased' …. She said on the day of the murder she'd gone to fetch fire-wood and that Ann Hannah had called out: "Are you coming here to steal more of my sticks?" …. Mary Timney claimed they came to blows …. She claimed, greatly angered, she went home and then went back to Ann Hannah's …. Mrs Timney said she only went with the intent of hurting her neighbour not killing her …. She claimed Ann Hannah kicked her above the knee and she did, indeed, have a scar there …. *She claimed Ann Hannah had used the mallet first* …. and that she had only used it after her neighbour had dropped it …. Now gripped in a frenzy, Mrs Timney, admitted delivering several blows …. there was no proof the mallet belonged to Mary Timney; and for some it was enough to begin a petition to save the woman from the gallows ….

On the Wednesday before the execution Mary Timney was visited by her husband and children. The scene at their parting was extremely emotional. Whatever hardness of heart may have been obvious in the unhappy prisoner at other times, she showed the agony of maternal feelings on this occasion. It was reported she screamed out her children's names and when this was reported in the media more petitions for mercy were begun …. The decision concerning Mary Timney's life was to be taken by the **Home Secretary in London, and Sir George Grey** met with MPs, who were opposed to capital punishment, lead by the famous abolitionist **William Ewart, who was MP for …. Dumfries**; whilst two Ladies travelled to Sir George's country house in Northumberland to plead for mercy …. Meanwhile Mary Timney began to adjust to life under the shadow of the noose – she began to eat and sleep well ….

The Ladies arrived at nine pm but courteously Sir George saw them …. They were greatly impressed by his knowledge of the case – he was able to answer all their questions in great detail …. Sir George said he could not – as a matter of the constitution - tell them his decision – and he needed more time with his advisors …. Sir George then arranged for a train to specially pick them up and take them to Newcastle that very night …. The key to the petition was the mallet – the judge said he believed Mrs Timney took it to the cottage, but this was never proved in court …. It was a point that Sir George had noted and requested a legal decision by the authorities in Edinburgh …. other petitioners said that since women were denied civil liberties then, they should not be judged as men, one stating, with a sense of sarcasm …. 'treat her with the leniency you would extend to one incapable of thought' ….

But there was to be no reprieve …. The judge had not referred to the mallet until after the jury had returned the verdict of murder …. The jury had clearly not thought this a case of manslaughter – indeed they had not recommended mercy, which was unusual in the case of a female …. Sir George felt he could not intervene – the execution would proceed ….

The famous London executioner, William Calcraft, arrived in Dumfries on the 7.40 am train on the day before the execution …. By all accounts, Mary Timney, thought she would be spared …. But on the preceding Saturday she was informed by the chaplain she was to die and had three days left – she was prostate with terror …. she seemed to loose all energy and on the next morning began to think it was her last …. But on the Monday as the hangman began his preparations, a realisation began to come over Mrs Timney – she wrote letters to friends …. However by tea-time she broke down again in a fit of hysteria – when the prison-doctor left her at nine pm she was semi-conscious …. And by this time large crowds were descending on Dumfries and making their way towards the prison …. However such was the position of the prison, that only between two and three thousand people were able to see the gallows …. They were mainly young people of both sexes and were generally well-behaved, in part due to the presence of a number of street preachers ….. and the presence of the ordinary police, 200 special constables enrolled for the day, and the local militia …. There were a number of street services and this meant it was not until 8.10 am that the execution could start …. At the correct time, Calcraft, had entered the death-cell and pinioned Mary Timney …. She broke down in floods of tears …. She kept saying 'Ann Hannah struck her first' …. But she could still walk …. However on seeing the gallows, she had to be helped up on to the platform – she was deadly pale and terror-stricken …. she asked to 'stand a minute' and cried out for her children …. As she was swaying, **two assistant hangmen – George Smith – known as the 'Throttler', and Robert Anderson - the 'Amateur Hangman' as he did the job for nothing**, helped her – one holding her arms - until Calcraft pulled the lever and she dropped – she died almost instantaneously – she did convulse for a few seconds …. It was now 8.23 am; the body cut down at five to nine; the crowds left and Mary Timney was buried within the prison grounds at three pm …. William Calcraft and his men left the prison at 11.15 am - jostled and booed as they made their way to the railway-station to catch the 11.25 train to England ….

The murder house no longer exists being now beneath a main road ....

<u>Matthew Spicer</u> – I assume that the Hannah brothers told the police that the mallet wasn't theirs ....

Case 6
"The Case Of The Dissenting Juryman"

" .... no expert, however eminent can be allowed to usurp the function of the jury." The trial judge, Mr Justice Avory ....

" .... eleven could carry a verdict" – The question asked by the foreman of the jury during the dramatic trial.

Thomas Rawcliffe (30)
[1910]
The Murder
Of his wife
Louisa Ann (27)

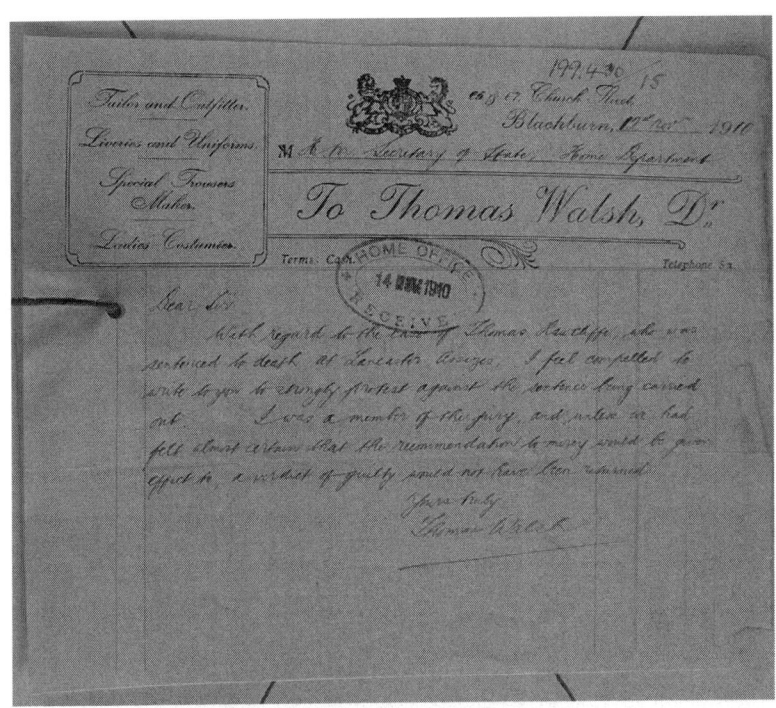

Domestic murder from Lancaster in the late Summer of 1910 with a dramatic twist in the trial at the Lancaster Assizes, which like the prison was, and as a Crown Court is, still a functioning part of the medieval Lancaster Castle. The gallows though were removed in 1956 when it was discovered they had been left in the 'spring position' from the last execution there in 1910 ….

Notes:

http://en.wikipedia.org/wiki/Lancaster_Castle

Number one Tyler's Yard, in the Cheapside area of the centre of Lancaster was home to a **30-year-old labourer Thomas Rawcliffe** and his young family in the late summer of 1910. Rawcliffe worked at Lord Ashton's River Lune (Lino) Works[14] and was married to Louisa Ann (27). Their children were aged six, four and one. Mrs Rawcliffe seemed to be a model wife – she was very tidy and didn't drink. Sadly Rawcliffe did and did so frequently and he would regularly threaten to hit his wife, but it appeared he never actually did so; instead he would bully her. Given Rawcliffe's behaviour it was not surprising that officialdom eventually took an interest in the family, and for some 2 ½ years an inspector of the NSPCC, a Mr William Thomas had been a constant visitor to the Rawcliffe's home. He felt particularly sorry for Louisa Ann as he regarded her as a 'decent' woman, who was very small and was not in the best of health because she was of a very frail build. On August 2nd, Mr Thomas paid one of his visits. Rawcliffe had said he was going to murder his wife. Mr Thomas calmed him down and left Tyler's Yard and didn't take the threat too seriously.

A month or so later Mrs Rawcliffe's brother, Mr Thomas Tarney came to visit and as usual Rawcliffe had been drinking. Despite the threats to his sister, Mr Tarney knew that his brother-in-law only became abusive when he was drinking; but that his problems with alcohol seemed to be becoming worse. On **Tuesday, September 6th, 1910,** Mr Tarney saw Rawcliffe again and he seemed quite normal. It was about eight pm and Mr Tarney could have no knowledge of the awfulness that was soon to be revealed at 1, Tyler's Yard ….

The following morning at 6.45 am Constable Thomas Wilkinson was doing his usual beat in Cheapside when he saw Thomas Rawcliffe coming up the road. In a slightly aggressive manner, he told the officer to come with him and 'see what I have done.' In Rawcliffe's kitchen the policeman asked him what exactly he had done. He was

---

14 "the present undertaking constitutes the largest manufactory of its class in the world; and further, we may say, without any fear of contradiction, that the mammoth works on the banks of the Lune, at Lancaster, are the most extensive in the universe, that are owned and controlled solely by one individual'." Lord Ashton's Lino Works.

soon to find out. Rawcliffe blurted out: "I strangled her last night[15] at seven o'clock." Constable Wilkinson was taken into the couple's bedroom and in the bed was the body of Louisa Ann on her back under the bedclothes and in her night-dress. There was no sign of a struggle. Incredibly their youngest child was asleep by the body and the other two had been asleep in a cot by the bed. The eldest child was awake but apparently not aware of what had happened. The body of the mother was quite cold and the officer could clearly see marks around the neck. Taken to the police-station and charged with murder, although excited, Rawcliffe gave a clear account of what had occurred, although he did say he must have been 'mad' when he did it. The following day Rawcliffe asked to speak to the Chief Constable of the local police, Mr Charles Harris to whom he claimed that the murder was in fact, a failed suicide-pact. He said his wife was ill and that he had taken some rat poison. He said he had been 'rambling' around the house all night before deciding to speak to Constable Wilkinson.

A Dr Arthur Barling had been called by the police and he noted that it appeared that Mrs Rawcliffe had retired to bed early – her day clothes were laid out on the bed. He noted some blood coming from her nostrils and that her tongue had been severely bitten and there was froth around the mouth. In all the doctor counted 13 marks on the neck. He concluded that the woman had died within the last 24 hours. The next day a *post-mortem* was carried out and Dr Barling could find no sign of any obvious illnesses beyond the victim being frail. The marks to the neck suggested that the strangulation had been carried out manually, and that given Louisa Ann's physique she would have been unable to resist her husband, who was himself only 5 ft 1 inches tall.

Thomas Rawcliffe appeared at the **Lancaster Assizes in Lancaster Castle before Mr Justice Avory on Thursday, October 27th, 1910,** before a crowded court. The **prosecution was undertook by Messrs Rathbone and Kennedy; whilst the prisoner was defended by Mr**

---

15 It is possible he murdered her at seven am and didn't realise – he does say he was in the house all day. Also he tells a Police Sergeant it was seven yesterday *morning*.

McKeever. Rawcliffe simply pleaded 'not guilty' but as we shall see, there was a surprise in store for the judge ….

Mr McKeever said that there was no question that his client hadn't caused the death of his wife, but he then claimed Rawcliffe was no 'ordinary man'. He said that at the age of just three the prisoner had fallen from a window some 30 feet, and had been unconscious for nearly two months: his skull was fractured and for nearly a year he was under the constant care of a doctor. He had an operation on the brain that had lasted three weeks, and that his family members considered him 'daft' and 'dangerous' and someone who lacked 'self-control.' Thus, but to the great surprise of the judge and prosecution, Mr McKeever now wished to put forward a defence of insanity; so a trial that would have lasted two hours would now take a whole day …. The defence called a Dr David Cassidy, an expert, indeed 'one of the greatest authorities on mental disease'. It was now necessary for the prosecution to either rebut the defence's case or accept that Rawcliffe should be found insane. Barely disguising his annoyance Mr Justice Avory told the court that the prosecution had been 'misled', but nevertheless the trial would have to continue with Rawcliffe now pleading 'not guilty' on the grounds of insanity.

The prisoner's mother told the court that after the operation on his brain her son had not walked for several weeks and that their doctor had told her that he would never be 'right': Given the level of health care available to the poor in the 1880s, his survival was miraculous. She said he became increasingly violent as he became older and was always in trouble[16], but somewhat paradoxically would always ultimately do what he was told, especially if done so nicely. She said he did badly at school but had worked in his present job since he was fifteen. He had married Louisa Ann after the birth of the first child, of whom Rawcliffe was *not* the father. His three sisters also told the court how they thought of him as strange. A work colleague said he thought of Rawcliffe as 'simple' – if he were spoken to he would look at the floor and walk off and then return to the conversation. Rawcliffe was thought of as 'absent-minded' and slightly paranoid as he would often join in conversations and ask if he were the subject

16 He served short terms for theft.

of them. But as a labourer he did his job well and no-one at work ever saw him drunk there, but on occasions he would not be able to work on Saturdays and Mondays due to his drinking over the weekend – indeed on the day before the murder was committed he hadn't been to work. The court was told that at sixteen Rawcliffe's father told his son to leave because of his drinking. Apart from his work at the Lune Works, Rawcliffe had done numerous other 'odd-jobs' and despite having a family, he would often spend nights in lodging houses.

Dr Cassidy was the Superintendent of the County Lunatic Asylum in Lancaster and had been so for the last 30 years and had been at Broadmoor for the previous seven to that, and in all had spent 42 years working with the insane. He told the court he had examined Rawcliffe's head and seen the depression in his skull. However before he could answer the defence's question as to whether Rawcliffe was indeed insane, the judge robustly ordered him not to answer, saying: " …. no expert, however eminent can be allowed to usurp the function of the jury." In the end, all Dr Cassidy could do was offer his opinion. To the prosecution he concurred that many people have suffered serious injuries to their skulls and brains without becoming mentally ill, and likewise to Mr McKeever he said the injuries Rawcliffe had suffered would be likely to have an effect on his mental capacity.

Dr Barling was recalled and said he had seen no signs of insanity when he first saw the prisoner just after the murder, and in the three or fours times that he had seen him since. Although he too had seen Rawcliffe's skull he could not say what damage had been done to the brain and all he could say was that whenever he spoke to the accused he seemed 'rational'. Mr McKeever then pointed out to the jury that Rawcliffe had stayed in the house with his wife's dead body for twelve hours, and to illustrate his mental illness, he had put the baby next to the body. Countering this Mr Rathbone suggested that Rawcliffe knew exactly what he had done – through drink he had lost his temper, something that accounted for the vast majority of murder cases, that the counsel had seen in courts. He suggested that the rat poison was merely a ruse by the prisoner, as was talk of a suicide-pact and his wife's supposed illness.

In his summing-up the judge explained the law and insanity and noted that when the victim's brother came around at eight, Louisa Ann was already dead and Rawcliffe had said that she had 'gone up the street for tea and sugar'. Was this the act of an insane man or something to say, giving himself time to think what he could ultimately say e.g. the suicide-pact? He pointed out that 'bad-temper' was not evidence of insanity and neither was being of 'low mental capacity'.

The jury were out for 35 minutes when clearly troubled they came back for further guidance; indeed asking whether 'eleven could carry a verdict'. They retired for another sixty minutes then after their re-appearance, dramatically the one 'dissenter' began questioning the judge and then what was described as an 'undignified discussion' took place amongst the jury in their box. The judge was blunt with regard to Dr Cassidy's evidence, refusing to go through it again in detail and directed them to reach a verdict. Many were surprised at this, as it was assumed Mr Justice Avory would simply discharge them and order a re-trial. After a short deliberation of a few minutes, the jury reluctantly or otherwise convicted Rawcliffe of murder, but recommended mercy in respect of the 'accident in his youth' – the recommendation possibly a compromise to the dissenter. There was absolute silence as the black cap was put on the judge's head and Rawcliffe was sentenced to hang. He was quickly removed from the dock, just managing to scan his eyes around the courtroom before he disappeared from view. He declined to appeal.

Over 1,500 people signed a petition asking for the death sentence to be commuted but on November 11th, the **Home Secretary, Mr Winston Churchill**, declined a reprieve. He had heard suggestions that the real reason Rawcliffe had murdered his wife was because of the involvement of the NSPCC, particularly as on one occasion she had reported her husband to them herself. On the following Monday he saw his children for the last time and then later in the day he saw his mother and other family members. All, heartbroken, left Lancaster Castle. Unbeknown until the case files were released a 100 years later one of the jurymen, a Mr Thomas Walsh telegrammed the Home Office complaining bitterly that if the jury had known that

Rawcliffe wouldn't have been spared, they wouldn't have returned a verdict of murder.

It had been 23 years since the last execution at Lancaster Prison [Alfred Sowrey on August 1st, 1887]. Rawcliffe would have to walk 75 yards to the execution shed, which was by the chapel. He had appeared indifferent in the death-cell, saying that he preferred to die rather than serve a life-sentence. He had told his mother that he had been suffering from nightmares where he constantly saw his dead wife's face. The execution was carried out on **Tuesday, November 15th, 1910, by John Ellis and his assistant William Willis** at eight am. Thirty minutes before, large crowds gathered outside the Castle and in keeping with the occasion the weather was gloomy and overcast. Rawcliffe had breakfasted well. As he and the chaplain, the Reverend Stanley Hersee sang a hymn, Ellis pinioned his arms and he was moved swiftly to the gallows. He appeared to die instantaneously; the body being, ironically, examined by Dr Barling.

The prison chaplain was so upset by the whole procedure, that he resigned and left the city. The gallows were brand new, but **Thomas Rawcliffe was the last person to be hanged at Lancaster Prison.** During the First World War it was decided that in future executions in Lancashire would either be carried out at Liverpool or Manchester. Incredibly the trap-door was left open after the hanging in the 'spring condition'. Over the next forty years or so the gallows fell into to disrepair and in 1956 it was removed after parts of the prison were closed in 1955. The inquest jury on the body of Rawcliffe requested that they be shown around the castle. It was pointed out that this was not immediately convenient but if they were to come between two and four o'clock the next day, then officials would gladly show them around.

Incredibly Lancaster Castle remains a working prison. The Castle is medieval and holds a Crown Court, and a Category C male prison. The castle buildings are owned by Lancashire County Council, which leases a major part of the structure to the Prison Service, whilst the land itself is owned by the Duchy of Lancaster. Due to it being a working prison access to the keep, towers, battlements and dungeons is currently denied to visitors just as they were to the inquest jury a century ago.

Case 7
"The Strict Law"

Oliver Butler

(1952)

Murder
of
Rose Meadows

A crime of passion, where the jury evidently did not believe Butler had intended to kill Rose Meadows, but had to follow the law. Despite their recommendation to mercy, Butler was subsequently hanged.

Some 25 miles north of Oxford on the A423 is the small town of Banbury. In total the town's police-force numbered just 15 in 1952 and on the afternoon of Monday May 19th one of them P.C. Robinson, who lived in the nearby village of Wroxton, made a grim and terrible discovery.

A little over two miles north of the town is the village of Hanwell and it was here in a field, some 250 yards from the main road, that the policeman found the body of 21 year old Rose Meadows. That P.C. Robinson had been sent to the field was part of the process that meant within hours of the body being found, Miss Meadows's killer would be in police custody.

The Banbury Police had been alerted by a 999 call made by Mr Arthur Phipps, who was responsible for the level-crossing at Horley, a few hundred yards from the murder scene. Mr Phipps had seen the young woman's body lying beneath a hawthorn tree and then with horror was told by a young man to call the police, as he had just killed his girlfriend!

Just after three o'clock Mr Phipps made his call and asked for P.C. Robinson to come to the level-crossing. From a quick examination of Miss Meadows by the local constable it was clear that she had been strangled.

Since P.C. Robinson was a local man he was acquainted with the victim and he preceded to her home at 2 Council Houses in Horley. At the house the police-officer had the painful duty of informing her parents that their daughter had been found dead and that foul play was suspected; after the initial outpouring of grief both parents 'knew' who was responsible.

Before P.C. Robinson broke the tragic news to her parents, he had discretely spoken to their neighbours and they said a young man, Oliver Butler, 24, had been living in the house for the past three days. Rose's parents told P.C. Robinson that Butler's actual home was at 37 West Street in the nearby village of Grimsbury.

With this information P.C. Robinson contacted Banbury Police-Station who despatched Det. Sgt. Morgan and Det. Cons. Hebert to Grimsbury. At just after four-thirty the two police-officers arrived at the small council house and found it empty. Believing that Butler was still in the district, the officers drove back to Horley. Their instinct was right for at 4.50 p.m. they spotted Butler by the level-crossing.

The two men were met by a distraught young man, who appeared to be in a daze and simply said to Det. Sgt. Morgan, when cautioned, : " Nothing to say now. " But then he turned to Det. Cons. Herbert and said, : " Can't you hang me now; I want to be with her. " With great speed Butler was driven to Banbury Police-Station, where he was formally charged with the murder of Rose Meadows.

Under the observation of the two policemen Butler wrote a detailed confession of the events that head led up to Rose's death. It appeared

Butler and Rose were walking through Wroxham Woods, when Rose, probably jokingly, said that this would a good place for a murder, since it was so quiet. However all was not as tranquil as it should be on a perfect Oxfordshire spring afternoon.

In the words of Rose's mother Iris, the couple were " desperately in love ", but Butler was married with three children and Rose wanted to marry him, but Butler's wife would not divorce her husband. It seems that the reference to Wroxham Woods being suitable for a murder provoked an angered response from Butler. In his confession he said, :

" I told her not to be so silly and she just laughed at me and told me that I would go back to my wife sooner or later. I asked why she thought that and she said maybe someday she would find another fellow. I told her that if she did I would do what I have already done .... She told me she never wanted to go home. A fortune-teller had told her that she would be murdered and she would sooner me murder her than anyone else.

I tried to stop her talking over it, to which she said that I was more nervous of it than she was. I asked her what she would say if I got hold of her throat, and she said she would not mind. She then said that if I did murder her I would hang and I would not mind for we should be in the same place.

She asked me why I did not do it, as her mother had heard that my wife had told someone in the town, that she would never divorce me. At that I got mad.

She said, : " We will never go no place, so why don't you do it ? I took hold of her throat and the next thing I knew she was dead. I felt her pulse and listened to her heart and I got scared and went to the Ironstone Gatehouse [The Horley Level-Crossing] and asked the fellow [Mr Phipps] to ring the police as I had murdered my girlfriend. If I had to do it again I would. I did not intend to let anything part us for long. "

Armed with this evidence, Butler was taken before the Banbury Magistrates on Wednesday May 21st, in proceedings that lasted only 11 minutes. He was remanded to appear before the County Magistrates on Thursday at which point they committed him to stand trial at the Staffordshire Assizes in July, as the Oxfordshire Assizes were not sitting until October.

When Rose was buried at Horley Parish Church all the villages around the north of Banbury were in mourning. Both Rose and Butler worked in the local Northern Aluminium Company factory. No doubt a few even felt sympathy for Butler as he languished in Oxford Prison waiting for his trial. Since Butler would have been assessed as a suicide risk he was no doubt guarded watchfully 24 hours a day.

At the assize court in Stafford, Butler stood before Mr Justice Hallett, on Friday July 4th. Mr George Baker Q.C. defended Butler whilst the prosecution was undertaken by Mr Ryder Richardson Q.C. .

For the Crown the case was simply that through jealousy and anger Butler had deliberately and intentionally strangled Rose Meadows. However the defence for Butler was to be somewhat unusual. Following Butler's time in Oxford Prison he had been purged of his suicidal tendencies and most definitely wanted to live. Mr Baker would attempt to show the jury that Rose's death was an accident in that Butler would admit placing his hands around Rose's neck but that her own medical disposition caused her death. Mr Richardson accepted that Butler was criminally responsible for her death but that the verdict should be manslaughter on the grounds that Butler did not intend to kill or cause grievous bodily harm to Rose.

Mr Baker attempted to show that there were medical reasons why Butler might have caused Rose's death, where if it had been inflicted on a fit person, it might not have caused any real injury at all.

Mr Baker, quoting from a book called *Medical Jurisprudence*, told the court that in most strangling cases the brooch bone was broken, but Miss Meadows's was not. However Mr Richardson called Professor Webster, Director of the Home Office Forensic Laboratory in London, who had carried out the post-mortem on Rose Meadows, and had been giving evidence at assize courts since 1924.

He agreed the brooch-bone had not been fractured but that he believed the breakage usually happened with old people. Professor Webster also said Rose did not die from pressure on the carotid nerve: some people can die instantaneously from this. Mr Baker also tried to have Rose's mother and sister say that she suffered from a weak heart, but they emphatically denied this.

The Judge asked Professor Webster to tell the court the exact state of Rose's health. He said that she was fit, healthy and strong. He told the court that she had died from asphyxia. Professor Webster told Mr Baker that it usually takes between two and five minutes for a person to strangle another, the implication being that Butler would have had to held his hands around Rose's neck for enough time for the law to imply he had done it intentionally. Professor Webster was quite clear that she had not died instantaneously.

Mr Baker next called a young girl Gillian King to tell the court what she and her younger brother had seen, as they were but a few yards from the whole incident. At about 2.50 p.m. they were paddling down the stream near the old mill at Hanwell, when unbeknown to Butler and Rose they passed by. However they did not actually see the killing only that when they moored and went onto the road, they saw the man leaving the field for the road. Miss King, 14, told the court that Butler looked worried, but she did say that from their boat they had heard the girl laughing.

Rose's mother Ethel was the next person called by Mr Baker to explain the couple's relationship. On the day in question - May 19th- Rose and Butler had eaten their mid-day meal. Mrs Meadows said in the three days that Butler was at her home, the couple never quarrelled. Tom Meadows, Rose's father, had let Butler stay at the house, on the understanding that he was not using his daughter.

Mr Phipps told the court of how he saw Butler at 3.30 p.m. and that, : " He was in a very bad way. He was crying and very distressed. He told me., : " There she lays upon the bank by the big thorn bush. I strangled her. I killed her she's dead. "

P.C. Robinson confirmed that when he arrived at the level-crossing Butler was sitting on a bench crying saying, : " .... she dared me to do it. ". Another policeman Det. Sgt. Morgan followed P.C. Robinson to tell the court that Butler's confession had been properly obtained: Sgt. Morgan had re-read the confession back to Butler and he had signed the bottom of each page. Mr Baker told the jury that Butler had no recollection of writing out or re-reading the statement.

Butler's trial only lasted one day and after lunch he was called by Mr Baker. He told the court he was very upset and distraught when he made his statement to the police and could not recall what he had written until it was shown to him a month later by Mr Baker.

Butler told the court that Rose constantly referred to murder and suicide, and that he thought she was trying to rile him by referring to his wife and her refusal to divorce him. Butler said that he and Rose had sex by the thorn-bush, as it was a very secluded part of the field, and that they had done this there, on several previous occasions. After sex Butler said he became angry by her referring to another fellow: and that this other fellow, she said, had tried to murder her.

Butler told the court that when he put his hands around Rose's neck he only intended to frighten her and that he still loved her. As he did this Rose pushed his right hand away and she began to hiss and her lips turn pale. Butler realised he had killed Rose.

In a question to the Judge Butler said he was using the word murder in the vernacular and not in the sense of that he had intentionally killed her. Butler also tried to clarify his position on the words, : " .... if I had to do it again, I would. ". Butler said he meant he would frighten her again.

To establish in the mind's of the jury that even if Butler did not intend to kill he did at least intend to cause serious injury, Mr Richardson said to Butler, : " You knew that in catching hold of a person's throat some grave injury might follow. ". Butler replied: Yes, but that he had not intentionally wanted to cause Rose grave injury. However Mr Richardson did have Butler admit that he might have known that death could result from his actions.

Unfortunately for Butler many of his answers to questions from Mr Richardson were confused and sometimes contradictory: whilst admitting he had killed her he also thought she had just fainted! In a dramatic climax Mr Richardson said, : *"You strangled her didn't you ? - I realise now I did sir. "*, was Butler's damming reply.

In his summing-up Mr Richardson said there was little to say other than Butler had, in the eyes of the law, murdered Rose Meadows.

Mr Baker's final address to the jury lasted a little longer. He said the whole affair was a tragic accident and that Butler was of low mentality and could not properly express himself. He said to the jury that Butler had shown no desire to harm Rose Meadows- Mr Baker reminded the court of the evidence of the schoolgirl Miss King who said Rose had been laughing.

Mr Baker also pointed out that by the evidence of Professor Webster that Rose was a strong young woman and yet there was no sign of a struggle: Mr Baker implored the jury to return a verdict of manslaughter.

Mr Justice Hallett directed the jury that they had to give a verdict in accordance with the law and that they must not shrink from their duty. The Judge told the jury that the crime of murder was proved if, : " .... it is committed when a man by an intentional act kills someone being at that time in that wicked state of mind we call malice aforethought. Also if he intentionally put his hands around her throat for the purpose of frightening her -a wholly illegal act- knowing it was likely to cause her death, that is also murder.

After 45 minutes the all-male jury returned a verdict of guilty of murder, but with a *strong recommendation to mercy.* As Mr Justice Hallett donned the traditional black cap women in the public gallery were heard to scream, but undaunted the Judge told Butler that he would, : " Suffer death by hanging ".

Immediately Butler had been condemned to die a petition was raised to save him from the gallows: his trade union, the National Union of General and Municipal Workers organised an appeal. In Butler's own village everyone signed the petition, organised by Butler's forgiving wife, and some publicans allowed their pubs to be used as focal points.

Meanwhile a legal appeal was launched in the Court of Criminal Appeal in London on Monday July 28th before the Lord Chief Justice, Lord Goddard and Justices Hilbery and Slade. The grounds of the appeal, again led by Mr George Baker Q.C., was that the trial judge had mis-directed the jury as to the law of murder, in that Butler could not have foreseen Miss Meadows's death.

However in dismissing the appeal, Lord Goddard said, that Butler was condemned by his own words in that he intentionally put his hands around the victim's neck in order at least to frighten her, and from that the reasonable man would imply the malice aforethought for murder.

Butler's fate was now in the hands of the Home Secretary- Sir David Maxwell-Fyfe. It is worth noting that he was a staunch supporter of capital punishment and that from death sentences passed in 1952, there were 22 hangings, the second largest number this century in England and Wales.

Many people have labelled the decisions to execute or reprieve a condemned person as a " lottery ", however in the words of a former Home Secretary, Sir John Anderson, the vast majority of decisions were clear cut and often it was because of information that could not be stated at the trial. Oliver Butler is a good example of the policy of executing murderers in the British Isles.

Although the jury recommended mercy in this case, he was executed. From the evidence of the case that was presented at Butler's trial it is difficult to see why he was hanged: Was there something in Butler's past that meant that the Home Office believed he deserved to die for his crime ?

Thus on the pleasantly warm summer's morning of Tuesday August 12th, 1952 a small crowd gathered outside the prison gates of Oxford Prison within Oxford Castle in the city centre. A four o'clock on the previous afternoon chief executioner Albert Pierrepoint and his assistant Harry Smith had slipped into the prison to prepare for the hanging.

At 9.07 a.m. two prison-warders emerged to nail the execution notice to the prison gate. As they did this a by-stander raised his hat. No-one from the Banbury area was present, the crowd being mostly house-wives and young errand boys.

The Prison Chaplain The Rev. D.K. Stather-Hunt had sat with Butler between 8.15 a.m and his hour of doom and after the execution the Prison Doctor Dr Patrick Molloy-Smyth held an inquest during which he said the hanging had been carried out " very skilfully."

Case 8
"The Writing On the Photo"

"The Swindon Hotel Tragedy"

Edward Palmer
(1903)
Murder
of
Miss Ettie Swinford

".... I have to pay for my folly next Tuesday."

By 1903 Miss Esther "Ettie" or "Het" Swinford was a bright and intelligent girl of 20. The daughter of a farm labourer from the small Gloucestershire town of Fairford, she decided in her mid-teens that she did not want the conventional life of a rural woman. However at the turn of the 20th century women still could not vote and so it took much courage at 17 for Miss Swinford to travel the short distance to Swindon. Although only 12 miles from

Fairford, the Wiltshire town was part of a different world. With the large G.W.R. railway works, the expanding "modern" town, was the ideal place for Ettie to start her new life.

By the summer of 1903, Miss Swinford was happily working as a barmaid, and she found herself in the Ship Hotel in Swindon, a place that at 17 she had first worked at, when she had first come to the town three years earlier. At 18 she briefly left Swindon and worked for a time as a servant in Bath to broaden her work experience, although she quickly returned to bar work. By the beginning of 1903 she was now an accomplished barmaid, who also ran the bar and was engaged in stocktaking and bookkeeping.

However as a young woman she was also interested in men and it was in her previous job before returning to the Ship Hotel, at the bar in the Rodbourne Road Club in the town in 1902, that she had finally decided on what she thought was to be the man of her life, one **Edward Palmer**. At the time the 23-year-old was working in the G.W.R works and lodging in Swindon.

In fact Ettie had first known Palmer from the Ship Hotel as early as 1900, when he was one of many young men from the G.W.R. works, who would come in there, and there were rumours in the works and hotel, that the couple had been first engaged in February 1901, something Palmer himself would later say was the case. Palmer became very friendly with the landlord of the pub, Mr Walter Matthews and his wife Isabella Ann, and when Ettie went to work in the bar in the club in Rodbourne Road, Palmer followed her and it was there they began going out with each other, on a more permanent basis.

The pair seemed very happy and at the beginning of September 1902, Palmer proposed marriage to Ettie. She happily accepted and the banns were read out in the local church and a date for the wedding was even fixed. Then it all began to go wrong. Their relationship finally ended, when Palmer took out a gun and threatened Ettie with it. Palmer then fled the town and was believed to have gone to Canada, but in September 1903, he was seen in Swindon again....

It was exactly a year since the pair had split up. In September 1902, Ettie was lodging with an aunt, and the three of them had decided to meet to discuss the purchase of furniture for their new home after their marriage. It was now only two days before the wedding and Palmer did not turn up. Ettie was naturally very upset and her aunt, more worldly wise, decided they should go to his lodgings and confront Palmer. Although the aunt, Mrs Ann Edwards, reassured Ettie on the short journey from Rodbourne Road, she was not surprised to be shown an envelope by Palmer's landlady, in which was the key to his room, and to be told Palmer had left with no forwarding address. It appeared as if Edward Palmer had vanished. However on September 6th, the day of the wedding he reappeared, and asked a friend, a Mr Brunsden, to go to Rodbourne Road and "fetch" Ettie. It seemed that even at the 11th hour the wedding could still be on.

This time with an uncle, Mr Brindle, Ettie listened with great interest to what Palmer had to say. Understandably the uncle told Palmer what he thought of him, and Palmer told him to mind his own business. Evidently still very much in love with Palmer, Ettie suggested they go for a walk alone and discuss the matter. However it was very a short meeting and in tears Ettie asked her uncle to take her back to Rodbourne Road. What Ettie didn't tell her uncle until much later, was that Palmer had pulled a revolver on her and threatened to shoot her!

Two days later Palmer once again gave his landlady his key, this time apparently for good, saying he was going to Canada. Except for a brief visit to the town in May 1903, all who had known Palmer assumed he had indeed emigrated. However just as Palmer had deceived Ettie, he didn't exactly emigrate to Canada. Far from it. For the next year he was employed as a gardener in three separate positions in Reading, Kintbury near Hungerford and Marlow, and it was in the last town that he was working just a week before he returned to Swindon in September. It turned out Palmer had never left England.

When Palmer had returned to Swindon briefly in May he had stayed with a work colleague called E. Workman, who did go to Canada. When Workman returned to Swindon himself at the beginning of September, he contacted Palmer and late on the night of September 2nd, Palmer came to Swindon and asked him to come to the Ship Hotel, but Workman said it was too late. Palmer took the late mail train to Reading to catch his connection to Marlow, but as he left he told Workman he would have to go to the Ship Hotel at some point.

On September 12th, Palmer handed in his notice in Marlow and travelled to Swindon and took lodgings. Although Palmer may have been preoccupied with the Ship Hotel, he certainly intended to return to work at the G.W.R. works, as he had written to them on the third of September asking for his old job back. However by the **Wednesday the eighteenth**, Palmer had not got his old job back, but on the afternoon of that date he was in the Mechanics' Institute club in the works, when to his shock he saw Mr Edwards, one of Ettie's uncle. The men saw each other but simply glared and no words passed between them.

Such was the high regard with which Mr and Mrs Matthews, the owners of the Ship Hotel, had for Miss Swinford, that at four-thirty on the eighteenth, when they went for their tea, they were quite happy for the 20-year-old to run the whole bar on her own. Then at about 4.45 p.m. Edward Palmer walked into the bar of the Ship Hotel. Palmer asked for a bottle of Bass and turned to speak to Ettie....

Ettie knew that the Matthews had shown great faith in her and so decided to treat Palmer like anything other customer. Palmer asked Ettie for a cigar and furthermore he requested that she bring it into the private bar. The pair went into the private bar and as Ettie was about to open the cigar box, Palmer took out a revolver and pressed it against Ettie's breasts. The Matthews later told the police that they heard a single gunshot at about 4.45. p.m. and that Mrs Matthews rushed into the private bar to find Ettie apparently dead on the floor.

Ettie had suffered a single shot from a revolver just about her heart. There was still a faint sign of life but within two minutes she was quite dead. Standing a few yards away was Palmer, the revolver still in his hand, but appearing like a lifeless puppet and he was quickly detained by Mr Matthews, and indeed placed the gun on a bar table himself. Mr Matthews ordered some children, who were in the bar to bring the police, and Palmer was alleged to have said: "You needn't do that, Walt. I done it: I loved the girl." Mr Matthews was wisely taking no precautions and Palmer was locked in a storeroom while they awaited the police.

At Swindon police station the police found a photograph on Palmer, with the words: " The curse of my life.". Palmer was charged with Ettie Swinford's murder and stood on trial for his life at the **Devizes Assizes on Wednesday, October 28th, 1903, before Mr Justice Wills**, in what had become known as the "*The Swindon Hotel Tragedy*".

At ten o'clock there was a large crowd outside the courthouse and when the doors were opened the police struggled to control the crowds as they surged forward to snap up the few seats in the small public gallery. Then with calm restored, the case against Palmer began at ten-thirty with words: " Edward Richard Palmer you are charged with having feloniously, wilfully and with malice aforethought, killed and murdered one Esther Swinford at Swindon on September 18th." Palmer replied "Not Guilty" to the charge and the defence would later suggest that the whole affair was a terrible accident or at most a case of manslaughter.

The Crown's case was put by **Mr John Foote KC and his junior, Mr Seton**, whilst Palmer was represented by **Mr Thornton Lawes**. Having outlined the basic facts of the case, Mr Foote called Mrs Matthews to the stand. The landlord's wife said she knew Palmer and knew he had been engaged to Miss Swinford and when cross-examined by Mr Lawes, she said that when she rushed into the private bar and saw Palmer, he looked "dumbstruck". The first officer on the scene, Constable Vincent also said that Palmer seemed "dazed".

It was when Superintendent Robinson took the stand that the court began to understand more about the relationship between Ettie and Palmer. The officer read out a letter, headed "Rodbourne Lane Club", which covered the period some time before the proposed wedding and which showed the couple were having some problems before September 1902. It began: "To my own Dearest Dick from H.S." One line read: "You have been in my mind and eyes, since you left Swindon." The letter went on to say that she wanted Palmer to go and see her father so they could start seeing each other again, and that she blamed herself for pressurising him into marriage, and she ended by saying she wanted to see Palmer again. As a footnote "broken-hearted Het" added:

" 69 kisses to you my darling own, because you were mine once, weren't you Dick, my very own sweetheart and me yours."

Another letter just before the wedding dated, September 1st, 1902 suggested that Ettie was being forced into marrying another man and she claimed: "They are watching me" and she ended the letter by saying, she was his "true sweetheart and true love".

After the court had heard the evidence of Dr Astley Cooper-Swinhoe concerning the cause of death, the court heard from a Mrs Selina Tocock, Palmer's sister, who lived in Reading and to whom he visited in September 1902. Mrs Tocock said her brother was in a "wild" state and that he had said he would never marry Miss Swinford. Mrs Tocock wrote to their brother Harold, and when Palmer visited him shortly afterwards, a revolver was taken off him. All Harold Palmer would tell the court was that his brother had heard "something" about Ettie and that he had spent all his money at the races.

Mr Lawes called a number of witnesses from Reading, Kintbury and Marlow in relationship to Palmer's employment as a gardener and all of them said he was "quiet, steady and sober". Then he called Mr Workman who said that Palmer had told him the simple reason why the wedding had been cancelled was that he had run out of money, and that he had "fled" Swindon as he was ashamed that he would be unable to provide for her. Mr Workman told the court that Palmer had also told him, that he blamed Ettie's relatives for the couple's problems.

On the morning of September 18th, Palmer's new landlady, Mrs Mary Huxtable said that he had told her: "I'm going to see the girl" and that in the short time she had known him, he had always behaved properly and was never drunk. Similarly his previous immediate boss at the G.W.R. works said Palmer was a good workman and had a very good character. After the court had heard from the Prison Surgeon at Devizes Prison, Dr Mackay, who said that Palmer was "perfectly normal", the court retired for lunch. When the court resumed there was a buzz of excitement, as it was believed Edward Palmer would be giving evidence on his own behalf.[17]

Walking firmly from the dock to the witness box, Palmer looked determinedly at Mr Lawes. Palmer said he had first met Ettie Swinford in April 1900 when she was 17 and he 21. On the day of the murder Palmer said: " I was at the [Mechanics'] Institute until twenty minutes past four.... I went to the Ship Hotel.... and asked for a bottle of Bass. Miss Swinford served me." After she served me, I said 'Hello Het', and she went round the other side of the bar without speaking. Then I went into the parlour and called for a smoke. Miss Swinford came in and I took the cigar from the box and said 'Het, aren't you going to speak to me, as I am going away tomorrow.' Palmer said that she replied 'I do not wish to have anything more to do with you'.

Turning to the jury, Palmer said he only pulled out the revolver to frighten Ettie, but she dropped the cigar box and Palmer claimed this caught his wrist and the gun discharged. Palmer said he was "stunned" by what had happened to Miss Swinford. In an answer to Mr Lawes, Palmer said he was devoted to Ettie and that he never had any intention of injuring her.

---

17 At the time this was still a novel idea as the law was only reformed in 1898 to allow a prisoner to give evidence on his own behalf.

Palmer said he had bought the revolver in May 1902 having seen an advert in the *Exchange and Mart* and that he carried it all the time, and that since working as a stable-hand and living above the stables at the age of 14, he had always kept a gun for protection. He told Mr Foote, in cross-examination that he no specific purpose in taking the gun to the Ship Hotel, and that as usual the gun was loaded, indeed all five chambers, was in his hip pocket, and the spare cartridges were in his ticket-pocket. Despite Mr Foote's obvious disbelief that a man would walk around Swindon with a loaded revolver and spare cartridges, Palmer seemed to think it was all quite normal.

Palmer admitted that he had pulled the gun out when Ettie had told him she no longer wanted anything to do with him and that he had acted on "impulse" in threatening her. Then Palmer claimed he had never threatened Miss Swinford before with a gun. When Mr Foote pressed him about the incident in September 1902, Palmer said: " As God is my Maker, I did not threaten her shortly before the day fixed for the wedding."

When asked by Mr Foote why he had written over Miss Swinford's photo with the words " the curse of my life", Palmer refused to answer. Similarly when asked why he did not tell the police and magistrates that the shooting was an accident, all he could say was: "I felt stunned." Pressed by the judge, Palmer said he had wanted to keep everything to himself.

In his final address to the jury Mr Foote said that as far as the Crown could ascertain Miss Swinford had never wronged Palmer in anyway and her letters to him showed she was deeply in love with him and wanted to marry him. On the other hand Palmer had bought a revolver in May 1902, for spurious reasons. In September of that year he was accused of having threatened Miss Swinford with a gun just before he was due to marry her. He had then "disappeared" for the best part of a year, telling people he had gone to Canada, a fact completely untrue. Mr Foote said that Miss Swinford's family were perfectly justified in not wanting her to marry Palmer.

Mr Foote suggested that a man who merely wished to "frighten" would not load a revolver. Suggesting the crime was "premeditated", he said that Palmer had gone to the bar at a time when few people would be around and Miss Swinford likely to be alone. Mr Foote suggested that Palmer was one of those men who, unable to marry the girl they loved, felt through jealousy, that they had no other option but kill them. He said such men feel they are called on to kill.

Mr Foote said that in law he did not have to show any motive, but he felt out of fairness to Palmer he should ask why he had defaced the photo of her, even though Miss Swinford was known to be of "excellent" character and "highly respected". Mr Foote said Palmer's response was telling - nothing. The Crown Counsel would say that this was because there was nothing to suggest that Miss Swinford had ever acted improperly towards the prisoner.

In his summing up Mr Lawes asked the jury to say that the prosecution had not proved any premeditation on the part of Palmer. He suggested the foolhardy practice of young men carrying loaded revolvers for bravado was far more common than ordinary people believed. He also stressed that everyone, except Miss Swinford's family, had viewed Palmer as a pleasant and hard-working young man. However he conceded that brandishing a loaded revolver against the victim's body was "gross carelessness" and the defence would accept the justice of a verdict of manslaughter. But nevertheless it was Mr Lawes' final words to the jury that Palmer should be acquitted as the whole affair was a "pure accident".

Mr Justice Wills was quite forthright in his address to the jury. He said that if they disbelieved Palmer's account of the shooting, then it was a case of murder and nothing less. The judge said he believed that the prisoner had been told some untrue rumour about the girl and this had lead him to the breaking off the engagement. He said he didn't believe it was simply a case of not having enough money for the wedding, as this did not explain the writing on the photo. Mr Justice Wills' final words to the jury were that they should look at all the facts "fully and carefully."

The trial of Edward Palmer lasted just seven-and-a-half hours. The jury retired at 4.15 p.m. and returned to their box, 30 minutes later. There was a deathly hush in the court as the foreman of the jury announced they had found the prisoner guilty of.... murder. Palmer was observed to have swayed slightly and his face to have turned a ghostly white. He said he had nothing to say.

Having assumed the black cap, Mr Justice Wills, said the jury had come to the right verdict and that the law of England knew only one sentence for murder. After the death sentence, Palmer was seen to loose his step, and had to be helped out of the dock, by the prisoner officers. He was taken the short distance to the condemned cell in **Devizes Prison**, to await the decision of the Home Secretary Mr Aretas Akers-Douglas.

There being no appeal court in England until 1907, the date of the proposed execution was set for **Tuesday, 17th November, 1903**. Two days before that date, Mr Akers-Douglas decided that nothing could be found in favour of Palmer and indeed that his execution should be a warning to those who carried loaded revolvers in public. There was to be no reprieve for Edward Palmer.

It was a typically grey and dull morning when Edward Palmer stood on the gallows at Devizes Prison **before the hangmen - William and John Billington at eight a.m**. Although there were only a few people outside the jail at the time of the hanging, up to the day before the execution it had been greatly discussed in the town. It was the first execution in Devizes since 1892, when John Gurd had been hanged for the murder near Warminster of his girlfriend's uncle in a fit of passion and a Police Sergeant who had tried to arrest him. Much was made of the fact of the "striking similarity" of the crimes of Gurd and Palmer and whether capital punishment was really a deterrent to murder.

Just before eight o'clock there was a glimmer of sunshine and then a flood of light, which caused the birds to break into song. Then a minute or so later the prison bell tolled and everyone in the town knew Edward Palmer had been hanged. That evening a letter was published by the press, by Palmer to a friend in Swindon. It read:

".... I have to pay for my folly next Tuesday. There's nothing for me to tell you, only that I repent and am more sorry than words can tell for that mad day. Oh if I can only undo it. But I trust in God to forgive me. I am going to Him truly penitent and trusting in His great mercy...." From your affectionate friend, Dick.

The execution over, William Billington, declined to be interviewed by the Press and the executioners left Devizes by the half-past two train. Like everyone else the hangman would not know that Edward Palmer would be the last person executed at Devizes Prison, and like everyone else he probably wondered why Edward Palmer had murdered Ettie Swinford and why he had written across her photo?

Edward Palmer was the last man hanged at Devizes Prison and the jail was closed in 1911.

Case 9
"The Curious Affair Of The Missing Money"

~The Many Lies of the Sibsey Drifters~

Henry Carey (24) & William Pickett (20)
[1859]
Murder
Of
William Stevenson (64)

" …. Let's kill the old bastard, I think he's got some money." A plot was hatched in a village pub ….

"A good view of the execution in this yard, admission 3d." Signs in two local pubs next to the execution site ….

Violent case of two young men, filled with drink, and short of cash, who decided to rob a fellow drinker from

their local in a village in Lincolnshire, in the Spring of 1859 ....

Despite being just four miles north of Boston, the Lincolnshire village of Sibsey has changed very little since the 19th century, and still has less than 2,000 people living there .... and just over 150 years ago, it was the scene of an extremely brutal and appalling murder .... On the evening of **Wednesday, March 16th, 1859,** one of the village's local pubs had just four patrons in it; and in the *Ship Inn* this night were two young men, who weren't exactly local – **Henry Carey (24) and his mate William Pickett (20);** although the latter's family were local .... Also in the pub was a local – **64-year-old William Stevenson** .... Everybody knew everybody in and around Sibsey, and most people tried to avoid the stranger Carey and Pickett, who had left the area some years prior – but the pair had been in the village long enough for people to quickly realise that they were bad news; they were anti-social and always short of cash .... But in small places like Sibsey, you couldn't help but avoid people like them .... This night they were determined to end their cash crisis; and as the beer flowed, they began to hatch a plan .... Soon this plan turned to robbery; and as they thought of what or who to rob, old Mr Stevenson ambled up to the bar for another pint .... A small local pig farmer – it was Wednesday, and he had been to market in Boston, and had made some money; and Pickett knew him somewhat .... The pair watched Mr Stevenson leave the bar, and under his breath Carey muttered menacingly: "Let's kill the old bastard, I think he's got some money." The young men left the pub early: it was about ten-thirty pm .... outside in the darkness they talked about putting handkerchiefs across their mouths; Pickett might have to cover his face completely bar his eyes, as he was sure the old man would know him .... They would way-lay Mr Stevenson en route back to his home: he had left a few minutes earlier .... it was about a mile to his home .... the landlord, David Richardson would later say that Carey was 'worse for drink', but that Pickett appeared quite sober .... He added that Mr Stevenson was also a bit under the influence ....

At about seven am the next day, a local woman, Mary Semper, was walking along one of the feeders from the *River Witham* that ran through the village; they were used as sewers and were 8 to 9 feet wide, and 4 to 5 feet deep …. She was near Mr Stevenson's cottage, and in the water she could see an old shirt – or that is what she thought it was …. As she went down to retrieve it, to her horror, she quickly realised it was …. the old man …. and it was obvious he had suffered terrible injuries to his head: indeed his skull had been fractured …. it must have been some kind of terrible accident …. he had slipped, stumbled and hit his head on the water's edge before drowning …. Very quickly the village police arrived, but they noticed blood before the water's edge on the path, and that a low hedge that boarded the sewer had been broken down or roughly gone through: this was easy to see as the hedge had recently been re-woven …. indeed there was a suspicious trail: it was about 80 yards back from the edge …. it looked like Mr Stevenson had been brutally assaulted some time before he ended up in the water …. What's more, there were other footprints on the path, along with marks, as if something heavy had been dragged across it; there was downtrodden grass and signs of a struggle on the field side of the path; and nearby, were three blood-marked fence stakes, broken into many parts; on closer inspection on the broken hedge were signs of blood …. By the hedge and down to the water was more traces of blood and hair, and the victim's son spotted a pool of blood about ten yards from the hedge ….

As news of the find spread to the village, people quickly came forward to say they had been surprised to see Carey and Pickett leave the pub so early; and others had seen them making their way towards Mr Stevenson's home …. The pair were quickly found: they were living rough in an old boat near the scene, and Carey was found in the *Ship Inn*; Pickett a few hours later in the village – the men clearly had bloodstains on their jackets and trousers; on one boot of Carey's – the right - was blood; but most incriminating was the fact that Carey's boots matched the prints on the sewer bank path; and when searched Carey had the victim's knife in his pocket, as well as two of his own …. Although there were other footprints on the path, they could not be identified; the knife was identified by the victim's son as belonging to his dad ….

In the village police-station to Superintendent James Strugnell, William Pickett admitted to being there when Carey attacked the old man – he said Carey had attacked the victim with the fence- stakes before throwing him into the water …. However to the young men's horror, Mr Stevenson, despite his age, was a strong man, who climbed out of the water and up the bank …! By now Pickett realised that he would be identified by the old man, and he and Carey re-assaulted him with the stakes, before, once again, pushing him into the water …. Just before he drowned, he called out: "Oh, Pickett, what are you doing?" Pickett admitted to the police that they assumed Mr Stevenson would have a large amount of cash on him from the market: all he really had was just a sovereign on him …. He said that when he had sobered up, he realised what a dreadful thing he had become involved in …. Pickett said both he and Carey were very drunk – although they had left the pub early, they had bought and taken with them a jug full of beer to consume on their way …. Pickett claimed it was Carey that had talked him into the enterprise and kept him involved …. Very early the next day, Pickett had gone back to the *Ship* and said to the landlord: "Good morning, I have brought you your bottle back, and another I have had sometime. *Stevenson was a strong man of his age ….*" Mr Richardson had no idea what the last part meant ….

Although seen frequently in and around Sibsey, Carey and Pickett were, in fact, homeless drifters: it was Pickett's dad and family who were local …. if they did work it was very casually; most of the time they begged and stole, and generally made themselves a nuisance …. As the police questioned the pair, it became 'obvious' that Carey was the 'brains' behind the plan, *or so it seemed* …. In the pub, it was clear the men were short of money, and as they argued with each other, they were warned by the landlord to be quite or to leave …. As the plan evolved, Pickett told his friend that he was sure Mr Stevenson knew him; but Carey said this was not a problem: the men would wear handkerchiefs; and with holes cut out for Pickett's eyes; the handkerchief could then cover his whole face …. Carey was sure that despite being on the boat, the old man would not remember him, after they fled the area …. It was Carey who had planned where to attack the victim, and that the old man would be using a big walking stick. Carey told Pickett: " .... you'll have to hold him while I do the rest ...." At first Pickett said that he had refused to hold Mr Stevenson, but Carey was undeterred, and said he'd take the old man on anyway ....

Mr Stevenson lived with his son in their cottage: Carey had decided to attack the victim some 500 yards away from his home; and that there were no actual fences between the path and the water, would make it easier to push the old man in after the assault and robbery .... As he made his way home, it didn't appear that Mr Stevenson was in any way drunk, despite what the landlord had said .... he saw Carey and Pickett and was certainly surprised to see *anyone* at all – especially at that time of night .... and he was aware of the two young men on the old boat .... but he wasn't afraid .... Carey and possibly Pickett launched into a ferocious attack on him with the fence-stakes – one dripping in blood shattered into pieces such was the force used: when the police re-constructed it, it was over four-feet long .... Eventually thrown into the water, old Mr Stevenson came back up coughing and spluttering, his head covered in blood .... It is probable that the old man had been revived by the cold water, and didn't appreciate how seriously injured he was .... Once out of the water, he was 'finished off' .... Dead or very nearly dead the pair robbed him .... Their great plan had resulted in just one sovereign, a few pennies (they actually missed a few more coins from the victim's rifled pockets), and the dead man's knife, which although Pickett took, he ended up giving to Carey .... This great booty, the pair took, and buried in a hole near another local pub, called the *Sun Inn* .... So drunk, the pair spent most of the night in a field near the home of a local called George Sands .... later in the morning they made their way back to the old boat .... However there was some mystery about the money that Mr Stevenson might have had on him, as his son told the police that when his dad left home to go to Boston about eight o'clock in the morning, *he had some £3 to £4, in his pocket*. The son said that he had lent him £2, the previous Monday, which had not been repaid. The son and the police searched their house after the murder; *but no money was found* ....

Henry Carey and William Pickett appeared at the **Lincoln Assizes on Wednesday, July 27th, before Mr Justice Edward Vaughan**

Williams: the trial lasted just over a day. **The defence for Pickett – Messrs MaCaulay and Flowers** was that he had helped the police – he had made a signed statement, which was read to the court: and that this should mean that he should be convicted of a lesser offence than murder – either robbery or manslaughter ….

"Carey and me left the public-house on Wednesday night between 10 and 11 o'clock, and went down to my father's house. I went up to my father's door, and he had gone to bed. Carey stood against father's gate when I came out again. He said let us go over the drain in your father's boat. I said, 'What for?' He said, 'I was working for George Sands, and I killed two rabbits in the close, and if you will go with me I will give you one.' I went with him till we came to Mr Teesdale's house. He drew a stick out of Mr Teesdale's fence. He said, 'very likely Mr Drury's dog will come out, you had better have one and all.' I said, 'No, I'll go without. ' Going on down the lane past Mr Coates' house we overtook Mr Stevenson. Carey said to me again, 'Lets kill the old b-----, I think he's got some money.' I said, 'No, don't meddle with the old man. ' He said, 'I will.' He hit him right on the side of the head, knocked him down, and put his hands in his pockets, and said, 'Let us have the old b------'s money.' He got off him again, and hit him three or four times over the head with the stick. He said to me,' Take hold of his head.' I said, 'No.' He said, 'If you don't I'll serve you the same.' I took hold of his head, and helped Carey to throw him into the sewer. He then went across the path again to fetch his stick. The old man was standing up in the dyke then. He hit him two or three more times, when the old man climbed up to get over the hedge. I went on as far as Mr Coates' yard, then Carey went the other way. I thought I would go round and assist the old man to get home. When I got within a few yards of him, I saw Carey coming up to him again, with a piece of wood or stick on his shoulder. When I got up to the old man, Carey struck him on the head and knocked him down, and hit him 7 or 8 times on the floor and broke the stick to atoms. The old man tried to get up again, when *Carey got a piece of hedge stake or thorn and beat him about the head till he was dead*, and trailed him down to the hedge next to the sewer dyke, saying to me, 'Take hold of his legs, and we'll throw him into the sewer.' I said, 'What for? Let him be.' He then reared him up on his head on the hedge-layers and tumbled him into the sewer. He then went on towards Mr Stevenson's house, and I went on to Mr Coates' house. When I got on the bank, Carey overtook me, and said, ' The old man is dead: he does not stir in the water at all.' He said, 'I've got a sovereign, a half-crown, a shilling, and a handful of papers, (I don't know what they are,) and two bags.' Going on for a while, I came to my father's seven acre field, when Carey said, 'I'll hide these papers here.' And he hid them under some grass on the bank side just against the tunnel. We went on till we came to my father's little boat, and went over the river in it, and when I got over I went up to my father's house. I said, 'I shall go and lay down a bit.' Carey said, 'I shall go and all where you do.' I said I would not take him there, so we went on as far as my brother John's house: went across his garden and across to Mr Sands' hovel, and tumbled over my foot. Carey and me then went to Mr Richardson's. There Carey took out of his pocket the two bags he had taken from Mr Stevenson with the money, and put a stone into them, and threw them into Mr Richardson's pit. *Signed, William Pickett.*"

For the **Prosecution, James Fitzjames Stephen** said that whilst it was 'obvious' Carey was more culpable; in law, both men were equally guilty of murder …. Carey had made no statement to the police; and in fact, was not defended in court, but when asked to plead said, in a loud voice, "I am guilty of the robbery, but not of the murder". Initially all the jury heard was Pickett's statement of how he was a passive individual, who had been easily led by the far more aggressive Carey …. However throughout the trial, Carey himself remained calm and seemed to bear no hatred towards his once friend, who now appeared more like a 'grass': The local newspaper said that Carey looked like a criminal: he had 'a low forehead, thought to distinguish murderers' …. The defence also suggested that Mr Stevenson had ill-used Pickett by employing him on his land as a farm labourer some years before, and paying him very poorly, and not providing any decent accommodation for him; although he had on occasion let him sleep in his cottage …. Then at the end of the first day, Carey was invited by the judge to speak to the jury from the dock, and he said in a firm loud voice that:

"He was very sorry for what he had done. He had promised Pickett he would not say a word about it unless he did. On the day of the murder he had been at work for Edward Sands. After they left work they met old Mr Stevenson and Pickett at the public-house. He wished to go home at ten o'clock, as he should be locked out if late, but Pickett would not allow him to leave, saying "he might sleep with him on board the boat." Pickett went out of the house first. He (Carey) wished to wait for George Sands, but Pickett said he did not want him with him. They went on towards where Pickett's father's boats lay when at home. Pickett said, "There is old Stevenson coming, let us go over and have his money." He (Carey) said, "You will not catch me going over tonight." Pickett said, "that was what he wanted him for; that three pence was all the money he had, and he must have some." He then said he had some handkerchiefs, and that they must cover their faces. They then went over in the little boat which Pickett's father used when he went farming. When they had got over, Pickett pulled out two pocket handkerchiefs and covered their faces. There were some holes in the one Pickett had, and he made some in the one, which he put on his own face. Pickett then found two sticks, one of which he gave to him (Carey), and the other he kept. They then went about half way down the lane where old Mr Stevenson was going towards his son's house. There they lay down, side by side, on the road side. Old Mr Stevenson was coming up and said, "Hello! What are you doing here? Get up lads, you will get your death of cold. Go in and lie down in the yard on the straw." They got up; and one clung to him, and the other placed a leg against his and flung him backwards. Pickett held his head down, and he (Carey) searched his pockets. He got what money he had. He then got up and ran away. He afterwards looked to see if Pickett was coming. He saw Pickett and old Mr Stevenson going on to the floor. He struck Mr Stevenson on the right arm with his weapon. He [Mr Stevenson] still kept hold of Pickett. He (Carey) then struck him on the head. Mr Stevenson tore Pickett's handkerchief from his face and tore it in two. He then took his walking stick and struck Pickett, who struck the old man with his weapon and knocked him down. He then took him by the collar and he (Carey) took him by the feet, and they put him in the sewer. He got up, and Pickett struck him twice on the hand. Then he struck Pickett, and went across the sewer, calling out, "What are you doing." Pickett then struck him on the back of the head. He (Carey) went across the road and flung his weapon in the dykc. He then saw Pickett run along the river bank. When Pickett rejoined him, he said he had got another weapon, and hit Mr Stevenson on top of the head and on the side of the head, and did not know that he had killed him, but wished him (Carey) not to be frightened. Pickett then sent him back for half of the handkerchief he had lost in the scuffle, because it was marked with his sweetheart's name; and when he had brought it, he (Pickett) tied the two halves together, and put a piece of brick into them and threw them into the river. He found a sovereign, one or two bills, and 3s 6d in Mr Stevenson's pocket. The sovereign Pickett took, and the bills were hidden near a tunnel of Pickett's father. They then went and slept at George Sands' hovel till five o'clock in the morning." The prisoner ended his statement by saying that he had prayed to the Lord to forgive him, and he prayed that the judge would be as merciful as he could ....

Late on the next morning **[Thursday, July 28th]** the jury retired: it took them just 25 minutes to find both Carey and Pickett guilty of murder. There was no recommendation to mercy for Pickett, who told the court: "My father has often told me that if I kept the company with Carey, I should be transported or hanged" .... Pickett then admitted that the victim had never been unpleasant to him saying: " .... Mr Stevenson was always a friend to me. He took me in when I was turned out of my own house." It was now that Carey spoke out again; now saying *he* was responsible for the whole affair, and that Pickett had not wanted to become involved; but had been cajoled by Carey .... It made no difference – **the Home Secretary, Sir George Cornewall Lewis**, felt no distinction should be made .... Furthermore he felt an example of the men should be made .... In 1836, the law requiring murderers to be executed within 48 hours of sentence, was abolished .... the new law allowed up to 28 days, and *suggested* at least *14* days[18] .... In this case the execution was set for **Friday, August 5th**: that was in just *eight* days time ....

The execution was to be held on top of the **Cobb Hall Tower of Lincoln Castle**, which also housed the County Prison: Carey was placed in cell C11 and Pickett in cell C10 .... The landlords of the two nearest pubs – the *Plough* and *Yarborough Arms* turned their

---

18 *Executions for Murder Act 1836*

front areas into viewing arenas: the admission charge would be 3d …. Reformers were outraged …. the area in front of the Tower was vast, and it was estimated that in all a crowd of over 25,000 would be in attendance …. The local 'paper reported that several 'notorious thieves' would be making their way to Lincoln for the event …. **The execution was set for noon**; and by then it seemed that this vast crowd had, indeed, turned up …. many were 'men following a respectable position in society' …. **The hangman was Yorkshireman Thomas Askern** …. The local clergy were out in force attempting to try and persuade the crowds to be more respectful and sober …. Sadly, it was not to be; and when the two men appeared on the drop, they were jeered and subjected to 'cruel laughter'. The execution had become a 'place of amusement' …. However apart from the crowd, the double-execution went *relatively* smoothly.

The castle gates were opened around 4.00 am for the workmen to come and erect the gallows; the work was all done by 6.00 am: Two of the workmen were brothers, Robert and George Panton; they had a joiners workshop next to the castle. At 6.30 am, the Prison Governor visited the prisoners, and reported they appeared well, considering their situation; and had forgiven each other ….

Friday was market day at Lincoln, and this August day was going to be another bright sunny day in a very long hot summer. For sometime before the appointed hour of the execution, crowds started to gather in the neighbourhood of the gallows, anxious to obtain a good view of the unfortunate men. There was a carnival atmosphere. People came to Lincoln by rail and all kinds of transport. Old and young struggled up the steep hill to reach the castle. They even went on crutches. Youths went truant from school to go and watch. Prostitutes dressed in their finest and most revealing attire, flaunting themselves in silk and ribbon, plied their trade below the gallows. As we know the areas attached to the *Plough Inn* and the *Scarborough Arms* were thrown open to the public, the landlords having large letters chalked upon the doors, "A good view of the execution in this yard, admission 3d." Judging from the number of people who paid their three-pences, there was no doubt the landlords made a considerable sum of money ....

Before 12 o'clock every spot where a sight of the gallows could be obtained was filled with a crowd so dense, that it was almost impossible to penetrate through it. It was the *Times* that reported the crowd as 25,000. One 93-year-old man gleefully said, that he had seen almost all the executions at Lincoln, and this was the biggest crowd he had seen .... At 10.30 am the prisoners attended the service in the Prison Chapel, and the Sacrament was afterwards administered to both of them. An hour later the prisoners were pinioned; Carey kept his composure, but Pickett cried piteously, and it was found necessary to give him a quantity of brandy. They and the official party left the prison at twenty minutes to twelve .... Carey, supported by a Prison Officer and Pickett similarly supported. On arriving at the foot of Cobb Hall, the two prisoners said farewell to the Chaplain. On reaching the roof of Cobb Hall, the prisoners said farewell with the prison-officers; there was not one present who was not moved to tears, the unfortunate men having earned the pity of all who had to do with them, by their exemplary conduct *since their confinement*. They spent a short while in prayer. Then each man with a firm step walked to his place beneath the beam. Pickett, on seeing the large crowd gathered to see his execution, held his head down. They both wore 'slops', Pickett a blue one and Carey white. A few seconds before the clock struck the fatal hour, the Governor appeared on the drop, and almost immediately all eyes were fascinated by two human figures, each standing motionless as sculptured marble (their outlines boldly defined against the deep blue sky) on the treacherous drop, and with the nooses swinging above their heads.

Thomas Askern, who was paid £11 8s for his services by the authorities, immediately drew a white cap over the head and throat of Carey, and then adjusted the fatal cord. While this operation was taking place, Pickett turned coolly round to his companion, apparently to observe the process: he next underwent the same operation. The excitement at this moment was intense, and the attention of the vast crowd was so steadfastly fixed upon the scene that scarcely a whisper was heard. The executioner left the drop; by the time the clock had finished striking the hour of noon, the fatal bolt was drawn, and both ceased to exist immediately, or so it initially appeared. Carey appeared to die without a struggle, Pickett remained in strong convulsions for two or three minutes. *Pickett had died hard in agony* …. The fall within the battlements of Cobb Hall was considerable, so the heads of the prisoners (now dangling to and fro in the wind) alone could be seen from the outside. At one o'clock the bodies were taken down and placed in coffins prepared for them, and then removed to a suitable room under the County Hall. A lot of the crowd remained until after the bodies had been taken down. As it turned out, the only trouble had been from a few pickpockets, from Nottingham. The next day, the coffins were taken to the Lucy Tower of Lincoln Castle and interred.

There was even better news for the authorities in that both men had left detailed confessions made before the executions; but which were now published:

On the Tuesday before the execution, the Rev Robert Rushton, Primitive Methodist Minister of Sibsey, had lengthy interviews with both prisoners, at their own request; when Pickett made the following confession of his guilt, showing that he was the actual murderer of William Stevenson, and admitting that his former statement was arranged with the view of clearing himself and throwing the blame onto his fellow prisoner ....

"On leaving the *Ship Inn*, between 10 and 11 o'clock, the first word Carey said to me after leaving the public-house was, 'We will go and rob old Stevenson.' I said to him, 'He will know us.' Carey said, 'No: I will stop him from that.' I was before Carey. We took two sticks from Mr Teesdale's fence; I pulled one, and the other was picked up by Carey. We went to Mr Coates' gate and altered our dress, walked some distance, and laid down on the side of the road with the sticks beside us. The old man came down the road, crossed over to us, touched me over the head, and said, 'What are you doing here, my boys. I don't know you, who are you: David, is it you? ' I suppose he meant his grandson. Carey got on his knees, and pulled the old man down; Mr Stevenson struck Carey with his walking stick while falling. I held his head while Carey robbed him. I got up and struck him on the ground until my stick broke all to pieces. Carey got off when he had robbed him, and beat him about the head; then carried him into the sewer. Carey went back across the road to fetch his stick, and struck the old man eight or nine times over the head until his stick broke all to pieces. Then the old man stood up in the sewer. Carey shoved at him with the broken part of his stick, trying to push him down into the water. Mr Stevenson got from him and walked to the other side of the sewer. Carey then threw the broken part of his stick into the sewer, and said to me, 'Go round to the other side and kill him.' [Matthew Spicer: There was a bridge nearby] I went round to Mr Coates' yard, got a piece of a rail, and went to the old man. Mr Stevenson had the thorn stick produced in court on his shoulder, and appeared to be going home. Carey said, 'Make haste, or he will get home.' I went behind him and struck him on the side of the head, and knocked him down; I hit him till my stick broke all to pieces. *I then took the stick Mr Stevenson had, and struck him about the head till he was dead.* I dragged him to the hedge: I was trying to throw him into the sewer, but could not. I told Carey I could not throw him over myself, and that he must come and help me. Carey said, 'Try again; you can get him over.' I then took hold of his legs, seated him up on end, and tumbled him over into the sewer. After that we both left, one on one side of the sewer, and the other on the other. We went on till we got to my father's seven acre gate. Carey had the papers produced in court, and threw the old man's tobacco box into the river opposite the gate. We went across the river in my father's boat, and went till we got to my brother's house. We were to go to George Sands' hovel to sleep. Carey said, 'We had better go across your brother John's garden, or the police will meet us.' We slept together in Mr Sands' hovel till morning; got up about four o'clock. Carey said, 'We had better look if there be any blood on our clothes.' We could not find any, but I had some blood on my face, which Carey washed off. We laid down again till six o'clock. Mr Sands came into his hovel to feed his beasts: he tumbled over my legs, and said, 'What are you doing here?' Carey said, 'We were locked out for the night.' Mr Sands asked Carey if he would sow him some onions. We got up and went to the *Ship Inn*; on the road Carey gave me the sovereign. Carey put a stone into the old man's bags, and threw them into Mr Richardson's pit. We went round to Mr Richardson's back door to see if they were up: I went home, and Carey went to his [Pickett's] brothers. We did not really think of robbing or doing anything else to Mr Stevenson when we first left the public house. I did not do as advised by my parents or friends in respect of Carey. I was very much frightened the night it thundered and lightened; I thought Mr Stevenson was coming to me in the cell. I am truly sorry for what I have done. The sentence passed upon me is a just one, and I deserve it. I feel for my parents, particularly my mother. I have no person to blame but myself. I felt relieved when the Chaplain visited me on Thursday, after the sentence was passed; and I earnestly pray to God to forgive me for murdering the poor man. *I believe I struck the blow which caused death.* The reason I made the statement at Sibsey was to clear myself. If Carey had been present at the examination before the magistrates, I should not have made that statement. The judge has done justice; if there was no justice there would be no living. I have been kindly treated during confinement: I feel resigned to my fate, and hope to have forgiveness; I am striving for it as well as I can. I hid the money (one sovereign) which Carey gave me, in the thatch of David Richardson's furnace house, about 16 inches from the end wall on the west side, between the first and second spar; and the knife that Carey had, is just outside the furnace at the corner by the chimney, which I should like to be given to Mr Stevenson's son. We never had any handkerchiefs, and Carey's statement about them is false. I have nothing else to state, and the above is the truth. *(Signed)William Pickett.*"

Henry Carey, also made the following confession to the Rev Rushton on the same day, admitting that his account given at the trial [from the dock] was prompted by a spirit of retaliation, for the false information given by Pickett. In it he admitted he also knew the victim, and had been helped by him ….

" Oh, dear Mr Rushton, my position is an awful one. I hope I shall be forgiven; it is all drink. I am truly sorry I did not take your advice. *Mr Stevenson was always a friend to me*; he took me in when I was turned out of my own house. I hope his friends will forgive me. I hope the old man's soul is in heaven. I feel reconciled, and the sentence passed is what I deserve. At the *Ship Inn,* I called William Pickett out doors, and asked him if he would go with me to rob William Stevenson. When we left the public-house we arranged to go into the house and say to people that we should sleep in the boat (Pickett's father's boat). We stayed till between ten and eleven o'clock; the landlord asked if we thought anything about going home, as it was bed time. I asked him to put a quart of ale into a bottle, as we were going aboard. He put three gills into a porter bottle. We went over the river in Pickett's father's boat; we got a stick each, and laid down in the lane where Mr Stevenson had to go to his son's. He came up and said, 'Hello, my lads; who are you? Get up and lay in some of these yards.' I think he did not know us. We both jumped up on our knees, and threw him backwards. Pickett held his head down till I got his money. I struck Mr Stevenson, and then Pickett struck him while on the floor several times. Pickett took hold of his head, and I took hold of his feet, and threw him into the sewer. Mr Stevenson got up on his feet while in the water, and we both struck him again. He turned to go across the sewer, and got out on the other side. I said to Pickett, 'Go round.' Pickett went round, got another stick, and struck him on the side of the head, knocking him down on the floor. I told Pickett to throw him into the sewer, which he did. I never went to the other side of the sewer. I know that I am the worst, and persuaded Pickett into it. We slept in Mr Sands' hovel until half past five o'clock, when Mr Sands found us. We then left there. Pickett took a sovereign: I kept a knife and 3s 6d. The two little bags were sunk in Mr Richardson's pit; the pocket-knife I hid in the corner of Mr Richardson's potato-house by the privy. I don't know what Pickett did with his money. It is false about having handkerchiefs. That is all I have to say, and the above is the truth. *(Signed) Henry Carey X*"

On the confession of Pickett being read to Carey, he signified that it was substantially correct, and that he did not wish any alteration to his own statement. Carey was unable to write, and so made his mark, in the presence of the Governor and prison-officers. Several farewell letters were written for the prisoners to their relatives, to be delivered after the execution ….

The last execution at Lincoln Prison was in 1961.

Case 10
"The Curious Affair Of the Dying Declaration And the Drunken Jury"

"You say Francy Hynes shot you" - The question asked of the victim by the Resident Magistrate.

"Leave off herding for Lynch." - A warning by masked men in the victim's farmhouse. But were they from the accused's family or from a more organised group?

"'Hallo, old fellow, all alone?'" - Did a drunken juryman say this to William O'Brien, a prominent Irish Republican, in his hotel room?

"A large force of constabulary will be drafted into this city to preserve peace and good order during the execution and subsequently." - The execution required a large police and military operation.

"I never executed a finer man, nor a man with so much nerve. He walked to his doom with the utmost composure and I cannot but admire him". William Marwood, the hangman.

Francis Hynes (23)
[1882]
Murder
Of
John Doloughty (60)

Incredible story from Ireland in the Summer of 1882 against the backdrop of the 'Phoenix Park Murders', rural unrest, special laws passed in London, where the police had uncovered an Irish Republican bomb-plot, and in Dublin allegations of jury rigging and of a Unionist jury being forced to spend the night in an Irish Republican hotel, where it was claimed they were drunk and played billiards ....!

Francis Hynes (23) was the son of a well-known Ennis solicitor Mr James Hynes, and the family lived a short distance from the Clare county town. He was a tall handsome man, well over six-foot, and his family also owned land around the town. In the village of Knockanean, some three miles from Ennis, for example, the Hyneses had some grassland which they let out in 1878 and 1879 to a person named Lynch, and another man called Doloughty, who at that time was also herdsman to the Hyneses. In 1879 Mr Doloughty began working for Lynch. He was a good-worker and served the Lynches as well he had served the Hyneses. However in 1880 the Hynes family began having financial problems and they were evicted from the land that they'd rented to the Lynches and the Doloughtys. Mr Lynch took over the farm and Mr Doloughty remained, in Mr Lynch's employment ….

The issue of land in rural Ireland had always been a problem. Many estates were owned by rich families in England or by wealthy Anglo-Irish families – the vast majority of whom were Protestant and the vast majority of the rural population were Catholic. During certain periods in Irish history the eviction, seizure and even the sale of agricultural land became violent and as we shall see the issue of land ownership also became intertwined with the issue of Irish Republicanism and the desire to end the Union with Britain. However equally so, much land passed hands peacefully in Ireland, and so the Lynches and the Doloughtys did not think they would have any problems, but unbeknown to them the Hyneses had also been influenced by others….

The head of the Doloughty family was **John and he was sixty**. He and his wife, Eliza, had one son, Michael (15) and seven young children, and they considered the Hyneses as family friends as well as employers. But this all changed after the loss of the land to the Lynches. Relations deteriorated very badly and in February 1881, Mr Doloughty fearing for his family, went to the police and Francis Hynes was prosecuted and was ordered by the courts to keep the peace for 12 months. The court had heard that when the Hyneses could not induce Mr Doloughty by threats to leave Mr Lynch's employment, they tried and failed to bribe him. The Lynch family had also been threatened by the Hyneses – their hay had been stolen and farm labourers had been warned to not work on the seized land.

Things became so bad that after the court hearing Mr Lynch gave Mr Doloughty a gun for his own protection ....

On **Sunday, July 9ᵗʰ, 1882,** Mr Doloughty went to Mass in Ennis with his wife but came back home on his own: he was fired at, hit, and was mortally wounded. His wife had left Mass at about two-thirty pm and whilst walking back home she met a boy running along, who said her husband had been shot. Mr Doloughty told his wife, son and eventually the local Resident Magistrate, Captain Hugh McTiernan, that the man who had fired at him was …. Francis Hynes, or so it seemed .... This all happened very quickly and Hynes was arrested about a mile from the scene of the shooting. Between the place of his arrest and where the attempted murder had been committed, was a stream, which had to be crossed to reach the point where the Royal Irish Constabulary arrested Hynes, apparently coming out of a local pub, *Hassets*, and eating some bread and butter. A Constable Richard Doyle said his trousers were tucked up to the knees, and the boots were grey, as if the black shoe polish had been washed off by water; he was slightly under the influence of drink; two packets of shot were found in his pockets, although not the weapon, which was believed to have been a hunting-rifle. It all suggested that he must have walked through this stream to reach the victim: it was certainly a dry day. It seemed an open and shut case ….

The two packets of shot matched exactly the shot removed from Mr Doloughty. The inquiry was led by Mr McTiernan and he knew all the families involved very well. He had been in charge of investigating Hynes over the intimidation of the Doloughtys. It emerged that on the night of a Nationalist meeting held by Charles Parnell in Ennis, a group of men came to his house, and warned him not to herd for any, except for former tenants or owners (i.e. the Hyneses); on the following day Mr Lynch brought over 20 head of cattle to the farm and after he had left, three sons of James Hynes, and a fourth man, an unrelated man called Hynes, drove the cattle off the farm onto the road, and they said they would not allow any cattle to be there until a settlement was reached with Messrs Lynch and Doloughty, who refused to negotiate. The Hyneses asked Mr Doloughty was he going to continue in Mr Lynch's employment, adding that he was a ' bloody schemer'. Not only was Francis Hynes bound over to keep the peace, but he had to enter a bond with the court.

Mr McTiernan dutifully recorded the statement of the dying Mr Doloughty, asking: "Who shot you?" The victim replied: "Francy Hynes." This was repeated for clarity: "You say Francy Hynes shot you?" and he said: "Yes." The Resident Magistrate then wrote the following on a slip of paper, using a pen and paper from a nearby school, the police having broken into the building to take the material. The dying man said. "I, John Doloughty believing that I am dying, declare that Francis Hynes killed me by firing shots at me." At that point Mr Doloughty was still alive but he died the following night **(July 10th)**.

Following news of the shooting the Resident Magistrate and Sub Inspector William Cloughan and two other officers had gone to Knockanean. They found John Doloughty on the side of the road, his wife cradling him: in his pockets was his own gun but it was unloaded. Other locals had also come to the spot too, as well as Father Loughlin. The victim had been shot in the head – the gunshot having entered his brain through his eyes. However the reverend would later testify that he heard the confession and the victim's mental capacity had not seemed to have been effected. Mrs Doloughty told officers that last autumn a number of men with blackened faces broke into their farmhouse and told her husband, forcing him on his knees to prepare to meet his Lord, that he should die, unless he would "leave off herding for Lynch." She could not see who the men were and had never actually heard the prisoner threaten her husband. She confirmed that before the issue of the land she had thought of the Hyneses as friends and Francis Hynes had given her husband several pieces of farming equipment during the past two years ….

The murder of Mr Doloughty came at a time of great problems in Ireland. Two months earlier on **May 6th the Chief Secretary for Ireland, Frederick Cavendish and his assistant Thomas Burke had been stabbed to death in Phoenix Park in Dublin** and there were Irish Republican plots to bomb London. In this period also,

Ireland was in the grip of the so-called 'Land War'. In October 1879 the Irish National Land League was set up to help the poor agricultural classes over issues such as rent and evictions; but it was also closely linked to the Republican cause. It was set up by Michael Davitt, a well-known Republican and their main targets were the wealthy landlords, nearly all of whom were Unionists. Their main weapon was boycotting but the league also associated with those who killed. Whilst Charles Parnell and the Irish Nationalist Party always condemned murder, many of his speeches shared the same aspirations as the Land League and ultimately Irish Republicanism. As a consequence of the Phoenix Park Murders, the government passed the *Prevention of Crimes Act* – officially at least this was to remove local prejudice from local crimes, but critics suggested it was to ensure that in the capital, a hand-picked jury of Unionists would themselves ensure that those that wished to disrupt British rule in Ireland would be punished. The bill was introduced into Parliament on the day of Lord Cavendish's funeral and became law on July 12th. On July 18th, the Ennis Magistrates committed Hynes to stand trial in Dublin under the new act.

The trial of Francis Hynes thus began at the Dublin Commission Court on Friday, August 11th, before Mr Justice Lawson, albeit before a so-called Special Jury under the new act. The trial was to last two days. The Attorney-General of Ireland, William Johnson, MP, QC, Mr Peter O'Brien, QC, and Mr Sullivan prosecuted. The MacDermott QC, and Mr John Roche defended the accused.

The Attorney-General, in opening the case for the prosecution, said it was one of a character unfortunately too well known in Ireland as an 'agrarian' offence, and which he said had "brought disgrace and dishonour on many parts of the country, and which would not have occurred but for the demoralised state of Ireland." He added that the crime with which the prisoner was charged was of a most "aggravated and cruel character." For the defence, Mr MacDermott said when arrested Hynes had told officers that he was out for a 'ramble' and that he had been in that vicinity for about two hours, and his clothing was wet because he had been fishing. When told he would be arrested, Hynes became very violent and it was under gunpoint that he was finally subdued. He was warned by the police that his behaviour in resisting might tell against him later and fortunately for the RIC other locals told Hynes to surrender.

The court heard from a Dr Cullinan who attended the dying man on the road. He said that Mr Doloughty was bleeding profusely and he said he was 'insensible'. He added that the victim had been shot from point-blank range. He disputed the police and family evidence that the farmer could have spoken coherently, although he was one of the magistrates who committed Hynes to stand trial! Mr MacDermott suggested to the jury that the victim was 'labouring under a morbid apprehension' that the Hyneses were trying to kill him, and that the killer had approached him from behind, and he would not have had time to properly identify him. Furthermore he said that three farm labourers who had been drinking in the pub near the shooting said that Francis Hynes had been in there since one pm and when he went out he was arrested almost immediately: The prosecution had suggested the shooting took place at two pm. These men were cross-examined by the Attorney-General and were forced to admit that they had been drinking a great deal and were now not sure of their timings.

The jury may have been picked for their supposed political beliefs but it is clear that they weren't just going to send a man to the gallows because the government didn't like him or his cause. Firstly they wanted to hear the evidence of the priest at the scene – the Reverend Loughlin – why had neither the prosecution nor defence called him? When asked by the *jury* he said he thought Captain McTiernan had asked of the victim: "*Is it* Francy?" - clearly a leading question, but something the Resident Magistrate denied saying. Furthermore they requested the recall of three other witnesses ….

One witness was Constable Doyle and he said that when he arrested the accused, he had a pair of spare socks in his pockets, as well as the pair he was wearing – the pair in the pockets were dry; the pair on his feet somewhat wet. He added that the Hyneses family had no firearm license, it having been revoked due to the issue with the Lynches and Doloughtys. He then added that the socks in Hynes' pockets were lighter and finer than those he was actually wearing, suggesting perhaps that he'd worn them to fire the gun to avoid getting residue on his hands. Earlier Hynes had claimed that the shot found in his pocket had been given to him two years before by a brother! Captain McTiernan was also recalled and he confirmed that Mrs Hasset said that Hynes was in her pub but it seems all she said was that he was in the pub between 'thirty minutes and one hour *before the police came.*' Mrs Doloughty wasn't aware of the murder until sometime after two-thirty and Hynes wasn't arrested until after her husband's dying declarations, so it would have been beyond three; thus if Mrs Hasset's times were correct, then the accused didn't really have an alibi. The Resident Magistrate also said it had been alleged that shots had been fired by the Hyneses at men working for Mr Lynch. The third person recalled by the jury was another religious witness, the Reverend McLaughlin, who had also come to see to the victim. He said he was 'quite unconscious and unable to speak.' Thirty minutes later he tried to speak. It was another hour before Captain McTiernan and the police came along. However under cross-examination by the Attorney-General, the reverend admitted that Mr Doloughty was able to say to him some of the act of contrition and the priest was able to understand it. He added he could not hear the victim say the prisoner had shot him.

In his summing-up Mr Roche said the jury should ask themselves why had not Mr Lynch been called to give evidence. He said that it was quite common for a 'country boy' such as Hynes to have shot in his pocket and a hunting-rifle. He said dying declarations were not to be relied on. In his final address to the court, the Attorney-General said that Mr Doloughty was an innocent man returning from church and he had been killed by an assassin: his young wife now had seven young children to look after. He bemoaned the fact that the police had found it difficult to take statements from locals and many people seemed not to want to become involved. He said the motive was clear – Mr Doloughty had offended no one else but the Hyneses and they had been inflamed by the speeches of Charles Parnell and other Nationalists and Republicans.

It was now that the Attorney-General suggested that other forces may have also been behind the Hynes family. He asked was there a band of masked men who would terrorise families – had the Hyneses employed them or had this group simply taken it on themselves to act for them? However he said he was in no doubt that Francis Hynes had shot the victim – he had been killed with a blast of snipe, which would not kill from a long distance. He said the killer had stepped out onto the road directly in front of the victim and so Mr Doloughty must have seen his assailant just inches from him. Addressing the jury Mr Justice Lawson said they must decide whether to accept the evidence of the dying declaration. As to the accused saying he had been fishing – where was his rod; where was what he might have caught? He suggested that he had not thrown away the shot, as Hynes assumed that Mr Doloughty was dead. The jury retired at 4.10 pm and returned at 5.25 pm. They found Francis Hynes guilty of murder and the judge ordered he be **hanged on Monday, September 11th, 1882 at Limerick Prison** as Ennis Prison had been downgraded to a district prison and the last execution there was in 1860.

After the trial and verdict it was revealed that the condemned man's father had fled Ireland, there being a warrant out for his arrest for forgery. The *Times* was also full of praise for Captain McTiernan, without whom, they suggested there would not have been a conviction. However the captain paid a price – under the Crimes Act, Special Resident Magistrates were to be appointed to areas affected by Republicanism and land problems and the 'gallant captain' lost his position and was moved to the North to Enniskillen in County Fermanagh. And within hours of the verdict the political problems in Ireland went on. At eight pm in Parsonstown (now called Birr), then in King's County (now Offaly) Constable Edward Brown (32) when out on patrol went into a pub. On leaving, a man fired four shots at him, one hitting his back. Although the streets were crowed and the assassin was seen by the publican's son, no attempt was made to detain him and no-one had apparently seen anything. Constable Brown died just before midnight but unlike Mr Doloughty was not able to make a dying declaration. Then five days after the trial Ireland was shocked by the "*Maamtrasna Murders*" when five members of one family were murdered in County Galway.

On the following Monday after the trial, as Hynes lay in the death-cell at Limerick Prison, Dublin was shocked by stories concerning the special jury. They had spent the Friday night in the *Imperial Hotel*[19] in Sackville Street, which given the contemporary disorder, was on the face of it, somewhat strange, as it was also the headquarters of the Irish National Land League, and was also the hotel that many Nationalist or Republican MPs would stay in when in the capital. One of the most powerful Republicans in Ireland at this time was William O'Brien, who was soon to be elected as an MP. Here is what he said in reference to the special jury from apparent first-hand knowledge:

"To the Editor of *The Freeman*.

"*Imperial Hotel*, Dublin,

"Saturday, August 12.

"Dear Sir,—I think the public ought to be made aware of the following facts. The jury in the murder case of the Queen v. Hynes were last night 'locked up,' as it is termed, for the night at the *Imperial Hotel*, where I also was staying. I was awakened from sleep shortly after midnight by the sounds of a drunken chorus, succeeded after a time by scuffling, rushing, coarse laughter, and horse-play along the corridor on which my bedroom opens. A number of men, it seemed to me, were falling about the passage in a maudlin state of drunkenness, playing ribald jokes. I listened with patience for a considerable time, when the door of my bedroom was burst open, and a man whom I can identify (for he carried a candle unsteadily in his hand) staggered in, plainly under the influence of drink, hiccuping, 'Hallo, old fellow, all alone?' My answer was of a character that induced him to bolt out of the room in as disordered a manner as he had entered. Having rung the bell, I ascertained that these disorderly persons were jurors in the case of the Queen v. Hynes, and that the servants of the hotel had been endeavouring in vain to bring them to a sense of their misconduct. I thought it right to convey to them a warning that the

---

19   The Hotel was destroyed during the Easter Uprising.

public would hear of their proceedings. The disturbance then ceased. It is fair to add that no more than three or four men appeared to be engaged in the roaring and in the tipsy horse-play that followed. I leave the public to judge the loathsomeness of such a scene upon the night when these men held the issues of life and death for a young man in the flower of youth—when they had already heard evidence which, if unrebutted, they must have known would send him to a felon's grave. The facts I am ready to support upon oath.

"WILLIAM O'BRIEN."

Afterwards a juror replied, writing to the *Limerick Chronicle*:

"Sir - Being one of the jurors in the case of the Crown versus Hynes, I think it right to lay before you what actually did occur at the *Imperial Hotel* on Friday evening the 11th instant.

On the court rising at half-past five o'clock the presiding judge directed the Sub-Sheriff to take charge of us for the night, and suggested that we should be taken to the *Gresham Hotel*. We were all much surprised when the Sub-Sheriff told us to choose between the *European* and *Imperial Hotels*. Knowing that these were chiefly patronised by the Land League and Nationalist party, we all remonstrated, requesting to be taken to the *Gresham* or *Shelbourne Hotel*, some jurors stating they would prefer to pass the night in the rooms at the courthouse. The Sub-Sheriff, however ended the matter by informing us we had no choice, and that, as we refused to go to the *European*, he would have us at once removed to the *Imperial*.

On arriving at the hotel we were taken upstairs to a passage at the top of the house, which, we were informed by the Sub-Sheriff, had been reserved entirely for our separate use. We were then immediately taken down to a room, where dinner had been prepared for us. After dinner some of the jurors asked permission to smoke. I and some others asked if it were allowable that the smokers might go together to another room, as the evening was very close. No objection was raised to this, and the smokers were taken, under charge of (the) Sub-Sheriff, bailiffs, and police, to the billiard-room of the hotel. There they remained, with the Sub-Sheriff or his son till they all went to bed together, shortly before 12 o'clock. This, I have since been informed, was irregular; but we were none of us aware that it was so at the time. I can only say that, as the Sub-Sheriff took us against our will to the *Imperial Hotel*, he could as easily, with the strong guard of bailiffs and police at his disposal, have prevented us separating as we did. On inquiry from the proprietor of the *Imperial Hotel*, I find that the whole charge against the jury is that one of their (our) number Mr (Charles) Reis, was under the influence of liquor when in the billiard-room, and afterwards behaved rather noisily when going to bed.

The foreman of the jury (Mr Barrett, of Kingstown) stated in open court on Monday morning 16th (14th) instant that he saw the last of the jurors to bed, which he considered it his duty to do, and that none of them were in any way under the influence of drink. This statement can be confirmed by those who were present at the time - one of them, Mr Phillips, of Grafton Street, being a total abstainer from intoxicating drinks. Major Wynne, one of those gentlemen not on the jury who were admitted into the billiard-room during the evening, also informs me that while there he saw none of the jurors under the influence of drink. The Sub-Sheriff and his son were there. If strangers were admitted into the billiard-room, it was their business to have had the jurors removed, who were under their charge, or to have arranged with the proprietor of the hotel that they should have had the room to themselves. As I have said before, I believe all the other members of the jury, were perfectly unaware of what the rules were to be observed under the circumstances. Now, as to Mr W O'Brien's extraordinary story, I was awake in room No 27, nearly opposite his, when the party from the billiard-room came upstairs. I heard Mr Reis speaking and calling out loudly (I have since been informed for slippers), as is his custom. I heard him knock over a bath and put it up again with more noise than was absolutely necessary. Mr Reis is short-sighted, and I am informed that at the time there was very little light in the passage. I heard someone go to two or three rooms knocking at and opening the doors; but I heard no singing nor did I hear anything that would lead me to imagine that drunken people were stumbling about in the passage. As to the opening of doors, the Sub-Sheriff had informed us that the passage was reserved entirely to ourselves. We had not all selected our rooms before dinner and I was most astonished that those last upstairs had some difficulty in finding a spare bed, particularly as it appeared that while some of the jury were doubled up two in a room, one had been reserved for the use of the editor or ex-editor of *United Ireland*. The Attorney-General has promised that a full inquiry is to be made into the circumstances of the case. This the jurors one and all are anxious should be made at once". - *Edward Hamilton.*

But another two letters to the same 'paper seem to back up Mr O'Brien:

"I Robert Boylan, coffee room waiter at the *Imperial Hotel*, Sackville Street, 21 years of age and upwards, make oath and say that I gave the jury the principal part of their dinner on the night of Friday the 11th instant. I supplied whisky and gave sherry and claret, to two of the jurors. They all had drinks, but Mr Reis ordered a bottle of champagne, and told me to bring only two glasses, for Mr Barrett, the foreman, and himself, and I supplied them with a large bottle of champagne, which they drank between them. That was at eight o'clock in the evening, in the jury room, where they were dining. Mr Reis asked me in a jeering way could they have a ladder to get down from the window. Shortly afterwards Mr Reis left the jury room to go down to the billiard room. Several other jurors left to go to the lavatory, and several remained in the jury room. They were then divided into three different parties in three different parts of the house, I went away for the night about nine o'clock, and know no more about it." - *Robert Boylan*

"I Patrick Tobin, aged 21 years of age and upwards, coffee-room waiter in the *Imperial Hotel*, Sackville Street, Dublin, make oath and say that during the evening of Friday, the 11th instant the jury in the Hynes' case were staying at the hotel. I remember having brought a couple of drinks to the billiard-room as ordered. One was for Mr Campbell, son of the Sub-Sheriff, who was in the billiard-room, apparently in charge of the jury. I also brought drink to Mr Reis, one of the jurors. Four or five of the jury were in the room at the time. Some ten or twelve persons were there, *including a number of strangers*. The billiard-room is on the ground floor of the hotel. The corridor to which the jury were directed is situated on the third storey. When I brought down the drink Mr Reis was very noisy and impudent. I think it was about 11 o'clock. The drink which I brought to the jury consisted of some glasses and half a glass of whisky and another glass of gin. It included a bottle of ginger beer and a glass of gin ordered for Major Wynne, a stranger not stopping in the hotel. I went upstairs, and my attention was again attracted by the jury at between a quarter and half past 12 o'clock at night. I went upstairs in consequence of a disturbance created upon the landing to which the jurors had gone to go to bed. The sound of a man's voice could be heard through the house. I tried to prevail upon the juryman to return to the jury room, or to go to bed. I did not succeed. I came downstairs then, but went upstairs again to the lower end of the corridor on which Mr O'Brien and the jurors had rooms. Mr Reis was standing there with another juror whom I can identify, but whose name I do not know. Mr Reis ran down as far as where I was standing, and let some shouts, and asked where was his bedroom. That corridor had been cleared for the night for the accommodation of the jurors, and the only person outside the jury who slept there that night were two lodgers, Miss Ca... (*illegible*).and Mr O'Brien. Reis was drunk at the time. He shouted and kicked the boots from the landing along the passage. He shouted along the passage three or four times. I tried to entice him to stay in a bedroom into which I had brought him but he jumped out again. Finding that the man was drunk I could do nothing else to induce him to retire. I have heard that the foreman of the jury stated that the last of the jurors had retired to bed before 12 o'clock. That statement is not correct. The bar as a rule is closed at 12 o'clock; but, on the night of the 11th instant the bar was kept open an additional quarter of an hour, till a quarter past 12 o'clock; and it was subsequently to the closing of the bar that night that I saw the man knocking about the hotel on the landing." - *Patrick Tobin*

and so the *Limerick Chronicle* felt obliged to speak out:

The trial of the unfortunate Francis Hynes, so prolific in startling incident; has now developed into quite a harvest of extraordinary and unprecedented consequences. While the miserable man in the loneliness of his prison cell counts the fast ebbing moments quite a storm of controversy has been raised in the outer world with reference to the several episodes connected with his fate. The well-merited condemnation passed by Mr Justice Lawson upon the High Sheriff of Dublin (*Edmund Dwyer Gray see below*), is, in noted importance, a mere bagatelle compared to the still more serious questions which arise with reference to the disposal of the jury by the Sub-Sheriff and the incidents, be they what they may, which took place in the *Imperial Hotel* on Friday night week. The letter of Mr Edward Hamilton, one of the jury, which appears in our columns, narrates with obvious veracity the whole story. Whether the bringing of the jury to the hotel in question, was a pre-arranged movement on the part of the Sheriff and Under-Sheriff, and that something in the shape of a pitfall was laid for them, we will not aver; but certain it is that to say the least of it, the conduct of the Under-Sheriff upon the occasion was most reprehensible. The Act of Parliament with reference to the treatment of jurors in criminal cases when trials are not concluded within the day, is most emphatic. It distinctly states that the Sheriff shall be responsible that the jury shall have no communication with any person whatsoever during the night.

and a week later (August 29th) the paper then reported, and with a clear inference that the murder was political:

"*The Dublin Evening Mail*" of last evening says - We are compelled to return today, much against our will, to the indecent attempt which is being made to arouse a morbid sympathy for the murderer Hynes. Now, we have the greatest respect for the persons who entertain conscientious scruples on the subject of capital punishment, and, therefore, we have not a word to say against any efforts which they may deem it proper to take for a commutation of the sentence upon Hynes. But there is another class which desires to see Hynes respited - *the class whose vile behests he so unhesitatingly and unflinchingly carried out. It is perfectly plain to this class the execution of one of their most efficient officers would be a fatal blow, and, therefore they leave no stone unturned to obviate that dire consequence.* In all that has been written and said in the way of sympathy for Hynes, not a syllable has been breathed, not a note of pity expressed for the widow and seven helpless children of his victim. No, their sorrow and their want are nothing in comparison with the shock which the execution of Hynes would have upon the sensitive feelings of the Moonlighters and their abettors, clerical and lay. Poor Doloughty's widow may appeal for bread, but it will be in vain. The public mind is too engrossed with the sufferings of Francis Hynes to spare a thought for them. Is this as it ought to be? The ostentatious parade of sympathy shown for the murderer of Doloughty reminds us that we ought ere this to have shown some material sympathy with the widow and orphans of Hynes' victim, who are at this moment in abject poverty. We now invite all whose hearts are moved in pity for these poor creatures who have been so ruthlessly and cruelly deprived of their support to join with us, in alleviating their more pressing wants and to give as they can to: "Doloughy Fund: *Dublin Evening Mail*."

There were then many attempts to have the death-sentence passed on Francis Hynes commuted and on September 9th, the *Limerick Chronicle* reported:

"The following reply has been received to a letter sent by the Lord Mayor to his Excellency the Lord Lieutenant last night, forwarding a copy of the resolution passed at yesterday's meeting at the Mansion House:-

Viceregal Lodge, 8 September 1882

"My Dear Lord Mayor - I am desired by the Lord Lieutenant to acknowledge the receipt of your Lordship's letter, asking his Excellency to receive a deputation to present a resolution in favour of the commutation of the sentence passed on the convict Hynes. I am to say that it is not the practice, either for the Home Secretary in England or for the Lord Lieutenant in Ireland to receive deputations on the subject of the commutation of the death sentence. His Excellency is not prepared to deviate from this rule, and must, therefore, decline to receive the deputation referred to by your Lordship. I am to add that the resolution itself shall be carefully considered by his Excellency. I have the honour to be your Lordship's obedient servant."

On receipt of this reply the Lord Mayor proceeded to Dublin Castle, and, in the absence of the Lord Lieutenant and the Chief Secretary, had an interview with the Under Secretary (Mr Hamilton), to whom he pointed out from the records in the *Freeman's Journal*, that in December 1867, the then Lord Lieutenant (the Duke of Abercorn) received a deputation on the subject of the commutation of the sentence on "General" Burke[20]. It was understood that the representations thus made were communicated to his Excellency. The Lord Lieutenant late on September 7th, sent a reply to the memorial. His Excellency regretted he was unable to alter his decision, and that the law must take its course. The Mayor had received the following reply to the memorial of the *Limerick Corporation*, adopted at its meeting on Thursday last, praying that the sentence might be commuted :

Dublin Castle, 8 September 1882

"J Counihan, Esq, Mayor of Limerick, Limerick, - Sir, - With reference to your letter of the 7th instant forwarding a Memorial from the Corporation of the City of Limerick on behalf of Francis Hynes, a prisoner under sentence of death in Limerick Male Prison, I am directed by the Lord Lieutenant to acquaint you, for the information of the Memorialists, that his Excellency has carefully considered the Memorial, and regrets that he cannot see any reason for interfering with the course of the law in this case. I have the honour to be, sir, Your obedient servant."

W.S.B. Kate

Meanwhile on Saturday (September 9th), **William Marwood, the executioner**, arrived in Limerick in the morning by the 1.45 am mail train from Dublin. He was received by a large party of police, who escorted him to the prison. The Sub-Sheriff of County Clare, Charles Mahon had made all the necessary preparations for the execution,

---

20 Thomas Burke was one of three men sentenced to death for high treason after the failed 1867 Rebellion in Ireland. All three death sentences were commuted.

which would take place at eight am on Monday, unless a last minute reprieve was ordered by Dublin. The local 'paper said: "A large force of constabulary will be drafted into this city to preserve peace and good order during the execution and subsequently." There was to be no reprieve by the **Lord Lieutenant, John Poyntz, the Earl Spencer**. The Monday morning was one of the finest which had come for over a year - fine glorious sunshine, a bright unclouded sky - all was warm and beautiful. As a local reporter approached the prison, a small knot of the 'lower classes' were collected on the pavement opposite the upper end of the building, whilst there was a doubled guard of police, who walked round the square, which the outer walls of the prison formed. Furthermore at about 6.15 am eight soldiers of the 70th Regiment marched into the precincts of the prison with loaded rifles and bayonets fixed. A short time afterwards a large body of more police took position in front of the main entrance to the prison. As the police marched to the prison the military guard turned out and presented arms. The authorities had sealed off Limerick Prison and would regulate the anticipated crowds outside.

At seven o'clock crowds of people commenced to flock towards the prison, and by 7.30 am, there were over a thousand persons present. The majority were of the 'lowest classes' from the poor areas of the city. The local 'paper said of them: "They came in all their repulsiveness and wretchedness for the purpose of gratifying a morbid feeling of curiosity and being near the scene of the execution of a fellow creature. But to their credit be it said there was a total absence of profanity and obscenity which formerly disgraced public executions when the full tide of life eddied and poured in rapid currents through the streets to witness an execution." Overall the police reported that the crowds behaved themselves and nothing was heard but prayers for the prisoner.

At about five am Francis Hynes rose and dressed himself with scrupulous care in a borrowed tweed suit. He ate a hearty breakfast and appeared to be in good spirits. He had spoken freely with the prison-officers, who were constantly with him in the death-cell, and said yesterday morning: "I don't care what they do with my body, but may God have mercy on my soul." At 7.30 am the Sheriff entered the condemned cell and informed the unfortunate man that his hour had come, and about five minutes afterwards Marwood appeared and pinioned the prisoner. The chaplain who had been with him since an early hour, and who appeared to be deeply affected, then handed the condemned a crucifix which he devoutly kissed. At 8.15 am a procession was formed, two Catholic clergymen lead with prayers. Next followed the 'doomed' man with a prison-officer on each side. Hynes walked firmly with his head held high and his eyes intently gazing on a crucifix: "Lord have mercy on us, Christ have mercy on us" was clear and distinct. Then followed the Governor, and Deputy-Governor of the prison, the Sheriff, and then the hangman in that order and the procession moved at a slow pace, the chaplain saying the prayers for the dead, the prisoner replying in a clear voice: his bearing was firm and dignified yet without bravado. The prison-officers and reporters stood aside [in the courtyard] with tears in their eyes, with heads bowed in sorrow in total silence. Francis Hynes was deadly pale; his eyes wandering alternately from the clergymen to the large body of soldiers and police, who had now come to the prison-courtyard. Hynes then gave a solemn prayer to God. On emerging into the courtyard a partition ran parallel to the inner wall and so now for the first time the prisoner saw the scaffold. By now some 15 minutes had passed since Marwood had first gone into the condemned-cell. The drop was reached by a short stair which the prisoner went up with a firm step. The clergymen still performed their religious duties, and still the voice of Hynes was heard in response. Then Marwood stepped forward, placed the noose around the condemned man's neck, pulled a thin white cap over his ashen face, and then stooped and tied his feet securely together. The pinioning of the arms allowed his hands to clasp his crucifix. Marwood was then seen to leave the presence of the prisoner, who stood for a moment before the persons present. The bolt was drawn and Francis Hynes was dead: he died immediately. A black flag was hoisted on the prison tower denoting that the execution had been carried out. Marwood afterwards remarked: "I never executed a finer man, nor a man with so much nerve. He walked to his doom with the utmost composure and I cannot but admire him".

Hynes never confessed and many in County Clare and Limerick believed he died innocent of the crime for which he was convicted. Marwood left Limerick for the last time in the same manner in which he entered - by the 'back door'. A covered mail-van and a large body of armed police was again needed to convey him to a specially cleared and deserted platform at Boher Railway-Station, some eight miles from Limerick, so he could catch the mail-train to Dublin. It was later said that on the trip from the capital the hangman engaged in a conversation with a young female civil servant, who had no idea who the Englishman was. Later the girl discovered who the man was and that he had come to hang her brother!

Before the execution took place, there were to be two inquiries held by the government. One was in regard to the behaviour of the jury in the hotel; the other the jury's initial make-up. On August 17th, Irish Nationalist MPs in Westminster had complained that of the 49 potential jurors called for the trial, whilst eleven had been challenged by the defence, the Crown challenged 26 of the remaining 38. Thomas Sexton MP for South Sligo said: "It was obvious from the first that the Crown had selected the panel from the County and City of Dublin, upon which they thought they could rely for a vigorous and rigorous administration of justice. But the Crown went further, and they still further filtered the panel by ordering 26 jurors to stand aside. I, therefore, call upon the right honourable and learned Gentleman the Attorney-General for Ireland to show to this House the reason why those men have been told to stand aside, and to explain, if he can, if there was any other reason except that those gentlemen were Catholics and Liberals in politics for their being cast aside."

The Attorney-General replied making a robust defence of the jury and said they were impartial and had done their duty. He also said that he had details of what the jurors had drunk that night during the trial. He said three had taken no drink at all. Six of them had played billiards, whilst the foreman ordered beverages for the other nine for their meal: half a pint of sherry, half a pint of gin; three bottles of claret, one pint of sherry, one bottle of champagne and a pint of whiskey. After their meal more drink was taken but in far less quantity. It seems the foreman paid for all this and no invoice had been sent to the authorities. However the Attorney-General accepted that by 12.20 am some of the men were misbehaving themselves. At this point, a Margaret Walsh, closed the bar and said the jurors were 'jumping across each other.' A night-porter said some of the men were moving boots from outside their door, and were playing other tricks on each other. Mr Reis admitted he had been somewhat noisy when banging into a bath. However the special jury believed they had all the third floor to themselves, which they should have had. Given the nature of the crime and politics in Ireland, the authorities should have made sure that the jury was segregated. There were two permanent guests. One Elizabeth Carberry said several jurors banged on her door and turned the handle. She said she feared what might happen had the door not been locked. The other permanent guest was …. William O'Brien. After his letter was published the paper's editor, Edmund Gray was imprisoned by the trial judge for contempt of court. Incredibly Mr Gray was also Sheriff of Dublin and a committed Irish Republican – *he had been given charge of a widely believed Unionist jury trying a man before a special court set up by the British Government* ....

And Francis Hynes wrote a poem in the death-cell:

Within my prison cell I sit penning down those saddening lines,
My age is scarcely twenty-four, and my name is Francie Hynes.
For the awful crime of murder, I am condemned to die,
But I will meet the scaffold without a sob or sigh.
I know that tears of sympathy from many an eye shall fall,
But one request I have to ask of friends and brothers all,
Let no man call me murderer of friends I humbly crave,
When I am cold and silent within my prison grave.
A Dublin Orange jury on that Memorial Day, mad drunk and blind with fury,
they swore my life away,
But I'm prepared to meet my fate, no tear will dim mine eye,
I never injured any man,
I swear by God on high.
My friends, they sought for my reprieve, but eloquence could not avail,
They will hang me in the morning in Limerick County Jail.
I give my blessing to my friends who beside me stood,
There's no more hope, they're thirsting for my blood.
My mother who watched me in my tender years,

Oh, joy she's gone before me,
Her form, it now appears as if in childhood's happy day,
she did me fondly clasp,
Little she thought she reared me for the hangman's grasp.
But I'm prepared to meet my fate,
No danger will I falter
For innocence will triumph o'er bloody hitch and halter,
And when the star of peace will shine again as in the good old times,
Let Irishmen remember the fate of Francie Hynes.

Written by Francis Hynes, son of James Hynes, solicitor, and Elizabeth O'Connell Hynes, the night before his execution in September 1882 aged, 24 years.

Francis Hynes was the last person executed in Limerick Prison. Although it is still a working prison today it was built between 1815 and 1821 and much of this facility has undergone extensive renovation of late. Many but not all of the old wings have been knocked down and replaced with new units provided with modern sanitation facilities. The original female section of the prison is generally not used except in cases of severe overcrowding, as a new modern female unit has been constructed.

There were political executions in Limerick between 1916 and 1923 both under British and Irish Rule – the last being in January 1923 ....

Case 11 "*The Curious Case* *Of* *The Twelve* *Footprints* *And* *The Mystery* *Of The Four* *Gates*"

"I would not harm the old woman. I was not there. I know nothing about it." - The man accused of murder ….

"All the evidence in the case seems to revolve about certain footprints." - The trial judge ….

"Perfectly innocent of the offence." - Charlton's last words on the scaffold and to the hangman ….

William Charlton (31[21])
[1861-2]
Murder
Of
Jane Emmerson (78[22])

In an absorbing case on a wild and stormy night in the late Autumn of 1861, an old lady who manned a level-crossing just outside Carlisle was brutally attacked and murdered with a variety of weapons including a hedge-cutter. The motive was robbery and the main and damning evidence was a series of twelve footprints at the scene, which the police diligently preserved and presented in court against a local engine-driver, who vehemently protested his innocence right up until the drop fell on the gallows, as he became the last person to be executed in public in Carlisle ….

Timeline:

9.40 pm: TT comes from Newcastle
11.00 pm: GH goes to work – sw gate out of position
4.20 am: JA drives through – all gates back in position
5.50 am: body found

---

21 Some sources have him as 35, but BDM has 31 – CHARLTON, William Head Married M 31 1830 Engine Driver Railway.

22 Some sources have her as 72 but she was 78: EMERSON, Jane Head Widow F 78 1783 Railway Gate Keeper

In the early 1860's Durran Hill[23] was an isolated and *superficially* lonely place. It stood at a point where the roads between the then villages of Botcherby and Harraby crossed a railway line on the *Newcastle & Carlisle Railway*. Today the area is just to the south-east of Carlisle city-centre. The level-crossing was maintained by **78-year-old Jane Emmerson** and she lived in a small cottage just a cricket pitch away, which also had a small garden. She was on old lady and by Victorian standards she was very old. However it was her duty to man the crossing, just as her husband, Anthony, who had died six years before, had done previously. The job was very constant and Mrs Emmerson only really had between 10.30 pm and 4.00 am off. Normally the last train would come through between 9.40 and 9.45 pm, but sometimes it would be as late as ten-thirty and in this period they were usually mineral trains coming from Newcastle-u-Tyne. By 4.15 am the trains would be starting up again. The evening of **Thursday, November 21st, 1861** was fairly typical, or at least it started off that way ….

At 9.40 pm Thomas Thompson's mineral train past through Durran Hill on its journey from Newcastle. He noticed the light on in the cottage, although he didn't see Mrs Emmerson. Once through the old lady would open the gates to let people and traffic across the line. It was just over an hour later at eleven pm that something was slightly amiss (see illustration). A railway-worker, George Hind was on his way for the night-shift in some railway sheds that were near the cottage, when he immediately noticed that the gates were all in odd positions, bar one. The two on the north side (by the cottage) were wide open. This was also the case for the (south-east) gate. However the (south-west gate) was across the line: all four should have been across the lines. This was most unlike Mrs Emmerson thought Mr Hind, but it would be some five hours before the trains would be coming through again, so he didn't look into it any further. And indeed by four am everything was back to normal …. At 4.20 am

---

23   It is now just a road – Durranhill Road

John Atkinson went through the level-crossing – all the gates were back in position. However just over one hour later (**Friday, November 22nd**), Carlisle was startled and horrified by the news of a terrible murder that had been committed during the night .... at the Durran Hill level-crossing. The crime was to be shrouded in mystery: for several weeks there was a great tension in the city as the police had a good idea who their main suspect was, but it was to be a month before an arrest was made ....

Mrs Emmerson had lived in the small cottage with a married daughter, Elizabeth Waite, and her two children, but they had just gone to Liverpool to see her husband who was a sailor returning home. They had left on the previous Saturday and so the old lady was left all alone. After the last train Mrs Emmerson would place the gates across the line and would take into her cottage two lamps, one of which hung on a signal post on the city side of the line, and the other in a small wooden cabin on the other side in the direction out of Carlisle. At 5.50 am the old keeper was found lying beside the line, within a few yards of the cottage porch by William Blaylock, a railway-worker. She was wearing, as usual, her very distinctive hat, which was made up of several layers of clothing and was described as a 'clout hat'. In a pool of blood the poor old woman was lying with her face covered with blood, one eye having been driven in with a sharp instrument, and there being several cuts on the face, one of them apparently inflicted with a stone: a few yards away was a second pool of blood. The body was warm, and the doctor and police who examined the corpse, believed she may have been attacked many hours earlier .... There were a variety of weapons that could have been used and it was possible that the attacker came back to 'finish her off', but it was also possible that she had taken a number of hours to die from the initial assault ...

Both of the warning-lamps were under the body, one of them having been broken by a stone found near the cottage. The garden gate was open, and in front of the cottage's only window was found a hedge-cutter with a wooden shaft about four-feet long, which belonged to the crossing-keeper. The blade was covered with blood, hair, glass and stone dust, and nearby were small pieces of glass: the window had been broken in three places, and it was clear that this had been done with the cutter, which was lying below. There was an indentation in the wall, and it seemed as if someone in striking a blow at the window had grazed the stone, whilst attempting to break in to the cottage. The framework of the window being of iron had prevented further damage being done, and the police thought perhaps that the attacker had probably thought that they were made of wood. He would then appear to have turned his attention to the door, after apparently not understanding how it was shut by a nail in a catch, and so it had been forced open. On it was a footprint, as if from a kick, and also the mark of a pick-axe, which, although usually kept in an outhouse in the garden, was found under a bed in the cottage, and was also covered with blood and it suggested that the attacker knew where it was kept. A drawer in the bedroom had been broken into – it too had marks from an axe on it - and it was believed that a considerable sum of money had been stolen: The victim's daughter said that the old woman would have had 25 shillings put by for her rent, as well as between £6 and £7 which she had saved to provide for her funeral expenses. Some silver spoons, a gold ring, and some jewellery also had been stolen, and likewise a pair of linen sheets. But Mrs Waite said, contrary to popular belief, her mother did not have a hoard of cash hidden away ….

The murder inquiry was led by the County's Chief Constable John Dunne and Inspector Alexander Taylor and they immediately noticed a man's footprints from behind the post of the south side, along the line, and across to the window, back to the south side of the tracks and then into the garden, the gate of which was undamaged and suggested the attacker had known how to open it. On one of the tracks was an iron-bar over two-feet long which was used to fasten one of the gates – it too had blood on it. Although described as a lonely spot, Durran Hill was part of an expanding railway system – indeed it was a system working 24/7, but the night had been wild and stormy, so that passers-by and workers in the railway sheds and yards might not have heard any cries for help. A reward of £150 for the discovery of the killer or killers was offered jointly by the railway company and the Home Office. An inquest on the body was opened at the *Plough Inn* in Botcherby on the following day by William Carrick, the County Coroner. On this occasion nor at any adjourned inquests was there any evidence available pointing to the identity of the attacker, and it began to look as though the tragedy was going to pass into the list of undiscovered crimes. Suspicion did fall on at least one person, however, and other arrests were made but no-one was charged, and the police soon came to believe that only one man was directly involved in the murder, and that he was not old, for some of the twelve footprints that were identifiable, indicated that the person had run ….

The police and everyone else agreed that the murder had been perpetrated by someone who was well acquainted with the locality, including the interior of the cottage, and even the precise place where the victim kept her money – of the three drawers in the cottage, the one that had been locked, was the one that had been broken into and searched. In this drawer, Mrs Emmerson did indeed keep her money and jewellery etc. The uncertainty over who the killer was continued for more than a month, by which time the chances of bringing the criminal to justice were fast diminishing so thought the general public, although hope was not altogether abandoned, and indeed the police were sure they knew who the killer was …. The vital clue in this case was clearly the footprints. A close examination of them showed that the sparables[24] or nails in the shoe soles were arranged in a peculiar pattern; and it was at once seen that, if the shoes worn by the killer could be traced, there could be irrefutable proof if they corresponded with those footprints. The prints had been covered by buckets and a local sculptor, Joseph Pickering had taken plaster-casts. Along with a number of pieces of circumstantial evidence, it was hoped that this would be the clear and direct evidence, needed to convict Mrs Emmerson's killer ….

Thirty-one days after the murder, the man upon whom suspicion had fallen was arrested at his house in London Road Terrace, Harraby Street – it was just a short distance away from Durran Hill. **William Charlton (31)**, the man in question, was an engine-driver for the

---

24 Small nail with no head used in shoe-repairs

same *Newcastle & Carlisle Railway:* he was a tall slim married man, with three children. He drove the second train to Newcastle, the 4.30. Throughout his police interviews he was cool and unmoved, but gradually he began to appear to feel the position in which he was placed, but part of his behaviour was probably due to the fact that he was .... deaf, and it was obvious he was unable to follow the police-questions and the subsequent court proceedings. Mrs Waite said Charlton would have known her mother very well – he had his own allotment near the cottage on the south side of the railway, and furthermore another railway-worker William Shepherd said that he had seen Charlton in her garden, and that he had used her pick-axe and he also said that he had seen him *inside* her cottage ….

When Charlton was arrested, Inspector Taylor found in his possession a pair of shoes. He had been asked to produce his footwear. Apart from his boots which he was wearing, he owned a pair of strong shoes. They had been newly nailed, and there were also marks of two semi-circles of nails that had been removed: in total there were 54 holes. Some of the empty spaces matched the empty-spaces on the plaster-casts. The police suggested that the killer might have realised that the *nails* would have been clearly been picked up by the plaster-casts, so they asked Charlton why his shoes had been re-nailed and he replied that they may have been 'knocked out by the engine'. He also said that his brother-in-law, 25-year-old Thomas Robinson, who lived with his family may have taken some of the nails out. Told the killer had worn his shoes, the engine-driver replied: "I would not harm the old woman. I was not there. I know nothing about it." When the police suggested there were traces of blood on his shoes, Charlton said it was engine grease. During a second search of his house the police found hidden in a wall by the toilet, 52 worn sparables wrapped in paper. Earlier a pair of pincers and chisel had also been found in the house. When the 52 sparables were put into the shoes, they matched the casts taken at Durran Hill ….[25]

---

25 *Carlisle Journal* Tues 18/3

Realising his predicament William Charlton sought to throw the guilt of the crime upon an entirely innocent man: his brother-in-law, Mr Robinson. The shoes had been recently soled, and the pattern of the nails was so peculiar as to be unmistakable. Round the front part of the soles there was a double row of removed nails, and there were also two curved rows which formed with the sides of the shoes two ellipses. Crucially one of the semi-circles of the ellipses was carried up further in one boot than the other, and that accidental difference was shown in the plaster casts, as was also a peculiar mark of triangular shape, imprinted by three nails in the heel. It was therefore necessary, if Charlton wished to clear himself, that he should endeavour to blame someone else, and that was what he tried to do, in a written statement, signed by him in the presence of Inspector Taylor. It read:

"On Thursday night, the 21st day of November last, I went home from my work about 5.20 pm. Afterwards I came out, and went .... over to the engine sheds. When I came from there Thomas Robinson, my brother-in-law, was standing at the railway yard gates. We spoke to each other. He asked me if I was going up street [into town]. We came up street, and went into David Hall's public house, and had each a pint of ale. We sat there a few minutes, not very long. While in there, he asked me to lend him my shoes as the roads were very clarty [muddy], and his boots were rather tight. So I lent him my shoes. They are the shoes which the police showed on Saturday at the Courthouse. We then came out and I left him at the door. He went down Crown Street. He said he was going to Ivegill[26]. I went down Botchergate. I called in at Mabel Andrew's in Union Street, and had two pints of ale, which I did not pay for until Saturday night. I then went home and went to bed. (William) Chambers called me up on the following morning (Friday) a few minutes past three o'clock. When I was coming out of the house Thomas Robinson came out of our petty [toilet] and gave me my shoes back again, and I gave him his own. I went into the house, and tied my shoes. He did not go in with me. When I opened the door again I asked him where he had

---

26   15 miles to the south of the city

been till this time in the morning. He said: "I have had a bloody good spree." He gave me 3d, which I spent at Hexham. I saw him no more till the Saturday night following, at the *Earl Grey Inn*. When I gave him my shoes in David Hall's the nails were *in*, and I did not observe them *out* until Saturday night, the 23rd November, when I was cleaning them. I have told Thomas Robinson never to come near my house again, as he was such a bad 'un. I wish I had never seen him."

Thomas Robinson had been in trouble with the police before, having been imprisoned for theft. Fortunately, however, he could prove a clear alibi, although not before he was arrested, and, he had appeared alongside Charlton in the dock at the magistrates court, charged with being an accessory to the murder. However through a succession of independent witnesses, he was able to prove precisely where he had been from the Saturday before the murder until the Friday following the date of the crime. On the evening of the Thursday - the night of the murder - he'd accompanied a friend named George Rayson, to a Mr Longcake's pub at Roe Hill[27], where they and other friends played cards until half-past ten. They then had adjourned to a "jerry shop" at High Bridge[28], kept by Thomas Jordan. By the time they'd left there - about midnight - it was so late that Mr Rayson invited Mr Robinson to sleep with him at his father's place. They went there, and slept - three in a bed – with another man. Next morning, at six am, they were awakened and he was seen leaving the house by a local timber merchant. Released he then gave evidence against Charlton: He said he had not seen his brother-in-law at all on Thursday or Friday ....

William Charlton stood trial at the **Carlisle Assizes on Monday, February 24th, 1862 before Mr Justice Willes, in a trial that was to last two days.** As the prisoner was deaf, there was some difficulty in getting him to understand the charge, but ultimately he pleaded: "Not guilty." When he entered the dock, his face seemed flushed - but as the case proceeded he became calm, and stood motionless.

---

27 Near Ivegill
28 Again nearby to Ivegill

Counsel for the prosecution were Messrs Edwin Price, QC, Maule, and J. Henry Fawcett; and the prisoner was defended by Mr Thomas Campbell Foster, who had with him, as junior, Mr W. C. Gully. Earlier the judge had told the Grand Jury: "All the evidence in the case seems to revolve about certain footprints."

By the time of the trial Inspector Taylor was a Superintendent. He told the court he'd arrived on the scene of the crime at 7.30 am. With some foresight he'd immediately took precautions to protect the footprints from contamination. Fortunately after Mr Blaylock only two other railway-workers had come to the scene and the officer then ascertained that two of the three men were wearing clogs, and that the other man's shoe-soles in no way corresponded with the prints. The sculptor, who made the casts, explained the resemblances in very great detail to the court, and the jury afterwards compared the casts with the shoes. In no one instance was there found to be any difference. The panel of the door marked with a footprint was produced in the court, and it also showed the same identical marking. Furthermore the paper in which the sparables were found wrapped contained some tobacco dust; and dust of exactly the same kind was found in Charlton's coat pocket, together with a loose sparable similar to the others. Marks on the nails showed that they had been removed with pincers and a chisel, belonging to the railway company, which should not have been in the prisoner's possession.

Apart from the footprints, the evidence for the prosecution contained many circumstantial details which pointed to Charlton's guilt. Amongst these were that he was intimately acquainted with the locality, including the interior and surroundings of the cottage. He knew the victim well, and was familiar with her duties, and the hours when she would be occupied with them. He had used the pick-axe in her garden and had taken it back to its owner, and knew where she kept it. On the morning after the murder he went to the engine shed soon after three o'clock, but did not take his breakfast with him as usual. He then left the engine shed, saying to one man that he was going back for his breakfast, and to another that he was going for a knife. He was, however, seen by a witness between half-past three and four o'clock, coming from …. the direction of the cottage, the opposite distance from his own home. The prosecution suggested that Charlton had replaced the gate across the line for the first train at 4.15 am. There was also a footprint in *coagulated* blood, showing that the killer had been there *hours* after the murderous assault, which corresponding with the time when Charlton was seen returning from the area of the cottage to the engine-shed.

Mr Price went on to say that Charlton had left for Newcastle on his engine at 4.30 am, and, when passing the crossing, diverted the fireman, James Mitchell's attention, by pointing out, and talking about cabbages in a nearby garden. Before he had left for Newcastle a fellow worker, James Carruthers had seen him approaching the engine shed (and indeed his own home) from the crossing at about four am and he told police that he had never seen Charlton come to work from *that direction at that time,* and he had been woken at *three* am for work from his home, so why had he walked towards the level-crossing. Mr Carruthers asked him what he was doing but did not receive any reply. Inspector Taylor had walked from the engine shed to the crossing, cleared the south-west gate from the line, walked up to the cottage and returned – it took him 13 minutes there and back. In Newcastle, when told about the murder, Charlton had said he saw a light at the crossing as they passed, that it was being carried from south to north, and that, in fact, he "saw the old woman in the porch", where as the prosecution would suggest Mrs Emmerson had been attacked shortly after the last train, a point further re-inforced by the fact that the victim's bed had not been slept in.

Mr Campbell Foster was forced to tell the jury that when his client had said that the nails in his shoes were burnt out on the engine, and that they were taken out by Thomas Robinson, that these were both lies. Indeed the defence called no witnesses; and, although his address to the jury lasted for more than two hours, many in the court thought it confused, and really it amounted to no more than pleading with the jury not to send Charlton to the gallows on the footprint evidence. He also pointed out that no blood had been found on the accused's clothes and what of the money and jewellery – none of this had ever been recovered by the police …. He also said that just because Charlton had tried to incriminate an entirely innocent man – his sister's husband - this did not prove his guilt, however reprehensible it might have been. As it was eight pm before the speech for the defence was finished, the judge postponed his summing up until the next morning **(Tuesday, February 25th)**. This occupied two hours, and was strongly against the prisoner; and in it the judge spoke highly in favour of the police, saying they had acted with great skill, which by the standards of the day they had. In order to ensure a 'fair trial', Charlton was given a newspaper report of the case so he could read the evidence against him. The jury deliberated for nearly six hours, again in this era, this was considered a long time. When they came back into the courtroom, they returned a verdict of murder, but strongly recommended Charlton to mercy on the grounds of 'previous good character'. Mr Justice Willes in passing the sentence of death, was greatly affected, but warned the prisoner that he could give him no hope of the sentence being commuted and indeed the **Home Secretary, Sir George Grey, 2nd Baronet, quickly said that the execution would proceed at noon on Saturday, March 15th, 1862, outside Carlisle Prison.**

Within six years or so public executions would be ended in Britain and William Charlton's execution was to be **the last public one in Carlisle.** Charlton for a brief moment turned his gaze down and away from the **hangman, William Calcraft, and turned to the crowd,** which was estimated to be between six and eight thousand. He met his fate firmly, and briefly on the gallows admitted that he had had a fair trial, and that he did not see how the jury could have come to any other conclusion, but somewhat inconsistently, he maintained that he was innocent. He told his wife, who was expecting another child, that innocent men had been 'hung' before and in this case he was adding to that number. The bolt was drawn at 12:05 pm. The execution was over in an instant: Charlton died cleanly. The drop was only partly elevated, thus rendering the sight of execution as difficult as possible for the crowd. Afterwards Calcraft told the press that the condemned had said to him: "Perfectly innocent of the offence." But was he really innocent?

Notwithstanding the clearness of the alibi proved by Thomas Robinson, gossip continued to cast aspersions upon him; and therefore a Mr Page, the prison surgeon, feeling that something further was really due to Mr Robinson, and to the public as well, to clear his name, went to Charlton before the execution, and robustly questioned him. The reply he received was that the statement made by Charlton was indeed quite untrue, and that Mr Robinson "knew nothing about the murder " - the implication being that Charlton knew all about it and therefore all about the 'twelve footprints and the four gates.'

Carlisle Prison was closed in 1922, and was pulled down in 1931. The last execution at the prison was in 1892 ....

Case 12
"Murder At
Pokehouse Quarry"

"I threw a stone at _____ my old wife, and hit her just behind the ear, and it is bleeding, and I can't stop it. If the poor old beggar is dead, I'll bury her in the brook." - William Haywood.

"Good bye, Dad!" - The tearful daughter, as she heard her father sentenced to hang for murdering her mother.

"They expected me to faint but I didn't." - Haywood's reply.

William Haywood (61)
[1903]
Murder
Of
His Wife, Jane (59)

SCENE OF THE TRAGEDY.
The X shows the spot where there were considerable blood stains and signs of a struggle.

Murder Scene

An appalling murder by a depraved and violent sexual offender – a man convicted of the rape of his own daughter whose mutilation, including appalling sexual injuries on his wife, led him to become the last person executed at Hereford Prison, ironically in a newly built death-chamber ….

Some five miles to the north-west of Leominster in Herefordshire lie the villages of Mortimer's Cross, Lucton and Aymestrey, and it was in this area that on **Sunday, July 12th, 1903** that locals began to hear of a truly shocking event that had occurred in their neighbourhood. At first information was not precise and all sorts of rumours were abound. Gradually people began making their way to a local quarry and the awful truth began to seep out …. *Pokehouse Quarry* was in the village of Lucton and nearby the body of a woman, horribly mutilated had been seen. She had been identified as being local and the police had quickly found out her movements on the day before. **Mrs Jane Haywood (59)** had left her home in nearby Yarpole between seven and eight am, taking her husband breakfast at the quarry, where he worked alone. She was not seen during the day, but she often stayed with her husband and helped him out at the quarry.

At about 9 pm, a local labourer, John Davies was near Mortimer's Cross with his wife, when he saw Mrs Haywood's husband, **William (61),** with a wheelbarrow at Foal's Yard. He bade him good evening but when he came up to Haywood to his horror he could see the body of a woman in a wheelbarrow that Haywood was pulling: the woman's arms dangling over the edge. He thought the woman had suffered some terrible injury at the quarry. Mr Davies told Haywood to stop and began questioning him about the woman, who was clearly dead. Haywood was evasive in his replies and by now a number of other locals had arrived on the scene. Haywood was told he would be detained and the village policeman, Constable Preece was sent for. A doctor was also sent for and rather strangely Haywood kept insisting the woman was only injured, despite the fact that the top of her head had been sliced off!

The locals decided to lift the body out of the wheelbarrow and lay the body on the grass and Haywood dutifully helped them. Haywood now seemed much more confidant and explained that the woman, whose face was unrecognisable, was his wife and that she had been struck by a piece of sharp slate in the quarry. Haywood then casually lay down by the body. Moments later Constable Preece arrived and after just a few short questions he realised that this was more than just an industrial accident – the woman had been battered and mutilated - and he arrested Haywood for murder. Haywood immediately jumped up and said he was going to drown himself in the nearby *River Lugg*, but he was held down by a number of local men. By midnight Haywood was in Leominster police-station being questioned by Superintendent Stephen Price.

The next day as locals began to realize the full horror of what had occurred at *Pokehouse Quarry*, a local doctor, Dr R. Williams conducted a *post-mortem*. Although he informed the police that he would have his full report by the 20th, it was obvious that Mrs Haywood's injuries were 'ghastly'. Apart from the scalp wound she had been horribly beaten around the face and a leg and arm broken, and there were other more shocking injuries .... Meanwhile the police and media conducted an intensive examination of the quarry, which was set in picturesque countryside and was becoming something of a tourist attraction. The quarry was, however, a hive of activity – there were crowbars, hammers, wire and bags of gunpowder everywhere. Haywood's wheelbarrow had been returned to the quarry and the bloodstains on it were immediately obvious. It had been put back where the murder appeared to have taken place as the ground around it was disturbed and there were traces of blood nearby: Constable Preece noted how the ground was impressed with a woman's dress and that a bucket of water was blood coloured. As to the time of the murder, the group noticed a basket on a nearby rock, which had in it some of Haywood's breakfast.

The Haywood family were well-known in the area and also in Leominster from where they originally came. Indeed on the Friday Haywood and his wife were in the town. Later in the evening Haywood went to his local pub, the *Bell*, and when Jane asked him to come home he said he would, but should she do this again, then she would regret it. In an angry mood Haywood took his tools and left their home that Friday night, sleeping rough, and at seven am the next day he was in a pub, the *Mortimer's Cross Inn*, drinking, including the purchase of a bottle of whiskey and beer. Haywood was a man who did not look his age and he was physically overbearing and was an ex-soldier. The couple had six children[29] and there was much local concern about the family's future. On the following Monday, William Haywood appeared at Leominster Magistrates and was remanded into custody. On the same day an inquest was held in Mortimer's Cross, with the prisoner in attendance, and Haywood's three daughters[30] were also there in mourning dress, as well as a son. The body of their mother was laid out in an outbuilding in the *Mortimer's Cross Hotel*. One of the daughters, Elizabeth (19), told the Coroner, Mr C.E. Moore, that she believed her father had left nearer eight than seven in the morning.

---

29 He had three boys and three girls – BDM.
30 Including one he was convicted of raping.

Since Haywood had been charged with murder, it was decided that the inquest should be adjourned and he was taken back to Leominster. As he was being put in a cab under guard, the crowd surged forward and saw how affectionately his daughters bade him farewell, but unbeknown to them, all was not well in the family. The police knew, but it could not be reported, that Haywood had been convicted in 1896 of raping one of his daughters. Indeed his criminal record went back some forty years: it was mostly for assaults and drinking, but he was also a 'wife-beater'. Throughout the three villages he was seen as anti-social and a bully, and much of his activity was never formally reported. On one occasion he attacked a police superintendent with a scythe after the police were making inquiries about another assault, but since the officer beat Haywood into submission, he was never charged.

William Haywood appeared at **Hereford Assizes on Saturday, November 28th, 1903 before Mr Justice Bigham.** Haywood, who had not shaved for days, appeared in a daze and when asked to plead said nothing. His **defence lawyer, Mr Ronald Bosanquet,** quickly interjected by telling the accused to say 'not guilty', which he did. The **prosecution was led by Mr Stamford Hutton, who was assisted by Mr Reginald Coventry.** In opening the case for the Crown, Mr Hutton said that at one pm on the day of the murder Haywood was seen in the *Mortimer's Cross Inn* drinking: his clothes were dishevelled and he had scratch marks on his face. He was alleged to have told a fellow drinker: "I threw a stone at _____ my old wife, and hit her just behind the ear, and it is bleeding, and I can't stop it. If the poor old beggar is dead, I'll bury her in the brook." Warning the jury of the shocking evidence that would follow, the barrister said that in the quarry the police later found a number of bloodstained stakes with human hairs attached to it. He added that he was sure the jury would reject any suggestion that Mrs Haywood had died from a terrible accident and as such the only issue would be the state of Haywood's mind.

At this time the only child living at home was Elizabeth and she told the court that her father's personality changed when he had been drinking. She said that her father would often threatened to hit her mother, but often it was only meant in jest. She added that a brother of her father's had died in a mental home in 1895, and that an aunt was also locked up in an institution, and that the prisoner's mother would often say she could hear voices in her head, and that Haywood himself had started to imagine people were around, when they weren't. Elizabeth said that about ten years before her father had fallen off a cart and injured his head, and after that even small amounts of alcohol had a dramatic effect on his personality. However a number of other witnesses told the court that Haywood rarely appeared to be *obviously* drunk and often only went to the local pubs once a week, although his daughter said he was a 'hard-drinker'. At the murder spot the police found a number of bottles of whiskey and beer as well as a hammer and axe that had bloodstains on them.

On July 13th, Haywood allegedly told a Constable Edward Rogers that his wife had been drinking in the quarry and that just before the 'accident' she seemed to have lost her senses and that he had washed the blood from her head and tied up her (broken) leg. However it was now that the court heard the damming evidence of Dr Williams. He began by saying that the body of the victim was covered in bruising from top to bottom. Apart from the top of the head having been sliced open, the brain was also severely injured caused by numerous blows to the head. Then the doctor explained how the body had been stabbed and cut all over and mutilated. He added he believed that the stakes had been used but not necessarily the axe. The doctor added he could find no trace of alcohol in Mrs Haywood's system. Next the jury heard the shocking evidence that Haywood had mutilated his wife's vagina by pushing *sharp* stones deep inside her, and later the jury were told that on one occasion he had pushed a stick into one of his daughter's vagina.

Dr Williams was also asked about his experience in dealing with insanity, and he agreed that mental abnormality was often inherited and exasperated by drink. He said that he'd seen the prisoner on many occasions and believed him to have fully understood what he had done. However after lunch the court heard from a Dr Morrison who was head of the *Herefordshire County Asylum*. He said he'd fully examined Haywood on two occasions and had taken evidence of his family back for some 40 years. He said he believed that the prisoner was mentally 'weak' and this had been made worse by his drinking, and that he was an 'imbecile of the highest grade'. He said he believed that Haywood had reacted to his wife's annoyance at his drinking and had 'over-reacted'. Asked what he meant by this by Mr Bosanquet, Dr Morrison said he thought Haywood was 'mad' when he attacked the victim. However the Medical Officer at Hereford Prison, Dr James Lane said he had interviewed Haywood twice and seen him frequently and considered him sane, although he seemed somewhat unconcerned that he had been charged with murder.

Dr Lane said he also had seen a number of letters written by Haywood and his family. In one Haywood complained that he had never been 'right in his head' since he suffered sunstroke in the Army, but this was over 40 years before. It was now that the court heard that Haywood had been given a 5-year sentence for the rape of one of his daughters in 1896. He had served four years but there was no record of insanity during this period. However Mr Bosanquet contended the injuries inflicted on Mrs Haywood were the work of a 'madman'.

In his summing-up Mr Justice Bigham said the fact that William Haywood might be a lunatic did not make him insane. He said the jury should take note of his demeanour before and after the killing – he certainly knew he had attacked his wife, as he said she was seriously injured in the pub, and indeed he had told a lie as to how it had occurred. As to familial insanity, the judge told the jurymen that it was for them to decide if this was evidence or not that the accused was insane. The judge also referred to the 'abominable' aspects to the crime and his conviction for a like offence. He said the jury might consider this a form of insanity, but it was far from it. The jury retired for just 17 minutes. They found the prisoner guilty of murder. The black cap placed on his head, the judge said he fully agreed with the jury's verdict. At this point the daughter who still lived at home burst into tears and cried out: "Good bye, Dad!" As he was being taken down Haywood replied with bravado: "They expected me to faint but I didn't."

The Home Secretary, Mr Aretas Akers-Douglas decided that it was best for two further doctors to examine Haywood, but they also concluded that the condemned was sane and so he was executed on **Tuesday, December 15th, 1903 at eight am, at Hereford Prison by Henry Pierrepoint and John Ellis.** In the death-cell, to the prison-officers at least, William Haywood was quite sane when away from drink. He complained about the 'shifty medical' opinion and then began issuing death-threats against a number of people were he ever to be released. At first he shunned any religious help but as the day of his execution drew nearer, he eventually succumbed. He took full advantage of the prison-rules and constantly smoked. Not unsurprisingly there was no local petition to save him. Although this was to be the last execution at Hereford, ironically it was on a brand new gallows built in a dedicated new death-chamber[31].

The execution was due to have been carried out by brothers William and John Billington but they were due to carry out a double-execution the following day at Winchester, and with two other men also under sentence of death it was decided to employ William Billington's so-called 'assistants'. The local media remarked how it was interesting that the media were barred from this execution yet less than 40 years before anyone could watch a public execution: how times had changed, they noted. The day Haywood was hanged was a grim grey day, and it was still not quite fully light as the execution party gathered outside the death-cell at a few minutes before eight. Prison-officers later told the media that William Haywood's callous indifference had gone and he looked very haggard as he walked to the drop. Moments later he was dead, death being recorded as 'instantaneous'. The time of the execution was 8.03 am as people in a workhouse next to the wall where the death-chamber was, could hear the thud of the trap-doors. At the formal inquest after the execution, Dr Lane, who had given evidence against Haywood, was shown a letter by the Coroner in which Haywood appeared truly penitent, and he replied: "Oh yes; drink being the cause of the crime."

During the First World War in 1915 Hereford Prison was closed[32] and in 1930 it was partially demolished: the only surviving parts of

---

31 The last execution to this one in Hereford was in 1891.
32 The next person STD at Hereford was Herbert Armstrong in 1922 who was, of

the prison today is the main building situated in the bus station car park, which is now a travel agent and flats; the bus station toilet block which is over the road of the car park is another remaining building that is left; these buildings were the Governor's and Deputy Governor's houses.

course, executed at Gloucester Prison.

Case 13
"The Last Public Execution in the British Isles"

Joseph le Brun
(1875)
Murder
of
His sister Nancy Laurens

Although the public execution of Michael Barrett outside London's Newgate Prison in May 1868 is stated to be the last public execution in Britain, the law abolishing public hangings did not extend to the Isle of Man and the Channel Isles …. Consequently when Joseph Le Brun was sentenced to death in July 1875 for murder on Jersey and his petition for a reprieve was rejected both in London and on the island, his execution was carried out in the public view from the island's Prison, which was ironically also called Newgate Prison.

All over Jersey everyone had heard of **Joseph le Brun**. He was known as a drunk and as a hopeless gambler, who owed money to many people. As his credit ran out so did the goodwill of the islanders and in October 1874 he moved to the village of Le Couvent renting a cottage near to his sister and her husband, as they were the only people who were still friendly towards him. The couple owned a small holding and sold fruit and vegetables.

Phillipe Laurens and Le Brun's sister, **Nancy**, were quite happy to help Le Brun out: He would dine with them in the evenings and then return to his nearby cottage to sleep. The couple felt sorry for the 52-year-old: He had no real job save that as a casual farm labourer and he had never married. To help him out the couple paid him a small amount to do small jobs around the house and in the garden.

Le Brun and his sister seemed to get on very well and on the evening **December 15ᵗʰ, 1874** he was invited to stay after his meal, as her husband was staying late in St Helier and would not be returning home until 10.00 p.m.

The village of Le Couvent had just one policeman (Centenier). During his whole career it is unlikely that he had even encountered a serious crime let alone murder, and so when a distressed villager ran to the police station screaming that a man's wife had been murdered and that the man he had been shot at, the officer himself became distressed.

Obviously Centenier Hamon knew the villager and was even more shocked when Clement Roudel said his neighbour Phillipe Laurens had returned to his cottage to find his wife dead and that her apparent assailant, her own brother Joseph Le Brun, had then tried to kill Laurens by shooting at him.

At the cottage the officer found Laurens lying on the couch in the front-room with a bandage around his arm. Although the wound appeared not to be life threatening, he had lost much blood and was very soft spoken when he whispered to the officer that it was Joseph Le Brun who had shot him.

Although the officer and Mr Roudel had walked through the open front door because it was dark they had unknowingly walked through a large pool of blood. The dead body of Mrs Laurens lay in the first room on the right, which had been converted into a kitchen. Mrs Laurens appeared to have been beaten beyond recognition though the gruesome wounds to her face and head had been caused by a shotgun.

Mrs Lauren's face was pitted with small holes and it appeared as if she had been standing by the window facing her attacker when shot, as the curtains were riddled with holes.

Earlier on in the evening Mrs Laurens had been seen by Mr Roudel on the sofa though he had thought she had been sleeping. Mr Roudel had popped into the cottage at about eight p.m. and had simply seen her lying down and had left. Unfortunately Mrs Laurens was prone to excessive drinking and often slept at the most curious hours, so Roudel didn't think to look extensively at Mrs Laurens. Roudel did say that he hadn't seen Le Brun in the house.

However Mr Roudel had heard several gunshots at 10.00 p.m. and quickly went to his neighbours. Although all the cottages were small they were all detached and even at 10.00 p.m. there was still some light and it was not uncommon to hear gunshots at that time, as people would shoot rabbits and birds. But the gunshots this time seemed uncomfortably close. Entering the cottage Mr Roudel found a shotgun in the hallway and pitiful moaning from the converted kitchen.

Mr Roudel was adamant he heard nothing before 10.00 p.m. Furthermore it was somewhat strange that the Laurens' cottage seemed quite peaceful: Apart from the damage to the curtains there was no apparent damage to any of the furniture – certainly there had been no attempt to ransack the house.

To add to the macabre was the fact that the injured Phillipe Laurens was sitting next to his dead wife, whose body had not quite managed to keel over and looked as she had simply nodded off. Her stockinged feet had been placed in a bucket of water by her husband Laurens, who whispered to Roudel that Le Brun had shot his sister and that he had lifted his wife onto the sofa.

By a quarter past ten a small crowd of people had arrived from the village and Centenier Hamon took Mr Roudel and some other men to Joseph Le Brun's cottage, which was only a few hundred yards from the Laurens' cottage. Le Brun gave the crowd no trouble and by one o'clock was under arrest in St Helier.

A local gunsmith told the police that the gun found at the Laurens' cottage had recently been fired and its protective cap was worn away, but that it would still require some effort to fire it.

Naturally enough the police seemed to have a watertight case against Joseph Le Brun. Also the injury to Phillipe Laurens was not that serious at all and on the following day he gave a statement to the police, which seemed to clinch the case against Le Brun.

Laurens said when he entered his cottage he was slightly surprised though not shocked to see his brother-in-law. Although Le Brun had stayed on after tea, he wasn't usually at the cottage at that late hour. However he said Le Brun launched into a torrent of verbal abuse, which culminated in him calling Laurens a "hangdog ".

He said that when he closed the front door he was faced by Le Brun, who said nothing but stood in front of him with a shotgun pointed at him. Then without a word le Brun pulled the trigger and Laurens fell to the floor having suffered an injury to his arm and face. As Laurens staggered out of the cottage, Le Brun then fired again hitting a lilac tree outside.

Despite his injuries Laurens pushed Le Brun aside and went into the kitchen to attend to his wound, when he saw his wife on the sofa. The clear implication was that Mrs Laurens had been killed sometime earlier, although no one seemed to have heard any gunshots coming from the cottage before 10 o'clock.

Faced with this horror as blood poured from his wounds, Laurens kept asking Le Brun why had done this, but he received only a deathly silence.

The police were told by two doctors that Laurens could not have shot himself and were keen to know why Le Brun would want to murder his sister and apparently his brother-in-law too. Laurens said that aside from his drinking he could think of no real reason. Laurens said he had never seen them argue and Le Brun regularly gave his sister money for his evening meals.

Laurens did tell the police that he had received £28 from selling produce from his farm, which he gave to his wife to look after. The police naturally enough searched for it and although they never found it, they were satisfied that Le Brun didn't have it: certainly Le Brun had made no attempt to ransack the house to find it. However the police did believe that Mrs Laurens had hidden the money, which may have angered Le Brun.

On the following day Le Brun was interviewed for over 12 hours but would say nothing. Furthermore the police were amazed that Le Brun simply said he was totally innocent.
Indeed Le Brun's whole demeanour was either that of a man who was totally indifferent to his fate or who was genuinely innocent. However he would say nothing further and made no effort to explain why he was innocent.

Although no gunshot had been heard the police were sure that Le Brun had shot his sister sometime between eight and eight-thirty, since a young boy, Peter Le Piez told them that he had seen Le Brun entering the cottage. They surmised that he must have left after tea only to return later.

Throughout the British Isles at this period a prisoner could not give evidence on his own behalf in court. In this case Le Brun refused to speak the other evidence had to be written out by the police, who did not begin their task until April 1875 and it took them a total of three months to collate it.

Between December 1874 and April 1875 the police hoped that Le Brun would break his silence. During these six months the police contacted many people on the island who knew Le Brun to try to understand why he would want to kill his sister. The police were sure that the shooting of Laurens was a reaction of shock at the thought that his brother-in-law would discover the murder of his wife.

On **July 7th, 1875,** Joseph le Brun appeared at the island's Assize Court at the beginning of a two-day trial. As well as the charge of murder, Le Brun also faced the charge of the attempted murder of Phillipe Laurens.

Under the island's ancient system of justice there were four judges headed by a senior judge (Bailiff). Bailiff Hammond was assisted by three other judges (Jurats) Mr Lerrier, Gruchy and Le Montais. Furthermore a jury in Jersey consisted of 24 men!

Although the Crown, whose case was put by the island's Attorney General admitted there was no obvious motive for murder, they alluded to the £28, that Phillipe Laurens had given his wife, though they said that Le Brun made no apparent effort to find it. The Attorney General suggested that Le Brun might have shot his sister, because she refused to say where the money was.

A number of villagers from Le Couvent told the court that on a few occasions before the murder, Mr Laurens had told them about the money, and whenever Le Brun was present, he would say that Laurens wouldn't have the money for much longer. However villagers took it to mean that Le Brun would drink it away rather than steal it. It was also shown to the court that one member of the inquest jury, Mr Perrot had pointed out that the dead woman's pockets had been turned out.

For the defence Advocate Westaway said that although everyone knew that Joseph Le Brun was a man "addicted to drink ", it was also case that his sister drank heavily, but at no time did they ever argue.

The court was told that when Le Brun was arrested an hour after the shooting of Laurens, the police found not a trace of blood in his cottage and yet the hallway and the kitchen of the Laurens' cottage, was splattered with blood.

Finally Mr Westaway implored the jury not to convict Le Brun on such slight evidence and launched into a speech outlining the dangers of capital punishment.

In his closing speech the Attorney General said that he had deliberately not relied on a motive because, firstly by law he didn't have to do this, but secondly it would be unfair to the accused. Also he told the court that he would not want the jury to take seriously the fact that Le Brun had told people in the village pub that " She (his sister) will die this time " or "there will be a funeral in the house. ". The Attorney General admitted to the court that the police could find no reason for such an outburst, except for Le Brun's drink problems.

However after retiring for just 35 minutes the foreman of the jury informed the court that all 24 of them agreed that Le Brun was guilty of the attempted murder of Phillipe Laurens, but that they were divided on the murder charge.

Under Jersey law if five of the 24 did not say Le Brun was innocent he would be declared guilty. The senior judge, Bailiff Hammond then summoned each juryman to him and each whispered their verdict in his ear.

After what must have seemed an eternity to Le Brun the judge said that under the law he was guilty of murder, but he would not say the split in the jury. However the judge also said that the jury wished to recommend mercy.

Unlike the rest of Britain the law in Jersey allowed any sentence, including death, to be passed for any serious crime, including murder. However by tradition in Jersey the sentence of death was always passed for a conviction of murder. In theory Le Brun could have been sentenced to death for the attempted murder of Phillipe Laurens too but instead a sentence of life imprisonment was recorded by the court.

Bailiff Hammond then turned to le Brun and told him to bow his head and then told him that he must repent to God and was told he would be hanged.

Under the unwritten constitution of the British Isles, although Jersey is a country in its own right, its legal system is subject to the control of the Home Office in London.

With Le Brun under sentence of death the Home Office decided that the issue should be decided by the Jersey government. This decision did not reach St Helier until August 8th. In the meantime Le Brun spent each day professing his complete innocence.

There was a brief exchange of telegrams between St Helier and London and finally it was decided that the Home Secretary would make the final decision. On August 10th, 1875 Mr R.A. Cross, decided Le Brun would hang, motive or not, and the execution date was set for **August 12th, 1875** at eight a.m.

On the previous evening there was a dramatic meeting between Le Brun and the man who he had tried to kill. Their brief meeting was reported fully in the press. Laurens said: " Joe, I'm sorry to see you here." However Le Brun replied by saying: " And you still wish today that it was I who did it?" When Laurens replied he had no doubt, Le Brun asked him what proof he had, but Laurens did not want to argue and simply said "Adieu".

It had been nine years since Jersey last hanged a murderer when Frances Bradley was hanged (on August 11th, 1866) – almost the exact date of Le Brun's scheduled execution. Much was made of the fact that Le Brun had witnessed that hanging, as proof that capital punishment had no deterrent value and could have brutalised Le Brun.

The day of the execution began with a huge thunderstorm. By six o'clock the Special Constabulary (Halberdiers) had surrounded the prison walls at Newgate Street to keep back the ever-growing crowds.

The regular police had set up barriers in the streets around the prison and the crowd was very well ordered. The gallows itself was put the day before. It had been constructed within the prison yard but was high enough for the head and shoulders of the man to be seen by the public.

The public would not be able to see the drop, though they would see William Marwood, the hangman, putting a hood over Le Brun's head and the noose around his neck.

At 7.30 a.m. Le Brun was given a shot of rum. At five minutes to eight Marwood escorted him to the scaffold across the grave of Frances Bradley and a plot already marked out for Le Brun! On the trap door Le Brun shouted to the crowd: " I am innocent. " Then Marwood pulled the lever and Le Brun was dead.

As the crowd began to drift away there ensued an exciting scene as the prison chaplain the Rev. Beaumont screamed out: "The man is innocent. It will be cleared up one day. It is a mistake: it is carelessness – it is carelessness." Finally as the last of the crowd left he said: "In Jersey you hang a man because they have a bad name."

The last execution on Jersey was in 1959 ….

Case 14
"Murder
In
Highfield Road"

"That's right. I did not think of it before till I got to my work. A man who kills a woman is not fit to live. I told her at dinner time today.... that if she came up I should cut her head off and that I should have no more to do with her. I found the hatchet in the market a while ago and had it ground at Topliss." The murderer.

**William Slack
(1907)
Murder
of
Lucy Wilson**

William Slack

It was an age when the postal service was omnipresent and deliveries would take place throughout the whole day. It was about five pm on <u>Monday, March 18th, 1907</u>, and Postman James Bennett was doing his teatime round in Highfield Road, Chesterfield. As he neared a bend in the road he saw a middle-aged couple talking on the pavement. The woman was gently rocking a pram back and forward and the postman had to walk in the road. It was a few seconds of normality in an average day, and Postman Bennett ordinarily, would never have thought about it again ....

<u>Notes:</u>

- .Slack was a well known amateur boxer
- .His own marriage was childless
- .He met Mrs Wilson whilst working as p&d at the Theatre – but also says he had known her for years and that they had been childhood sweethearts, so that could tie back to 1899 [*see below*].
- .Says area of the town where the murder took place is Stonegravels.

A further walk away, perhaps the length of a cricket pitch, the postman heard the sound of wood being chopped. It was early spring and so it wasn't that surprising, but nevertheless the sound stood out and he was curious as the more he concentrated on the sound, it seemed to be in the road itself. The postman turned and saw an incredible sight: it was the couple with pram, but now the woman was lying, face down in the road, with the man standing over here with an axe. Holding the weapon in his right hand, the man appeared to have been chopping at her. The assailant briefly looked up and at Postman Bennett, but seemed unconcerned and began chopping again at her head.

Momentarily stunned, the postman looked around and saw a familiar face from his rounds, a Mr Tom Wright, coachman to a local doctor, Dr Sidney Worthington. Mr Wright was working in the stable-yard and quickly ran over to the postman and they cautiously approached the woman. As they neared the scene, they could clearly see the woman was dead and her head covered in blood, and there was blood trickling away into the gutter. The man was now yards away and on seeing the two men coming towards him pointed to a nearby garden, saying that the axe was in there. He then added: ".... I'm going to give myself up. She fetched me from work this afternoon."

With incredible man management and coolness both the postman and Mr Wright sensed that the man was not going to give them any trouble, and it was agreed all three would walk towards the nearest police station. Even more amazingly as they started their journey, the postman asked Mr Wright if he would all right on his own, as he wanted to finish his round! One could say it was taking natural English reserve and calmness to an extreme! Postman Bennett then returned to delivering his letters, presumably unconcerned by what he had just seen. However it then seemed things were not going to plan, for the man said he wanted to look for the axe and bring it with them....

The surreal atmosphere continued as Mr Wright persuaded the man to leave the murder weapon, but then it occurred to him that there might be a baby in the pram. The man said it was his child and that he would fetch it. He also added the murdered woman was what he called his wife. As the pair reached the pram, the man bent down and kissed his dead wife, before taking the baby out of the pram. Now the two men made their way to the police station wheeling the pram along. Perhaps the adrenaline was now beginning to wear off, for in Newbold Road, Mr Wright saw two men in a pony-and-trap and told them of what had occurred and that a policeman should be summoned. As the men rode off, the man turned to Mr Wright and said: " She has been and bought me from work this afternoon and wanted some money. She has been the ruination of my life." By now the local police-station had received a 'phone call saying there had been an 'incident' in Highfield Road.

Sergeant Samuel Fisher immediately left the station with a constable walking towards Highfield Road when he saw the two men and the pram. When he saw the men, he sighed to himself and thought that he wasn't surprised. The murderer was a man he had known for the last 15 years, **Wilfred Slack, a 47- year-old** local. A painter and decorator by trade, Slack was in his work clothing. The officer could saw paint stains, but he could also see splashes of blood on the clothing and on the man's wrists and hands. Even more gruesomely the pram was marked with blood and human brain and other matter. The sergeant ordered the constable to take Slack to the police station, whilst he went to the murder scene. As the trio parted, Slack said: " Its Mrs Wilson, her [that] caused that other trouble when my wife went away[33]. Knowing Slacks' background, Sergeant Fisher realised the man had murdered his girlfriend and not his actual wife. The dead woman was **42-year-old Mrs Lucy Wilson**.

Sergeant Fisher arrived at the murder scene at 5.40 pm, where he met Dr Worthington, who had already carried out a preliminary examination of the body and noted down that the victim had suffered several deep wounds in her head and neck. The murder weapon was quickly found by the officer. The bloodstained axe was in a gooseberry bush. It had recently been sharpened and stuck into the

---

33   I assume he doesn't mean 1899 [see attempted murder case below], otherwise he'd have known her for eight years

blood were long black hairs and they appeared similar to those of the victim's. Returning to the police station with the axe, Sergeant Fisher interviewed Slack and charged him with murder. Slack told him: "That's right. I did not think of it before till I got to my work. A man who kills a woman is not fit to live. I told her at dinner time today.... that if she came up I should cut her head off and that I should have no more to do with her. I found the hatchet in the market a while ago and had it ground at Topliss."

The next day William Slack appeared at the town's magistrate's court where he was more than keen to tell the court why he had killed his new woman. He said: "We've been going together several months. I didn't go with the forethought of killing her. I tried to frighten her. I told her that if she followed me to work I..." Warned that all this would be recorded against him, Slack continued: " I struck her. She said: 'There's your bloody bastard' and I didn't deny it. Of course everyone knows it's my child." Remanded after a full hearing on April 3rd, Slack was sent for trial at the **Derby Assizes** in the summer.

William Slack stood trial on **Tuesday, June 25th, before Lord Coleridge. The case for the Crown was put by Sir Ryland Adkins and Mr Henry McCardie, whilst the prisoner was defended by Mr Harold Wright**. The court's first witness was Mr George Wilson, the victim's real husband. He said his wife was a ticket collector at the *Chesterfield Theatre*, where he worked also, and that she also worked as a cleaner during the day. They had been married for some 15 years, said Mr Wilson. On the day of the murder, the husband had been at the theatre with his wife. He left at 12.30 pm, and his wife returned to their home in Spa Lane at one-thirty. Mr Wilson returned to the theatre at twenty to five. He told the court his wife was dressed with the baby in their living-room and appeared as if she were going to go out. Despite her apparent relationship with Slack, Mr Wilson said he had never seen or heard of him. He added that as far as he was aware the baby was his and he had no suspicions of his wife.

It was all too much for Slack. He began screaming abuse at Mr Wilson saying it was his child. He said that on the very day of the murder Mr Wilson had seen his wife and Slack in the theatre bar, and that he had also been to the Wilson house. Pressed by Mr Wright, Mr Wilson stuck to his story. He pointed out that the baby had been born in June 1906, yet in March, Slack had said that he'd known Mrs Wilson for only 'several months'. Mr Wilson said, that there's was a happy marriage.

The next witness was a work colleague of Slack, a Mr William Madin. He and Slack had been working on the same property for several weeks. He had seen Slack at seven am, and the pair worked through till 11.45 am, when Slack asked him if he could go and collect 15 shillings that was owed to him. Slack then walked off towards the town centre. At one o'clock, Slack returned but said he didn't have his money, but that a woman might be brining it along later. Mr Madin said the woman he described was wearing dark clothing and had a baby in a 'cart'. Slack said to Mr Madin that if he saw her, would he give him a shout, as he was going to be working at the back of the house. Then at three-thirty, Mr Madin watched as Slack walked off again in the direction of the road where he had gone before, but this time he did meet with a woman, who fitted the earlier description exactly.

As Mr Madin worked on the house he watched Slack and the woman. They spoke for about 20 minutes during which time, Slack made to leave two or three time, but each time was stopped and called back by the woman. Eventually Slack returned to the house and the woman walked off in the direction of Highfield Road, but to Mr Madin's now annoyance, Slack asked another painter and decorator to cover for him, and some 15 minutes later Slack himself headed off, towards the same road. Mr Madin pointed to the pram in the court and said it was the same as he saw. He added that the murder weapon was not part of the tools used by him or his men, but that he had seen Slack with one at one job at a hotel, and Slack had indeed been sharpening it.

Mrs Elizabeth Osbourne also worked at the theatre, as a cleaner. At some point between midday and one o'clock on the day of the murder, Mrs Wilson went outside and Mrs Osbourne saw her talking to a dark man with a moustache, and she had picked Slack out in an

Identity Parade. Both Postman Bennett and the doctor's coachman told the court that Slack was perfectly sober. Dr Worthington then was called to give the results of his *port-mortem*. He said that out of all the wounds to the head and neck, two would have proved fatal, as they had gone into the head some four inches deep. The carotid arteries on the right side of the head had been severed. Another wound on the left side had cut through the spinal cord and this would have also caused death too. In addition the skull had been fractured, exposing the brain. One wound was not in the head and neck area. Mrs Wilson's left little finger had been severed and this was a defensive wound. Bar this wound, Dr Worthington believed that all the wounds were inflicted as the woman was lying on her face on the ground.

Sergeant Fisher told the court that he knew Slack. He said he had served in the Army and in India. Although his discharge papers were stamped 'good', the officer said he knew that Slack was a man who lost his temper easily, was prone to be violent and indeed had a criminal record for a serious assault on a policeman, and had been given a seven-year sentence, for attempted murder. The prosecution was keen to show the jury that the murder was 'premeditated'. A Mr Bartholomew Murphy, a close friend of the accused, said he had been with him, when he bought the axe, and that it was about eight or nine months before the crime. A Mr Arthur Butler, who worked at *Topliss'* wood-yard said that three months before the murder, he saw Slack sharpening the axe.

The defence suggested that the crime was one of manslaughter, and Slack went into the witness box to give evidence. He said that before his present job, he had also worked as a carpenter, and had often bought and used axes, and that's why he purchased the present one. He said he had served in the Army for five years leaving in the summer exactly 10 years before. Slack now claimed he had known Mrs Wilson for two years, and that they had had sex on their first meeting. He claimed they had even had sex in her house, whilst her husband was downstairs. He said she had told him that her husband hadn't given her any money for seven years and since she claimed he had slept with other women, she thought she'd do the same thing.

Slack said she suggested they elope, particularly as his actual wife had given evidence against him in the police assault case.

Slack said that on the day before the murder, the Sunday, he and Mrs Wilson had met in an empty house in St Helen's Street, where he had been working. They agreed to meet at the theatre the next day to finally decide what to do. They indeed did meet and planned to leave for Coventry. They agreed to meet later in the evening back at the theatre. However in a departure from the plan, Mrs Wilson came to Avondale Road, where Slack was working. It seems she had been annoyed, as he had told her he wouldn't be in Avondale Road that afternoon, and she thought he was going to renege on their agreement. He said that to placate her he agreed to meet her later in the afternoon. When they did meet in Highfield Road, Slack said that she was hysterical, threatening to drown herself in a local stream, known as the Donkey Racecourse. Slack claimed that as he tried to walk away, she grabbed his coat and almost knocked the pram over. She called him a 'rogue' and insulted his wife. Slack pulled out the axe and lost his temper...

Mrs Elizabeth Slack told the court that her husband had said the axe was to be used to repair some steps at his sister's home, and a boy assistant had bought some wood for the job. Mrs Clara Ford told the jury that Slack did indeed come to her home at just before one. She said that he would be back later and that since he had returned from India his character had much changed and the family suspected that he had been affected by sunstroke. Her husband, Patrick said that he and Slack had been in a local pub, having a drink once, when suddenly Slack said that a man was staring at him and that he would 'go for him'. Mr Ford said that, had he not held him back, there would have been a serious situation.

A now Sergeant James Hudson told the court how he had been attacked by Slack in March 1899. It arose over a domestic dispute when Slack wanted the police to intervene after his wife had left him. When Slack believed the officer wasn't going to do much about the case, he stabbed him with two knives, inflicting nearly 20 wounds, and he also accused the officer of talking to his wife, something that was untrue. At the Derby Assizes four months later, he was convicted of attempted murder and sentenced to seven years in prison. When arrested he said he had intended to kill his wife and the officer.

A Dr C.A. Greaves, the Medical Officer at Derby Prison, where Slack was being held on remand, told the court that he found him 'excitable, touchy and irritable', but most importantly that he was perfectly sane. Throughout the day long trial and during the judge's summing-up, Slack had angrily interrupted the court proceedings. Slack was told to be quiet on a number of occasions, but angrily told the judge that things were being made up, to suggest the crime was premeditated. In a final desperate plea, he shouted at the court, that any man would have behaved as he had done, had the woman insulted their wives. Without leaving their box, the jury found William Slack guilty of murder. There was no recommendation to mercy.

Asked if he had anything to say why the death sentence should not be passed, Slack told the judge to "…. off" and tried to leave the box, before being held by a number of prison-officers. He then told the judge where he could put his black cap! As Lord Coleridge began to speak, Slack, undefeated, said: " I've told you what to with the cap. It's no use talking." Once again Slack struggled in the dock, and as he was being told he would be buried in the prison after his execution, he pulled a small clump of hair from his head, threw it in the air, exclaiming: "That's what I care. That's the man I am." By now the judge had had enough, ordered Slack removed and kicking and screaming, he was dragged to the cells below.

The new appeal court was still 12 months away and so Slack's case was very quickly decided on, by the Home Secretary, Henry Gladstone. He was advised, that should Slack's life be spared, he would almost certainly attack and seriously injure a prison-officer. There would be no reprieve. **William Slack was hanged on Tuesday, July 16th, 1907 by Henry Pierrepoint and John Ellis – the last execution at Derby Prison**. By all accounts until the lever was pulled, Slack was abusive to everyone, shouting to the priest at the very end.

With Slack dead the local 'paper published a letter penned by him. It began by reiterating how he met Mrs Wilson and that he would visit her at her home, sometimes as much as four times a week. He maintained he had known her for two years, being misquoted when he had said 'several months'. He said she maintained the child was his, and he said she even suggested murdering her husband. The gist of the letter was that he had tired of her, but she would not let go. Where the truth lay however was hard to tell. It was suggested in Chesterfield that Slack may have been stalking Mrs Wilson and had never slept with her and made the whole thing of their affair up, just as he had in the case of the attempted murder in 1899.

The Times, Thursday, Jul 13, 1899; pg. 11D - The attempted murder case.

Cases 15 and 16

Case 15
"The Killer In Cell 727"

"I have experience of the prisoner Edwin Alfred Preedy, who I have recently learned is in your charge. I advise that your staff take great care, as this man is violent and I fear may one day seriously injure or even kill a prison-officer." A letter from a prison-governor before the murder ….

"I meant to kill him. I ate my dinner, read from my Bible, and was then able to make the decision to kill Evans. I had good reason to kill him." - The Killer.

"Shake hands, you bloody fool and make up." – Part of the most bizarre and extraordinary scenes at the trial of Edwin Preedy ….

Edwin Preedy (20)
[1862-3]

Murder
Of
Prison-Officer Charles Evans (39)

Absolutely extraordinary case involving the murder of a prison-officer at Portland Prison in the late summer of 1862. The court and the Home Office decided the killer was sane but this was a man who acted in a most bizarre way from his time in prison, whilst on trial for his life, where he was chained and shackled, and finally to giving a number of prison-officers signed copies of the Bible as he sat in the death-cell ....

It was eight o'clock on the evening of **Monday, September 8th, 1862** in Portland Prison in Dorset and three inmates, Thomas Moore, John Ashton and James Schofield had been tasked to collect cutlery from the cells, as it was then the custom for prisoners to eat their evening meal in their own cells. The men were being supervised by **Prison-Officer, Charles Evans (39)**. As they approached Cell 727, Schofield glanced at the officer and smiled .... The prisoner in this cell was known to scream and yell at nights. A family man the officer had some sympathy for this young prisoner and said the others should not make fun of him – the other prisoners said this prisoner played the hard man during the day; but couldn't hack the nights. The prisoner in question was one **Edwin Preedy (20)**. Born in the West Midlands, he had spent most of his life in London. At the age of four he had cracked his head open – but his family were desperately poor and he was simply put to bed and eventually after some time, he *appeared* to have re-covered. After that Preedy was regarded by most people who met him as not normal. Long after he should have done so, his fear of the night meant he slept with his mother, although it did stop, when his mother began living with a man, William Edwards, who had not the time or patience for Preedy, and used his fists to control the young boy. Edwards said his mother was soft on Preedy – and so he had his own bed and would scream at night. As time went on Edwards began to enjoy hitting the boy – and he began to use a cane and on occasions a heavy metal knob ….

Preedy took comfort from an aunt – she had been there when he had had his fall, and she tried to speak to his mother, but she feared Edwards would hit her. Ultimately the aunt did nothing and Preedy suffered this abuse until at the age of thirteen, he left home. He slept rough until two men took him to a workhouse in central London. He had been found frothing at the mouth and with great effort the men delivered him to the workhouse matron. It actually seemed that Preedy had gone mad and eventually the matron agreed to him being taken in and he was tied down to a bed until morning, when a doctor examined him. The diagnosis was that he was suffering a form of insanity caused by typhus. During his treatment the boy's head was shaved and the matron and doctor were shocked to see the scars across his skull from his repeated beatings. Eventually Preedy appeared to become normal and even likeable and then the matron said he would have to leave the workhouse.

Preedy said he didn't believe he had been suffering from typhus fever – he said that he breathed in charcoal fumes from a fire in an old building that he had been squatting in. Indeed when his mother came to collect him, the now Mrs Edwards was told that he had been simply insane and typhus was not mentioned. Back home it seemed that a new relationship with his step-father was beckoning and he began working with him at a printers. However it was clear that Edwards enjoyed punishing and hitting the young boy for his own pleasure …. Soon Preedy began showing signs of insanity again. This time Preedy ran away to his home county of Warwickshire and a hope that he might find his real father. He didn't find him, but he did commit his first crime, receiving an eight-month sentence for theft. Incredibly for a youth abused by an older man, upon release Preedy joined the army, but equally incredibly he seemed to have found his vocation in life, as he quickly rose to the rank of corporal.

However Preedy's mental instability soon re-surfaced. Having been promoted and as soon as the stripes were sewn onto his uniform, he promptly deserted. Preedy lived by stealing until he was caught in

June 1860 in South Wales. This time he was sentenced to ten weeks in custody. But worse was to come; the court hadn't realised he was a deserter but soon after he began his sentence, he was handed over to the military authorities. But Preedy didn't want to go – he hit one prison-officer and then jumped at the prison-governor. He was wrestled to the ground by another officer, but his prison-issue shoes – heavy wooden clogs had come off, and he used them as weapons – in a split second he laid both prison-officers out with blows to the head. More officers piled into the governor's office and the prisoner fended them off with a chair. After a vicious melee, he was eventually overpowered by sheer weight of numbers. As he was dragged away Preedy added that he would rather hang, than be handed over to the army.

When the military authorities arrived to pick Preedy up they found a madman heavily chained and shackled and took him to an army base in the region. Did the army beat this young man? No – they took the easy way out and 'dishonourably discharged' him. Despite his apparent hatred of the army, Preedy felt desperately rejected by the military and soon afterwards he now started a three-year sentence for stealing clothing in South Wales. On reading of Preedy's latest conviction, the prison-governor, who had been attacked, decided to contact the authorities in the prison that he might now be sent to. Eventually he was sent to London and to Millbank Prison, where he was soon in trouble with the system, although not for being violent, but that was on its way …. At Millbank Prison, Preedy was put on report for being idle and lazy and time was added to his sentence. The officer who reported him was called Beldon. As the officer was seeing Preedy back to his cell, the inmate snapped. Snarling and spitting he began hitting and clawing at the officer. Such attacks were dealt with in a quick summary fashion back then, and Preedy was flogged. Having inflicted this on him, Millbank Prison quickly had him transferred to what was then one of England's most toughest and grimmest prisons – Portland Prison on the island just to the south of Weymouth. In his report to Portland, the Millbank Prison governor referred to Edwin Preedy as 'crazy'. Portland Prison had long been home to the toughest of prisoners and many of them had mental health issues, so Preedy was nothing new and indeed he didn't *seem* that difficult. He certainly didn't seem violent, but he certainly was odd, as he was on that evening in the late summer of 1862 ….

Moore opened the door to Cell 727. Preedy was there, as per the prison rules, ready to hand over his cutlery etc. He began handing over the knife, fork and spoon but then dropped the last two and then sprang forth onto the landing, holding the knife. In a split second he grabbed Officer Evans from behind – plunging the knife deep into his throat and pulling it hard across, screaming madly, as Ashton grabbed one of Preedy's arms, and Moore the other to try and stop him. This forced Preedy into releasing the officer, who staggered about in agony until dropping dead on the floor. Covered in blood Moore and Ashton kept shouting for help, as Preedy still could reach the knife. Officer Thomas Roberts soon arrived, drew his sword and turning it flat-wise, hitting Preedy over the head with a heavy blow, rendering him unconscious. When he regained consciousness, Officer James Douglas asked him why he had done it. Nearly all the prisoners liked Officer Evans and Preedy shocked everyone by saying: "I meant to kill him. I ate my dinner, read from my Bible, and was then able to make the decision to kill Evans. I had good reason to kill him." Preedy refused to say what the motive might be …. Locked in a cell, Preedy was then told by the Prison Chaplain, Mr Duke, that the officer was dead. Preedy simply screamed abuse at the chaplain. The shocked man was told to leave by the prison-officers, who feared for his life, and were shocked at the verbal abuse that Preedy had given Mr Duke. Then Preedy calmed down and said he had been abusive towards the chaplain as Preedy said he was a Catholic.

The murder case was now handed over to the police and a Superintendent George Underwood arrived at Portland to take Edwin Preedy to Dorchester police-station. The senior officer was amazed to find a polite, contrite and pleasant young man, and he assured the Portland authorities that he needed no help in taking the prisoner to the county town. As they left Portland, the young man laughed at some street entertainers, and Superintendent Underwood, noted that Preedy seemed completely detached from what he had done. He said he had pushed the murder to the back of his mind, but added: "I'm really sorry that I killed Mr Evans. Do you know that? Since I did it, the other warders have told me, that he was a nice man with a large family. I feel very sorry for his wife and family." Preedy now admitted there was no mysterious motive for the murder and that he had simply wanted to kill a prison-officer, such was his hatred of authority, and what he claimed was the system picking on him. Officer Charles Evans was the first officer to 'come along'.

Held on remand in Dorchester Prison, Preedy once again 'fooled' the authorities into thinking he was normal, until he attempted to break his own legs by pushing them through his cell-bars and bending them back. The local magistrates had ordered Preedy to be kept in solitary confinement and despite an appeal by the prison-governor, they had feared housing him in the general prison population. Preedy continued to cause problems and for two days he was left naked, as he kept destroying his clothing. Some of the more backward prison-officers not only feared Preedy physically, but they thought him possessed by the devil, as he seemed impervious to the cold. It would be six months until the next county assizes, and after a month on remand, Preedy seemed to calm down and acted quite normally, indeed almost a model prisoner. He began taking an interest in the birds that came into the prison, looking after the injured ones, and then taking in other prisoner's injured birds, although tragically he trod on one by accident and was extremely upset.

On **Tuesday, March 10th, 1863, Edwin Preedy appeared before Mr Justice Shee**. He was smartly dressed and very composed as he heard **Messrs Poulden and Cole outline the undisputed facts for the Crown**. The court proceeded normally until Thomas Moore told the court of the point where the accused cut the officer's throat as his arms were being held. Preedy shouted out across the court to Moore saying: "Was it you who jerked my arm?" A startled **Mr Prideaux for the defence** calmly told Preedy that he should discretely ask *him* to ask questions of the witnesses. Suddenly as Moore continued with his evidence, Preedy tried to climb out of the dock, hitting out violently against any prison-officer, who tried to stop him and six of them were injured until the prisoner was finally subdued, at least by his hands and feet; but then amazingly he swung his head back so far that he was able to bite out part of his clothing on his back, in an attempt to commit suicide by choking. When the officers forced his head forward Preedy began biting chunks out of the dock!

Forcing his way through the body of officers, a Mr Good, the surgeon in Dorchester Prison spoke to Preedy saying he was very upset as the accused had promised to behave, but all Preedy could say was: "I am very upset." He screamed at the doctor to shake hands and when he refused he shouted at the top of his voice: "Shake hands, you bloody fool and make up." Sensing that the whole proceedings were falling apart Mr Justice Shee left the court saying he would consult his fellow judge at the assize, Mr Justice Byles. On return he asked Mr Good, if the trial could proceed, and he was told it could. The judge asked Preedy if he would like ten minutes to compose himself, but was met by silence, followed by a bizarre conversation with the clerk of the court, who repeated the question. Preedy then said he thought he knew the clerk and wanted to shake the puzzled man's hand. He then refused to speak to Mr Good, saying he would only deal with the clerk. By now Preedy appeared to be rambling and all the judge could suggest is that Mr Good stay close in case the prisoner had another breakdown. Unfortunately this seemed to provoke Preedy again and he screamed at the doctor, saying: "Get away from me, you bloody bastard!" All Mr Justice Shee could do is try and finish the trial as quickly as possible, but Preedy was shouting and screaming and so the judge ordered him restrained – his arms and legs were held by a leather belt and strap. But despite the judge ordering the hearing to re-start, Preedy kept screaming and the restraints snapped! Once again a group of prison-officers smothered the prisoner. Mr Justice Shee quickly left the court again as chains and shackles were ordered and put on the prisoner, who was then put on a chair, although he continued to thrash about. It was decided to let him do this, until exhausted he slumped forward and the judge returned to court.

However there was still energy left in Edwin Preedy – he began shaking violently and shouting, so much so that the judge told the jury he would be adjourning the case for a short period again. He said he would consult with Mr Good, as well as the Portland Prison doctor and a local doctor, adding he had serious doubts as to the sanity of Preedy and whether he was fit to stand trial. But all three doctors said the accused was not insane and so the judge returned to court and said the trial must go on. Preedy's 'fight' did appear much reduced, although he did scream abuse at Officer Douglas when the court was told that Preedy would often be stripped naked and left in the cells. When Mr Good gave evidence, the accused smiled and told the witness to speak up and not be frightened! Preedy also tried to tell the court about his real father from Warwickshire, whom he said was a lay-preacher, but the judge was told that the man was traced and denied the allegation completely. Eventually the day-long trial ended and after just 20 minutes, and despite Preedy's performances in court, the jury found him guilty of murder. As he was being sentenced to death, the prisoner broke down in tears as the judge recalled the evidence of his mother, concerning his childhood fall. Indeed during her evidence she had collapsed and desperately, despite his chains, Preedy had tried to move towards her to comfort her. The judge said he praised the jury for sticking to the hard facts and not falling into a trap of emotion and for not taking the 'merciful' way out, by finding the accused to be insane. In sentencing Preedy to hang the judge said that if he wished to be seen by a Catholic priest in the death-cell, that would be arranged. Mr Justice Shee informed Preedy that there could be no question of a reprieve in his case, although ultimately it was up to the **Home Secretary, Sir George Grey.**

In the death-cell, as difficult as ever, Preedy did not turn to a Catholic priest, but to a Protestant vicar, the Reverend Henry Moule, and the pair spent many hours together. When a member of a prominent local Catholic family heard of this, he, out of kindness, came to the prison, thinking that Preedy had been denied his right of religious expression. Dismissively, however, Preedy told the man: "I am not, nor have I ever been, or ever will be, a Catholic!" In the death-cell the condemned also made beads. He did make a final statement, in which he said he was facing a just punishment. In it he explained why he murdered the officer, saying if he had only hit the victim, he would have only been flogged! Curiously whilst Preedy was on remand in Dorchester Prison, the letter from the prison-governor in South Wales eventually caught up with the prisoner and it prophetically read: "I have experience of the prisoner Edwin Alfred Preedy, who I have recently learned is in your charge. I advise that your staff take great care, as this man is violent and I fear may one day seriously injure or even kill a prison-officer." Bizarre to the end Edwin Preedy ordered a number of Bibles and then requested all the prison-officers, to whom he had been involved with at Portland and Dorchester to visit him in the death-cell, where he handed them out! Each Bible was personally signed by Preedy!

The execution date for Edwin Preedy was to be on **Friday, March 27th, 1863 outside Dorchester Prison**. However it was to be a double-event for the anticipated 5,000 strong crowd. The day before Preedy had been tried and sentenced to death another man, had also been convicted of murder, in the case of ….

Case 16

"In The Shadow Of Incest"

~The Curious Affair of the 'Laughing' People~

"I'll shoot that man like a rook."; "I don't never feel well." - The killer.

Charles Fooks (49)
[1862-3]
Murder
Of
His cousin, Daniel Stone (30)

By all accounts Charles Fooks was an odd man: he was convinced people were listening into his conversations and laughing behind his back; he also claimed he was offered two first cousins in marriage, but rejected them on moral grounds as he regarded them as sisters and therefore considered it incest; he was also living with two young nieces …. Unfortunately Fooks was a man who collected firearms ….

Charles Fooks

(49) had had a troubled life. He looked 20 years older, a shy man; he was also a hypochondriac. In the Summer of 1862, he lived in the then village of Walditch, but which is now part of the town of Bridport, some 12 or so miles to the west of Dorchester. To people in the village Fooks was 'not quite like other people'. Although he ran a small farm employing five people, everyone thought of him as a bit 'eccentric'. Fooks' problems seemed to have started in 1845 when he called a doctor to his farm …. Fooks was laying on his bed, covered in a blanket, and with a vinegar-soaked cloth wrapped around his head. The whole farmhouse had been sealed off and was completely airless. The doctor said what the patient needed was a good dose of fresh-air and when the doctor tried to take off the head-cloth, Fooks angrily shouted at him, saying: "Leave that alone, and get out of my house." When the doctor told him, Fooks had called for *him*, the farmer dismissed the doctor. A new doctor was called, who played along with Fooks' 'illness' and eventually Fooks 'recovered.' However Fooks' behaviour became very odd. Towards a cousin and neighbour, **Daniel Stone (30)**, he started to believe the latter was laughing at him. This was not true, but to add to the complexity, Stone had *apparently* refused to allow a sister or sisters, and therefore also Fooks' cousin (s), to marry the farmer ….

Fooks did not seem that short of female help and company, however, and there was much wagging of tongues for by 1862 he was living with two nieces, Martha Hallett (20) and Jane Fooks (18). Martha soon became somewhat concerned about Uncle Charles' behaviour. For example, one night the pair were talking, when all of a sudden, Fooks motioned with his hand for his niece to stop talking, and then said that Daniel Stone was listening at the window. When Martha looked puzzled about all this, Fooks looked at her rather oddly, as if there was something wrong with her! A close friend of Fooks, a local solicitor's clerk, Daniel Read also thought his friend was becoming odd. Fooks was also the local church treasurer, but he couldn't handle the accounts, and so Mr Read did them for him. Also on the church committee was Mr Stone and the solicitor's clerk soon realised Fooks didn't like his cousin. One evening he spoke to them both in the vestry …. by trying to imply that both men were to blame for the bad-feeling and he told them not to be so silly and asked them to shake hands. Daniel Stone immediately agreed and offered his hand, but Fooks snapped: "Never" and tried to leave the building. It was too much for Mr Read, who followed Fooks home and was asked inside. Fooks seemed to have calmed down and did offer an explanation of the problems with his cousin, saying: " …. my head gives me agony." Holding his head in his hands, he cried out that he didn't know what he was saying at times and why he was saying it. Asked about his doctor, Fooks said he had explained all this to him, and had visited him at his practice in Weymouth, but it was all to no avail. Sensing the moment, Mr Read suggested he make it up with Mr Stone, and then everything would be all right. However the solicitor's clerk had judged it wrongly, the farmer shouting back: "I'll shoot that man like a rook." This cut a chord with Mr Read, as Fooks was an avid gun-collector and his home was full of them. The two men continued to talk, when suddenly half-an-hour later the farmer jumped up, grabbed a gun, and proclaimed that Mr Stone was outside, 'listening' and he ran out of the house to 'confront' him. Of course there was no-one there, and Fooks came back in. No shots were fired, but what would have happened, had Daniel Stone been there? The answer appeared to quickly come, when after Mr Read left, and Fooks was eating with Martha, he once again grabbed his gun, went outside and did fire …. Fortunately there was no one there, but things were becoming worse on the farm. For no good reason Fooks sacked two brothers who worked for him. He had always looked after them and had given money to their mother. When he dismissed the pair, Fooks had been muttering about Mr Stone.

Another friend, who tried to help, was one Stephen Hawker, who had heard about the two farm labourers. However Fooks needed no lecture from a friend: he agreed he shouldn't have sacked the boys and once again blamed the situation on his head and said he was having trouble controlling his temper, so much so that he would have shot even his best worker, the mood he was in. He then said he would shoot Mr Hawker, if this mood grabbed him. Like Mr Read before, the friend looked apprehensively around the farmhouse, at all the guns. Another long-term friend of the farmer was one George

Allen – he'd known Fooks for some 20 years. He went to see him, although he began the conversation by noting that a Somerset man had shot himself. Fooks solemnly replied that he felt that way sometimes himself, especially when everyone was 'laughing' at him.

In August 1862, a local farmer, George Major was walking along the road in the nearby village of Shipton Grange, when he saw Mr Stone, and the two walked along having a chat. As they approached Charles Fooks' land, Mr Major swore he saw the top of the farmer's head, just above the hedgerow, and to his shock he saw a large stone come flying over the hedge and hit Mr Stone full against his head. The blow knocked Mr Stone's hat off and he was sent reeling. Mr Major immediately tried to help his friend, and as he did so he could sense someone looking over them: it was Fooks, who seemed fascinated by the very large lump on Mr Stone's head. Fooks then muttered: "I didn't exactly intend that," before he ran off. This news was too much for Martha. She left the farmhouse returning to her mother, Fooks' sister. She told her mother everything, and Mrs Hallett said she wasn't that surprised. She thought her brother odd, although she had never thought of him as *violent*, and she asked her daughter if it were really true. Martha's step-father did believe her though, and suggested she not return to Fooks. In the end it was decided Martha would go back, but that the step-father, Thomas Humber would come back too and find out what was going on. Fooks was very candid to Mr Humber, saying his stomach and head were constantly hurting him. Somewhat surprisingly considering what Fooks had done to Mr Stone, Mr Humber concluded that the farmer wasn't mentally ill, but in physical pain: it was therefore safe for Martha to return to him ….!

On August 28th, Charles Fooks came back to the farmhouse in the evening and to Martha's deep shock he began ranting and raving at her. It was the same story as before – his niece was 'laughing' at him. He then accused her of having been friendly with Mr Stone. Tearfully the girl protested she hadn't been friendly, but Fooks was having none of it, saying that the two of them had been meeting and had been talking about him. Martha went to her room and spent a terrified night, fearing every sound. After a sleepless night she left the house early for her mother's. That same morning **(Monday,**

August 29th) another villager, William Parker, had planned to meet Mr Stone at 7.30 am, and indeed saw him approaching his home. As he did so, he passed Charles Fooks' home ….

What happened next would stay with Mr Parker for the rest of his life. Fooks opened his front-door, put his gun to his shoulder, took aim at Daniel Stone and fired. The shot hit Mr Stone in the head and he slumped to the ground. Two other villagers, Jesse Parker and John Bishop rushed to help him, dragging him back to his own house, where his distressed father tried to help him. However there was little anyone could do: the two men who had come forward to help in the road were covered in blood and brain matter, and they had to tell Mr Stone, that his son was dead. Then there was the sound of a second shot and everyone assumed they knew what that was. The shot had come from inside Fooks' home and the front-door was locked. A trio of men, including one of Fooks' farm labourers and a cousin, went round the back of the house – the back door was not locked ….

Once inside they headed for Fooks' bedroom, which was upstairs, but which was also locked. The door was kicked in and lying on the floor was the apparently mortally injured Fooks – a shotgun laying beside him and blood pouring everywhere from a head wound. However Fooks was still breathing – just – and the men picked him up and put him on the bed before going to fetch a doctor and the police. Strangely enough Fooks' second doctor, Dr Smith, was in the village and he quickly could see that incredibly, despite the blood, Fooks' life was not in danger – he had fired but had hit his upper lip and the gun-blast had grazed his head. Still Fooks had used a 12-bore shotgun and so it was amazing that the gunshot alone had not killed him as it had been from point-blank range in a small space. However the first officer on the scene, Police-Sergeant Lavender could quickly see that this was not a real attempt to commit suicide – one barrel was empty; the other had just wadding and powder, but not *shot*. It was the wadding that had caused Fooks' injuries, although the wadding was powerful enough to have blown a hole in the ceiling!

Remanded to Dorchester Prison, where just under two weeks later Edwin Preedy would join him, the authorities seemed to think that Fooks might be insane. A Dr Tukes from the Hanwell Lunatic Asylum in west London was summoned, where he and Dr Good examined the farmer. Fooks said he had woken up on the morning of the murder feeling 'terrible', adding this state applied both physically and mentally. He then said: "I don't never feel well." He then blamed Martha for the actual shooting, adding that on that day, she was supposed to be getting his game licence for him, adding: "I ain't got the game licence now, have I?" Then realising the bizarreness of what he had just said, Fooks burst into laughter. He then said he had killed Mr Stone for laughing at him; just as he had sacked the two boys for doing the same thing – they all deserved it, he said. When asked specifically what Mr Stone had done, it took Fooks several minutes to reply, before he began talking about some of his land, on which he claimed his cousin had planted it with dock to render it useless. Fooks now denied saying, that the victim had ever been outside his home eavesdropping, to his niece, although when Dr Tukes pushed him, he now claimed Mr Stone had been listening in, but that he hadn't told his niece about it. When asked about mental problems directly – was Fooks insane? - the farmer emphatically denied he wasn't, although he said when he shot Mr Stone, he thought no more of it, than when he would shoot a rabbit in the field.

And so Charles Fooks appeared before **Mr Justice Shee on Monday, March 9th, 1863 – The prosecution was Mr Collier, QC, and this time Mr Prideaux for the Crown; whilst the prisoner was defended by Messrs Coleridge, QC, and Stock**. Dr Tukes gave evidence that he considered the accused to be insane – he called it 'homicidal mania' and he said that he was amazed that Fooks hadn't killed before. The judge pointed out that this man had been surrounded by guns for years, yet now, aged 49, he had decided to kill for no real reason. Dr Tukes explained this by saying that, in his opinion, the mental illness had come on in stages, adding: "I think it is mania and delusion that occasionally got beyond his control." The doctor further added that he did not think that Fooks knew the gun would kill and he believed that the prisoner didn't actually want to pull the trigger but was driven by a compulsion to do so. However after a trial that lasted just hours, the jury were out for just 20 minutes and they rejected the defence's claim that Fooks was insane. Sentenced to hang, in his death-cell Fooks caused the authorities no problems.

Curiously enough local opinion was that both Preedy and Fooks were *sane*: A local clergyman, William Templer organised a petition to save Fooks' life, but few people signed it. Indeed Fooks himself petitioned his own landlord, Lord Wynford asking for his help. His lordship did approach Sir George, but he was told the Home Office officials believed that Charles Fooks knew what he was doing, and indeed eventually he confessed, fully, to the prison chaplain, Benjamin Watson, although he put a different slant on the argument with Mr Stone. He said it was the *victim* who wanted Fooks to marry his sister, and he had even offered another one, both of whom agreed to marry Fooks, but as they were the condemned man's *first* cousins, he considered it immoral, putting them on a par of sisters and therefore incest. Fooks also returned to a recurring theme saying that the reason he stopped going to church was that the congregation were 'laughing' at him. Fooks would only speak to the Reverend Watson in the death-cell: no relatives or friends came. Even as his execution date approached, Fooks wouldn't say he would ask for forgiveness at what he had done – he still blamed the 'laughing' people for the crime. He even claimed the victim was a 'murderer' for taking Fooks' life away! And so Charles Fooks and Edwin Preedy, strangers, found themselves on the gallows outside Dorchester Prison ….

THE EXECUTION – Friday, March 27th, 1863:

Edwin Preedy and Charles Fooks walked out of their death-cells and onto the flat roof of the North Lodge part of the prison at just before eight am. Contrary to popular belief, the last public execution at Dorchester was not that of Martha Brown in 1856 – indeed there was also one in 1858. Many in the crowd thought Preedy would put on a performance on the scaffold. In the death-cell he had reverted back to destroying his clothing and appeared now in a torn shirt. He also once again indulged in his odd behaviour of wanting to shake hands, requesting the Under-Sheriff and Prison Governor to do so. They refused, poignantly turning their backs on him. **The hangman, William Calcraft** was not so bothered, shaking hands with Preedy and also taking some of his hand-made beads from him.

Charles Fooks was crying on the gallows. He had been wearing a hat but this was removed by a prison-officer. It seems that Fooks didn't wish to shake hands with Preedy either. Fooks was capped and had the noose put around his neck first. Crying even louder he heard the same procedure carried out on Preedy. Down below the crowds surged forward for a better view. Meanwhile one local man had hired out a view and had even built a gantry, although this collapsed injuring a number of people. They were not seriously injured and some of the injured looked on as the London executioner pulled the lever and the trap-doors opened. Fooks appeared to have died almost instantly – there was just one twitch; but Preedy 'died hard' – his body twirling around and convulsing as he died in extreme agony – it was almost as if he was trying to get out of Calcraft's 'strait-jacket.'

The crowd had not been allowed to see where the men had dropped to, as the under part of the gallows had been screened off, and so they didn't see the death throes of Edwin Preedy. But once it was clear he was dead, the screens were removed and the bodies kept on view for the customary hour. For the rest of the day the police reported much anti-social disorder in Dorchester mainly centred around drunkenness. It was a scene often repeated around England until just over five years later public executions were banned throughout the country in May 1868.

Case 17
"The St Erith Tragedy"

William Hampton
(1909)
Murder
of
Emily Tredrea

Tragic case of a young Cornish girl engaged at 15 to a young man, who she later decided she longer loved. Unfortunately he still loved her...

In 1881 the Hampton family left their home village of St Erith in Cornwall for a new and hopefully better life in the U.S.A. However in November 1907 one of the family, **22-year-old William** returned to Cornwall following the footsteps of his father, who had returned a couple years before. However his mother and his brothers and sisters stayed on the other side of the Atlantic.

William Hampton was welcomed with open arms in the village. In May 1908 he began lodging with a family who were friends of his father's. The Tredrea family lived in a tiny four-roomed cottage near the village church in St Erith and Hampton found work in a local tin mine at Cambourne.

In 1908 the Tredrea family there were four children - a new baby, a girl aged six, a boy aged nine, **and 15-year-old Emily**. Emily was already a young woman in her physic and she and Hampton were immediately attracted to each other, something, which her Mother did not disapprove of. Even had she objected, with her husband working in a mine in South Africa, there were still six people living in four rooms and it would have been impossible to stop them seeing each other, and the family needed the rent money.

At Christmas time with Emily just a few weeks from her 16 birthday, she and Hampton became engaged, once again with her parents' approval. The intention was that they would marry when she was 20 after they had saved enough money. Part of the plan was that Hampton would return to the U.S.A.

Before the *Marriage Act (1928)* it was quite legal for girls to marry at the age of 12, and although it was rare for it to actual happen at 12 or 13, before the First World War in rural areas, marriages of girls at 14 or 15, were not viewed as particularly strange. In January 1909 a telegram was sent to Emily's father John in America and he replied that he had no objection to their match.

Unfortunately everyone to this agreement had a different view of the arrangement. The Tredrea family were poor and Emily's parents understandably saw the proposed marriage in terms of much needed finances, whilst Hampton wanted Emily as he loved her and after several months together thought that that entitled him to sex as well, whilst for young Emily she soon tired Hampton.

Although Hampton was a tall handsome man with dark sallow looks, which matched young Emily's own, he was known in the village as a miserable young man, who preferred to stay in during the evening and not drink in the village pub.

Everyone in the village knew that Hampton and Emily were seeing or " walking out " with each other. However they didn't seem to be doing much physical walking with each other. The rumour in the village was that Emily felt she was too young to commit herself to

Hampton, although she told her friends that she loved Hampton, for the sake of her parents.

As the warmth of the Cornish Spring emerged in April 1909 people began to notice that on Sunday picnics Emily would come along and Hampton stayed in the cottage. Then on Friday
April 30th, Emily told her mother that she no longer loved Hampton and wanted to stop seeing him.

Mrs Tredrea did not know what to do. They family needed Hampton's rent money but as her daughter had turned 16 she could simply leave home, if she were forced into marrying Hampton. She hoped the couple would patch things up.

Two days later on Sunday morning Hampton went to nurse his grandmother who lived in nearby Church Street. On the way he met Emily coming out of the church saying that she was going to help with the Sunday School. By teatime he returned home.

Mrs Tredrea would often go to Hampton's grandmother's herself to help out and on Sunday evening she left her cottage at just before ten o'clock. When she left Hampton and Emily were looking after the baby in the kitchen, whilst the two other children were asleep. Emily had just returned herself, having spent the evening with a girlfriend and not Hampton.

William Tredrea who was nine had to sleep with his six-year-old sister, Gwendoline, because of the lack of space. As with most children of that age he did not go to sleep straight-away, but he drifted off until he was woken at just after ten by a noise.

Peeping through the rails on the landing he was shocked to see his elder sister lying on the kitchen floor. Even more shocking was what Hampton was doing to her. Although only nine, William, clearly knew that he was trying to hurt his sister.

Hampton had one knee on Emily's chest and was trying to strangle her. The little boy bravely shouted: "Get back ". However Hampton simply ignored him, so William returned to his bed and dressed.

Returning to the landing, William now saw that Hampton had picked up Emily and was banging her against a side-door that led to the garden.

This time William asked Hampton why he was trying to hurt his sister, but the young man said that he was trying to help Emily as " she was sick. " Not unnaturally the little boy was slightly confused as Hampton put Emily in a kitchen chair and she rolled about before appearing to fall to the kitchen floor.

However William sensed something was not right when Hampton blocked his route into the garden to call for help. The boy was given a chance to escape when Hampton tried once again to put Emily back in the chair and he ran out into the street towards where his mother was in Church Street.

Mrs Tredrea naturally was shocked and ran back to her cottage, fortunately meeting the village policemen, P-c Ashford, who took charge of the situation.

P-c Ashford quickly realised that Emily had been strangled and tried in vain to revive her. P-c Ashford clearly saw the marks on the girl's neck, which showed that the strangulation had been deliberate and intentional.

At about 11.30 p.m. two constables were patrolling in the nearby seaside town of Hayle, when a young man announced that he had just strangled his girlfriend. The officers had no idea about the St Erth murder, but took him to the police station as a precaution.

Although the villagers knew that Hampton and Emily were a couple there much anger towards Hampton because of the age difference between them and the belief that Hampton had killed her because he had rejected his demands for sex.

At Hayle police station Hampton said he " had choked her with my hands. " He explained that he done this because, " I was going with her and she won't have anything to do with me. I suppose that it was anger that made me do it. "

However at St Erith, P-c Ashford believed that Hampton had killed Emily out of more than just anger at being told that she no longer wanted to see him, because the attack on was sustained and designed to kill her.

Dr Llewellyn Davies said that Emily had received no other apparent injuries other than that to her throat, which estimated would have taken four minutes to kill her. He conducted the post-mortem in the room that Mrs Tredrea and Emily slept, and in the background a sobbing mother cried out: " Why did he do it?"

On **Thursday June 24th, 1909,** William Hampton appeared at the **Bodmin Assizes before Mr Justice Phillimore and was defended by Mr Seton, whilst the prosecution was led by Mr Raymond Asquith.**

Mr Asquith said that the couple had never appeared to argue, either in the cottage or on the few times they were seen in public. He said it appeared that Emily simply no longer loved Hampton, and that on Sunday night Emily may have told this directly to Hampton. Mr Asquith said that in fairness to the accused there was no evidence that Hampton had wanted " Emily to submit to his desires. "

Nevertheless Mr Asquith said that it was still a case of murder, as it had never been held in law that a case of provocation could not reduce a murder charge to manslaughter, when a young lady wanted to change her affections from one man to another.

Mr Seton said that he would be calling no witnesses for the defence but that Emily was not in good health. On occasions that she and Hampton had been out walking, she had fainted when they returned to the cottage. Mr Seton suggested therefore it would not take a great deal of pressure on her throat to kill her and consequently Hampton would not know that he was *intentionally* killing her, and should be convicted of manslaughter.

In his summing-up the judge said it was for the jury to decide if it were a case of murder or manslaughter. However it was his duty to tell them that legally there was no provocation that Hampton could claim. It could only be manslaughter if Hampton had not intended to kill Emily when he squeezed her throat.

After 15 minutes the jury returned saying that it had taken them that long (!) because although they found Hampton guilty of murder, they wished to recommend mercy, because they believed Hampton had acted from passion and jealousy on account of his own young age.

Despite the jury's recommendation there was no sympathy in St Erith for Hampton, and after his appeal was dismissed in London on July 2nd, he was hanged at **Bodmin Prison on July 20th.**

During the early hours of the execution day a large crowd had gathered outside the prison gates. Many of them tried to gain access to a neighbouring field hoping to see Hampton being led the 50 yards across the prison court-yard to the gallows from the death-cell, which because of the infrequency of executions at Bodmin, had to be erected in the yard. There was a rumour in the crowds that even the gallows could be seen from the field, and so the prison authorities had erected a screen along the prison walls.

At one minute to eight Henry and Tom Pierrepoint hanged William Hampton, in what was also Bodmin's last execution.

After the execution the governor of the prison, H.L. Browett, said it was only fair that he report Hampton's last statement, which was that there were circumstances about his relationship with Emily that no one knew of and that these were " locked in his bosom and would die with him. "

He said he was desperately sorry for Mrs Tredrea and hoped she would forgive him. Hampton also said that he died happily, as the bible was a "new book to him."

Case 18
"The One-Eyed Bruiser"

"They are a murdering the man" - The shout of a neighbour in Jamaica Street.

"She may escape punishment here, but God Will punish her." - *Philip* Murray, in the dock for murder at Edinburgh High Court, referring to his girlfriend who had originally been charged with murder with him ….

"I must thank my counsel for the defence he has put up on my behalf. I do not think it was very fair of the jury to accept Mrs Donoghue's evidence against me. I am fully prepared to meet my God. I never put that man through the window as is alleged against me. Thank you." - *Philip* Murray having been sentenced to death.

Philip Murray (31)
[1923]
Murder
Of
William Cree (30)

Phillip Murray Aged 31

It was a normal Saturday night in the New Town area of Edinburgh in the Summer of 1923: drinking and prostitution. But what made this night different was one of the prostitute's clients came crashing out through a window and was mortally injured on the pavement below. Was he pushed, did he fall or was he trying to escape …. The answers lay in a prostitute who turned 'King's Evidence' and her pimp who ended up on the gallows; the last person hanged at Calton Prison ….

Notes:

http://www.scotland.gov.uk/About/sah-70/caltonjail

Philip Murray (31)

cut an imposing figure – a big bruiser of a man with his right eye missing. He supposedly worked as a news-vendor in Edinburgh and lived in a small one-roomed flat at 40, Jamaica Street in the New Town area of the city, with his girlfriend, **Mrs Catherine Donoghue**, in whose name the property was, and her 15-year-old daughter[34]. Another man, **30-year-old William Cree** from Dunfermline was also in this tiny flat on the late evening of **Saturday, June 23rd, 1923** and in an explosion of violence one of the men ended up out of a window on the street below and died later in the evening in hospital at 11.40 pm ….

William Cree was a railway worker who lived with his parents. He was unmarried and during the war had served with the Black Watch. Injured three times, he was nevertheless a strong man in good health. As far as his family were aware he usually went to Edinburgh to watch a game of football or to go out and would always return on the last train. And so on June 23rd, he left home in the late afternoon saying he would see his parents later that night …. The next day at about five pm a policeman called at the family home with some very distressing news …. Mr Cree was laying dead in the Royal Infirmary in Edinburgh.

The police believed that Mr Cree was something of an amateur boxer, something his family denied. Meanwhile other officers had visited a pub near Jamaica Street in Rose Street. A barman, Mr William Mitchell told the police that he'd known Catherine Donoghue and Philip Murray for about two years and that he had seen her in the pub after eight-thirty when his shift began. He went on to say that after about 45 minutes Mrs Donoghue left, returning to the pub with a different man – a complete stranger to the barman. He said this man had three pints of beer, whilst the woman drank whiskies. He said the pair were being very friendly towards each other. At ten pm, the man, later identified as Mr Cree, bought a bottle of whiskey and beer and left the pub with Mrs Donoghue ….

---

34   Three people in a room 14 ft by 8 ft

Some twenty minutes later another occupant of 40, Jamaica Street, chauffeur William McDonald was in his room with his wife when they heard shuffling sounds on the landing. Then there was a terrible rumbling sound in Mrs Donoghue's flat – then the piercing sound of wood shattering. They could also hear a man screaming and Mrs McDonald said to her husband: "They are a murdering the man." The woman knew the voice of Mrs Donoghue's boyfriend, Philip Murray and knew it was not him pleading: "Oh don't, oh don't." McDonald rushed onto the landing and saw a complete stranger who had a terrified look on his face. The chauffeur darted back into his flat and slammed the door tight as he thought this man was trying to follow him. Then there was silence …. this quickly ended 30 seconds later with the sound of breaking glass. Mr McDonald rushed out again from his room and went downstairs after hearing more glass breaking. Outside on the pavement was the stranger, gravely injured.

Moments later the first police arrived on the scene, and Mr McDonald told them that after the first sound of glass breaking, he had heard, Mrs Donoghue plead: "Don't Phil; my Phil" The man on the pavement was in a terrible way and the whole of his face was badly mangled and dripping with blood. He was barely alive and appeared to be choking. Another neighbour, a Mrs Catherine Laing told police that she too had heard "terrible bumping and thudding" and on looking out of her window and down below to Mrs Donoghue's flat she saw the head and shoulders of a man appearing through the window. Then to her horror she saw this man fall through the window and a pair of hands disappearing back in from the window. Mrs Laing screamed out: "…. dirty blackguards: They have pushed him through the window." Mrs Laing said that Mrs Donoghue had shouted for the attacker to stop. The police would soon claim that Mr McDonald had said that Mrs Donoghue had said: "*Go on*, Phil" and not "*Don't*, Phil" and she too was arrested and charged with murder. Although Mrs Laing knew Murray and his voice she could not say if it were his hands she had seen drawing back inside the flat.

Mrs Laing's husband George told police that he was outside in the street when the commotion started and although he could not see what was going on in the flat, he believed Mr Cree was hitting Murray and winning until Mrs Donoghue started hitting the victim. He agreed with his wife that the woman had, at some point, been trying to stop Murray from hitting Cree but as the dispute continued it was her doing the hitting.

When the officers went up to Murray's flat it had been bolted and they were forced to break in. Murray was in bed and tried to suggest he had no idea why the police would want him to come to the police-station. Incredibly he began attacking the officers and force had to be used to subdue him and take him away. Another witness, Mr Andrew Lamb claimed to have seen the victim clinging to the window sill and worst of all that Mrs Donoghue was hitting him on the fingers to loosen his grip. Indeed he claimed to have not seen anyone else pushing the man out of the window. Another local, Mr Archibald Mullett said that he too had seen a man clinging from the sill. He ran to help but just as he arrived outside number 40 the man fell. Mr Mullett said he had seen no-one pushing or forcing the man out and said it did look like someone trying to escape from the property.

At this time New Town was an area with a poor reputation including that of prostitution. The police were aware of this and so not overly surprised when another local, Mrs Jessie McPhail said that she had seen Mrs Donoghue returning home with a man, and she said to her husband that "Kitty" was bringing home another 'victim.' Having witnessed the fall from the window, she told the police she certainly thought that the man had been pushed out. Other neighbours said they regularly saw Mrs Donoghue taking different men back to her flat, so it seemed incredible that Murray didn't know what his girlfriend had been doing and if he did know why had he apparently turned on William Cree? Mrs Donoghue told the police that her husband was one John Donoghue but that they had long since stopped living together. She said she had moved to Jamaica Street some two years prior. She said that she alone paid the rent – 14 shillings a month. She said she had met Murray at the same time of moving in. They had met in a pub, got drunk, slept together and Murray had considered it his home ever since.

Mrs Donoghue went on to tell the police that although Murray had a job he never gave her any money for the flat. She said that as far as she was aware Murray didn't have a problem with her bringing men back to the flat and so she did this night. She and Mr Cree went into the flat and Murray was lying, fully dressed, on their bed. She and the victim were kissing and whispering when she said that suddenly Murray sprung up and headbutted Mr Cree. As the men stumbled towards the fireplace, Murray hit the other man across the head with a smoothing iron. Mr Cree was badly dazed and Mrs Donoghue said her boyfriend dragged him across the room towards the window where he began hitting him around the head again, before …. pushing him out of the window. Asked by officers what if anything was said before this, the woman said that Mr Cree had said he had not come to fight and offered to have a drink with Murray. Murray refused, asking the victim how much money he had on him.

Mrs Donoghue said that Murray was very drunk and after the man had hit the pavement he said to her: "If he had given me money, he would not have been out there." She candidly told the police that she was living as a prostitute and that she earned £7 a week. She now admitted that Murray was her pimp and lived "immorally of her earnings." Apparently unbeknown to her he had been earning some money singing in the street. She said that she wanted to leave Murray but he "would not stay away from the house." Wiping a tear from her eye she emphatically denied ever hitting or encouraging Murray to hit Mr Cree, and she had done her best to stop the fight. She said after the man had hit the pavement, Murray hit her and pulled her by the hair back into their flat and then locked the room. Eventually after legal advice the murder charge was dropped against Mrs Donoghue and she agreed to give evidence *against* Murray.

Philip Murray appeared at the **City's High Court on Monday, October 8th, before Lord Constable in a trial that was to last for two days.** The court was full to capacity and even when the proceedings had started there were still hundreds left outside. **The Prosecution was undertook by the Lord Advocate, William**

Watson, KC) and two Advocate-Deputes, Mr Fenton KC, and Lord Kinross, whilst the accused was defended by Messrs MacLaren, KC, and Menzies.

Constable John McTaggart was one of the first officers on the scene and he told the court how he and another policeman broke into Murray's flat. He said Mrs Donoghue was doing her best to prevent them from entering. Once in, he described the flat as in great disorder. He said Murray refused to come with the officers, and he was forced to strike him across the chest with his truncheon. Murray still would not give in and other occupants in the building had to help the police carry Murray to the police-station. Constable McTaggart said that the neighbours had warned him to be wary of Murray as he was described as 'dangerous'.

The man leading the murder inquiry, Inspector George Hall said that he saw William Cree's body in the hospital and it was drenched in blood as was his clothing. When charged with murder, Murray told him: " I am making no comment." He told the jury that having read the statements of the neighbours he charged Mrs Donoghue with murder but on June 27th, she asked to see him on remand in Calton Prison. She said she had hoped that Murray would have told the truth by now: that she had nothing to do with pushing the victim out of the window. She said that Murray had told her to tell the police that she and Cree had gone back to the flat alone and that when Murray came in, Mr Cree got out of the bed and jumped through the window to escape.

A Professor Harvey Littlejohn said that on the day after the murder he had examined Philip Murray and he could only see minor injuries to him: a slight wound to a finger and some bruising on his back. He said Murray was a very powerfully built man. He had examined the flat and told the court that a very great struggle had taken place. Along with a Professor Lorrain Smith he had conducted a *post-mortem* and he believed that the blows to the head *before* the fall from the window were the ultimate cause of the victim's death. One blow above Mr Cree's eye had cut right through to the brain and this could have killed him and it was most likely to have been caused by the blow from the iron. He added that even the other blows to the victim might not have been fatal and it would have been difficult to have pushed the man through the window. He said he had read some witness statements suggesting that Mr Cree had fallen on his feet, which Professor Littlejohn thought was quite feasible. The professor added that he did not think for a minute that any woman could have dealt the blows to the victim other then using the iron and he didn't think a woman could have forced a man through the window.

Cross-examined by the defence, Professor Littlejohn said the wound above the right eye could have been caused by a heavy fall on a sharp object, but he was absolutely sure the victim had not tried to jump through the window as it appeared too small for a man to get through. Surely Mr Cree would have more likely broken the door down to escape, he suggested. Furthermore he did not think the man would have the energy to force himself through the window, as he would have been considerably dazed from the initial beating.

On the second day of the trial Philip Murray went into the witness-box. He said that on June 23rd, having earned 3 shillings singing in St Andrew Square and having had his evening meal he went out, retuning to 40, Jamaica Street about 10 pm. He said he was alone. He lay down on the bed being woken by voices, one of which was Mrs Donoghue's. When he woke up he saw a man, a complete stranger, sitting in a chair by the fire. Murray said the man said that: " .... this young woman fetched me up." Not explaining why he would be bothered by this man more than any of the others, he said he took the man by the sleeve and told him that he ought to leave. A struggle began which intensified when it was clear that Mrs Donoghue didn't want the man to go. Murray said he agreed he had hit the man first, but only after the victim had grabbed him by the collar.

William Cree was himself a big strong man and Murray claimed that in addition to saying: "Go on Phil.", Mrs Donoghue made no attempt to stop the fight. He said that during the fight the pair fell onto the fireplace and the victim's head struck the fender. Furthermore as the pair fell onto the bed, Murray said his girlfriend hit Mr Cree. Murray said he had been 'winded' by the struggle and stood back for 30 seconds, to recover. He claimed that he now saw Mrs Donoghue by the window and that the man had apparently 'disappeared.' Mrs Donoghue then went and locked the door and helped Murray undress and bath his wounds. Turning to the jury Murray strongly denied hitting the victim with an iron. He also denied being Mrs Donoghue's 'pimp' saying she had never given him a penny. He said he was jealous of the way she carried on adding: "She may escape punishment here, but God will punish her." Cross-examined by the prosecution, Murray said he'd earned about two pounds a week, and it was he who had given Mrs Donoghue money. He also asked the prosecutor a question - why if Mr Cree had been pushed out of the window, did he fall feet first?

In his summing up, the Lord Advocate began by addressing this point by saying there were a number of witnesses who'd seen Mr Cree hanging on by his fingertips and that would explain how he came to fall onto his feet. He went on to say that he would suggest that Murray had simply lied to the jury – why if Murray were "winded" would the victim choose going through an upstairs window as his preferred method of leaving the building? He would suggest that Murray *alone* had dragged Mr Cree over to the window and dropped him out feet first. He said he could see no other verdict than 'guilty of murder'. However Mr McLaren, in his final address, said that it was shocking that Mrs Donoghue who also really knew what went on in this tiny flat was herself not in the dock charged with murder. He said she was a woman of 'bad character' and yet the law viewed her as a witness. Mr McLaren said the jury should simply reject her evidence out of hand. He said there was no independent evidence that Murray had thrown the victim out the window and that at best his client should be afforded a verdict of 'Not Proven.' However given the fact that the prisoner had admitted hitting Mr Cree, Mr McLaren said he would accept a verdict of manslaughter.

The trial judge quickly dismissed any talk of 'culpable homicide' in this case. He said it was either murder or an acquittal. He then explained the position of Mrs Donoghue and that even if the jury now believed she too had been party to the murder, this would not diminish the prisoner's role in the crime. He said he did not think the jury could reasonably think that the victim had jumped of his own accord.

The jury, which included six women, retired at six pm on **Tuesday, October 9th, 1923**. Just 27 minutes later they came back into court – they had a verdict – by an 11 to 4 majority they had found Philip Murray …. guilty of murder. They then added they wished, *unanimously*, to recommend mercy. Under Scottish law the Prosecution would then ask the judge to pass sentence – in this case, of course, … one of death. Lord Constable said he had no power to deal with the jury's recommendation but would pass it on. Then donning the dreaded black cap he ordered that Philip Murray **be hanged on October 30th**, "between the hours of eight and ten." Dramatically rather than meekly leave immediately, Murray cleared his voice and said: "I must thank my counsel for the defence he has put up on my behalf. I do not think it was very fair of the jury to accept Mrs Donoghue's evidence against me. I am fully prepared to meet my God. I never put that man through the window as is alleged against me. Thank you."

As Murray was lead away from the dock, a friend in the public gallery called out: "Cheer up, Phil." At this time there was no appeal court in Scotland and so Murray's legal team put all their efforts into saving him from the **gallows in Calton Prison**, ironically where Mrs Donoghue had also been held before she turned "King's Evidence." The condemned man's solicitor, Mr G. W. Hoggan said her evidence was one of four points being presented to the Scottish Office, as to why Murray should not be executed. The others concerned how the judge had directed the jury and the question of whether they should have been allowed to consider a verdict of manslaughter. By Thursday, October 25th, over 15,000 signatures had been gathered. **The Scottish Secretary of State, Viscount Novar**, told Mr Hoggan that the decision would be left as late as possible and was not made until the following Saturday, just 72 hours before the scheduled execution. There was to be no reprieve.

Mr Hoggan said he was very angry with the Viscount's decision. By now he had amassed over 22,000 signatures on his petition and said he would continue to plea for mercy right up until the end. Monday was a day of feverish activity in Edinburgh as Mr Hoggan now petitioned the King, George V. The solicitor also went to see Viscount Novar. Mr Hoggan also pointed out that there had been a reprieve in the famous "Brixton Taxi-Cab Murder", a case which had resulted in Alexander Mason (22) being spared, in part, because of the inadmissibility of evidence of an alleged accomplice. He told the Secretary of State that the case needed to be "gravely reconsidered."

Mr Hoggan's efforts were to be of no avail. The Scottish Office refused to change their mind and **executioners, John Ellis and William Willis** were already in the prison when this was communicated to him. Philip Murray was hanged at eight am: he died instantaneously and remained calm to the end. He had said Mass in the death-cell and walked on his own to the gallows. As the prison-clock chimed eight am a crowd of some hundreds gathered on Calton Hill, itself not far from the murder scene. There was no sound in the crowd. Many noted that the old tradition of hosting a black flag appeared to have been discontinued and with that the crowds simply melted away into the cold autumn morning. A note on the prison gate said the hanging had been carried out at 8.01 am. Officers guarding Murray in the condemned cell said his only regret was that his mother and sister (his only family) who were living in England had found out about the case.

Philip Murray was to be the last person executed at Calton Prison and indeed only the ninth person executed there. Calton Prison was opened in 1817 on the site of a previous prison and was described by Jules Verne who visited the city in 1859 as resembling a small-scale version of a medieval town. It was closed and demolished in 1930. After that executions in the Scottish capital were carried out at Saughton Prison.

Case 19
"The Case Of the Missing Chinaman"

~Murder and Castration in Warley Woods~

"I wantee tellee very true. I have very good mother and four good brothers. I wantee tellee true because such a disgrace to my country to tell lies to big chief." – The start of the murder suspect's statement to the police.

" .... that Zee Ming Wu business, the Englishman do not take the trouble to find out." - Djang Djing Sung.

Djang Djing Sung (33)
[1919]
Murder
Of
Zee Ming Wu (41)

Djang Djin Sung Aged 33
The Murderer

Revolting murder from the Birmingham area just after the First World War. The body of a 41-year-old Chinaman was found in wooded area on a golf-course in parkland: the victim had received many serious injuries, but most sinister of all, the left scrotum had been cut open and the testicle removed, and the right had also been slashed with a cut wound leading up to the penis ....

Notes:

There was another murder in Warley Woods Golf Course in 1957 – unsolved murder of Frederick Jeffs (see True Detective Summer Special (2002) pg. 8)

Warley Woods, Park and Golf Course together forms a rather unique, beautiful and much-loved open space to the south of the west Birmingham suburb of Smethwick near to the Wolverhampton Road and is known collectively as Warley Woods[35]. It contains remnants of ancient oak and beech woodland, overlaid by a bold landscaping plan created in

---

35   At the time of the murder it was in Worcestershire.

the early 19th century by the renowned designer Humphrey Repton, for the Galton family of Birmingham gun-makers. It became a golf-course in 1896. In 1906 those parts of Warley Woods that had not already been built over were saved by the combined efforts of local people led by the Smethwick glass-maker Alexander Chance. Warley Woods then became one of the area's finest urban parks and gold-courses, the latter becoming open to the public in 1921 and since 2004 it has been run by the Warley Woods Community Trust.

Two years before the public were allowed open access to the golf-course on the late afternoon of **Friday, June 27th, 1919**, a young man, Henry Wilson was out walking through Warley Woods, when he decided he needed to urinate. He left the pathway and went into a small wood. As he unzipped his trousers his attention was drawn to a dark object in a slight undulation in the fields and which stood out against the greenery of the surroundings. As his eyes focused the young man realised it was a man lying on his back, his head turned to the right, and he thought he was asleep, but then it seemed strange that there was no movement at all. As he crept closer he could then see a heavy wooden log across the man's face. The man was absolutely motionless and his face had been horribly disfigured and so young Mr Wilson ran as fast as he could to raise the alarm.

Officers at the scene could tell that, despite the facial injuries, the man appeared to be Chinese or from the Far East. Marks around the body seemed to suggest that the body had been dragged to its present spot, although there had been no effort to hide the corpse. The body had started to disintegrate, suggesting the murder had taken place some days before, although the exact time would need to be ascertained by an expert, due to the warm weather. A Dr Louis Broughton told Detective-Inspector Francis Drew of the Worcestershire Police, who was leading the murder inquiry, that he thought the murder had taken place at least four days before. The police decided that they would focus their attention on **Monday, June 23rd,** as a starting point.

Given the proximity to Birmingham and the fact that the city had a significant, albeit small, Chinese population, the police began asking questions within the community and examining police records. This provided an immediate result as just two days before, on Wednesday, a Chinaman, Mr Li Ding Jig had gone to Birmingham Central Police-Station, asking to speak to the officer who dealt with immigrants in the city. The Alien Registration Officer, Detective-Inspector William Tudor, was told by Mr Jig that he had some concerns at a lodging house, used mainly by Chinese men in the city, at 109, Coleshill Street in the city-centre, where he was himself lodging. The house was run by an Italian family, the di Mascios, who were themselves worried about the apparent disappearance of one of their six Chinese lodgers, **41-year-old Zee Ming Wu**, who had been last seen on at least Sunday evening [June 22nd], although he had been heard in his room the next morning [June 23rd], that is assuming it was him.

The police duly noted Mr Jig's concerns, but on the next day a member of the di Mascio family went herself to the police. Teresa di Mascio, whose parents owned the lodging-house told the police that Mr Wu had come to their home in April. She repeated what Mr Jig had said, but said that Mr Wu had gone to work with the other five on Monday morning – she had seen him. At eight pm that night, Mr Jig spoke to Teresa saying that he was worried about his friend as his non-appearance was totally out of character. With the discovery of the body of a man, who was almost certainly Chinese, it emerged that the concern for Mr Wu was the only report that the Birmingham police had regarding Chinamen that week. Mr Jig was taken immediately to the city's mortuary, where he quickly identified the body as that of Zee Ming Wu. A nephew of the victim, Mr Li Si Shin, told officers that Mr Wu came from Chekiang Province[36]. Although married his wife and three children had remained in China and Mr Wu would send them money. The victim worked for the *John Wright & Eagle Range* factory, who made gas ovens and stoves. After his disappearance a letter had arrived at the lodging house from his homeland with the good news that a daughter was due to be married.

A *post-mortem*, carried out by Dr Broughton revealed that parts of the victim's body had been mutilated. Around his ears were some 10

36 Now called Zhejiang Province.

cuts (and they had penetrated the brain); he had been stabbed through the right side of the forehead and his lower jaw had been broken; his skull had been fractured and three ribs had also been broken, possibly by someone jumping up and down on the victim. Most gruesome of all Mr Wu's left scrotum had been cut open and the testicle removed; whilst the right scrotum had also been cut with a cut wound leading up to the penis. Dr Broughton surmised that since there was little blood around the genitals, mercifully the victim must have been dead at the time of the castration. Furthermore since Mr Wu's trousers had not been cut they must have been removed and replaced after this. The doctor said the stab wound to the forehead would have most likely caused the Chinaman's death and the most likely weapon was a screw-driver or thin chisel, but that a hammer had also been used in the assault. Given Dr Broughton's earlier belief that the murder had taken place at least four days before and given Mr Wu's disappearance on that day, this seemed the most likely day of the murder **[June 23rd]**.

Whoever killed Mr Wu must have had a deep hatred of him. Having killed him with the wound to the head, he could have fled there and then, but instead decided to castrate him. This indicated perhaps passion and jealousy lay behind the crime, but the police also quickly discovered that Mr Wu was a man of sober and frugal habits, who in his time in England had put away some £240 in a Post Office Savings Account, a considerable sum of money in 1919. A search of the victim's room, the rest of the lodging house and his workplace failed to locate the book, suggesting robbery was behind the crime, although why did the castration take place – was the killer trying to mislead the police?

All the country's police and post-offices were given information about the post-office book and very quickly it came to light, although not directly from police information, as we shall see. On June 24th, at some point between two and two-thirty pm a Chinaman went into the Post Office in Blythe Road in West Kensington in west London. The cashier was one Arthur Powell and he received an account book in the name of 'Zee Ming Wu'. Since it had been opened there had only been two transactions. On May 24th, £200 had been deposited, and £40 on June 7th. 'Mr Wu' said he would like to withdraw the whole amount. This, *per se*, was not overly unusual, but Mr Powell became suspicious when 'Mr Wu' asked for the book back, apparently to enable him to fill out the withdrawal slip. 'Mr Wu' then seemed to copy out his name from the book. The man then made a basic error – the real and dead Mr Wu could not write, yet this 'Mr Wu' signed his name. 'Mr Wu' was then asked to come to a private office.

The man in charge of the branch, Herbert Brigden asked the man to explain the difference in signatures, but was faced with a barrage of quickly spoken Chinese. As best he could, Mr Brigden told 'Mr Wu' he would be escorted to the local head-office in nearby West Kensington Gardens where the matter would be dealt with. One Peter Marr was given the account book and withdrawal form and he was to escort the Chinaman. However once on the pavement outside, 'Mr Wu' shouted out: "Me no go", but Mr Marr tried to hold him, telling him he must come. The Chinaman tried to grab back the documents and said he would be late for his dinner! Having failed to get hold of the book and form, "Mr Wu" disappeared into the crowd. Later in the day the post-office received the information about the murder in Birmingham and officers were immediately informed about what had occurred in West Kensington. Detective Inspector Drew and his team were deeply frustrated – if only West Kensington Post-Office had known about the book - for very quickly the case seemed to be slipping away from the police. Another local Chinaman was arrested and charged with the murder on July 10th, but the city's magistrates threw the case out. Soon a month had past after the murder and the police had no clues. But once again we must return to the capital ….

Ernest Dyson lived in Aldine Street in Shepherd's Bush in west London in yet another lodging-house. The room above Mr Dyson's was occupied by a Chinaman, Kwo Doung Dsou. What happened next was most bizarre. During the early hours of July 25th, Mr Dyson heard noises coming from Mr Dsou's flat. As he looked out of his window to try and look up he saw another Chinaman walking down the street. An hour or so later Mr Dyson left the house to go out and to his shock found a bloodstained hammer outside his door! The police were called and Mr Dsou explained that a friend had been staying with him in his room, had attacked him with the hammer, and left. The injuries to Mr Dsou were not life-threatening, but the name of the friend was **Djang Djing Sung (33)**, whose home address in England was in …. Edgbaston, Birmingham. He was married with a young boy in China.

The Worcestershire and Birmingham police were immediately told and returning to Coleshill Street they were told that Sung knew Mr Wu. Every policeman in London and Birmingham was told to look out for Sung and fortunately he was found three days later on July 28th, in Birmingham at his lodgings: in his possession was a …. chisel. In order to avoid any chance of the local magistrates in west London granting Sung bail, he was charged with the attempted murder of Mr Dsou and remanded into custody. Indeed Mr Dsou had received a number of blows to the forehead, a shattered elbow and fractured rib. The arresting officer in Birmingham, Detective-Sergeant Algernon Sprackling wrote down in his note-book that Sung had said that Mr Dsou owed him 'Fifty Dollars'. Sung said he wrote to him asking for the repayment, received no reply, and so decided to burgle him. When Mr Dsou woke up Sung decided to 'tap' him on the head with a 'small stick' – he denied it was a hammer. A frightened Mr Dsou had told police that Sung was a friend staying for a few nights. When the hammer was examined by the eminent pathologist Dr Bernard Spilsbury he believed it had been used in the Warley Woods murder and it bore traces of human blood.

Having been remanded for attempted murder, Detective-Sergeant Sprackling now informed Sung that he was going to be arrested for the murder of Zee Ming Wu. He was told he would be put before an Identity Parade to see if he was the man who used the victim's account book on June 24th. Sung immediately confessed that he had been in the post-office in West Kensington, but …. that he hadn't killed Mr Wu. He said the real killer was …. Mr Jig, who had then told him to travel down to London and cash the book in. Sung was taken across the capital to the docks in the East-End, where in Limehouse, home to many thousands of Chinese sailors, he was put before an ID Parade in the local police-station. Mr Marr picked him out as the man in the post-office; Mr Dyson that he was the

Chinaman, who walked past his window. Furthermore a doorman at the post-office, Philip Besien also picked the suspect out.

Back in west London at Paddington police-station, Sung now allegedly said he wanted to tell the truth and was interviewed by Detective-Inspector Percy Savage and made a detailed statement, which he signed and which he began by saying: "I wantee tellee very true. I have very good mother and four good brothers. I wantee tellee true because such a disgrace to my country to tell lies to big chief." Sung said he had left the factory at which he worked at 5.30 pm on Monday, June 23rd, meeting up with four other Chinamen, including the victim and Mr Jig. He claimed that Mr Wu asked Sung to steal a hammer[37] from his place of work – *W.H. Briscoe & Company* – who made brass stamps. Sung went back inside and duly stole the hammer. When he returned only Mr Wu and Mr Jig were outside and all three of them caught a tram to Warley Woods, where they intended to hunt for rabbits using the hammer to kill the animals. In the small wood where the body was found Sung said that Mr Jig called out that there was a large rabbit and then smashed the hammer down onto …. Mr Wu's head …. repeatedly.

Sung said he was deeply shocked and asked why Mr Jig had done this, his friend replying that it was an 'honour-killing': Wu's family had cheated on his family back in China. Sung said he feared for his life and therefore did whatever Mr Jig wanted and accordingly he took the post-office account book and helped move the body off the public path. He said that moments later the two other Chinamen from outside the factory, Zee Bing Zar and Ling Gai Wu, who were both unemployed, arrived, having caught the next tram. Sung said that as soon as they saw the body of Mr Wu they shook their heads and returned back to the city, although Sung also said that this Mr Wu helped moved the body (Sheet 9). Sung said he was so traumatised by what he had seen that he asked his landlord in Edgbaston to sleep with him. He also claimed that Messrs Zar and Wu were at the railway-station when Sung returned empty handed from London.

---

37 This was the hammer stolen from the factory

Over the next six weeks Sung was re-interviewed by the police many times, but refused to change his story. Naturally Mr Jig denied any involvement in the case and, of course, he himself had been to the police and on September 6th, Sung was charged with Zee Ming Wu's murder. During the preceding period the police had found letters in Mr Dsou's room which alluded to the murder. One letter, dated July 7th, read (in Chinese): "Zee Ming Wu is buried, but has had no revenge yet. I think Englishman is careless of it', implying the police weren't doing a very good job! However another letter, on a post-card, on July 10th, merely said: "After all the real offender has been caught[38], and that I am not the one. One would not murder Ming Wu for anything, and if the book was taken to London, that must have been the object." It emerged that the man arrested, one Ah Chee, had not been picked out of an ID parade. On the post-card Sung also noted: "Today I saw in the newspapers that there were four Chinamen concerned in the murder of Ming Wu, I do not know, if it is true."

Djang Djing Sung appeared at the **Worcester Assizes on Wednesday, October 22nd, before Mr Justice Rowlatt**. He pleaded 'not guilty' and he followed the trial through a translator. Mr Jig told the court that Sung was a regular visitor to the lodging-house in Coleshill Road, and that he had been there on June 22nd, the day before the murder, a fact confirmed by Teresa di Mascio[39]. Mr Jig said he overheard the accused and the victim talking about 30 shillings that Sung owed Mr Wu. It appeared quite friendly as Mr Wu said he didn't need the money straight-away, as he had four or five pounds on him.

A time-keeper at *Briscoe's*, George Aston, told the court that Sung, who had worked at the factory since August 1916[40], had been clocked out at 5.41 pm and that he had indeed seen him with 'Mr Wu' outside the factory gates, but he had seen no other Chinamen.

---

38 The Chinaman arrested, whose case was thrown out by the magistrates court.
39 Although according to a Birmingham City Police report Sung was keen to avoid other Chinamen and always lodged in 'respectable' neighbourhoods. He said his parents were wealthy and that he had been to University in China.
40 He arrived at Bristol and was Registered as an Alien Chinese Subject selling soap.

Sung did not report in for work for the next two days, but returned on June 26th. On the next day he was sacked for poor time-keeping. On the same day Sung had told his landlord, Arthur Grosvenor, that he could not sleep properly and with a candle in his hand, had asked if he could sleep with him: Sung specifically referred to the murder in Warley Woods. Mr Grosvenor suggested the Chinaman return to his own room, but was then to tell the court that on June 29th, the prisoner had himself been to the mortuary and had viewed the body of Mr Wu. When he returned to Edgbaston he was once again greatly upset. Mr Grosvenor also told the court that on the night of the murder Sung did not return home until 11.20 pm, which was unusual.

For the prosecution, Messrs A. Powell and A.E. Jordan, told the jury that no suspicion must be attached to Mr Jig as it could be proved beyond any doubt that he could not have been at the murder scene on June 23rd, as he left work at 5.45 pm and was back home at 6.15 pm, and indeed by Sung's own statement (Sheet 8) the murder took place at around seven pm. This was a major problem for **Mr Reginald Coventry, who defended** the prisoner, and the jury were out for just nine minutes in finding Djang Djing Sung guilty of murder. An original execution date of November 11th was cancelled when the defence appealed but after this was rejected and Sung's case for mercy was rejected by the Home Office, **he was hanged at Worcester Prison on Wednesday, December 3rd, 1919 at eight am by John Ellis and Edward Taylor, the last person executed in the prison.**

It seems that Djang Djing Sung was something of a strange character. At the lodging houses that he stayed in, he was thought of as a student, and he often spoke of going to Birmingham University. In the summer months he would often be seen in the city's parks with a tennis racket and balls, wandering around but he was never actually seen playing. His room was full of books and writing material but he was thought to be not very well educated in China and someone who actually came from a poor background. Indeed in a letter to the West London Police Court he claimed to be actually 29, although he had said he was born in 1885 when he arrived at Bristol. It also seems that Sung thought he had escaped justice as in one of the letters he said: " …. that Zee Ming Wu business, the Englishman do not take the trouble to find out."

Worcester Prison was closed and partially demolished in 1922, some of its buildings being used for flats.

Case 20
"The Tragic Case Of the Rejected Valentine's Gifts"

"Oh Mr Giles, that scaffold at Aylesbury. Am I to be buried in a prison? To die there and be buried in the gaol yard and be covered up with hot lime. I cannot. Let me die on the bed as I am. I wish Dr Death had been out at the time, and then I should have been dead and I should now have been in heaven with my Annie." Williams Stevens, the murderer ….

William STEVENS (24)
MURDER
Of
Annie Leeson (17)
[1864]

*__Aylesbury Prison – William Stevens was hanged outside
the Arch/Entrance on a Summer's Day in 1864 ….__*

*Had a young
Buckingham tailor not travelled to London for his
apprenticeship, he may not have become the last person
publicly executed outside Aylesbury Prison in 1864 ….
His sojourn in the capital changed him from a hard-
working soul, into a man who returned and acted
'inappropriately' with women; and whose interest
focused in on a 17-year-old girl with whom he tried to
'take liberties' with; and who when she showed no
interest in him, he threatened to shoot her or cut her
throat ….*

By the middle of the 19th
Century the town of Buckingham had lost its status as the County
and Assize Town to Aylesbury, and so had reverted back to a small
and usually quiet market town in the North-West of the county with
a population of about 4,000 …. But like everywhere else, it had its
stresses and strains, and in early 1864, this centred around a young

man and a young girl, whose families also happened to live next door to each other in Nelson Street in the town centre ….

William Stevens (24), a tailor by trade, like his father, was completely besotted with **Annie Leeson (17)** …. The Stevens family were well known and respected in the town and its surrounds – his father being described as 'sober steady and quiet' ….. Annie lived with her widowed mother and family and worked, as a domestic servant, a few doors along in a local shop run by a relative Mr James Uff, with whom, in fact, she spent most of her time, as he also had a home nearby, where she was also employed ….

As he grew up, William Stevens seemed to be the absolute mirror of his dad – and their employer, a Mr Ladd, sent him to London to gain further experience in the trade …. However when Stevens returned to Buckingham after two years away, he had picked up a lot more than just more knowledge for his job …. Whilst in the capital, he had mixed with 'dubious company', and people of 'questionable morals'. Stevens also developed a new way of talking and behaviour with the opposite sex, and on his return home, became completely obsessed with Annie Leeson …. Unfortunately, the teenager was not in the slightest bit interested in Stevens, and told him so to his face, and anyone else who would listen …. This included Stevens sending Annie two expensive Valentine's gifts on February 14th …. Stevens was seething and he also was becoming very jealous in the manner in which she chatted to other men in the town. One of the reasons why Stevens was so attracted to Annie, was her naturally bubbly and outgoing nature; but Stevens had mistook this when directed towards him, as a sign that she fancied him; he was mad with jealousy, as she behaved like this around most men ….

In the aftermath of the rejection of his Valentine's Day presents rebuff, things came to a head nearly a fortnight later on **Saturday, February 27th** …. With hindsight, many in the town would say that Stevens had threatened to cut Annie's throat; but nearly everyone dismissed this as the talk of a jealous young man, who would soon turn his attentions elsewhere; others actually thought Stevens was trying to 'impress' Annie with a 'hard-man' image …. Regardless of what the young man did, the young girl kept ignoring him, *for the most part* …. However nearer to home the Stevens' family were slightly more concerned – at the back of their minds was the thought of what Stevens had seen and done in London …. When Stevens' dad discovered that after Valentine's Day, his son had taken to carrying a razor around with him, Mr Stevens spoke to him and took it away …. By the twenty-seventh, Stevens had it back in his possession …. And at around six pm, he noticed young Annie in the street below …. Back home from work and changing ready to go out for the night down the pub, Stevens saw her going along with a bucket to the local water pump, which was at the junction with Hunter Street and Tingewick Road …. It was just a short distance away, and now fully dressed, Stevens slipped outside and waited for Annie's return ….

Outside the house of a Mrs Elizabeth Spicer in Nelson Street, William Stevens pounced ….. creeping up behind Annie Leeson, Stevens pulled out his razor and cut her throat …. A second later he delivered an even more vicious blow cutting deep into the flesh: young Annie began to collapse onto the road spilling her bucket of water in the process …. However such was her determination that she staggered onto Mr Uff's shop …. She stumbled in trying desperately to stem the flow of gushing blood from her throat …. She saw Mr Uff and extended her arms for help, but she could not speak and fell into his extended arms …. It was a truly shocking sight: as young Annie fell into Mr Uff, her head nearly came off. He took her into his back room where he tried to stem the flow of blood with a piece of cloth …. It was proving a great ordeal for Mr Uff, who despite being a young man, had to sit down; young Annie collapsing on him, and drenching him in blood …. Within a minute she was dead, having let out one final deep sigh of life ….

Quite by chance the very moment Annie had entered the shop, one of the town's local officers, Constable Richard Seaton had entered the premises. He immediately ran to the town's police-station and to seek medical help. Just a few streets away lived Dr Robert Death, and he was in the shop within minutes, having dramatically arrived on his black horse …. Having quickly established that Annie was dead, he was then summoned to the Stevens' house, where William lay gravely injured – he too had cut his own throat …. Moments after cutting Annie, Stevens did likewise. In an almost mirror-like attack, he had cut himself *twice* – using the same razor as the murder weapon …. His own mother had watched the suicide-bid, and prevented him from cutting himself a third and almost certainly fatal time; incredibly also present was the victim's mum, who'd popped around for a Saturday night chat .... For several hours, it was assumed that Stevens would not survive, and initial reports of the case, described it as one of 'murder and suicide' .... However Dr Death had done a good job in sewing up the wound .... As the doctor began his work, Mrs Leeson ran to Mr Uff's shop to tell him and her daughter what had happened – one can only imagine the horror she must have felt, when she found her daughter dead ....

For the next five weeks, William Stevens lay in his own bed, guarded night and day by the police, until at the beginning of April, he was placed on remand in Buckingham Prison .... Stevens regularly asked to be 'left alone'; but not unnaturally this was refused .... At one point he went on 'hunger strike'; but he still continued to drink water, although this caused the medical staff in the prison problems, as the water would seep through the wound to his throat ....

Two days after the murder, an inquest was opened in the *Red Lion*, near, ironically, to Mr Uff's house. The Coroner, Davis King, took the jury of sixteen men first of all to the shop to see where Annie Leeson had died, and where her body had remained .... The first witness back in the *Red Lion* was Mr Uff, and he cut a pathetic figure – he had been greatly affected by the tragedy, and despite being in his mid-thirties, appeared like an old man .... He told the hearing that both he and Annie had often heard Stevens threaten the victim, but the teenager had laughed it all off, which had meant he didn't take it seriously either .... The next witness was Annie's older sister Elizabeth, who agreed that, to some extent, Stevens and Annie had been seeing each other, as on a number of occasions, she had 'walked out' with him; but Annie had told her she was not interested in him .... However the last time was just a week before the murder, and a week after the Valentine's Day presents .... However on this occasion, Annie had returned home and was extremely annoyed – Stevens had behaved 'inappropriately' towards her, and had tried to take 'liberties' with her .... After that, the normally bouncy Annie vowed to avoid Stevens .... On the Thursday before the crime, Annie had visited another sister in the town, and had asked Elizabeth to accompany her .... Elizabeth couldn't; but the reason she was needed soon became clear – Stevens had followed Annie, and had waited outside the other sister's place ....

Two days later the Leesons heard Stevens come in from work, and when they heard him in his kitchen, they thought it would be safe for Annie to leave to fetch the water; the young girl herself calling out: "Lizzie, he's gone down the yard and I'll go." To Elizabeth's horror just after she saw Annie leave the property, she saw Stevens creep out – minutes later she heard the sound of a scuffle, the sound of a bucket and water crashing to the ground, and the sound of something terrible …. At the same time Stevens' mum came out with a candle to see what was happening, and it was at this point, the mother saw her son trying to kill himself, and Elizabeth running off for help …. Elizabeth said that as well as threatening her sister with a razor, Stevens had also said he would shoot Annie, were she to marry someone else ….

A local 13-year-old, Richard Woolhead had actually witnessed the murder …. He said he'd watched Stevens follow the victim in complete silence – she had no idea he was behind her …. He watched in terror as Stevens grabbed Annie from behind with his left arm and cut her throat with his right …. Annie Leeson said just one word – "MURDER!" Two local men, both of whom knew Stevens, then saw him as he made the short distance back home …. John Billing, a drinking friend of Stevens, and George Finch, both said he had known what he had done, and that now he was truly repentant – indeed, previously, in the pub, Stevens had frequently told Mr Billing that, were it not for the law, he would kill Annie …. The men also saw him after he'd try to kill himself, and both said that he was genuinely distraught that he hadn't succeeded ….

Dr Death said that the second cut wound to Annie was quite deadly – it had sliced through the windpipe and the gullet; as well as the major blood vessels in the neck …. The evidence against William Stevens was clear-cut, and he was committed for trial at the next assizes in the following month; the first day on which, Annie Leeson was buried …. However he was deemed too ill to appear, and he stood trial on **Tuesday, July 19th, before Justice George Bramwell**, in front of a packed court in Aylesbury …. Standing in the dock, William Stevens looked quite ill – he was very pale and withdrawn …. He was a short and thin man, and he cut a quite pathetic figure …. His own ghastly neck wound was covered with a blue handkerchief, and as an act of mercy, he was allowed to sit during the trial, which lasted just a few hours …. Although he pleaded 'not guilty'; it was more of a technicality, as he offered no real defence ….

Opening the case for the Crown, Mr David Keane, QC, said there could be no question of *provocation* in this case; and indeed said there was plenty of *premeditation* …. Giving evidence, Elizabeth Leeson, in full mourning dress, fainted on two occasions, and had to be roused by smelling-salts …. To add to her distress, Stevens constantly starred at her, as she tried to give her evidence …. **For the defence – Mr Payne** – suggested that the officer leading the inquiry – Superintendent William Giles - had not properly cautioned the prisoner. Indeed the officer said this was quite true! But this was because he had not actually interrogated Stevens due to his illness …. He said that the prisoner had freely given a number of statements in front of a number of different witnesses on many occasions; and since Stevens knew all the police as acquaintances – it was such a small town - legally, the superintendent didn't believe he had to be cautioned ….

Justice Bramwell agreed and Superintendent Giles read out one statement made by Stevens, which read: "Oh Mr Giles, that scaffold at Aylesbury. Am I to be buried in a prison? To die there and be buried in the gaol yard, and be covered up with hot lime. I cannot. Let me die on the bed as I am. I wish Dr Death had been out at the time, and then I should have been dead, and I should now have been in heaven with my Annie." Although convicted murderers were, by law, buried within the prison after the 1868 law abolishing public executions; in theory, after 1823, they could be buried in a church-yard, although this was rarely, if ever, used; and so most were buried within the prison …. One of the officers, who had guarded Stevens on remand was Constable Humphrey Ray – he had also retrieved the murder weapon, and said that Stevens told him: "How could I do it? I wish she was alive and I was dead!" The officer said that George Finch had told him, that Stevens had said that outside Mrs Spicer's, Annie started mucking about, and refusing to speak to Stevens, and that he had attacked her as she was annoying him …. When Stevens heard Mr Uff describe Annie Leeson's dying moments, William Stevens broke down in tears ….

Despite the evidence against the prisoner, Mr Payne made a gallant effort to save his client's life …. Despite the fact that Stevens was carrying a lethal weapon on him, he suggested that the crime should be one of *manslaughter*, as he said the killing had taken place during a moment of frenzied passion …. He laid into the police, saying that they had made up the law in suggesting they didn't need to caution him …. Stevens had seriously injured himself, and therefore could the jury really be sure he knew what he was saying, especially as this was all written down by the police! Mr Payne then demanded that were the jury to reject the defence of manslaughter, then they should request the judge recommend mercy to the Home Office on behalf of the prisoner …. Mr Justice Bramwell said this was not possible, but Mr Payne said it had been done before ….

In his summing-up, the judge told the jury that, in strict law, there was no evidence of manslaughter – he said that since 'ancient times' in England, a man had no right to kill a woman, who rejected his advances, and no right to claim provocation …. The jury were out for just 13 minutes – their verdict was murder and no recommendation of mercy of their own …. Stevens said nothing and simply gazed aimlessly at the judge, who donned the black cap, and told the prisoner, that he would be hanged outside Aylesbury Prison ….

Soon afterwards, the execution date was set for **Friday, August 5th, 1864, and the executioner, William Calcraft was contacted in London** ….In the death-cell, William Stevens met with his family for the last time …. The time set for the execution was 8.00 am and by five, Aylesbury Prison was surrounded by a crowd of about 4,000 …. Those that could afford them brought binoculars and took positions in the neighbouring fields that once surrounded the prison …. Around forty policemen were on duty – some on horseback – but there was no trouble …. As eight am approached, the crowd watched as Calcraft checked the scaffold – situated against the prison arch and entrance – before going back inside the prison ….. Here he pinioned Stevens and listened as the murderer asked forgiveness from the prison chaplain ….. Stevens was then led onto the drop by the hangman, where upon seeing the beam, he promptly began to faint, but was stopped from completely collapsing by a prison-officer …. As the rope and white hood was placed around his neck, Stevens began praying loudly …. The lever was pulled, the trap-door opened, and to the crowd's horror, William Stevens didn't die cleanly – for a whole *five* minutes he twisted and turned at the end of the rope – he had died in agony …. For another hour the body was left at the end of the rope – a few hundred people watching it, before Stevens was, indeed, buried inside the prison ….

Afterwards the prison released a statement, saying that William Stevens had cleared his conscious – he had admitted fully his guilt ….

The last execution at Aylesbury Prison was in 1880 ….

Case 21
"The Castletown House Outrage"

'.... typical Victorian country gentleman who gave to many charitable works' The victim ....

"We left the man settled." - Allegedly said by a third man on trial for the attempted murder ….

"I ask you to have nothing to do with secret parties or Ribbonism." - One of the men on the gallows ….

James Kirk (50) & Patrick McCooey (35)
[1851-2]
Attempted Murder
Of
James Eastwood (54)

It was Christmas Eve 1851 and all was not well in Ireland: She was just emerging from the terrible ravages of the Famine, which Republicans said illustrated all that was wrong with British Rule, and why it should end. A focus of their anger were the landlords, especially those that evicted tenants, such as James Eastwood, one of whose family homes was just outside Dundalk, the County Town of Louth. The fact that he was a kind man, who advocated women's and children's rights did not stop his name being put onto a 'hit list' by a secret group called the Ribbonmen ….

Notes:

http://www.stlouisdundalk.ie/oldcastletownproject/normans.html

1) Photo of the Eastwoods' 'hatch' where the tenants would pay their rent so the family didn't have to interact with the peasantry

http://www.faughart.com/local-history-page22740.html

A Ribbonman was a member of a 19th century Irish Republican group, The Ribbon Society. The Ribbon Society was originally conceived to stand as opposition to the Orangemen rather than Unionists *per se*, but later it became a group of tenant farmers who joined together to prevent eviction by their landlords. They are called Ribbonmen because they wore a green ribbon to identify themselves.

Although the 1848 Rebellion in Ireland had failed from a Republican point of view, the disorder connected with it rumbled on, particularly in hotspots such as South Armagh, North Louth and East Monaghan and on December 4th, 1851 a pillar of the established order one Thomas Bateson was beaten to death near the town of Castleblayney in County Monaghan. A landowner in his own right he was most pertinently of all a bailiff; his name was at the top of the list of the

'Ribbonmen', who whilst their long-term objective was the end of the Union with Britain; in the short term they targeted landlords and their agents in rural areas, especially after evictions[41] ....

However common such events as the murder of Mr Bateson were, they still had a huge impact on the community, and so it was a great shock that the newspapers in this part of Ireland learnt of another "agrarian crime", this time just outside the County Town of Louth, Dundalk. As one 'paper put it, it was " .... enough to curdle the blood." In this part of the North of Ireland many in the landed classes and their allies, feared who would be next. Indeed in and around Dundalk it was said that a 'hit-list' had been drawn up and that certain people had been told their time would come .... sooner or later. One family who were talked off in such a fearful way were the Eastwoods. They lived just a mile west outside Dundalk in one of their ancestral homes – *Castletown House* – although most of their land was a few miles to the north in South Armagh. Although in normal times they played their full part in the community and were, indeed, valuable local employees, when the wind blew the other way, some saw them, as 'legitimate' targets, and the Eastwoods knew this .... Indeed less than 20 years prior one of them James Robert Eastwood was murdered in Dundalk! Such was the importance of this Anglo-Irish family, that this case was reported in the *Times* on July 4th, 1835:

" DREADFUL MURDER IN LOUTH. An inquest was held in Dundalk on Sunday and Monday on the body of James Robert Eastwood, a tithe and rent collector, who died in the Louth Hospital on Sunday morning. He had been employed on Wednesday last by the agent of Robert Hall, Esq.; to sell some goods detained for rent at Carrickedmond, about two miles from Dundalk. After the sale, the deceased, the agent, and several of the tenants, adjourned to a public house, where they drank rather freely. All of them appeared in good humour, with the exception of one person, who alleged that Eastwood had treated him ill, some

---

41 Three men were hanged for their parts in the crime at Monaghan on April 10th, 1854: the last execution at Monaghan.

time before, regarding the payment of the tithe, which the deceased had been in the habit of collecting. Eastwood, it is stated, was rather tipsy, but not unable to transact his business. On his way home to Dundalk, about 5 o'clock in the evening, he was met by four men armed with sticks, who came from the adjoining fields, where a great number of the peasantry were collected. They knocked him down and beat him in a most brutal manner. Scarcely an inch of his body was free from contusions, and his hands, in an ineffectual effort to preserve his head, were beaten to pieces. The unfortunate victim was, however, able to reach the gatehouse of the Rev. Gervais Tinlay, at Fort Hill, from whence he was conveyed in the gentleman's jaunting car to the Louth Hospital. This shocking outrage occurred in a very thickly inhabited part of the country; and although it was witnessed by a number of persons, 13 of whom were examined at the inquest, yet not one could be induced to discover the perpetrators of the murder. Under these circumstances, the verdict of the jury was: "Wilful murder by persons unknown."

In December 1851 the new incumbent of *Castletown House* was **54-year-old James Eastwood**. He was described as a 'typical Victorian country gentleman who gave to many charitable works'. He was particularly interested in education and was involved with the churches in the running of the infant school in Dundalk. His income came mainly from his land and unlike many landlords of that period he was described as "not unpopular" among his tenants. But the Eastwoods were not just Unionists they were from a different class, and this new Mr Eastwood wished to *appear* to maintain a distance from his tenants and employees: rather than have them call to his house with their rent, he had a "hatch" installed for this purpose beside his gate. This, now blocked up, window can still be seen today (see photo). However when he was sure no-one was around Mr Eastwood would talk to the 'humblest persons'. The Famine (and it was only just ending in 1851) had caused an even greater tension throughout Ireland between tenants and their landlords and it was against these backgrounds that James Eastwood walked from Dundalk to Castletown on the afternoon of **Wednesday, December 24th, 1851, Christmas Eve** ....

At about four-twenty pm Mr Eastwood was approaching a farm and orchard of his about ¾ of a mile from his house. Aptly enough it was on the Castleblayney Road and going across the fields this led into the gardens of *Castletown House*. The landlord often went this way as a short cut. It was a very isolated place – apart from the farm, *Castletown House*, and a small school, the nearest place was the country house of Lord Roden. Mr Eastwood climbed over a style at the entrance to the farm and orchard and once through the farm, he could then see his house just a few hundred yards away. However he was now aware that three men were following him, and he had been aware of them before on the main road out of the town …. Mr Eastwood knew the men wanted to speak to him and they appeared angry, but he was after all, a member of the 'ruling class', so he stopped and asked them what they wanted; it was imperative he showed no obvious signs of fear …

The men started swearing at him. Then worst was to come – he was attacked with sticks and stones; kicked and punched. Mr Eastwood considered himself a fair landlord and didn't think the 'talk' in Dundalk would amount to anything and so he wasn't armed - all he had to defend himself with, was …. his umbrella. It was useless and the men continued their attack. Badly beaten he was thrown unconscious into a quarry – there is no doubt the men thought he was dead – that had been their plan; but fortunately the quarry was only three feet in depth. At four-thirty, a passing teenager, Richard Loudin, saw Mr Eastwood in the quarry, but fearing the consequences of helping he went on: furthermore it was dark by now and later the boy said he thought the man was a drunk. Fortunately just a few minutes later a farm employee came to fetch some milk. She saw the umbrella and immediately recognised it as belonging to Mr Eastwood. She thought he had dropped it, but then she saw the man in the quarry. He had been so badly beaten that she did not realise who it was and his speech was so badly impaired by the assault, that she thought he said his name was 'Mr Reed'.

Like the boy earlier this woman thought the man drunk and that he had fallen into the quarry and so she initially refused to help. Summoning up, what he thought must have been his last breath, he shouted out: "Mr Eastwood" and the woman replied: "Are you the master?" When he replied affirmatively, she went into the quarry and helped the victim to sit up. Despite a policy of dignified distance between master and employee, Mr Eastwood recognised the woman and that she had been working on his estate for some 20 years. She then went off to fetch help and returned with some men, including the teenager, from the farm and he was carried into his house, blood dripping from several wounds, and where he was met by his wife. The family doctor and another from Dundalk, Drs Pollock and Edward Brunker were soon at *Castletown House*. Mr Eastwood had suffered three severe wounds to the side of the head, and his skull was fractured; his right ear split and the right side of his face was badly swollen. The landlord was hopelessly incoherent and it was feared he would soon die. On undressing him the doctors could see that Mr Eastwood had also been robbed – his gold watch had been wrenched from its chain that he was still wearing; but it was damaged showing that it had been violently pulled. He did have some coins on him. He had been in the town selling a cow, but the proceeds had been banked. At the scene of the crime was a large pool of blood and a stone, large and oval, covered in blood and with hairs attached to it ….

There was a genuine shock in Dundalk over the attack – this Mr Eastwood, whilst maintaining an aloofness, was thought of as a good and even kind employer – labourers on the quarry farm earned the princely sum of 6s 9d a week, way above the average for Ireland. He was also forward-thinking and had been trying to build a manufacturing base on his land and was a keen advocate of women's and children's rights, employing many females in a small clothing factory. And of course every Christmas he would distribute money to the local poor.

However he was also a businessman and in the previous August he had been to court to evict half-a-dozen families from his land in South Armagh, for rent arrears. Indeed it was said in court that some had not paid any rent for years.

Over the coming days as Mr Eastwood regained his facilities he said the three men said they wanted to speak to him about the August evictions. He said they went a bit further into the fields, so they could look back passed him to see if there was anyone on the main road into the town. Then the attack began. Fortunately Mr Eastwood was making excellent progress, but for many months, he was still described as being in a 'critical condition.' For the Government in Dublin two such cases in such a small area meant something had to be done quickly. A £100 Reward was immediately offered; extra police were drafted into Dundalk, whilst the mainly Unionist press in Dublin demanded 'repressive measures'. However the authorities were already moving quickly – they had an informer. With this apparent evidence three local men, **James Kirk (50), Patrick McCooey (35) and Thomas Belton (23) stood trial at the Dundalk Assizes in the following July, before Mr Justice Greene**. The trial opened on the **Tuesday, the sixth** and such was the importance that the government placed on the case, the men faced both the **Attorney and Solicitor-Generals for Ireland** - **Sir Joseph Napier and James Whiteside**. The men were charged with attempted murder, still then at this time, a capital offence throughout Britain and Ireland.

It was clear the men regarded the attack on Mr Eastwood as 'political': they all refused to recognise the court to the extent they would not participate in the jury selection; but as it was a capital case they would use the services of a barrister to defend them. Overall the case would last three days, as since the men would not take part in the jury selection, each would be tried separately, with Kirk first. Sir John said the prosecution would pay for the men's defence and James Kirk said he would like a Mr Gartlan, a somewhat strange choice as he was a Crown Prosecutor for the county. Summoned to the court, the prosecutor said he did not wish to defend prisoners and he was excused. He did, however, suggest a Mr McMahon. He too declined. The men had already asked him, offering him a sum, smaller than that now offered by the Crown. Plus he did not think he would have enough time to prepare an adequate defence. Next a Mr Dickie refused – one of the prosecution witnesses was employed by him! He fully admitted to being prejudiced against the prisoners as this witness had told him a great deal about the case! Pressured by the judge, eventually Mr Dickie agreed to help and said a Mr McMeehan would do the job ….

But still the trial could not commence. After twelve men had been picked for the jury, a shout went out that one of them was a minor – he wasn't eighteen and furthermore, he wasn't the person he claimed to be. Looking at the person, the Attorney-General agreed he could not sit on a capital case. This young lad now admitted he wasn't even the person on the jury list, but his son – he had done this as his father had not turned up at the court and would therefore be fined. A new juror was called, but Mr McMeehan said this was illegal as the boy had sworn the oath and whilst eighteen may have been a guideline there was no law preventing someone other than an 'obvious' child being a juryman. It was agreed that the boy, Henry Parker, would be on the jury.

Sir John said that the main evidence against Kirk would be that of an informer, Owen Hamill and, of course, to some extent the testimony of the victim himself. Mr Eastwood told Mr Whiteside that he'd suffered greatly for three to four months and even now he could not fully recount what had happened at the quarry – he could not now even describe his attackers; but he did say that the watch was definitely his. Although cross-examined by Mr McMeehan, nothing in his evidence could be seen to actually incriminate any of the men. The stone was also produced in court and the two doctors agreed that the hairs attached corresponded to that of Mr Eastwood. It was now that the Attorney-General told of the arrest of the men and he called the informer, Hamill ….

Hamill said he knew all the men and he had, himself, lived in Dundalk for the last two years. He said on December 23rd, he had cooked McCooey's evening meal and later he met him and Kirk. He said on Christmas Eve he met all the accused by a smoky railway bridge in the town in the morning, where he said McCooey told him: "We have met that man, but he had a steward and dog with him." Hamill said he then saw the men later on at four-thirty pm – Hamill was asked to be a witness by the men. He claimed Belton said: "We left the man settled." He said Belton described the gold-watch and showed it to Hamill, and it had the victim's name on it - Hamill was ordered to keep the watch and that he would be contacted later. Hamill claimed, he could see blood on Belton's hand and that the latter had then wiped it off ….. The informer went on to say that on the day before the attack he had seen Kirk and McCooey in Dundalk and they were shouting in the street. Hamill said they should be quiet or the police would arrest them. He said Kirk said the men were on a 'job', adding: "I am going up for Thomas Belton; and we are going to shoot Mr Eastwood." Asked why, Kirk referred to the recent evictions. Hamill then went and fetched Belton for Kirk. Hamill said on the early afternoon of Christmas Eve he also saw Kirk, and two other men, strangers, and these men were discussing using pistols and whether any of them had any usable shot. Despite a fierce cross-examination by Mr McMeehan, Hamill stuck to his story ….

In his address to the jury, the judge said they must solely concern themselves to the facts not the *consequences* of a guilty verdict. He said that in law, attempted murder, had been committed – whoever attacked Mr Eastwood intended to kill him. After two hours the jury found James Kirk guilty of attempted murder, but they recommended him to mercy due to the prosecution's use of an informer. The judge said he would take note of it, but it could not be part of his sentencing decision. The next day **[July 7th]** Patrick McCooey was put on trial ….

Once again the trial was caught up in the legal arguments over jurors. Using the threats of fines, the prosecution had a reasonable amount of men to choose from, but they wanted the jury from the Kirk case! Mr McMeehan vehemently opposed this but the Solicitor-General said in law this was a *separate* case, but sensing the case could be delayed he agreed to 12 new men, but he managed to obtain a majority of them from an apparent Unionist background. The evidence was broadly the same but it was clear from the direction of Sir John's arguments, that the prosecution would say it was Kirk and McCooey who had actually inflicted the life-threatening wounds on the victim. This time the jury was out for just *five* minutes and there was no recommendation to mercy …. And so it was onto the trial of Thomas Belton **[July 8th]** ….

Mr Whiteside said he felt it his duty to inform the court that whilst he believed Thomas Belton to be guilty of attempted murder, in law, since he would not put forward evidence that Belton actually *struck* the victim, he could not be guilty of a *capital* offence. The jury were out for ten minutes – they also found Belton guilty of attempted murder. All three men were then sentenced. Since Kirk and McCooey were deemed to be the actually attackers then the judge could do nothing but impose the death sentence. As regard Belton, the maximum he could receive was a life sentence, which the judge imposed due to the 'aggravating nature of the crime'. James Eastwood made an emotional plea to have the death sentence commuted but an execution date was set for **Saturday, July 31st, 1852 at mid-day**. Ironically near to the quarry was being built a new prison, but the execution, if carried out, would be in front of the old gaol in Crowe Street in the town centre.

The **Lord Lieutenant, Archibald William Montgomerie, 13th Earl of Eglinton, KT, PC**, decided there could be no reprieve. Unlike in England, public executions in Ireland, did not attract large crowds – many intentionally stayed away. In this case given the 'political' dimensions many refused to watch but instead would follow the funeral cortèges, as since the men had not been guilty of *murder*, their families would be allowed to bury them. By ten am a large body of the police were in the town, with a back up of lancers should the need arise. At daybreak the men were visited by two Catholic clergy – both had slept soundly during the night. For over two hours the men prayed and then ate a good breakfast, although the crust of the bread was cut off, in case the men should choke on them! After breakfast there were more prayers. The police lined up in double file in front of the gallows and also used their numbers to close off streets. Nearly all the shops in the town-centre shut in protest over the execution. It seemed that the only people who wanted to witness the hangings were 'country folk'. At eleven am the Under-Sheriff of Louth went into the condemned cells, but the priests had not finished their work and it was not until 12:10 pm that the men were lead to a room, which would then lead onto the drop. There they met the hangman, who incredibly seemed just a lad. He had come from **Queen's County [County Laoise] and for 'obvious reasons' his name was not made public and he wore a black mask**. Using leather straps and buckles he pinioned the two men before allowing them a few more minutes of prayer.

The rope used for the execution had been made in Cork Prison. White hoods over their heads Kirk and McCooey were lead onto the scaffold. It had been said that McCooey had been responsible for many murders over the years in County Louth, but he denied this. He also denied that there ever was a *plan* to murder Mr Eastwood, but he did not deny attacking him. His final words were: "I ask you to have nothing to do with secret parties or Ribbonism." He then claimed it was *Hamill* who had organised the whole plot! Kirk said nothing. The lever was pulled; the men fell together; in less than 10 seconds they were dead – Kirk's body had twitched momentarily. The bodies were left for 45 minutes, then taken inside the prison before being handed over to the respective families. Ironically it was Dr Brunker who examined the corpses! Outside the prison the police were determined that there be no demonstrations en route to the churchyard and there were no subsequent disorders. By three o'clock the men were buried, the gallows dismantled **and it turned out to be the last execution in Dundalk**. Indeed it was the first for nearly 25 years – In March 1828 a man and woman had been hanged for separate murders. **And what of Dundalk Prison …. ?**

This prison finally shut in 1854 to be replaced by a new one – the one by the quarry. In 1915 it was taken over by the Army and during the Civil War (1922-3) the new Irish Army used it as a base and **six IRA men were executed there; the last on January 22nd, 1923**. The prison closed in 1931. **And what of James Eastwood …..**

James Eastwood died childless in 1865 and was buried in the family vault at Creggan in South Armagh. His widow, Louisa, inherited much of his estate. At this time the majority of landlords were experiencing financial difficulty in Ireland and the Eastwoods were no exception and much of the estate had to be sold off in 1868 to pay off creditors. James' will gives us a good insight into his character. He left money for the establishment of an industrial school for girls with a religious plaque inscribed over the door. Some £75 was to be given to a missionary society to preach the gospel in Dundalk and missionaries were to be given the use of land at Castletown for a yearly rent of just one shilling. Another £10 per annum was to be made available "for a mistress of a good spiritual school in Castletown" and £5 was provided for books for a library at

Castletown. The will also stipulated that no public house was to be allowed on his property!

The two men were to be the penultimate execution for attempted murder in Ireland – the last was a week later in Armagh ….

Case 22
-"Horror at John-
de-Bois Cottages"-

"If I am locked up, it will not be for nothing, and she will know of it" ..... *" ..... I cannot stand her nagging any longer: she is a complete devil."*- Alleged to have been said by the prisoner about his wife who had left him a week earlier.

Frederick Southgate (52)
Murder
Of
His Wife, Elizabeth (58)[42]
[1924]

---

42 Her age is given variously at between '50 and 60': BDM has 58 which is what I've used.

THE ARDLEIGH MURDER.

EXECUTION OF SOUTHGATE.

The above is a photograph of Southgate and his wife on their wedding day.
Frederick Southgate, the Ardleigh labourer,

Frederick Southgate & The Victim

In the Summer of 1924 a tiny hamlet in Essex witnessed a shockingly brutal murder of a woman by her husband, from whom she had separated the week before on the grounds of his 'persistent cruelty' – the man was disarmed by a brave 16-year-old boy before fleeing on a bike to a mental home, where he was arrested by the police. Since executions had ended at Chelmsford Prison, the husband was hanged at Ipswich Prison, the last ever execution there …..

Midway between Colchester and Manningtree in Essex, on the A137, lies the village of Ardleigh and less than two miles from it back towards Colchester, is the hamlet of John-de-Bois Hill, said to be of Norman origin. In the Summer of 1924, two of the inhabitants were a married couple,

Frederick Southgate (52) and his wife Elizabeth who was six years older than him. The woman had been married before and was relatively wealthy, owning three cottages in the hamlet: her husband, who was just 5' 3" tall, on the other hand, was a farm labourer and gardener, who also worked as a road-worker in Colchester. The couple lived in one of the properties, John-de-Bois Cottages near the village pub, the *Fox & Hounds*. Unfortunately the couple did not get on well and eventually Mrs Southgate had taken out a summons against her husband for 'persistent cruelty'. The magistrates granted a separation order and instructed Southgate to pay five shillings a week to his wife. It was clear Elizabeth wanted rid of her husband and on **Saturday, July 26th, 1924,** put all his belongings outside their home ….

That evening at about eight-thirty pm, Frederick Southgate demanded that he be let into the cottage but his wife refused. The commotion was heard in the hamlet and minutes later Southgate was seen jumping on his bike and leaving in the direction of Colchester. Something dreadful appeared to have happened at John-de-Bois Cottages and shouts went up to stop Southgate. The police-station in Ardleigh was alerted and officers began scouring the countryside for him. However soon afterwards a man appeared at a mental asylum at Severalls in the Mile End area of Colchester, claiming to have lost his memory ….

Meanwhile back in John-de-Bois, Mrs Southgate was dead – a long (7 ¼ inches) butcher's knife had been thrust, with great force, in between her shoulders. She had tried to run for safety to a neighbour's cottage, but had been attacked near a water butt and died almost immediately. At the age of 22 the victim had been left a widow with seven children to look after: two sons had been killed in the war and one daughter killed in an air-raid. In 1920 for purely practical reasons she married Frederick Southgate who had been a lodger of hers at her home in Colchester, and unemployed at the time. But Southgate was not going to play the role of the grateful husband and demanded control over her bank account, which Elizabeth refused ….

In 1921 Mrs Southgate bought the three cottages in John-de-Bois, but the couple were very unhappy living together in Colchester, eventually moving in to John-de-Bois Cottages in April 1924. The villagers thought the pair oddly matched – she had money, kept her home spotless, and the husband was a road-worker and very untidy. When it became clear to the villagers that all was not well, Southgate began telling them his wife was "carrying on" with another man, which few believed. After the separation order Southgate had to move out of the cottage, and had been lodging in Ardleigh. On July 13th, he had punched his wife and a neighbour, a Mr Robert Bruce, had had to rescue Mrs Southgate. After the separation order, Southgate had written to his wife saying he wouldn't do it again, pleading: "For God's sack write back to me", adding that he had only ever "wiped her down" the once. Under arrest in the police-station, Southgate was alleged to have said: "I did not know what I was doing when I struck the blow. I did not do it with the intention to kill, but only to frighten her." A few days later was Mrs Southgate's funeral. Somewhat sadly there were no mourners, only her solicitor being present and his was the only wreath too.

Frederick Southgate appeared at the **Chelmsford Assizes on Thursday, November 6th, 1924 before Mr Justice Swift in a trial that lasted just one day.** The prisoner was dressed as if he had just done a day's work on a farm and he pleaded 'not guilty' to the murder charge. **Mr Cecil Whiteley, KC, (assisted by Mr Ansley) for the prosecution**, in outlining the case, said that the son of their neighbours, 16-year-old John Bruce, whose parents were out at the time, had bravely seized Southgate's arm and forced the knife out of his hand and onto the ground. A few days before the attack Southgate had bought a butcher's knife in Colchester. Mrs Bruce said that the couple were always arguing, mainly about food rather than money, but it was Southgate who was the more argumentative, and a fellow worker on a local farm said the accused had a "nasty temper", although he was never drunk. To another work colleague, Southgate said that he'd become depressed over the court order and the prisoner had added: "If I am locked up, it will not be for nothing, and she will know of it", further adding: "I might knock her." At his new lodgings his landlady told the court that Southgate kept asking if any letter had arrived for him.

John Bruce graphically told the court of the stabbing. He was sitting on the back step cleaning a cycle lamp, when he began talking to Mrs Southgate in the back gardens, when the prisoner came to the garden gate asking to speak to his wife, to which she'd replied: "Go away: you have no right to be here." Nevertheless she did go to the gate, although only to tell Southgate to leave. Southgate ignored this and opened the gate. To the boy's shock he then chased his wife manically waving the butcher's knife in the air. Within a few feet of the cottages the prisoner plunged the knife into his wife's back and the boy bravely seized Southgate's arm. John Bruce tried to hold onto Southgate but he broke free and fled on his bike. He told the court that Southgate appeared "astonished and terrified" that his wife appeared to be dead. The boy then carried Mrs Southgate's body into his kitchen before running to the village police-station. The next day the police found the murder weapon in a field next to the cottages. A Dr Robert Erskine told the jury that the knife had penetrated through the victim's clothing and into the skin to a depth of 1 ½ inches causing an immediate haemorrhaging and immediate death: the aorta was completely penetrated.

A brother of the prisoner, Robert Southgate told the court that the accused had been very unwell recently. He had been suffering from fainting fits and he had been constantly complaining about his head. A Mr James Emms of the Severalls Asylum said that Southgate had turned up at 9.15 pm saying his memory had gone but also that he had 'killed someone'. Mr Emms immediately called the police and had Southgate detained. When taken away by the police, one officer found a letter in his jacket, addressed to his brother Robert, which said: "Everything I have belongs to you and my brother Edgar. I cannot stand her nagging any longer: she is a complete devil."

Dr William Fryer, the Medical Officer at Ipswich Prison, where Southgate was held on remand, told the court that he could find no evidence of insanity. He said the prisoner had complained of headaches and was suffering from sleeplessness, which he had received medication for from the doctor, and in August had not been able to appear at the magistrates hearing as he was taken seriously ill. Asked by the prisoner's **defence barrister, Mr E.A. Digby**, whether

Southgate was suffering from 'temporary insanity', the doctor said he was not sure, saying that going to the mental home could be a sign of it, but it could equally be part of a premeditated plan to *appear* insane. At this point Mr Justice Swift interjected asking whether there was not some confusion between insanity and 'bad temper', to which the doctor agreed that, that was often the case.

Mr Digby declined to call any expert medical witnesses to say that Southgate was insane instead he addressed the jury directly saying that the murder was "committed in the heat of the moment." As to any threats before the crime, he suggested that, they were far from a real intention to kill and the butcher's knife had been bought some days before the crime took place. Furthermore Southgate had to pass his old home on his way back from work to his lodgings in Ardleigh and he suggested that he had the knife to merely *threaten* his wife into her having him back, however reprehensible that might be, although the prosecution had pointed out that there was no legitimate reason why the prisoner had bought the knife, known colloquially as a 'sticking' knife, in the first place. Mr Digby posed the question of whether a man could be guilty of murder even if the act he had done, he believed would not kill.

In his summing up Mr Justice Swift said that although Frederick Southgate had pleaded 'not guilty', on the evidence before the jury and after what his own defence barrister had said, it was clear that a defence of manslaughter and/or insanity had been put forward. As to the first point the jury would have to consider whether plunging a butcher's knife into someone was an intent to cause 'serious harm' – if it were, then that was murder. Secondly on the question of insanity the jury would have to believe that Southgate did not know what he was doing. The jury, which included three women, retired for just 20 minutes before finding the prisoner guilty of murder, although they added a recommendation to mercy, the foreman saying: "We think the murder was committed under great provocation[43]." Southgate appeared unmoved having heard the death sentence, and then with a quick step, was taken from the dock.

---

43 Although provocation was never put forward by the defence!

Frederick Southgate decided not to appeal and the date of execution was set for **Thursday, November 27th, 1924. Because there were no longer facilities at Chelmsford Prison to carry out executions, the decision was taken to hang Southgate at Ipswich Prison**. Although the **Home Secretary, Mr William Joynson-Hicks** received information that there had been evidence, not presented at the trial, of insanity in the condemned man's family history, he was informed that the Home Office appointed doctors did not believe Southgate was insane. Furthermore although the judge had originally informed the Home Office that he agreed with the jury's recommendation to mercy, having been visited by Whitehall officials he changed his mind. At nine am on the appointed day Frederick Southgate was duly executed, there being just a few people outside the prison gates. **The hangman was Robert Baxter and his assistant Robert Wilson**[44]. Indeed after the execution one juryman asked why the hanging had not been carried out in Essex, to which the Coroner replied that he could or would not answer the question. Furthermore the same juryman asked why the prisoner had been executed when a jury of 12 had recommended mercy. The Coroner at first did not want to answer but then added he was sure the matter had been fully gone into. Before any more questions could be asked, the jury foreman stepped in, saying that the prisoner had been executed "according to law."

Frederick Southgate was the last person executed at Ipswich Prison. In 1925 the prison was closed and the male prisoners were transferred to Norwich. The prison was demolished in the 1930, although part of the site survived at the County Council's office buildings.

---

44 The first choice of assistant had been Seth Mills from South Wales but he could not obtain time off work

Case 23
"A Killer Resigned To His Fate"

"I am going to die for a bad woman, you know." The killer to a prison-officer on the steps of the gallows ….

"It's jolly funny she has not." - The prisoner asking why his dead wife had not come to visit him in hospital!

John Eayrs (59)
[1914]
Murder
Of
His wife Mrs Sarah Ann Eayrs (53)

THE CONDEMNED MAN.

John Eayrs

The First World War was just weeks old and the local newspapers throughout the land were full of stories of German atrocities in Belgium, when after a series of domestic rows and fights, John Eayrs turned on his wife chasing her with a razor ....

John Eayrs (59) and his wife Sarah Ann, who was six years younger, lived at 4, School Place, Albert Place in Peterborough[45] city-centre. A tinsmith, Eayrs had only married his wife, a widow, some three years ago and he now bitterly regretted it. To one friend, a Mr Thomas Hawksworth, he said that unless she changed her ways he would have to do something 'desperate' about it, although his friend dismissed it, as the drink talking once again. However Mr Hawksworth kept his thoughts to himself as both of the couple were alcoholics and they frequently argued with each other, although when free from drink they were pleasant enough, and Mrs Eayrs had a job herself working in various local pubs and city hotels as a cook. Their neighbours across the street, the Griffins, were well aware of the couple – they heard them often enough, and on one occasion Mrs Elizabeth Griffin heard Eayrs shout out: "I will do her in before the night is out." Later she saw Mrs Eayrs at her window sticking her tongue out at her husband. Eayrs had complained to neighbours that his wife was pawning their belongings for drink and that the house was filthy.

As most people knew and certainly had heard Eayrs and his wife, when on **Saturday, August 22nd, 1914,** between five and five-thirty pm, one local, Mr Harry Masters saw them apparently fighting on the street he didn't think too much of it, although the pair did not *seem* drunk. After they'd stopped hitting each other, Mrs Eayrs

---

45 Until 1965 Peterborough was part of Northamptonshire: now it is in Cambridgeshire.

laughed at her husband and he replied: "All right you bugger. You will get all you want before morning." She then shouted out to the neighbours: "Don't believe the old liar. I caught him with a woman." As one neighbour told the police, the Eayrs' led a 'cat and dog life'. However Eayrs didn't wait until later that night, as about an hour later at seven pm, Mr Masters heard the sound of breaking glass and then saw Mrs Eayrs running out of the house and into the backyard quickly followed by her husband ….

Approximately 2 ½ hours later at about 9.40 pm another neighbour, a Mr William Rodgers said he could hear moaning coming from the Eayrs' backyard – and he too had heard the couple arguing before at tea-time. Everyone was somewhat used to the Eayrs' anti-social behaviour but what Mr Rodgers saw was truly shocking – Mr Eayrs was lying on the ground having suffered a wound to his throat; his trousers half way down his legs. Neighbours, led by Mr Rodgers, quickly called out into the street and moments later a patrolling officer, Constable Frederick Powley came rushing to the house, followed quickly by a number of other policemen. The officers quickly determined that the wound to Eayrs, whilst it looked quite shocking, was, in fact, superficial and that he smelt of drink. They too were aware of the domestic problems at number four and so quickly looked around the yard ….

Just a short distance away from the back of the house was the outside toilet. The door was slightly ajar and on opening the door the officers found the body of Mrs Eayrs, who was fully-clothed: she was lying face down in a pool of blood and was quite dead: her throat had been slashed open and she had three bruises to the forehead, and her fingers had been badly cut as if she had been trying to defend herself. Inside the kitchen Constable Powley found a bloodstained razor as well as a coat and jacket belonging to Eayrs that were also bloodstained. A Dr Robert Jolly, the police-surgeon, who carried out a *post-mortem*, pointed out to the police that the wound to the throat extended down to the breast bone some six inches– once the throat had been cut the knife had been dragged down towards the breasts, severing the main arteries and veins. The doctor confirmed what Constable Powley thought, namely that the wound to Eayrs was not serious and most probably inflicted with a pen-knife, and one was found on the prisoner. He also told police that Mrs Eayrs' stomach was free of, and the smell of, drink.

John Eayrs was immediately interviewed by the police in hospital and he told a Detective-Sergeant William Smith that he and his wife had been arguing since Friday night "over a ha'penny". However he claimed she came at him with a knife and even 'worse' had refused to make his tea. During the quarrel Eayrs claimed his wife threw a sugar-basin at him and hit him on the head and one was, indeed, found lying broken on the floor. Then looking straight into the eyes of Detective-Sergeant Smith, Eayrs said: "I can't tell you anything more after that, because I don't know anything." Both Mr Rodgers and the police had gone straight into the backyard and didn't enter the house through a side-door which had been forced open with a stool, although the house itself was unlocked, although Mrs Eayrs had locked herself in. Eayrs himself told the police that after his wife had thrown the sugar-basin at him she went outside via the side-door and he never saw her again. He said the next thing he could remember was being in hospital. Police notes from the hospital revealed that the first thing Eayrs said to officers, was asking if his wife had been to see him yet! When told 'no' he then added: "It's jolly funny she has not." It seems that it was not until August 28th that Eayrs realised his wife was dead, unless of course he was trying to deceive the police ….

John Eayrs appeared at the **Northampton Assizes on Wednesday, October 21st, 1914 before Mr Justice Avory in a trial that lasted just a few hours. The prosecution was undertook by Mr C.E. Dyer and Mr Drysdale Woodcock; the prisoner was defended by Mr Bernard Campion**. There was drama in the court when Eayrs did not enter a plea simply saying: "I know nothing at all about it!" Following a glance from Mr Campion the accused then quickly said: "Not guilty!" In the witness-box Eayrs was asked by Mr Dyer if he had ever threatened his wife, but he replied he hadn't or couldn't remember and had absolutely no idea how her throat came to have been slashed. The prosecutor said that given the large amount of blood by the sink in the kitchen, as well as a bloodstained flannel, it was quite likely that the attack on Mrs Eayrs started there and she then staggered into the outside toilet. It was on the kitchen window-ledge that the bloodstained razor was found and there were no blood splashes inside the toilet.

Mr Campion asked Dr Jolly about Eayrs as he was also his family doctor and he confirmed that the prisoner had suffered a blow to the head some years back and suffered from dizzy spells, caused by ageing of the arteries or high blood pressure. He also agreed that Eayrs had suffered a recent blow above his left eye, which the doctor agreed could have come from a blunt instrument. He also told the jury that any threats that Eayrs had made about his wife should not be taken seriously as they were common in that area of Peterborough at the time. He suggested that this was a case of manslaughter; after his wife had thrown the sugar-basin at Eayrs he chased her around the kitchen, slashing her throat before chasing her outside into the toilet and that he had attacked her without thinking what he was doing. Mr Campion said that the assault on the prisoner was sufficient to prove 'provocation'. He added that although Eayrs had suffered from dizzy-spells the defence would not wish to say that he was insane.

In his summing-up Mr Justice Avory told the jury that the law of provocation was naturally open to interpretation. He suggested that if Eayrs had struck his wife immediately after having been assaulted that would be manslaughter, but in this case the prisoner then went and found a lethal weapon and pursued his wife around the kitchen and then cut her throat. The judge's advice to the jury was that this was completely disproportionate to the initial assault, which of course, the jury only had Eayrs' word for, that it actually took place. The jury seemed to have completely dismissed Eayrs' version of events. Retiring at 3.45 pm, they were out for just ten minutes before finding him guilty of murder and they added no recommendation to mercy, which many observers in the court thought they may have done, as this was quite common in 'domestic' murders, in the era of capital punishment. Eayrs was seen to swoon in the dock and was unable to speak properly as the death sentence was about to be pronounced. It duly was – the judge saying he fully agreed with the verdict.

John Eayrs declined to appeal and the execution date was set for **eight am on Tuesday, November 10th at Northampton Prison**. The **Home Secretary, Mr Reginald McKenna** took the view that the victim had been pursued and that Eayrs had been *determined* to kill her. Eayrs walked unassisted to the gallows where he was met by the **hangmen, John Ellis and William Willis**. Indeed on the way he stopped and said 'good morning' to one prison-officer. A few steps later and as he was about to mount the scaffold he turned to the same officer and said: "I am going to die for a bad woman, you know." Ten seconds later John Eayrs was dead, all that was visible to the watching officials and pressmen was a white hood slightly tilted to one side. Indeed the whole episode was over in 30 seconds and the drop given was five feet. Eayrs died in the same drab suit that he had appeared at the assizes in.

The condemned cell at Northampton Prison was usually used to house the prison van and was just a matter of yards away from the death-cell, fifteen at the most. The prison authorities had taken the precaution of shrouding the building with a large screen in case anyone in the town was able to look into the prison from a vantage point outside. During his period in the death-cell Eayrs seemed quite resigned to his fate, almost longing for death: he ate and slept well. And as with many a man in the condemned cell he eventually took some interest in what the religious personages had to say to him. On the morning of his execution John Eayrs ate a full breakfast and spent an hour talking with the Chaplain, the Rev. J. Evan-Hopkins. There was a large crowd outside the prison, who when the bells of a local church chimed eight, they began to disperse. Ninety minutes later after the body of Eayrs had been cut down an inquest was held in the prison and it was noticeable that Eayrs' face had the same expressionless features that he had displayed in life at his trial.

John Eayrs was the last person executed at Northampton Prison, which closed in March 1922 and was demolished in 1931.

Case 24
"The Death of Constable Ebenezer Tye – A Case of Murder ?"

~Hanged for a Bale of Hay ~

John Ducker (63)
[1862-3]
Murder
Of
Constable Ebenezer Tye (24)

" .... all police-officers, and all ministers of justice are protected, and if killed under circumstances which, were they only private individuals, would make the crime that of manslaughter, the killing of these persons, even though it be involuntary, amounts to the crime of wilful murder ...." The Coroner ....

" .... that it was to be a policeman's death that was to be accounted for .... It would be in a certain sense highly dishonourable to them as a body, if they could not avenge their comrade's fall, and it could easily be believed that the police would be in such a case, induced to show an activity, which perhaps they would hardly show in other cases .... " Was this really a case of murder .... ?

".... this sad event should be a warning to Constables and others against excess of zeal in discharge of their duty .... we may lament the consequences, which ensued from an attempt which was (in this case) unnecessary!" A letter in the *Ipswich Journal* just after the execution of John Ducker ....

Intriguing case from Suffolk in the early 1860s of a man, who if he had told the truth would have probably been convicted of manslaughter; but who, instead told a number of lies, and falsely accused a neighbour, and so who, ended up on the gallows ....

Notes:

There are 3 Benjamin Warnes – aged 76; 44; and 22 – *snr* **and** *jnr* **are the latter two [44 and 22] .... Stephen Warne (48) is the brother then of Warne** *snr* **....**

Clothes (Ducker's):

Mon a/noon – HW says JD has a pair of drabbett trousers on and drabbett waistcoat; no coat

Tues morning – (Later morning) HW says JD was wearing clothes he would be arrested in (therefore the drabbett trousers must have been the ones under the cushion (see below)); FS says there is a spot of blood on JD's waistcoat (JD says he lent a waistcoat to BW the night before).... HW says it is a different w/coat to the one on Mon .... (Earlier morning) HT says JD was wearing a coat and drabbett trousers ....

Tues evening – JD shows a suit to the police; old pair of trousers under cushion (they smell and have traces of mud and weeds on them)

Wed morning – pair of leggings; coat and boots – all bore traces of mud and weeds

"**T**he deceased was in full uniform with his greatcoat on. He had no belt or cutlass on, and he had no staff or handcuffs about him ....."; so said Sergeant Daniel Taylor, at the inquest into the death of a colleague, **Constable Ebenezer Tye (24)**, who had died during the early hours of **Tuesday, November 25th, 1862**. The slightly built officer had been in the force for only sixteen months; the last seven of which, he had spent in the small mid-**Suffolk town of Halesworth**; but he was well known in the town, where he had established a reputation as a fair, but above all, fearless young officer. Regard for him was enhanced after he was seriously beaten by two men, whom he had interrupted while robbing a barn; an intervention for which he was subsequently commended by the courts. The Monday evening started normally enough for Constable Tye. He was on night-duty, so a little before ten pm, he went to the town's police-station, where he met Sergeant Taylor and Constable William Lucas: the trio would patrol

Halesworth that night. The three men had a short discussion, during which Constable Tye was told by the sergeant to watch the house of one **John Ducker (63)**. He lived in **Clarke's Yard off Chediston Street,** and was 'well-known' to the police as a 'professional criminal': the sergeant hoped to see him return from some illegal nocturnal venture. It was agreed that after patrolling in the town, Constable Tye should then keep observation from five am until breakfast time on Ducker. Constable Lucas meanwhile would continue patrolling in the town ….

John Ducker was a familiar figure in Halesworth and the surrounding countryside. Local people were used to seeing his stocky and powerful figure, and many were frightened of him …. As a younger man he had been a well-known wrestler; but now he worked as a hay-trusser at the business of a local corn-merchant Thompson George. Several times Ducker had been spotted returning home in the small hours — indicating, to the police, at least, that he had some illegal means of supplementing his low agricultural wages. However this night seemed to be about to pass off uneventfully …. Both Sergeant Taylor and Constable Lucas had suggested to their colleague, that he wear a pair of galoshes before commencing his watch on Ducker's house …. to deaden the sound of his footsteps. Constable Lucas twice spoke briefly to his colleague, the second time at quarter-past four, five minutes before he went off duty ….

At about 5.40 am, soon after John Winter, a labourer on his way to work, had said 'good morning' to Constable Tye, the officer became aware of Ducker's approach …. He heard his uneven-sounding footsteps – the consequence of a hard and bruising life, that had left Ducker with a hobble - and then saw his shadow as he entered Clarke's Yard, apparently on his way home …. In the moonlight, the policeman noticed that Ducker was carrying what appeared to be a truss of hay, so he followed him into the yard and challenged him …. After they had spoken for several minutes, it seems Ducker handed Constable Tye the hay, and then walked on down the yard, the policeman following. Suddenly Ducker broke away and ran across a stream at the bottom of the yard onto some rough ground opposite. The officer, throwing the hay to one side, pursued him and caught up with his quarry on the far side of the stream. A heated argument ensued, which soon developed into a fight between the two men .... Constable Tye, although young and fit, was physically disadvantaged against the older and slightly disabled, but stronger man. Back and forth they struggled, splashing into the stream, punching, kicking and gouging, the origin of their conflict to some extent lost, as they fought desperately for mastery over each other. The young officer succeeded in landing two heavy punches to Ducker's face, and struck the older man on the head with his staff, opening up a terrible-looking gash on his scalp. Ducker, greatly angered, retaliated by half-strangling the policeman with his leather-whip, which he always carried. Breaking away, gasping for breath, Constable Tye paused to recover. It was Ducker's opportunity: summoning up his last reserves of strength, he launched himself at the younger man and landed a final, crushing blow to his forehead .... Whether this was delivered by his fist, a handy piece of wood or even by the policeman's own staff was never determined .... Whatever the means used, the blow knocked the younger man unconscious. With two audible groans he collapsed to the rubble-strewn ground. Grunting and gasping for breath, Ducker dragged the officer's body to the stream, into which he pushed it in with one last effort, tossing the policeman's top hat in after him. The stream, polluted with the effluent of a dozen nearby toilets, was barely sufficient to cover Constable Tye's upturned face; nonetheless, within seconds of his immersion, the final measure of air bubbled from his lungs: Constable Ebenezer Tye was dead ....

It was several hours before Constable Tye was missed .... Had he not been detailed to keep observation on Ducker's house, he would have gone off duty between 4 and 5 am, returning to work about noon the same day. He failed to arrive, and when Constable William Lucas arrived back at the station at 2 pm, he immediately joined in the full-scale search that by then was in progress. Initially it seems not to have occurred to anyone that John Ducker might have been able to provide a clue as to the officer's whereabouts, least of all that the hay-trusser might have been involved in his disappearance! — that is, until Sergeant Taylor returned to the police-station just before six o'clock: incredibly no-one thought of contacting him about the missing policeman .... Once told, he went with Constable Lucas to pay Ducker a visit ....

They found Ducker at home, sitting in an armchair eating his supper. Both policemen immediately noticed his two black eyes, prompting Sergeant Taylor to leave his colleague in the house, while he went to fetch Superintendent Jeremiah Gobbett. During the sergeant's absence, in response to Constable Lucas's questioning, Ducker denied any knowledge of Constable Tye's disappearance, stating, that he had not left his bed until seven o'clock that morning. When Sergeant Taylor and Superintendent Gobbett arrived, the former asked Ducker to account for the black eyes, an injury to his face and a head wound under blood-matted hair. Ducker's replies were unconvincing: he explained that the injuries to his eyes had resulted from a piece of wood he had been chopping the previous Friday flying up and hitting him in the face; and that the wound to his head had been caused by a comb. When he was asked for his clothes, Ducker showed them a suit and said that, apart from what he was wearing, this was the only clothing he possessed. As he rose from his armchair, however, the policeman caught sight of an old pair of trousers under the cushion. 'Ducker, what do this mean? Ain't these yours?' Constable Lucas asked. 'Yes, they are an old pair,' Ducker admitted. Although still damp after an apparent attempt at washing them, the trousers stank and traces of mud and weeds remained on them .... This find persuaded the officers to delay no longer; they told Ducker that he was being taken to the police-station, where he would be detained while the search for Constable Tye continued ....

The police then went to Clarke's Yard, where they searched Ducker's other property - opposite the house where he lived. It was used as a store for lumber and other bits and pieces. There, concealed in a cupboard, Sergeant Taylor discovered a truss of hay .... For several hours, policemen, and by now townsfolk alike, had all been desperately looking for Constable Tye. The police concentrated their efforts in and around Ducker's home, and it was Constable Lucas, who just before ten pm saw some outstretched fingers of a left-hand breaking the surface of the stream, as if reaching for the willows draped across the water: there was no doubt who it was .... The dead policeman lay on his back just beneath the surface about forty yards downstream from where he had fought with Ducker. Apart from his top hat, which was floating a few yards away, Constable Tye was still fully dressed in uniform. As Sergeant Taylor later told the courts, '...his clothes were saturated with mud, water and weeds ... and the smell of the mud was very offensive ....' The body was then removed to the *Corn Hall* in Halesworth for a post-mortem carried out by a Dr Frederick Haward.

The police gave little credence to Ducker's explanation as to the cause of his injuries. As far as the police were concerned, the circumstantial evidence already pointed unerringly to Ducker as the person responsible for their colleague's death .... Soon they hoped they would seek out all the other corroborative evidence .... But Ducker denied any knowledge of the policeman's death. A few local people wandered down Chediston Street and into Clarke's Yard, an area that most of them generally avoided. With its dilapidated tiny houses, many of which were unoccupied and boarded up, and the stream at the bottom carrying sewage and effluent away from the town, it had little appeal, and was thought of, as a place best not to go to, especially after dark .... When news came that Constable Tye's body had been found, excitement mounted and many people remained out of doors Tuesday night, anxious not to miss any further drama. One local, Thomas Mills, who was helping with the search was raking through the mud and debris at the bottom of the stream, when he found Constable Tye's handcuffs from the spot where his body had lain. Next morning, a Constable Henry Cattermull, searching the rough ground bordering the far side of the stream, recovered the officer's staff a few yards from where he had been found .... Soon after arriving at the police-station on the Wednesday, Sergeant Taylor went again to Ducker's address ....

A more thorough search of Ducker's home revealed a pair of leggings concealed under the bed upstairs, together with a coat and a pair of boots in the room below. The boots and men's stockings were soaking wet, and all three items .... bore traces of mud and weeds ....

The inquest into Constable Ebenezer Tye's death opened at the *Angel Hotel* promptly at 5 pm on Wednesday. The **Coroner, Mr B.L. Gross**, told those in court: "I regret to say that there can be very little doubt that a frightful crime has been committed in this neighbourhood" .... Addressing the inquest jury, Mr Gross went on to explain the law of murder with regarded to police-officers: ".... all police-officers, and all ministers of justice are protected, and if killed under circumstances which, were they only private individuals, would make the crime that of manslaughter, the killing of these persons, even though it be involuntary, *amounts to the crime of wilful murder* ...." When the coroner had finished speaking, the jury went to an adjacent room to view Constable Tye's body. Scarcely had they returned to their seats, than the door of the room opened and John Ducker entered, escorted by two policemen. Burly, ruddy-faced and with large, strong hands, he gazed round the room through his swollen and blackened eyes, which, together with the barely concealed head wound, bore testimony to the violence involved. Asked by the Coroner if he had anything to say, Ducker's reply was brief and succinct: "No, Your Honour, I haint got nothing to say. I am innocent."

The only other witness to be heard before the proceedings were adjourned until the following morning, was Mrs Hannah Tooke, a neighbour of Ducker's in Clarke's Yard. After she had told the inquest that she knew both Constable Tye and Ducker, the widowed Mrs Tooke went on: "I heard the town clock strike six .... I knew Tye's voice very well, and I heard him talking to Ducker .... The voices were very loud, but I could not distinguish what they said. I swear positively that the voices were those of the deceased and Ducker .... I saw Ducker on Monday afternoon and he had no marks or scars about his face then ...." At 10 am on Thursday the inquest reconvened at the *Corn Hall* instead of at the *Angel Hotel*, the former having more room to accommodate the large number of spectators it was expected would attend the hearing. Ducker arrived from the police-station looking pale ....

Sergeant Taylor told the inquest of having examined Constable Tye's soaked and muddied clothing, and of his discoveries, when the day before he had searched Ducker's rooms: "The mud, weeds, and dirt on the stockings are of the same description as those found on the clothes of the deceased. The weed is what is called duck-weed. There was the same offensive smell as upon the clothes of the deceased ...." The sergeant illustrated his rudimentary forensic evidence with three samples of the duck-weed for the jury to examine. Constable Lucas was the next to testify. He described first going to Ducker's address on Tuesday evening and retrieving the trousers from under the armchair cushion, and then later finding Constable Tye's body in the stream. Constable Lucas said that, when found: ".... the body was stiff and swollen and when first taken from the water a great deal of blood came from the mouth and nose. The right eye was much swollen and very red. The hands and face were covered with mud .... I could distinguish the features, but the mud was smeared all over." Smelling-salts were produced by some of the ladies present when Dr Haward told of his post-mortem findings and of Ducker's injuries .... The post-mortem examination of Constable Tye had been more revealing after the preliminary examination had shown little external injury. 'There was a contusion on the forehead over the left eyebrow ....' the doctor began and went on, that ' .... on dissecting the scalp the veins were found much congested, as also those of the neck. On examining the skull, the veins and sinuses were filled with dark venous blood, otherwise the brain appeared healthy. I examined the internal surface of the skull, especially that part under the place where the blows had been received, but could discover no fracture. On examining the chest the lungs were congested .... The stomach contained a small portion of food with mud and water. From my examination I am of opinion that the deceased died from .... *asphyxia, caused by immersion in the water.* The contusion on the forehead was sufficient to have caused insensibility.' In reply to the coroner, Dr Haward said that the blow to the forehead had been inflicted while Constable Tye was alive, and that it was possible, although unlikely, that it had been delivered by a fist. He went on: "I examined his face, and found both eyelids much swollen, and of a dark, livid colour. The nose was scratched in several places, and there was a wound on the left cheek. On examining the scalp, I found the hair matted together on the left parietal bone. On removing the hair from this, I discovered a scalp wound one and a half inches in length, extending down to the periosteum." The doctor dismissed Ducker's explanation as to how *his* injuries had arisen, and in reply to a juryman's question, said that: "The injuries, in my opinion, were all received at one time in some recent, severe struggle." After Mr Seaman Garrard, a surgeon who had assisted at Constable Tye's post-mortem, had confirmed Dr

Haward's findings, there seemed little doubt as to what had taken place between the policeman and Ducker ....

There followed a succession of witnesses, all of whom were neighbours of Ducker. It was a unique situation for most of them: for unsophisticated, mainly illiterate country-folk, to be thrust unexpectedly into the limelight before their friends and neighbours, was an unnerving experience .... Spectators craned forward, anxious not to miss a word, as Elizabeth Sawyer, the widowed mother of a 14-year-old daughter, told Mr Gross that she lived in Clarke's Yard, four doors away from Ducker's house. She had risen early on the morning of Constable Tye's death, and had heard a scuffle at the top of the yard; it was about six ... after the noise had ceased, she said: "I heard a man coming down the yard. I cannot say whose footsteps they were, but I have heard this man walk [indicating Ducker], and I thought it was him ...." Mrs Sawyer added that she had, in fact, heard the footsteps of two people, one of whom .... "walked heavier than the other". Soon afterwards, she '... heard a shriek as if they were struggling in the direction of the bottom of the yard, and I heard a man's voice ' Can you swear whose voice it was?' asked Mr Gross. 'No, sir, not at all ....' the witness replied. Despite this, her evidence hammered another circumstantial nail into Ducker's coffin. Fanny Sawyer, well scrubbed and wearing a clean pinafore, followed her mother into the witness-box. She told the inquest that on Tuesday morning, when calling on Ducker with some cooked bullock's feet, she had seen him cleaning a spot of blood from his waistcoat, and he had told her that his eye had been blackened when he had been cutting hay. In reply to a doubting juror, Fanny said: "I am quite sure it was blood I saw upon his waistcoat ...." She then identified a waistcoat when it was shown to her in court. Ducker became agitated as Hannah Tooke described the clothes she had seen him wearing on Tuesday morning, and then in the afternoon after he had apparently changed. His discomfort increased when she also told the hearing: "I am able to speak so positively to the prisoner because I saw him come home three mornings last week, Thursday, Friday and Saturday. I had often seen him go out early in the morning, before daybreak." At the end of this damning testimony, Ducker complained to the coroner: "She will swear to anything ...."

Worse was to follow. A Miss Harriet Warne (16), who lived with her father [BW *snr*] in Clarke's Yard, and who worked at the hay-yard with Ducker, told the inquest that, at work on Monday afternoon: "He had on a pair of drabbett trousers and a drabbett waistcoat. He had no coat on.' 'Had he any bruises or marks about his face on Monday?' asked Mr Gross. 'No, sir,' Harriet replied. 'What clothes had he on Tuesday?' the Coroner inquired. 'He was dressed the same as he is now,' was the reply. 'Did you notice anything particular about his face?' 'He had a black eye and other marks about his face on Tuesday morning ....' Harriet ended by identifying clothes, including a pair of drabbett trousers, as those Ducker had been wearing. One of the last witnesses to testify was Charles Todd, a painter who lived in Rectory Lane less than a hundred yards from where Constable Tye's body was found. He said that at about six o'clock on Tuesday morning, as he was about to awake, he had heard 'two groans'. 'Was it quite close to the house?' asked Mr Gross. 'It appeared to sound close, but I cannot tell how near it was,' Mr Todd replied ....

Before summing up, the Coroner asked Ducker if he wished to make a statement under oath. Ducker gave it a few moments thought, before telling him: "I leave it to the gentlemen." After pointing out that murder is seldom witnessed, Mr Gross went on to tell the jury that an accumulation of circumstantial evidence could nevertheless have much the same impact as direct evidence: '.... if the general tenor of the evidence points out to you that the prisoner Ducker was present in company somewhere or other with the deceased, and it is clear to you he was afterwards in the osier [willow] ground with the unfortunate deceased, and that a struggle ensued between them, and that a blow was struck by the prisoner, which struck the unfortunate man into the water, that evidence alone would be sufficient to justify you in finding a verdict of wilful murder, if you are persuaded that the prisoner Ducker entered into the conflict *knowing the deceased to be a policeman in his uniform* ....' This direction left the jury little choice. After a short retirement they returned to announce to the crowded room a verdict of 'wilful murder against John Ducker'. The accused, looking ahead grim-faced, then listened as the Coroner committed him to stand trial at the next assizes. Watched by a large crowd, Ducker was then escorted back to the police-station, where he contemplated a bleak future. The case against him was formidable and his principal hope lay in the absence of direct evidence ....

Later on the Wednesday evening Dr Haward was summoned to the police-station. Anticipating either a prisoner or policeman in need of examination and treatment, he was surprised to find Captain John Hatton, the Chief Constable, and Mr Read, the prosecuting solicitor, awaiting him. Mr Read said that Ducker wanted to speak to Dr Haward about the case, and had agreed that the solicitor should be present. 'The prisoner spoke to me,' the doctor later testified. 'He said he wished to speak the truth to me for it could do no harm. What he said was most dramatic .... He said: "*It was old Ben Warne*". He [Warne] asked me: "Had I seen the policeman?" and he said, "I'll be damned if I have not done for him." This clumsy attempt by Ducker at accusing one of his neighbours of killing Constable Tye does not appear to have been given much credence by the authorities, although Benjamin Warne's [*snr*] brother and his wife, Stephen and Emily Warne, were later arrested on suspicion of having been accessories after Constable Tye's murder. As we shall see, however, the case against the couple, was later dropped ....

Ducker had to go through the formality of appearing before the town's magistrates. Sergeant Taylor told the court that, apart from the truss of hay found in Ducker's storage house, he had found other pieces of hay in his living-accommodation, examples that matched some obtained from the hay-yard where he worked. There then followed an extraordinary outburst in the court: 'Pray ain't you ashamed of yourself? Where wor you to see me? You said you never opened the window. How could you see me in the dark? You could not see; I should be ashamed to say so.' This outburst by Ducker was directed at Hannah Tooke, after she had again told of having looked out of her window on Tuesday morning, after having seen him on other mornings returning home laden with wood. She then identified the coat and drabbett trousers that she said he had been wearing. Likewise Harriet Warne was harangued by Ducker. During her examination she identified the waistcoat she said Ducker had been wearing on the Tuesday. This was too much for the prisoner. 'Had not I this same waistcoat on Monday?' he asked her. 'No,' she replied. 'I had my best slop on and you could not see it ....' he insisted. When

Harriet told the court that: "…. Ducker generally calls me up when I go with him [to work] but he did not do that [Tuesday] morning", the prisoner disagreed: "I called you, and your mother said she would send you," he told her. 'If you did call, I didn't hear you,' the witness replied. Captain Hatton stated that a recently washed shirt belonging to Ducker had been found in the Warne house on the morning of Constable Tye's death, whereupon the husband and wife – Stephen and Emily - were remanded in custody accused of helping Ducker after the crime ….

Meanwhile preparations were being made for the funeral of Constable Ebenezer Tye. It was a sad affair attended by the officer's colleagues and watched by silent townsfolk. Constable Tye's father collapsed as his son was lowered into the ground, and was helped from the cemetery, as the mourners dispersed. Over the next week or so, John Ducker's physical condition had severely deteriorated. When he reappeared before the magistrates on December 3rd, he looked thinner, his former jauntiness had disappeared; and his face was pale and haggard, despite the fading black eyes. Despite the efforts of Ducker's family to obtain the services of a solicitor, he was still unrepresented. Once again the hearing was frequently interrupted by Ducker's arguing with witnesses .... The proceedings opened dramatically, with Superintendent Gobbett telling the court that early on the previous Sunday morning Ducker, after asking to see him, had requested him to write a letter on his behalf to his daughter. He had afterwards alleged to the senior officer, that on the evening before Constable Tye had been killed, Benjamin Warne *snr*, who was a sweep, had borrowed his old clothes, returning only the waistcoat the next morning after he had gone to work. Ducker had again spoken to the superintendent later on Sunday morning, this time to tell him that on the Monday afternoon he had seen a man in Clarke's Yard with 'a long dark coat on', carrying a truss of hay, which he had thrown down upon seeing Ducker. Ducker told the policeman that he had decided at the time to '…. take this into my old house and keep it until I heard of an owner for it'. It seemed that with these unlikely stories, Ducker had been preparing the ground for his defence.

Sergeant Taylor once again entered the witness-box to say that two days before the resumed hearing, he had again been dragging the stream, and had found an old battered glengarry hat, similar to one he had previously seen the prisoner wearing. Hannah Tooke was recalled and to Ducker's disgust confirmed that she too had often seen him wearing such a cap, *including early on the morning Constable Tye died*. Ducker disputed this, saying that he had left the hat at work on Monday, and had retrieved it later the next morning. 'It is no use to ask her anything. If you speak to her fair, she will swear to anything,' he ended dismissively. This remark amused the spectators, some of whom even clapped, indicating, perhaps some measure of agreement with the prisoner's sentiments. Harriet Warne said that she had seen Ducker wearing the hat at work on the Monday, but the following day he was wearing a different 'wide-awake' hat, one she said she had never seen him wearing previously at work. Asked by the clerk, if he had any questions to put to the witness, Ducker replied resignedly: "No, it is no use; she will say anything."

The Warne family were to figure prominently in the prosecution case. Harriet's father, Benjamin Warne (44) [*snr*], followed her into the witness-box. He said he had gone into his brother Stephen's house in Clarke's Yard at eight o'clock on the Tuesday morning, and had there found Ducker examining his eye in a looking-glass; this caused further merriment among the spectators. 'Jack, you have got a rum one,' he had remarked to Ducker, who he said had replied, 'Yes, it is, I have had a scurry along with the policeman.' At this, Ducker erupted: 'No, no!' he shouted at the witness, who remained unperturbed: 'You did, John. I stand here, between God and man, and I o'nt swear to lie for none on ye. You said: "It was a rum one". Stephen's brother, Benjamin Warne *snr*, had entered the courtroom dressed in his sooty working clothes. He denied ever having borrowed any clothes from Ducker, so repudiating the statement the latter had made to Superintendent Gobbett. There followed a minor sensation as Stephen and Emily Warne were brought into court to hear Captain Hatton say that, as he had no evidence to offer against them, they should be discharged and examined as *prosecution witnesses* ....

Stephen Warne said both he and his wife said that Ducker had called at their home on the Tuesday with a shirt which he asked to be washed. Ducker was not having this, shouting: "Didn't your wife ask me for my shirt — didn't she come and ax me and said, "Ar'n't you going to have your shirt washed this week, because you hadn't one last week?", he demanded. Stephen Warne replied with equal force: "That is a lie. I have told the truth, and I will tell the truth." 'It ain't the truth,' Ducker persisted. Mr Warne went on to tell the court that on the day before Constable Tye's death, Ducker had confided in him and his wife, that he proposed stealing some wood from a local brickyard. When Mr Warne had warned him that he would probably be caught in the attempt, Ducker had said that he '…. would not be stopped by one policeman — if there were only one, he would go "life for life".' 'He said he would go "life for life", were those the words he used?' asked one of the magistrates. 'Yes, sir,' replied Mr Warne. Emily Warne largely corroborated her husband's statements, although she was more specific about Ducker's reply, when her husband had cautioned him against stealing the wood. According to Emily, Ducker had said: "If Mr Tye or any other policeman come after me, I have got something in my old house that will satisfy him." When asked by magistrates, she was unable to clarify what Ducker had meant by 'satisfy him'. Emily Warne's evidence ended with a sarcastic exchange with the man in the dock. 'Didn't you come here to speak the truth?', he asked her. 'Yes,' she replied. 'Well, didn't you come and ax would I have a shirt washed?' Ducker went on. 'You liar, you. I never said such a word.' 'You did.' Emily was beside herself with anger: "You wicked old story-teller you — why don't you hold your tongue?" 'What did your husband say to me when I came on Sunday night?' asked Ducker. 'My husband never spoke to you.' 'Didn't he say, 'There's plenty of wood at Mr Smith's brickyard?' 'No, you old villain — you liar — how could you say so?' And so it went on, until the magistrates said, they had heard enough of the evidence against John Ducker ….

Soon afterwards the prosecution case ended …. A public meeting in Halesworth a few weeks later typified the attitude and concern of the Victorian middle-classes to crime. The recent events in Halesworth had focused local attention on the town's inadequate police resources; it emerged during the debate, that two years before police manpower in the Halesworth area had been redistributed, leaving only a superintendent and a lone constable to serve 2,500 people. At the end of the meeting a resolution moved: "That in the opinion of this meeting an increase in the permanent staff of the police-force stationed in this town is absolutely necessary for the efficient protection of the person and property of the inhabitants", and was given to the authorities. Of course, it is doubtful whether additional police resources, had they been available, would have helped Constable Tye. He was a brave, but also an impetuous young man, who had tended to act without thought of the possible consequences to himself ….

John Ducker's trial opened at the county assizes sitting in **Bury St Edmunds on Thursday, March 26th, 1863, before one of England's most senior judges – the Deputy Lord Chief Justice, Sir William Erle**. There was a noticeable improvement in Ducker's appearance since his committal: gone were the bruises and other injuries, and his face had regained some of its colour. He gazed enquiringly about the crowded courtroom, occasionally nodding at and giving a fleeting smile of recognition to one or two of his former neighbours .... Ducker pleaded 'not guilty' and looked relaxed. The Crown's case was thus: "…. that the policeman early in the morning saw the prisoner in the act of taking this hay, and followed him, and endeavoured to apprehend him …. seeing him [Ducker] disappear at the bottom of the yard, Tye …. went after him. That Ducker made his escape over the brook …. followed by the policeman. That Ducker made a violent resistance, and in that resistance the policeman met his death ....' The prosecution denied that any of the Warnes had been coerced into giving evidence, and that the arrest of Stephen and Emily was to frighten them ….

Under cross-examination Hannah Tooke admitted not having mentioned the first hat [glengarry] until the second day of the committal hearing. 'Did you tell Harriet Warne to swear to the cap to make your story come true?' asked the defence. 'No,' Mrs Tooke replied. 'Did you not go to the second meeting of the justices for the purpose of swearing about the cap?' was the next question. 'Yes,' she admitted. 'Did not Harriet Warne go for the same purpose?' 'Yes,' 'Well, then, did you not, before that, tell Harriet Warne to swear to the cap, because it would make your story come true?' she was asked again. 'No, I did not,' insisted Hannah Tooke. 'Did not Hannah Tooke say to you, "You must swear to the cap because it will make my story come right?" The defence was now questioning Harriet Warne about the first hat. 'Yes,' she replied. Ducker looked round the court in satisfaction at her answer. The prosecutor was on his feet. 'Was that not after you had given your evidence before the magistrates about the cap?' he said to Harriet. 'Yes, but she did not know that,' the witness replied. 'Will you tell us how it happened?', the prosecutor pressed. 'It was outside the court. Some people were standing about. She did not know I had been swearing to the cap. Mrs Tooke said: "Do you swear to that there cap, and make my tale come right?" I had sworn to it then.' 'What answer did you make?' 'I said nothing.'

Counsel between them had confused the issue and cast doubt on the veracity of both Hannah Tooke and Harriet Warne; were they lying? The answer may not have been critical to the outcome, but it could raise doubts in the jury's mind as to the reliability of the evidence as a whole; and that had to be in Ducker's favour. However Ducker had said two completely contradictory things – one he had been in a 'fair-fight' with the officer and had killed in self-defence: the other that he was completely innocent, and that the real killer was his neighbour. Benjamin Warne *snr*, the sweep, emphatically denied Ducker's allegations and was not cross-examined. His father, Benjamin (76), was confused under cross-examination, and there was laughter among the public at his discomfiture. After administering a mild rebuke, Lord Erle himself gave up trying to make sense of the old man's replies. Not so Stephen and Emily Warne; both stood up well to the defence's questioning .... However Ducker's lawyer further tried to discredit Stephen Warne by extracting an admission from him, that he had served three prison terms, albeit for minor offences ....

The final prosecution witness was Dr Frederick Haward .... The defence tried to establish that, after Constable Tye had fallen to the ground, as a result of non-fatal blows, his heavy and restrictive uniform would have made it difficult for him to stand up, and caused him to drown by accident. The doctor said that this was possible; but equally he replied to the prosecution, somewhat ambiguously, that: "I certainly think there would not be anything sufficient to prevent him from getting up." The defence were able to show from the doctor's evidence, that Ducker had been severely injured. 'Were any of the wounds on the prisoner the result of violent blows?' Dr Haward was asked. 'Yes, the wound on the head was from a very violent blow.' 'With a policeman's staff, do you think?' .... 'I should think so,' agreed the witness ....

In their summing-up, the defence made this impassioned plea: "…. that it was to be a policeman's death that was to be accounted for .... It would be in a certain sense highly dishonourable to them as a body, if they could not avenge their comrade's fall, and it could easily be believed that the police would be in such a case induced to show an activity, which perhaps they would hardly show in other cases …. " The defence questioned the legal basis of the Crown's case. Speaking of the hay, which it seemed had been the cause of Constable Tye's stopping Ducker originally, they submitted that, as there was no evidence of the hay having disappeared, equally there could be no evidence of the prisoner's having stolen it. It followed, said the defence, that Constable Tye had no power to arrest Ducker, and that any attempt to do so, was an assault, that the accused had been entitled to resist .... The defence asked the jury that, knowing the prisoner at the bar was an unarmed man, that he was an old man, that he was a lame man, was he the person to attack the armed man, the young man, the strong man, the policeman?' It was suggested that the reverse was the case, that Constable Tye had carried out an unprovoked attack on Ducker, who had struck him in self-defence, partially stunning him and knocking him into the water. If the jury came to the conclusion that Ducker had used excessive force; at worst, he would be guilty only of *manslaughter* – if not excessive, then it was self-defence, and no crime had been committed ….

In his summing-up, the judge said he did not believe any of the neighbours had lied and he had no doubt John Ducker was involved in the officers's death …. As these words were uttered, Ducker slowly shook his head in disbelief. Worse was to follow …. Lord Erle continued: "There was no reasonable ground to suppose that he [Tye] took any steps to apprehend the prisoner till he saw occasion"

.... As to the evidence of Stephen and Emily Warne - the jury would also weigh the fact that the evidence was given at a time when the witnesses were in custody of the police; and it would be for them to say whether that story was fabricated by the Warnes to gain their freedom .... However, Lord Erle saved his most devastating comment until near the end of his address: 'It appeared that the evidence was strong that the death was caused by the prisoner being in the water with Tye and using violence ....' In other words Ducker carried on the fight too far .... **The jurymen were out for just 45 minutes** considering their verdict, before returning to announce that they found the prisoner, John Ducker, guilty of murder, and there was no recommendation to mercy either. Ducker remained silent and stood white-faced and tight-lipped as Lord Erle formally sentenced him to hang. He stepped down from the dock as the crowd spilled out into the street after the **ten-hour trial**. Many of them surged round the horse-drawn prison van hoping to catch sight of the condemned man, as he was taken back to **Ipswich Prison and the death-cell** ....

The execution was set for Tuesday, April 14th, 1863, and Ducker was not devoid of hope during this time, as there was a sizeable number of people, including three of the jurors, who, although agreeing with the verdict, considered that the sentence should be commuted. A petition urging a reprieve was submitted by Ducker's supporters to the Home Office, accompanied by a letter written by his solicitor Mr Salmon. The letter referred to the doubtful evidence given by some of the less reputable witnesses, and more pertinently submitted that the crime had been unpremeditated; and that it had not been proved that Ducker was, or had been, engaged upon a criminal enterprise [the stealing of the hay]. However four days before the execution, all hope of a reprieve was finally dispelled in a reply received by Mr Salmon from the Home Office:
" .... after a careful consideration of the evidence, and of the observations of the Lord Chief Justice on the case, and on the arguments pressed by your defence and yourself, **Sir George Grey,** can see no reason to doubt the correctness of the verdict; and he regrets that he does not feel justified in advising that the law should not take its course. I am Sir, your obedient servant H. Waddington."

The construction of the scaffold proceeded on the lodge roof of the County Hall where the prison was also housed. Ducker stayed composed while awaiting the end. He was said to have eaten and slept well, and like others in a similar situation he found solace in religion. Apart from the prison chaplain, the Reverend J. Daniel, he was ministered to by the Reverend Bolton from Ipswich and by Archdeacon Hankinson, who journeyed from Halesworth to visit him. It was perhaps as a result of these ministrations that on the *eve of his execution*, Ducker confessed to killing Constable Tye, although still insisting that his death had been unintentional. In a final confession he also absolved Benjamin Warne [*snr*], the sweep, from involvement in the crime: "I am sorry for what I have said to set that about him .... I could not go out of this world with this false charge against him .... I admit the justice of my sentence." — so the Reverend Daniel reported Ducker as having told him. Shortly before 8.00 am the next morning, John Ducker, dressed as he had been at his trial, with the addition of an old felt hat, was helped up the narrow staircase to the lodge roof. Seconds later, in front of 4,000 people, who had been assembling outside for over three hours, **executioner William Calcraft** launched the 63-year-old man into eternity; **the last person executed in public at Ipswich and Suffolk (The last execution at Bury St Edmunds was in 1851)**.

It is interesting that some people felt Constable Ebenezer Tye contributed to his own death: they considered that the situation, which had culminated in his death should never have arisen, and that the policeman had precipitously arrested John Ducker. A letter published in the *Ipswich Journal* four days after the execution said that: ".... this sad event should be a warning to Constables and others against excess of zeal in discharge of their duty .... we may lament the consequences which ensued from an attempt which was (in this case) unnecessary!"

Case 25
"When Death
Came
To The
Black Plantation"

~Murder Near Alton Towers~

William Collier (35)
[1866]
Murder
Of
Thomas Smith (23)

" .... I'll tell you what I shall do; I shall either knock their necks out, or blow their bloody brains out!" - Did William Collier really say this …. ?

That William Collier had cold-bloodily murdered a young farmer whilst out poaching in the Staffordshire countryside in the Summer of 1866, eventually came out, as he awaited his doom in Stafford Prison; he said he

was quite resigned and ready for death; but there is no doubt, he wasn't ready for the 'horrible scenes' on the gallows, at the hands of the hangman George Smith ….

Notes:

1) TS was 23 – he would have been 24 in August ….

Just over ten miles to the south-east of Stoke-on-Trent lies the small market town of Cheadle: today it is best known for the amusement park at *Alton Towers*. Three miles to the north is the village of Whiston Eaves in the beautiful Churnet Valley …. A 150 years ago, it was solely an agricultural area; and this meant, as well as the legitimate trades, there was the never-ending problem of poaching; and the man, who all landowners and farmers and their employees hated and feared the most, was …. **William Collier (35)** …. a notorious game-poacher, and neighbouring farmer with seven young children .... And so on the night of **Wednesday, July 4th, 1866,** local farmer **Thomas Smith (23),** and one of his men, John Bamford, went out for the night looking for poachers …. Although it was a well rehearsed routine; and although the men would not meet during the night, they both knew where each would be – each had his own 'spot'. Between about two and three am **[Thursday, July 5th],** Mr Bamford found himself in his usual 'spot' at *Cotton Bank* …. ½-a-mile away was Mr Smith near a wood …. At 6.30 am Mr Bamford went to the Smith farm to report that nothing untoward had happened on his watch; but there was no sign of Thomas Smith …. after about 2 hours, the farm labourer became quite concerned, and went back to try to find his 'master' - he found him an hour later at 9.30 am …. The body of Mr Smith lay in a wood about ¼ of a mile from the farmhouse, and was on part of his watch …. The farmer was in a strange position: he was lying on his knees and his right hand was under his chin …. Strangely he didn't look dead, but when Mr Bamford took him by the left arm he simply fell over. The young man's face and head were stone cold; but his stomach was warm ….

Mr Bamford feared his employer had been attacked – there were two viscous cuts on his forehead, and the back of his head, had been badly bruised, as if he had been repeatedly struck there with some blunt instrument; and when he moved the body he saw part of a gun – it was a trigger, and a few yards away, was what was called the ramrod – a stick used to load the gun with powder or shot …. By the body was also a large pool of blood; and nearby there appeared to have been a deadly struggle, as the ground had been trampled down …. Mr Bamford knew of the 'obvious' suspect – this night, as on many others, they had been watching out for …. William Collier in particular: his small 30-acre farm called *Oldfield* was not far from the scene - a wood called the *Black Plantation*, which covered the area, where Mr Smith had been found dead …. Collier's farm was on the northern edge of the wood, and not on the Smiths' land ….

Mr Bamford was fairly sure that Collier had been out that night …. before he had found Mr Smith's body, he had been to a place called Monystones Commons, and found a number of articles belonging to Mr Smith in a quarry hole …. there was an overcoat, a pair of leather-leggings, a pair of straps and a sack-bag …. Collier's farmhouse was within sight of this spot, and the sack-bag was used by the farmer to lie on …. It was less than a ¼ of a mile from where Mr Smith appeared to have been murdered …. Other employees helped bring the body back home, and one employee Thomas Moorcroft went looking for the rest of the gun …. very quickly he found more parts of a weapon in a field belonging to …. William Collier, after his wife said that she had seen Collier acting suspiciously in the field by a stone wall …. it was two barrels and was lying in a drain called a sough: the barrels had been broken off at the stock …. On the barrels was what appeared to be human hair (of the same colour as Thomas' - dark), although there didn't appear to be any blood …. Mr Moorcroft went to the wood, and found a gun-lock near to where Mr Smith had been found … A police-officer, Constable John Goodwin, who had been sent from Cheadle gathered up all the parts of the gun in the wood, and noted the name of the manufacturer *"R.H.Bate"* on it …. Another officer from a neighbouring village, Sergeant William Gaunt, found more bits of the gun in the wood, including discharged wadding, and in particular the gun-stock. This officer searched Collier's home and found more bits of the gun .... During the search, Collier was not placed under arrest, and when the sergeant came back later in the day, he noticed that the poacher had removed a number of wads from a shot-bag, leaving just two .... Collier denied he had removed anything ....

Some 12 miles or so to the south-west of Cheadle, is the village of Hollington; and just before the previous Christmas, a local gunsmith, Rupert Mellor, told officers that he had sold the murder weapon to William Collier .... He suggested that the gun-stock had broken off, when Mr Smith had been struck around the head; and that to break such a stock, would require a very heavy blow or blows .... When Mr Mellor took the barrels away from the remaining stock, to show them his mark, blood marks were noticed .... The gunsmith also said that he had sold Collier the ramrod and some shot too .... He said he also was sure he sold him the shot-bag, but would not swear to it .... A police sergeant, Thomas Perkins, had also come from Cheadle – he had seen the remnants of the gun, and asked Collier, if he had recently bought a gun, which he denied; he simply denied knowing Mr Mellor .... Asked more firmly by the sergeant, Collier know admitted that he did know Mr Mellor, and had, indeed, bought a gun off him 'six months ago': the officer also noted, that there were marks of blood on the accused's clothing, as well as attempts to wash away the blood .... William Collier was then charged with the murder of Thomas Smith and taken to Cheadle ....

In the woods, the victim's dad, Thomas *snr* had found his son's hat – it had two holes in it, that appeared to have been caused by blasts from a shotgun ... and in the wood on a rock and trees there also appeared to be the markings of shotgun blasts .... Old Mr Smith, who was also *Lord of the Manor at Whiston Eaves*, had been with Mr Bamford, when they had found the items where Thomas had been watching; and he believed that his son had left them in a hurry there, when he spotted Collier near the wood .... The old farmer said when his son did not return for breakfast at six-thirty, he knew something was not right .... Mr Smith said that his son and his employees never went out armed, simply taking with them a flask of whiskey to fend off the cold .... The whiskey had been found, as had the victim's watch and wallet .... At around eight pm on Thursday, a surgeon, Thomas Webb, arrived from Cheadle to examine the corpse

…. He found three separate wounds on the forehead, and he concluded that the back of the head had been completely battered in – the hair was saturated in blood …. At a later post-mortem, Mr Webb, found two gun shots in the head – at the top and in the back …. The shots and blows from the gun had fractured the skull into sixteen distinct parts, which the surgeon collated …. He said the blows were 'fearful'; and any of them would have caused almost instantaneous death – there were some defensive wounds on Mr Smith's arms and head, as if he had tried desperately to grapple with his killer; given the circumstances, the surgeon believed the victim was hit several times from behind and then shot, although when Mr Smith *snr* found the hat, it was some eighty yards from the body: in it was a white rose that the son had put in the night before …. The surgeon believed the killer was standing behind the victim, a little behind on the left, when the first blows were delivered …. He felt it was possible that, in themselves, the two shots would not have proved fatal ….

William Collier said nothing to the police, at the inquest or before the magistrates, except to say that the blood on his clothing had come from a cut finger. Just three weeks later on **Wednesday, July 25ᵗʰ, Collier appeared at the county assizes in Stafford, before Mr Justice Shee, in a trial that lasted just a day** …. Collier entered the dock with a firm step and a defiant smile …. Having pleaded 'not guilty', he sat down …. The defence's case was that the area was rife with poaching, as it was known as good 'game country'; and, as we shall see, there had been some gypsies in the area too ….

The court heard from John Bamford, that when the police and employers went to Collier's home, the prisoner, had taunted him by asking how he would have felt, if he had been in Mr Smith's position. He said that Collier then asked him if Mr Bamford had seen him that night, but he gave no reply …. The witness was asked if he had heard any shots in the night, and he replied he had - one; but it was in the opposite direction to where Mr Smith was; and he thought it had come from a gypsy camp that was also in the *Black Plantation*, although most of them had left some two weeks prior …. Mr Smith *snr* told the court that Collier's dad had farmed the same land, and apart from a misunderstanding about the use of water, they had never *apparently* quarrelled …. The old farmer said it was he that had sent Mr Bamford to look for Thomas in the wood …. Mr Smith *snr* seemed to think that his son had been shot first: he said that the two shots in the hat had been fired from a distance of five yards and about 15 yards …. Next morning, he saw Collier hoeing some turnips on his land; and since he had ordered his men not to say anything of the murder, he believed Collier didn't know that his son had been killed, and this also confirmed to him, that the poacher had fired at some distance, and was not sure that he had hit Thomas …. A local woman, Eliza Taylor, tending her ill mother, said that at three am, she had heard two gunshots close together …. However she said gunshots at that time were not uncommon, particularly when there were gypsies in the area …. Another local was more precise – Henry Goldstraw - said the two shots were at 3.15 am and were from the *Black Plantation* …. He said that there was about 60 seconds between the shots ….

Cross-examined by the defence, Rupert Mellor, admitted that whilst he examined the wadding and shot, he had not brought them with him for the trial …. He also said that he kept no gun registry – the law did not require him so in this era – and he kept records only when he sold weapons on credit …. Mr Mellor said the gun, which he had sold for 50s to Collier, had been fired a matter of hours, before it was found …. The gunsmith's dad, William, admitted to the court, that the gun in question was a very common type of shotgun …. All he could say was he was sure that it was the weapon sold to Collier …. He said the gun had been shortened by the Mellors, and he remembered doing it …. A local in Hollington, Louisa Fower, said Collier came to her home, and asked where he could buy a gun, and she sent him to the Mellors …. On the night of the crime, William Collier had a farm labourer staying at his farmhouse …. George Hill told the court that the next morning, when he and Collier were working in the fields, and they noticed activity near the *Black Plantation*, Collier simply said, that the Smiths were probably having a gathering of employees for a meeting …. Mr Hill said he was unaware of the murder, and was sure Collier didn't know either …. he said he had seen the prisoner use a shotgun – to shoot pigeons ….

Sergeant Perkins said that when he searched Collier's farmhouse, he had found evidence of poaching – rabbit nets etc, as well as two other shotguns, both of which were old and disused, and clearly hadn't been used for some time …. Asked about the gun from Hollington, which Collier finally admitted he had bought and where it was now, the accused told the officer, that he had lent it to another farm labourer of his, called Bowler …. Bowler did exist and was, indeed, a convicted poacher, although the sergeant only knew this on the eve of the trial …. Thomas Bowler, a cousin by marriage to the prisoner, had left *Oldfield* in May – he told the court that one of the guns that Sergeant Perkins said were disused was his: he denied emphatically taking any gun away with him; and furthermore he said he went with Collier to Hollington to buy the shotgun in question! The officer in charge of the inquiry, Superintendent Thomas Woollaston, said he had seen the dusty shotguns in Collier's house; and that the prisoner had told him, he had no other weapons …. This officer said he did notice an abrasion or blister on Collier's hand, which could have bled; but in the inside of his trousers was a patch of blood, that had hardly dried – it looked as if Collier had knelt down in a pool of blood …. and the outside of the trousers, which had no blood …. *had been washed* …. there was clearly a stain, and it was the size of the officer's palm …. However, the superintendent admitted that such staining could have come from killing and skinning rabbits ….

A Mr William Brindley, who had lived near Collier, and worked as a servant locally, said that when he had spoken to the prisoner about the Smiths and Mr Bamford, Collier had said: "I'll tell you what I shall do; I shall either knock their necks out, or blow their bloody brains out!" The surgeon, Mr Webb, now told the court, that the two shots found in the victim's head could have brought him down, before the blows inflicted with the gun …. possibly Mr Smith was trying to rise, when he was bludgeoned to death …. He said both the gunshots and the blows had been from behind …. Shown a shirt of Collier's by the police, Mr Webb, said it looked to him that the blood spots on it were caused by arterial blood, such as when someone is struck around the head as Mr Smith had been …. He also said that the wrist area of the shirt had been washed, and appeared to have been stained with blood …. The surgeon also examined

William Collier and found no marks of violence on him at all …. He said he did not think the blister on the hand would have caused much blood …. Given the importance of the case, the forensic material was examined by a Dr Alfred Taylor at *Guy's Hospital* in London …. On the question of the crucial staining at the back of the knee, the doctor said he could not tell if it were recent or not; it was possible, that it appeared new, due to having been dampened down in an effort to clean it …. However on the shirt, the doctor said he believed the stains of blood were recent, and from someone recently attacked …. To the fascination of the court, Dr Taylor said that *under the microscope*, he could see other blood spots on the shirt, that were invisible to the naked eye, and these too were of the same splash pattern as the others …. The expert said he could not find any blood on Collier's boots …. He noted a lot of blood on the prisoner's overcoat, the inside pockets of which, were heavily stained; but also had traces of pheasant feathers and rabbit fur …. It was notable that whilst Collier seemed disinterested in most of the trial, he leant forward and listened intently to what Dr Taylor had to say ….

In his summing-up, Mr Justice Shee, said it was greatly in his favour, that Collier went about his normal business the next day, *apparently quite composed* …. But the judge felt, that his evasiveness and lies about the gun when questioned, told greatly against him …. The jury retired at 9.00 pm; an hour later they returned to court: they wished to hear the evidence of Thomas Bowler again …. this time he said that he had seen Collier use the *Hollington gun* …. to shoot birds, having earlier not mentioned, which gun he had used, when like, Mr Hill, he had said that he had seen Collier with a *shotgun* …. Without re-retiring, the jury foreman quickly looked at the others, and said 'guilty'; but that they wished to recommend mercy on account of Collier's 'previous good character'; no doubt, they did not regard poaching as a real crime …. Collier then smiled and bowed at the court, before he was sentenced to hang …. The judge said he did not think it fair of him to suggest, that there was any hope that the Home Office would act on the jury's recommendation; and as he was led away from the court, it appeared from Collier's facial expression, that he was about to break down …. And the Home Office didn't act on the jury's recommendation, and **Tuesday, August 7th, was set for the execution outside Stafford Prison; the hangman would be**

George Smith, who had participated in executions at the prison for the last quarter of a century; and what happened was to make headlines throughout the country. Before this, fortunately for the Home Office, William Collier made a full confession, and admitted the justice of his sentence ..... a catholic, he conversed greatly with the prison's priest, and said he was quite calm and composed about being executed .... He explained that he had shot Mr Smith first, before beating him to death .... He said he realised that he hadn't killed the farmer with his gunshots, and fearing a life-sentence for attempted murder, determined to kill Thomas Smith, who knew it was Collier .... During visits from his wife and other relatives, Collier would keep his face covered with a handkerchief, as if he did not wish to betray emotion ....

"HORRIBLE SCENES ON THE SCAFFOLD"

Just before eight am, George Smith pinioned William Collier's arms, and for the next few minutes, he was left with his priest .... As the time approached, it was noted that only 2,000 people had turned up to watch .... Unusually the prison-bell was not tolled, as Collier approached the drop .... The gallows at Stafford was effectively a huge wooden box on giant iron-wheels, that was moved up to the prison-wall .... However not all of the front was covered, so that the full drop could be seen by the public .... The noose and rope were already in position, and it was noted that the one on there, was not very long.... normally after an execution the bit used would be cut off and kept by the hangman – in theory, what was left was long enough for the next job, but it was now quite short .... A new rope was therefore due, but only arrived at 8.30 pm on the previous night .... Consequently, in the morning, the prison-officers, put out the old short (execution) rope: it was, indeed, too short, and they spliced it to another piece of rope; the noose being formed from the old short rope .... the other bit of rope was attached to the beam; to most people watching it looked too loose and frail .... William Collier was 5 ft 7 inches tall and weighed 11 ½ stone; and it was thought he would drop 4-feet ....

Having put the white cap over Collier, Smith pulled the lever with a violent jerk …. There was a terrible screeching whistling-type sound – Collier had dropped; but the rope had broken …. worst still the separated rope acted like a whip across the condemned man's shoulders, and he screamed out in agony …. Smith ran down below to the gallows to find a disorientated Collier slumped against the side of the scaffold, moaning, the white cap and the noose still around his neck …. George Smith seemed incapable of acting, and a prison-officer took charge – he ordered Smith to take off the cap and rope, whilst the new rope was brought out …. Collier had gone very pale, and there was a severe red weal around his neck, as Smith led him back onto the drop …. Collier began reciting prayers as Smith was offered the new rope – but the hangman rejected it, instead using the old rope, but without attachments to it …. With Collier re-positioned with the white hood back on, the crowd hooted 'Shame!' …. the lever was re-pulled – this time Collier did die …. but in agony; it took 2 ½ minutes for him to be *strangled* …. this time the drop was too short ….

The last execution at Stafford Prison was in 1914 ….

Case 26
"The Stranger In The Boiler-Room And The Bakehouse Mystery"

"I am a bad boy" - George Reynolds, as he looked in a mirror ….

"I fired the boiler for 14 months, and I can still fire it for another 14 months. He is an Englishman and you are an Englishman." Was Reynolds racially abused and acting in self-defence, or was he a cold-blooded killer who had murdered in order to rob …..?

George Reynolds (41)
[1928]
Murder

Of
Thomas Lee (24)

Duke Street Prison, Glasgow

In the early hours of a morning in March 1928, an Englishman, somewhat drunk and wild-eyed, came into the home of his ex-landlady in Glasgow, wearing two scarves and with a most extraordinary story to tell ….

Lang's Bread Factory was a well-known local landmark in Wesleyan Street in the Bellgrove area of Glasgow near the city-centre. It was a hive of activity and operated for 24 hours a day and at just before one am on **Thursday, March 22nd, 1928** one of the employees went to check on the boiler-room, when he saw a work colleague, **Mr Thomas Lee (24)** apparently asleep! A married man, it seemed as if he'd nodded off on an improvised chair, and had duly put a coat over his face to help him sleep. Somewhat annoyed the employee pulled off the coat only to be faced with a truly shocking sight ….

Mr Lee's face was caked in blood, some of which had dripped down onto his clothing below. On closer inspection the man had also suffered a terrible wound to the back of his head. With the aid of other colleagues Mr Lee, who was still just alive, was taken first to the factory gatehouse and then to hospital in a company car. The doctors quickly diagnosed that Mr Lee had suffered a fractured skull. Despite his injuries it was thought, at first, that Mr Lee had been involved in some tragic industrial accident .... but then someone mentioned that, unusually a stranger had been in the boiler-room at around 12.30 am .... and he had been stoking the fire, and curiously it was thought Mr Lee had been asleep at that time too. The stranger had been seen by other workmates and quickly said he had been helping Mr Lee with the fire ....

The police were informed about the incident and so every available man in the City's Eastern Division was looking for the stranger armed with a description of the man, and equally importantly that he had an English accent and that it was from the North-East. Tragically Mr Lee never regained consciousness and died late on the following day **(March 23rd)**, and on the next day, the police had arrested a man in connection with the affair. The man had been seen in the city-centre and was quickly taken into custody. At the police-station it was quickly ascertained that the man was **41-year-old George Reynolds** who said he was originally from Sunderland, although he had tried to say his name was 'John Smith' and that he was from London, and later he changed his story saying he was from Newcastle-u-Tyne. In addition to being charged with the murder of Mr Lee, Reynolds was also charged with stealing some overalls from the bakery. He was committed to stand trial at the **City's High Court in the summer, where he appeared before Lord Hunter on June 25th, in a trial that was to last three days.** He was also charged with robbing the victim of a scarf and two shillings.

Under Scottish law the defence were obliged to state what the grounds of the defence were and **Messrs Walter Watson, KC, and W. Ross McClean** said that Reynolds would be pleading 'not guilty' on the grounds of self-defence and the court was to hear some remarkable evidence. A female witness, a Mrs Gordon, told the court that Reynolds had come to her house, somewhat drunk and wild-eyed in the hours after the incident, saying that he had committed a 'desperate action'. Reynolds and his wife had previously lodged with her and knew her well. She said the Englishman was overcome with 'emotion and fear' and was weeping uncontrollably, as he tried to explain what had occurred in the boiler-room. At first the woman could not take in what was being told to her but Reynolds said it was 'too true'.

The **Crown, the Advocate-Depute, Mr H. MaConnachie (assisted by Mr J.R. Milligan)** had earlier told the jury that they would say that the accused had hit Mr Lee over the back of the head with a branding iron and other blunt instruments in order to rob him. As this was said, Reynolds' knuckles went white as he grabbed the iron-bar at the front of the dock. Mrs Gordon told the court that Reynolds had come to her home in Tennant Street at about one-thirty am, and she noticed his hands were black from soot and dust. Reynolds said he had been on a night-shift at the bakery and had been helping a man called 'Lee'. As the witness spoke Reynolds leaned forward eagerly listening to every word she spoke. She said that the prisoner had told her, that he had struck Mr Lee with a fire-bar, adding: "I have done it this time; I did not mean it."

Mrs Gordon said that over the years that she had known Reynolds he had been prone to telling stories but he told her: " …. believe me this time." So far Reynolds had mentioned nothing of being attacked by Mr Lee and even told his ex-landlady that he had continued hitting the victim to stop him screaming and so that Reynolds could escape. However he then told Mrs Gordon that he had not gone into the boiler-room to attack Mr Lee, but in order to rob an office next door. However he said that having attacked Mr Lee he tore off his overalls and took coins from the injured man's pockets. Reynolds added that should Mr Lee die, he would give himself up. Pointedly when he had come into Mrs Gordon's home, Reynolds had been wearing *two* scarves, one of which belonged to the victim. The ex-landlady explained that during his 'confession', Reynolds had noticeable sobered up and became more and more frightened as his story unfolded. The pair stayed up all night and went for the first edition of the morning 'papers at five-thirty, but there was no mention of the case …. had Reynolds been lying again after all, pondered Mrs Gordon?

Reynolds then left Tennant Street saying goodbye to Mr Gordon as well. He left the scarf and overalls saying that the couple could sell them if they wished. By four in the afternoon there was still no mention of the affair in the press and when Reynolds knocked on their door, Mr Gordon would not open it. However soon afterwards they saw the early evening newspapers and references to the 'bakehouse mystery'. Mr Gordon gathered up the scarf and overalls and took them to the police. He too confirmed to them, that Reynolds was always telling them stories about fights that he had been in, and they never actually believed him. On one occasion, Reynolds had looked into the mirror and said: "I am a bad boy", said Mr Gordon, who also told the court that the accused had told him that he dealt a *second* blow to Mr Lee, as he thought the victim was going to attack him. It was the Crown's case that this second and further blows were dealt when Mr Lee was on the floor and that Reynolds had then picked up him and put him back on the chair, but that the *first* blow was dealt when the deceased was asleep on the chair.

This question of self-defence was central to the case and Mr MaConnachie asked a Dr John Glaister to explain if he thought a struggle or fight had occurred in the boiler-room. In the centre of the court a chair had been placed and the doctor simulated what he thought had happened. He said he thought it was most likely that the victim had been sleeping or dosing on the chair when the first blow was dealt. He said the most likely weapon for this blow was a fire-iron. He said the deceased was taller than the prisoner and the first blow was a clean swipe, and given their relative heights, he thought it would have been difficult for Reynolds to have hit Mr Lee had he been standing and awake. He said such were the force of the blows that Reynolds must have replaced the victim on the seat as he would have fallen to the floor.

On the third and final day of the trial **(Wednesday, June 27th)** George Reynolds went into the witness-box. In a quiet and composed manner he recalled the events on the day of the incident. He said that he considered Mr Lee a friend, having first met him in a poorhouse and that on March 21st, he said 'hello' to Reynolds in the street. The pair then spent the rest of the day drinking. It was pay-day and they discussed work and money, but although Mr Lee received £2 10s a week, he bemoaned the fact that he had to give his wife nearly all of it, leaving him just 10s to spend on drink. The pair had left the pub at the then closing-time of nine pm and according to Reynolds, Mr Lee suggested they carry on to the bakery. They had first gone to Mr Lee's home in Cathedral Street, where an angry Mrs Lee told him he was stupid to let Reynolds into the factory, as he might lose his job, but, probably under the influence of drink, he said there'd be no problem, and that Reynolds could be his 'stand by'. The pair, singing loudly, went off to the bakery, where Mr Lee, having punched his ticket in, went in and opened the factory gate to allow his friend in. It would appear that Mr Lee was much more drunk than Reynolds, who explained to the gate-man that he was going to cover for Mr Lee, and that he had worked as a ship's fireman: Reynolds was duly given a boiler-suit. Incredibly the gate-man then gave the accused an impromptu display on how to work and maintain the boiler!

Once inside the boiler-room, it would appear that Reynolds quite comfortably took to the job: on one occasion an engineer came to see him telling him not to let the pressure drop below 65lbs. When it was approaching one am, Reynolds told the court that he could hear Mr Lee stirring, and half-asleep the latter motioned towards his coal-shovel. According to Reynolds, Mr Lee's mood was now quite different and that he racially abused him and the engineer by saying: "I fired the boiler for 14 months, and I can still fire it for another 14 months. He is an Englishman and you are an Englishman." Reynolds claimed that Mr Lee had lifted the coal-shovel in a threatening manner and that he had taken if off him and told him not to be silly.

According to Reynolds, Mr Lee once again sat back on his seat and nodded off whilst he continued to keep an eye on the boiler. However once again he claimed Mr Lee woke up and aggressively reached for the shovel, and so this time Reynolds said he decided to face up to Mr Lee or "go under". Reynolds said he took the shovel away but that the deceased pushed him up against the boiler, skinning his nose in the process. Reynolds said he tried to remain calm but pushed Mr Lee away. He said the pair began to fight and his now ex-friend fell to the floor on his knee. Reynolds now claimed that Mr Lee put his hand on the fire-bar and that in an 'excited' state he swung at Mr Lee with the shovel, hitting him on the head. It was to a hushed and intent court that Reynolds gave his own demonstration as to what had gone on. He said: "He sort of sank down on his knees but he still had hold of the fire-bar. He got up again and I saw it was either one or the other of us." Reynolds said he once again hit Mr Lee around the head with the shovel. Seeing that the other man had collapsed, the Englishman said he threw the shovel to one side.

Asked by Mr Watson what he did next, Reynolds said that when he touched Mr Lee and heard him groan, he panicked and fled the boiler-room. Reynolds was allowed to demonstrate in the court how he attacked the victim with the shovel and obviously it was in sharp contrast to how the doctor had suggested that Mr Lee had been killed. The Advocate-Depute asked Reynolds why, if he had acted in self-defence, he had not reported the incident to the gate-house, and the accused said that he was frightened, as he ought not to have been working in the bakery in the first place. Asked why he had robbed a dying man, Reynolds had no answer. Could it have been that robbery was the motive all along, Mr MaConnachie asked the jury? The jury obviously thought so and that George Reynolds hadn't acted in self defence – after just 25 minutes absence, they found the Englishman guilty of murder, and it was a unanimous decision, 15-0.

The judge, Lord Hunter, said he could not see how the jury could have come to any other decision and sentenced Reynolds to be executed on July 18th, although this was postponed when he appealed. Now once again wild-eyed Reynolds shook hands with Mr McLean and waved at Mr Watson. As he was being led below, someone in the public gallery called out: "Cheer up, Geordie." An appeal was duly dismissed the following month and a new execution date was set for **Friday, August 3rd, 1928**. Executions in the city had taken place in the **Duke Street Prison** since the abolition of public hangings in 1868.Duke Street Prison, in the Drygate area near the city-centre (and not far from Bellgrove), housed the city's criminals from 1798 to 1955 - and where female inmates were sent from all over Scotland. It was demolished in 1958, being replaced by a housing scheme in 1961. The only remaining structure of Duke Street Prison is some of the boundary wall.

The **Secretary of State for Scotland, Sir John Gilmour**, decided there could be no reprieve and George Reynolds was **executed by Robert Baxter.** There was only a small crowd outside the prison, described as 'morbid' by the media. When the official notice was affixed to the prison gates at just after eight am, they left. **This was to be the last execution at Duke Street Prison** and indeed the last in Glasgow until 1946, from which point executions would be carried out at Barlinnie Prison until the end of capital punishment for murder in 1965.

Case 27
"The Sinister Case
Of
The Eerie Hand
And
The Two
Candlesticks"

"It was the duty of the jury to stand between the avenging hand of the Crown and the prisoner, whose mouth was sealed by an undeniable seal, and who must depend on them for whatever mercy he was likely to get." - Defence at the trial ….

"The law expects that you will do your duty, as you have sworn to do by the Evangelists, and that you will not regret your conduct hereafter, what ever your verdict be." - The Judge ….

Thomas Keel(e)y (35)
[1901-2]
Murder
Of
Mary Clasby (60)

Athenry

       Absorbing and sinister case from County Galway in the Autumn of 1901. The body of an old lady was found horribly murdered in her lodging-house; killed as she prayed. As her body lay in a bedroom, an eerie hand protruded into the street and asked a boy to buy some candles, which were later found, ritualistically lain out by the body. Soon afterwards the main suspect, a deformed cripple with a lump on his back, was seen making his way from the murder scene ....

Notes:

It is KEELEY on all the official documents

                                            Some eight miles to the east of Galway City lies the small town of Athenry and in the late Autumn of 1901, it was home to **60-year-old Mary Clasby,** who ran a single-storey boarding house at her home in North Gate Street – she lived with no relatives, just her lodgers, and she had spent most of her life in the USA. Everyone knew everyone else in the town and everyone quickly got to know a deformed lame man, who was also a painter and decorator. He'd come to the town looking for work, or so he said, some five weeks before and, of course, lodgings and was pointed in the direction of Mrs Clasby's. The man cut a pathetic figure telling those he asked for help and food, that he was short of money and had nothing in the world except a hammer …. his painter's hammer. On the day he first came into town, one local, Patrick Murphy, gave the man 2d for his rent and eventually the man was seen leaning over a half-door at Mary Clasby's house and then he went in ….

Within a few days of arriving the deformed man was a familiar face in and around Athenry and on the morning of **Monday, November 18th, 1901**, at just after ten am, a boy, Richard Burns, selling turf, was passing by Mrs Clasby's, when he heard a voice calling him. He went over and to his shock he saw a hand and arm stretched out from the door, which was partly closed, and the voice told him to go for two candles, in a spine-tingling voice. The boy took two pence and went to purchase the candles and coming back put them into the hand. The hand drew in and closed the door. Later in the morning an acquaintance of the lodging-housekeeper came by – Mary Seize would bring the milk, but on this day the deformed man said Mary Clasby had a sore leg, was laid up and could not be seen until night. Whilst in the kitchen Mary Seize attempted to open the bedroom door, but when she had her hand on the latch, the man pulled her away and would not allow her to open the door. After this incident he was seen over the half-door looking up and down the street in a most sinister way ….

Later at around mid-day, a young girl, Delia Spelman, came into the house to do some chores, calling out for Mary Clasby; but received no reply what so ever. She was, however, able to look through the opening in the bedroom door, which was just off the kitchen and which was ajar and …. to her horror saw the hand of the old woman on the floor. Gathering herself she ran to fetch the police: Mrs Clasby was dead on the floor, her skull battered in with a hammer …. a painter's hammer, which was covered with blood lying beside her. The victim's knees were bent and her head resting against the foot of the bed. Most peculiarly and somewhat sinisterly …. two candles, half-burnt down, were alighted about a yard from her feet.

The deformed man was called **Thomas Keeley (35)** and he was the obvious suspect and the following day, he was found in Tuam, some 20 miles to the north-west of Athenry. He had a considerable sum of money on him, along with brooches, rings, rosary beads and other small things, all of which would be identified as having belonged to the murdered woman. The murder of Mrs Clasby was regarded as one of the most cowardly murders ever committed in County Galway …. Keeley's father was originally from Tuam but had emigrated to the USA, where the prisoner was born – he had then been brought back to Castlegrove near Tuam by his mother. The boy, who'd bought the candles, heard the prisoner speaking at the police-station under arrest, and he recognised that as the voice of the person who asked him to go for the candles, whilst the man who directed him to the lodgings, Mr Murphy, also identified him, as did Miss Seize. The Royal Irish Constabulary also set up a hand ID parade! The boy viewed the right hands of three people put through a door, one after the other, in the same position he had referred to at the house. He said one of the hands had a slight resemblance and the coat sleeve very like it – it belonged to the prisoner. Many witnesses knew Keeley well and he had been caught out by just knowing and by being seen by too many people in the locality of Athenry.

Thomas Keeley appeared at the county assizes before **Mr Justice Kenny on Monday, March 24th, 1902**. The case exited great interest and the court was abuzz with great tension; whilst the accused listened to the proceedings apparently quite unconcerned. **Mr James Campbell, KC, the Solicitor-General for Ireland; Mr Fetherstonhaugh, KC, and Mr Edmund Coll appeared for the Prosecution. The prisoner, who pleaded not guilty, was represented by Mr F.W. Price.**

Mr Campbell said the accused was well-known in Athenry – many people had seen him looking for casual work, walking and wandering around, begging, being offered food etc. One local, Robert Lannon, a coachman, said that on the day of the crime, that he was riding in the direction of Athenry, and that at 11:30 am he saw Keeley opposite the cricket pavilion outside of the town, about 200 yards from the *Railway Hotel*: Keeley was slowly walking up the hill in the direction of .... Tuam. At 12.20 pm Patrick Lynch, a groom, said that the prisoner was coming from Athenry and was walking *very fast*. Also there, was a stable-boy called Cusack, who asked for a match from Keeley but the prisoner refused in a *very serious tone*. Once the prisoner had passed Mr Lynch, young Cusack turned around and looked at Keeley .... wiping his boots on the grass ....

Thus with a limp and a hump on his back many people remembered Keeley on the day of the crime – one lady told police that he had asked the way to Tuam. About half past seven the prisoner was in *Patrick Browne's* pub standing at the bar in this town. He was recognised by a farmer, John Gormley: although Keeley had asked the way to Tuam, he had once worked in Tuam Workhouse and as we know, he knew the place rather well .... The two men then drank some beer in the pub. Keeley appeared to have some money, indeed rather a lot of it. The prisoner bought two pipes, one at 6d and the other at 9d, and Mr Gormley was given the 6d pipe, and the prisoner kept the 9d one. The prisoner also purchased tobacco. Mr Gormley saw the prisoner take a bead case out of his pocket and then ten sovereigns, giving the pub landlord half-a-sovereign. The prisoner told Mr Gormley to come into a room off the bar, as he wanted to talk to him. He handed Mr Gormley a bunch of notes, which he asked him to count for him. There were eleven pounds, and the prisoner remarked that he earned this money since he was last in

Tuam, which was only in September. The prisoner then asked Mr Gormley to retrieve a suit of clothes which he'd pawned in the town. Both of them went there. The men then both went to *Burke's* pub next door and where he also treated two other men to drinks. After leaving this pub, the witness said to Keeley that he was going to go home soon and welcomed the prisoner to stay; Mr Gormley saying that he had no separate room, but if the servant boy was willing to share, Keeley could stay. The prisoner then gave his friend half-a-crown to send him for a 'naggin' of whiskey and a gallon of porter! The drink was later consumed by the prisoner, Mr Gormley, and two other men. Keeley eventually slept that night in the kitchen.

The men then spent the next day together, taking some more drink at *Keeley's* pub. Next the two men went back to *Browne's* and the accused brought a razor for 2s 6d. Once again, the prisoner paid for another drink. Next the prisoner bought some clothes: one pair of underwear, one inside-shirt; two pairs of socks and a neck-tie, giving 5s to Mr Gormley to buy them for him. The men went back to Mr Gormley's house around two o'clock. By now the shocking news of the Athenry murder had fully reached Tuam. A man named Thomas McGovern saw Mr Gormley and Keeley and began speaking about the murder: Keeley became frozen, as if he had seen a ghost. Mr Gormley began thinking about the money his friend had on him and told both men not to leave the house until they'd had dinner. Mr Gormley duly went to the police when Keeley became very agitated when told Mrs Clasby's head had been cut off with an axe! Soon afterwards Sergeant Thomas Sheehy came to Mr Gormley's house and saw the prisoner. Keeley was in a terrible state, shaking and mumbling and the sergeant asked him to stand up, saying: "I am going to ask you questions regarding the Athenry Murder." He asked the prisoner about all the places he had been to. Keeley told him that he came to Tuam *two* days ago; that he was from Loughrea and had left that district a couple of days ago on *Sunday*. Mr Gormley knew this was not true, as his friend had told him he'd come from Loughrea yesterday, and so Sergeant Sheehy interrogated Keeley more directly, which made the prisoner become more and more slow at answering the questions. Keeley also told the sergeant that he had slept on the side of the road at Gort, which was not true. He also claimed that he came from Gort – in the opposite direction from

Athenry as was Loughrea. The sergeant asked the prisoner was he in Athenry at all? To which the prisoner replied: "No, I wasn't'."

Arrested, the prisoner made no statement. Searched he had 3s 3d and a gold ring in a purse, which had no money in it. Keeley was then fully searched and an accompanying constable found £19 4s in Keeley's pockets. All the sovereigns had been in a rosary bead case and they had found other items too; whilst the money had been wrapped in a brown tissue roll – all items later found to have come from the murder scene. Sergeant Sheehy found cut marks on the prisoner's shins, as if they had been caused by kicks and the prisoner told the sergeant that he had scratched them. Taken back to Athenry, Keeley was put before the ID parades and on November 21st, under the direction of District Inspector Feeley, the murder house was thoroughly searched. In the bedroom, the police found three boxes of clothing with a petticoat and bodice with blood stains on. The items were then sent to Drs Lapper and Edwin of the *Royal College of Surgeon's* in Dublin to be forensically examined along with the hammer. Dr Edwin said he had found *mammalian* blood on almost every part of the head and smears of blood on almost the entire length of the handle of the hammer but not on Keeley's clothing. Meanwhile Dr Lapper had examined items taken from the bedroom – they were all bloodstained, including the paper wrapped round a candle, adding they were 'tolerably recent.' A Dr P.J. Quinlan carried out the post-mortem later on in the day of the murder at about six pm, and he believed Mrs Clasby had been murdered some 10 to 12 hours earlier, so probably around six am. He said that there were five large wounds penetrating through the skin to the bone of the head and skull, which had been fractured. Mrs Clasby was not short of money. A schoolteacher, Thomas Higgins, said that the victim had consulted him about some money. She'd received over eighty pounds from the USA in February 1901, whilst a Mr James Corry, manager at the town's *Ulster Bank*, said that the deceased had deposited over £155 recently.

Despite all this, Mr Price claimed that: had there been a more mysterious affair than this one? He said: "It was the duty of the jury to stand between the avenging hand of the Crown and the prisoner, whose mouth was sealed by an undeniable seal, and who must depend on them for whatever mercy he was likely to get." On the following day **(Tuesday, March 25th, 1902)** the judge summed up saying that: "The prisoner seemed to be a man not inclined to do his own work so long as he could get others to do it for him, and was offered employment and would not go to get it. Don't let any feeling influence you other than, did this man commit the crime?" He said there was no issues of insanity but if there was any question of 'diminished responsibility', the judge said he knew that the Lord Lieutenant would see that: "No person goes to his Maker who could for one moment have *not* been held to be responsible for the crime for which he had been sentenced." The judge noted that lighting the candles at the feet of his victim was peculiar, but peculiarities don't make a man 'mad.' In his final address, Mr Justice Kenny said: "The law expects that you will do your duty, as you have sworn to do by the Evangelists, and that you will not regret your conduct hereafter, what ever your verdict be." The jury retired for 90 minutes and returned with a verdict.

Mr Justice Kenny had assured that this Irish jury would bring in a guilty verdict, but
they did recommend mercy, at which point a deep groan of horror went up from assembled spectators, many of whom were from the business classes in Galway City. The prisoner said nothing. The judge, the black cap on his head, then said: "Thomas Keeley, you have heard the verdict of the jury and your own fellow countrymen, which has been come to after a patient and exhaustive trial ….. The crime was a brutal one, and you hurried this unfortunate victim before her God without a moment's notice. The law is more merciful to you and you will get time to repent of your crime, and I hope you make the best possible use of that time which is now left to you to reconcile your soul to your maker, and make your peace with God. I must say that I thoroughly agree with the jury in their verdict, which was a proper one; and I may say in my opinion they could, conscientiously and as reasonable thinking men, have arrived at no other verdict than they did." Thomas Keeley was then ordered to be executed on **Wednesday, April 23rd, 1902, at Galway Prison**.

Keeley's case was rejected by the **Lord Lieutenant, George Henry Cadogan, 5th Earl Cadogan, KG, PC, JP** in Dublin. The recommendation to mercy was seen as either a sop to opponents to the death penalty on the jury, or unwarranted sympathy for Keeley due to his physical deformity. When told there was no hope, Keeley, became terrified of the future. Indeed after the trial Keeley had collapsed, and was taken to hospital, where it was also discovered he was terminally ill with a tumour on his back-bone, which ironically was successfully removed, although it was also thought he would not have lasted much after the execution anyway, as he was generally in very poor health. Returned to the condemned cell, he was never out of the sight of two prison-officers. At first he refused to eat, and it was thought that he would starve to death, but when told his case was being discussed in Dublin, he did begin to eat and drink again. Finally when told there was no hope, he stopped again. Before the day of the execution, he was constantly either praying or crying at times. Somewhat shockingly on the day before the hanging Keeley would lapse into an unconscious state and at one point it was thought he had actually died! He did not have a great sleep the night before, suffering, 'fitfuls of starts, mutterings, crying and groaning.' Fortunately for the authorities Keeley confessed several times to killing Mary Clasby, admitting attacking her whilst she was praying.

It was to be the first execution in the city since 1885 and required the building of a new gallows and three prison-officers were rewarded with a bonus of one pound for seeing that it was built on time. (See photo 236)

The men appointed to carry out the execution were the Billington brothers, William and John. They had stayed the night before in the prison. While Keeley was unconscious the hangmen had strapped the prisoner. He briefly regained consciousness but on the scaffold, he fainted a couple of times: he'd groaned, moaned and cried out aloud; but two Catholic clergymen had managed to calm him down. William Billington pulled the bolt: Keeley was 'swung into eternity with an awful thud'. Everyone bar the Billington Brothers seemed to be terrified and greatly affected. The body was left hanging for an hour: The black flag was raised. The local 'paper said: "There was about 4,000 people present outside the prison who had been expecting to hear the crack of the bolt. A shout of horror went up from the assembled multitude, who now knew of the awfulness that had taken place." The Billington Brothers were late for the ten o'clock train and were followed about by crowds, although somewhat surprisingly [for Ireland] they were not hostile; although the longer they didn't leave, the more worried the police became. Eventually the pair left Galway on the three o'clock train after the station was thoroughly searched by the RIC. Overall the local media congratulated the jury on the case, by saying: "To suppose the Jury would let the prisoner go would be to establish upon your country a stain which centuries would not remove. What would become of helpless women and children of this county? They would have to shut their doors, uncertain to the projection of their neighbour, and might be found brutally murdered some morning."

And what of Galway Prison? Thomas Keeley was the last person executed at Galway: there were no political executions there (1916-1923) and the prison closed in 1939 and eventually became home to a new cathedral in 1965, with just a few parts of the wall remaining.

Case 28
"Murder By Mistake"

"Your pigs are on the road." - The false words that were to lead to the murder of a 10-year-old boy, by mistake.

"Evil is good and good is evil" - The criminal code of John Logue.

John Logue (21)
[1865-6]
Murder
Of
Thomas Graham (10)

Absorbing and extraordinary case from County Down. Lurking in the shadows by the porch of a large house on a moonlight night in the summer of 1865, lay a gunman bent on revenge, a feeling he'd nurtured for some years....

Notes:

http://www.passagewestmonkstown.ie/spike-island.asp - Spike Island

Some three miles to the west of Lisburn lies the small County Down village of Ballymacbrennan. A community wedded to the countryside, it seemed outwardly content and peaceful but within the community was a one-man crime-wave. This man, only 21[46] years of age, caused no end of problems for the villagers, but most of his behaviour affected the Graham family, who lived in a large house on Saintfield Road. The house was somewhat run down and so the family had converted the kitchen into a bedroom, where the father, George Graham, and his **10-year-old son Thomas** slept, whilst his wife Susannah and their two young daughters slept in another converted bedroom. When they went to bed on the night of **Thursday, August 10th, 1865**, whilst they were well aware of the troublesome young man, they probably had no thought of the awfulness that was about to befall them....

During the night Mrs Graham was woken by the sound of gentle tapping on the back door from their kitchen. The sound was so light that the woman ignored it and returned to her slumber; indeed so soft was the noise she assumed it was the soothing sound of the passing wind. As to the time, well, she would later recall that she believed it to be around one-thirty am **(Friday, August 11th)**. And so Mrs Graham continued her sleep. But then at some point between two and two-thirty am, Mr Graham was woken by the much louder sound of banging on a kitchen-window. Although somewhat annoyed at being woken, such things were not uncommon in rural areas when neighbours needed help and so it was, in this case, that it appeared that a friend had come to help the Grahams....

Mr Graham went to the kitchen door and asked who was there to be met by the reply: "Your pigs are on the road." The farmer quickly fully woke up and he and his son, who had also been woken, went into the hall to go out of the front door and onto the driveway, which led to the road. As the pair emerged into the driveway, they noticed a man in the shadows standing by their piggery, with a white handkerchief around his neck. Initially they assumed it was the 'friendly neighbour', but then to their shock they saw that the man

---

46   Some sources say he was 23; but he said he was born in May 1844.

was pointing what seemed to be some sort of weapon at the pair. Mr Graham pushed his son back into the hallway and then he himself started back into the relative safety of the porch. However the armed assassin followed Mr Graham into the porch and fired, aiming at his head and upper chest....

The bullet whizzed into the hallway, missed Mr Graham, but hit young Tommy who had remained in the hallway waiting for his father. The young boy had been hit in the spine as he had turned, as he saw his father coming up the hallway. Screaming and in agony the boy stumbled through the porch and collapsed outside against an elm tree, which formed a natural shelter over the front door. Mr Graham ran into the house shouting at the top of his voice that Tommy had been shot. Mrs Graham lifted her son back inside the porch. Mr Graham now seething with anger and therefore immune from danger approached the shadowed assassin and shouted out: "I know you", to which the killer retorted that he would shoot him. Although followed by Mr Graham towards a cornfield, the assassin disappeared into the County Down night....

Mr and Mrs Graham were sure the man was one **John Logue,** the troublesome 21-year-old. They knew all about him: they had once employed him and four years prior Mr Graham had given evidence against him when he was accused of sheep-stealing. However Logue also was also disliked by the whole of the village and it was with a mixture of annoyance and dread that Logue had returned to Ballymacbrennan. The epitaphs that accompanied Logue were usually couched in such words as 'vile'. In today's language Logue would be described as anti-social, but he was almost a "professional criminal", as we shall see....

Just over two hours later poor little Tommy died in his mother's arms. Incredibly unbeknown to the Grahams, Logue had not fled the village and had been lurking in the vicinity of the house …. for his intended victim was Mr Graham: the boy had been "murdered by mistake". There was a huge manhunt, throughout Ireland for Logue and this spread to Britain as Logue had spent time in England, where he had committed a number of crimes and picked up a strange English accent. However Logue was determined to murder Mr

Graham and so remained in the general area of Lisburn until August 30th when the police finally received the information that they needed.

The contemporary Logue family were well-known to the police. The original family had moved to the Lisburn area in 1830 from County Donegal. One of Logue's uncles had been fatally wounded having been shot whilst stealing potatoes. Logue's father, James, had been employed by the Grahams for many years and he himself had worked for the family from a very young age. He had first left Ballymacbrennan at the age of 15, when he was slapped by Mr Graham for taking a horse without permission. Logue told locals that he then left for Russia where he travelled around in the company of an ex-soldier and he became involved in "all manner of vice". On returning home he vowed to become a "professional criminal", and take revenge on Mr Graham.

However Logue's career as a 'master criminal' didn't last long. In 1861 having stolen some sheep from a local farmer he was seen by Mr Graham and other members of their family, and along with evidence of his bad character from Mr Graham and a Mr Carson he received a four-year sentence, which he was to serve in full. On being taken from the court he swore vengeance against Mr Graham blaming him for all his problems from the time of his beating. Viewed as a dangerous criminal Logue was sent to the much-feared Spike Island in Cork Harbour, at the time Ireland's top-security prison. Logue was to later comment that the system on the island was the "perfect hell for wickedness" and that he'd learned how he would become a better criminal there, as there was no segregation of criminals, new or old, and he picked up many new tips for his new would-be life of crime. Logue left the prison on June 28th, 1865 telling prison-officers that he now found crime irresistible. Logue had been regarded by the authorities on Spike Island as one of the worst criminals they had ever come across, although whilst in prison Logue had improved his writing skills.

John Logue went first to England committing a number of crimes that went undetected. He stole one valuable watch, which he sold, and was able to return to Ireland. He was seen locally on July 7th, and broke into the village school on the eleventh. He then attacked the property of Mr Carson and said that he then went to Dublin, where on July 20th, he witnessed the public execution for murder of Patrick Kilkenny outside Kilmainham Prison. During the police investigation it emerged that Logue had tried unsuccessfully to kill Mr Graham on previous nights, using such activities as stealing the family dog to lure Mr Graham outside, and he'd been sleeping rough in Dowling's Wood near the house in order to watch the family and its movements.

After the murder John Logue had found a job working as a servant for a local magistrate, Captain James Whitla. A fellow employee recognised his description from the newspapers and the police were alerted. Logue was quickly identified by Mr Graham as the man in the shadows and on **Thursday, March 15th, 1866, he appeared at the Downpatrick Assizes in a two-day trial before Mr Justice Fitzpatrick.** Putting the case for the **Prosecution, Messrs McDonnell, QC, and Dr McBlain,** said that the evidence of Mr Graham was overwhelming and there was drama in the packed court as the father of the victim pointed to the accused in the dock as his young son's murderer.

The court was told that it was a bright moonlit night when the boy was shot, and Mr Graham had three distinct opportunities to make Logue out: twice by the porch and the third by the cornfield. Mr McDonnell then told the jury of other evidence connecting Logue to the crime. Another villager, Daniel Maguire said that two nights before the murder his home had been burgled and a number of items stolen, including: a coat, a (long) service-rifle and a powder flask. Maguire had later told the police that he had seen Logue wearing the coat. Another villager said that he too had been burgled, on the Wednesday night, and he too had seen Logue with items from his home. Furthermore with Logue safely under arrest other locals had said they had seen him on the main road from Lisburn to Belfast on the morning of the shooting between four and five am. However despite an intensive search by the Irish Constabulary, the murder weapon was never found.

Between the murder and his arrest Logue had tried to obtain work at a number of farms and large houses in the Lisburn area using the name of 'Bill Shaw'. Once employed he would constantly refer to the murder giving detailed knowledge to those that were prepared to listen. Logue was known for being wild and irresponsible and had also threatened another local man and former employer, Mr George Carson, who had given evidence against him back in 1861 (see above), and during this period, in July, a great deal of his property and animals was stolen and burnt.

On the second and final day of the trial **(Friday, March 16th), the defence, Messrs McMechan and Hamill** informed the judge that they would put forward no defence but Mr McMechan said that he would seek to discredit the prosecution's case. Firstly he suggested two shots had been fired: the police had found a second bullet lodged further down the hallway in a chest of drawers, and he said there was no proof that the murder weapon was Mr Maguire's stolen rifle. Mr McMechan said the bullet marks in the boy's body and the furniture were the same shape, and Mr Graham had never described the gun. After the murder Logue had been seen on the Belfast road and had been given his breakfast by a kind local: "Murder did not make a man hungry", said Mr McMechan, who also pointed out that Logue began to doze off: again surely not the behaviour of a man who had just committed murder[47]. Why did Logue not flee Ireland, asked the barrister? Why not go to another part of the North of Ireland as it was harvest time and the large farms in that part of Ireland were awash with casual labour. That Logue was apt to sleeping rough in haystacks should not be taken against the prisoner, as he was, by virtue of his reputation, an outcast, said his counsel.

Mr McMechan said that although it was said to be a moonlit night why couldn't Mr Graham see this 'long rifle' by the porch or as he followed the assassin to the field? In cross-examining Mr Graham, he forced him into saying that the night was, in part, *grey*, and that he was confused (he certainly hadn't said that there had been *two* shots), as his mind was on the condition of his son. Despite the defence's best efforts after an hour's deliberation the jury found

---

47   Although of course he didn't know he had committed murder at that point ??

Logue guilty of murder and he was sentenced to hang on **Thursday, April 19th, 1866, outside Downpatrick Prison**.

Despite the cold-blooded nature of the crime a number of petitions were sent to the **Earl of Kimberley, John Wodehouse, the Lord Lieutenant in Dublin**, asking him to spare Logue's life. These were based on the belief, in some quarters, that Logue was somewhat mentally backwards and therefore not fully responsible for what he had done, and that the evidence was not conclusive. However, in addition to the fact this was a clear case of premeditated murder, Logue was viewed as a very dangerous man, who whilst on remand had, in October, tried to escape from Downpatrick Prison. He had moved a piece of gas-pipe into his cell and during the night had started to dig a hole. The night the tunnel was discovered, he had incredibly almost broken through the wall. From then until his trial he was watched 24 hours a day by two guards.

Until he was actually sentenced to death John Logue seemed quite indifferent to his fate, saying he would escape anyway. But then he broke down in tears and then he would spend hours walking up and down the death-cell with a menacing look and swearing revenge. When told he was not to be reprieved, he said he would tell the truth of the shooting and claimed he was not the killer. However Logue soon gave up on this tract and returned to his previous seemingly unconcerned state and once again, like so many in his position, he accepted the kindness of the prison's religious ministers, in this case the Protestant clergyman, the Reverend George Douglas.

John Logue became something of a *cause celebre* in Ireland. Many people wrote to him urging him to embrace God and this seemed to appeal to his vanity, and he spent many hours writing, often turning his prose into rhyme. He vacillated between an almost child-like excitement of his new found fame and his desire for revenge and how he had no fear of death. On one occasion his anger seemed almost bestial, and this was used by those that said he should not be executed as an example of his low mentality, although no-one would say he was insane. However on the eve of his execution he said he'd repented to God and confessed to his "wicked life" blaming much of his problems on drink. However he returned to the idea that he had not committed the murder, but he admitted he had committed all the other crimes. He told the religious ministers: "I will not go before my God with a lie on my tongue." Logue ate his final evening meal and went to bed, sleeping soundly until six am, incredibly having to be woken by one of the death-watch officers.

Logue was due to be executed at eight am and the weather was wet and stormy. He enjoyed a full breakfast and then prayed with the ministers. At 7.40 am the execution process began when Logue was moved from the condemned cell along the corridor to a large window that opened on to a porch and the gallows which had been built around the latter. He was reported as looking somewhat pale, but otherwise quite unmoved. Dressed in his own clothes, they were somewhat faded and worn and he appeared quite bedraggled, as since his conviction he had not shaved and his moustache and beard had grown long. With tears rolling down his face, Logue's hands were tied behind his back and he was helped up a ladder onto the gallows. The white sack was then placed on top of his head and the executioner asked him if he had anything to say to which he quickly replied: "No, No!"

The sack was then pulled down over his face and he was moved onto the trapdoor. The knot adjusted, the hangman twice asked the Under-Sheriff, Mr Hutchinson-Boyd if he was happy. The nod came and Logue dropped - again in Ireland the drop was very long – some 14 feet. Logue appeared to have died without a struggle. The body was cut down and buried within the gaol. As with the execution of Patrick Power the crowd was small, no more than five hundred, even though, as at Wexford, it was the first execution at Downpatrick in 30 years[48]. Indeed the last time someone was under sentence of death in Downpatrick was exactly 10 years before and so the gallows needed much repair to them.

Once again we don't yet know the name of the hangman. It was reported that two men had vied for the job. One came from the North from Armagh, whilst the other came from Wexford in the South. The latter was given the job and was known as the "Irish Calcraft". He

---

48   David Anthony hanged for murder on March 19th, 1836.

was described as being in his mid-fifties, workman-like, and who liked to smoke his pipe after he had completed his grim task. John Logue was the last person to be publicly hanged on the island of Ireland: just over two years later legislation throughout Britain and Ireland had outlawed them.

So was John Logue really the killer?:

.Mr Graham spoke of his suspicions of a neighbour, a Mr Kearney, and one-time friend with whom they fell out.
.Logue was never picked out of an ID parade.
.Graham said he did not mean "'I know you'" to mean it was Logue only that he knew the man ….

Case 29
"Horror on the Gallows"

John Tapner
(1854)
Murder
of
Mrs Elizabeth Saujon

In August 1965, Guernsey became the first part of the British Isles to completely abolish capital punishment for murder. However it had been well over a 100 year prior, that a murderer was hanged on the island, and it was execution so gruesome that it was not reported in the Press, and it's true secrets were kept locked away in a Home Office file for over a century.

John Tapner was an Englishman by birth, and to whom the phrase "to die with their boots" on was very apt. In England, in the middle of the 19th century a child of seven could be guilty of an offence and by the age of 13, Tapner had a string of offences to his name. Not that his family could be blamed because they were extremely religious, although Tapner confessed himself an atheist at an early age. There was one break in Tapner's non-religious beliefs when he was 17, but it was event that was to lead him to the gallows.

Tapner had wanted to marry his girlfriend of the same age, but her family had spotted he was a non-believer and forbade the marriage. Even when Tapner said he would be confirmed they still objected and in the end the couple never married. Tapner's heart was torn apart and he decided to embark on a proper life of crime. In 1847, now aged 24, he left England and went to Guernsey. Guernsey would seem an odd place to become a master criminal but Tapner had married a young Guernsey girl who became Mrs Mary Tapner.

On the face of it, Tapner seemed to have put behind him his wild youthful ways, for soon the couple had two children, both boys, and by 1853, Tapner, now aged 30, was working as a clerk in the offices of the Royal Engineer Department. By July 1853 Tapner, although he used a different name, was living in the small village of Canichers and appeared to be quite happy but his other darker side had already taken over.

Tapner lived in a room in a house, which was owned by **Mrs Elizabeth Saujon, a widow of 72 years,** and a woman remarkably fit for her age, who as well as running her home ran a small market garden. After a short period at Mrs Saujon's, Tapner's two boys disappeared leaving what Mrs Saujon thought was just man and wife, a "Mr and Mrs Simmer". For a short period Tapner and his "wife" persuaded Mrs Saujon that the children were being cared by Mrs Tapner's sister but soon the old lady realised that "Mrs Tapner" was really Tapner's sister-in-law. Such behaviour may have been tolerated in London but in Guernsey it was a moral sin. But of course Tapner was a man of no religious persuasion and he couldn't see the problem.

Despite many lecturers on the subject Mrs Saujon hadn't actually asked the new couple to leave until the middle of October, but the old lady had kept reminding Tapner of the sin he was committing and then began to question the character of his sister-in-law, suggesting that she must be a very low type to betray her sister. It all came to a head on a mild autumn night on **Tuesday, October 18th, 1853**.

That night, just before ten o'clock, for about 10 minutes the pair spoke in the kitchen, when for no *apparent* reason something quite amazing and inexplicable happened - Something Guernsey folk only thought could happen in the darkest and vilest parts of London.

During the conversation Tapner began pacing up and down like a caged animal when it is agitated. Then when behind Mrs Saujon he suddenly began hitting her on the back of the head with a wooden stick, a club, which he had concealed on his person, when he entered the house. After several blows the old lady collapsed and was taken by Tapner into her bedroom. As to why Tapner should have attacked his landlady *appeared* clear as he began pulling out draws and searching through her clothes: Tapner was after money and jewellery.

However the reality was that in Tapner's mind he was determined to put an end to the old lady's constant remarks about his sister-in-law - After all she was quite happy to take the rent for three months. However both Mrs Saujon and Tapner could sense a feeling between them that his relationship with her daughter and sister-in-law would end in tragedy. As Tapner began pouring white spirit over the woman, he believed was dead, he wondered whether there was a God after all and this was his punishment.

Believing Mrs Saujon dead, Tapner placed some wood on her body and set her alight. Around the house he started other fires hoping that all trace of the crime of murder and theft would be erased. It was all part of his plan to make it look like an accident or if the police did suspect foul play they'd think that a burglar had killed Mrs Saujon having been caught rifling her bedroom.

There was one problem, however. Tapner was no master criminal: The fire was not sufficiently ablaze when Tapner left. Mistakenly he believed by locking every window and door tightly he would help the fire. Instead the opposite happened - the fire was starved of oxygen. The following morning the terrible crime was revealed.

The police quickly discovered that the Mrs Saujon had spoken to a friend about a man called "Simmer" who was going to call on her late about buying some furniture, but about whom the friend, felt Mrs Saujon was not being entirely open.

Such was the size of Guernsey that the police quickly established "Mr Simmer" and John Tapner were one and the same, and he was arrested, indeed with a large sum of money on him. The police had also established that some #30 pounds (a considerable sum of money at that time) had been stolen. Underneath Mrs Saujon's bed the police also found a bottle of white spirit, which later was proved to have belonged to Tapner.

To the island's police, who had no experience of such a terrible crime, Tapner came across as indifferent and callous. In one letter to his sister he wrote: "I am accused of having murdered an old lady here, but I expect they'll find it a hard job to prove me guilty."

In December 1853 John Tapner appeared at the **Royal Court in St Peter's Port in a trial that was to last 13 days**, and which included just one rest day. At the time it was one of the longest criminal trials in the British Isles. Unlike in England John Tapner faced two other charges, that of robbery and arson, both of which still were still capital offences on the island. He appeared genuinely disinterested in the proceedings and had to be prompted into saying "Not Guilty" by the judge, an Englishman brought in especially for the case. His disinterest was more than compensated for by the excitement the case had cause on the island. Even the normally cautious *Evening Star* on the island said: " We have no hesitation in saying that the trial.... is one of the most remarkable that can be met.... and that it is entitled to take its place amongst the *cause celebres* of modern times".

For the **Crown, the Queen's Procurer, Mr Utermack**, said all the evidence against Tapner was "almost entirely circumstantial" but that it was damming evidence. The Procurer went through the finding of the white spirit and the money found on Tapner and also told the court that other items from Mrs Saujon's house were found in a haystack nearby and witnesses would say that they had seen Tapner moving to and from the house to the field. The Procurer said they were very valuable items - plates, trinkets, and furniture.

Advocate Falla, on behalf of Tapner said that he would suggest to the court that the Crown had not proved Tapner guilty and that he would put forward an alibi - that he was drinking in a pub in St Peter Port - and explain why Tapner suddenly had a large sum of money on him, when previously he was a man a meagre means. However he was not helped by Tapner, who when he was called to the stand simply replied "Not guilty" to any question put to him. The court were to never hear Tapner's explanation as to why he had such a large sum of money on him, when he was arrested.

On **Tuesday, January 3rd, 1854** the trial ended. Despite the length of the trial the jury, called a *jurat*, found John Tapner guilty. However in Guernsey the jury are joined in their deliberations by a magistrate, a *Bailiff*, and make up a "jury" of 13, and their deliberations are in public. In Tapner's case all 13 unanimously found him guilty after a short retirement. The execution date was set for January 27th, a Friday; a day set down by custom on Guernsey for executions.

In the death-cell Tapner played a long and tortuous game with the authorities. At first he seem to welcome his execution, then after five days he had a *volte face* - he wanted to be spared and wrote to the Queen begging for mercy. Whilst his case was discussed in London, the execution date was reset for February 3rd. By now the case was beginning to excite interest in London, since there was a belief that if not innocent, was the evidence strong enough to hang Tapner? The Home Office asked the Guernsey government to look into the case.

The island's government passed the case back to the Royal Court, who rejected any idea of a re-trial and breaking with tradition set Monday, February 6th, 1854 as the new execution date. What the government in London wanted was a watertight confession. Three priests were set the task of working on Tapner. They took it in turns, although one was asked by Tapner not to visit him again, when like Mrs Saujon, he passed moral judgement on Tapner's relationship with his sister-in-law.

Tapner still maintained his innocence, although all three priests believed it to be a sham. Eventually on February 1st, a compromise was reached: The remaining two priests would write the "confession" and Tapner would sign it. Even then Tapner only suggested guilt, but it was enough for the Guernsey Government to issue another temporary stay of execution.

The two priests worked frantically on Tapner and four days before the next scheduled execution date of February 10th, Tapner began to confess. Tapner said he was doing it because of his children. Tapner acknowledged the verdict of the court and went further by saying that the murder was entirely premeditated. Tapner had entered the house with the sole intention of killing Mrs Saujon out of revenge, because he was sick to death of her morality. He said: " I considered that she (Mrs Saujon) had behaved very ill to my sister-in-law and had made very ill-natured remarks about her. And I was always very vindictive. Perhaps you do not know what revenge will make a man do, but I do, to my cost"

Tapner's time in the death was made the subject of a book called the *Eleventh Hour* in which the author, a Guernseyman and one of the three priests who regularly visited him in the condemned cell, the Reverend Frederick Bouverie and the Prison Chaplain, interviewed him at length in the weeks after the death sentence. Tapner then said that the cause of all his adult troubles was his lost love of the girl he wanted to marry when he was 17.

When Tapner finally confessed in writing to the Chaplain he also said that he had acted quite alone and that his sister-in-law had played no part in the crime, including after the murder, since the island was abound with rumours that there was a "love angle" in the case. He said: " There should be no longer any doubt on the subject. I now declare that I alone was guilty of the crime for which I am condemned" J.C.T.

Once absolved in the eyes of the Chaplain, Tapner then began confessing to other crimes he had committed. In October 1852 he had burgled a large house at Fort George, near where he worked. He delighted in saying how he had spoken with the owner shortly afterwards to give himself an alibi for being near the house. By the time the police interviewed the owners they were confused as to the time and so the police, who suspected Tapner, did not even arrest him.

Another daring crime Tapner confessed to was the stealing of deer belonging to an army regiment stationed on the island. The animal, meant for meat, had become violent so was destroyed. After it was buried Tapner dug the animal up and tried to take it home. It was heavy but he still hacked off the best bit and took it home. In full flow Tapner confessed to dozens of burglaries in Guernsey and England.

At 7.30 a.m. on the morning of **February 10th, 1854,** the execution party entered the death-cell. The first in was the Queen's legal representative, the Procurer, Mr Utermack, who had prosecuted Tapner, his deputy the *Greffier* and four policemen called *Bordiers* on Guernsey. The Procurer had been to see Tapner many times during the six weeks that Tapner had languished in the death-cell and now Tapner wanted to apologise for his attitude to the man. The legal formalities having been completed, Tapner was allowed to spend his last 30 minutes on earth with his *now* friend the *now* author Bouverie.

Firstly Tapner wrote a last letter to his wife. The men then talked until three minutes before eight when a loud voice boomed out "Mr Tapner". The death-cell door opened and Tapner was walked to the prison's garden, where it was decided Tapner would hang. By tradition executions on Guernsey normally took place on the sea front at St Peter Port, which would have meant parading Tapner through the streets of the capital[49]. However this was only tradition and the Guernsey government decided to redefine "in public" and restricted the execution to just 200 "special guests", although such was the position of the garden it could be seen from houses nearby and a good a number of women took up vantage points. Furthermore

---

49 After the Napoleonic Wars there were only two executions on Guernsey that of Tapner in 1854 and the previous, on the sea-front of a Frenchman called Beasse for murder of his newly-born child, in 1829.

a hole was made in a wall by the garden so that Tapner only had to walk less than a 100 feet to his doom and to the hangman, a local man, a man, whose identity is still not known.

What happened next was not reported by the Press and remained locked away in the Home Office until well over a hundred years after John Tapner was executed, although it was viewed by a number of the good folk of St Peter Port. On the gallows, the dreaded white hood over his head, and his heart beating apace, Tapner managed to untie his hands, which had been pinioned in the death-cell. **The executioner [John Rooks]** quickly pulled the lever and the trap-door opened, but then the real horror began - the drop was hideously too shoot and the whole too small - John Tapner grabbed on to the side of the drop and hung on. To kill Tapner, the hangman had to pull hard down on the condemned man's legs, whilst he screamed in agony and the white hood turned blood red. In all it took 15 minutes to execute John Tapner.

After the execution the novelist Victor Hugo[50], who had petitioned the Home Secretary, Lord Palmerston, for a reprieve for Tapner, visited the death-cell. He described it as being white, clean and well lit. At one end of the room was a fireplace, and in the left-hand corner, a bathing-tub. He noted that one of the condemned man's bed's legs was broken, and the bed itself was no more than a straw mattress.

In 1875 a public execution took place on Jersey; **but the Guernsey Government did not abolish public hangings on their island and bring the law in line with England until 1937.** In 1955 a local paper was shown around the new death-cell and reported that little had changed in the death-cell itself, but that now the gallows were adjacent to it. In 1967, never having been used and two years after abolition, the gallows were dismantled and the wood was used to make bunks for the cells that the authorities used for men arrested for being "drunk and disorderly" on the island.

---

50 Victor Hugo (1802 to 1885) was expelled from France in 1851 and lived on Jersey, from where he was also expelled in 1856, living on Guernsey until 1870, before he was allowed to return to France.

Case 30

"*The Last Execution in Britain*"

Peter ALLEN & Gwynne EVANS
[1964]
Murder
of
John West

Evans and Allen

On August 1st, 1998 the Crime and Disorder Act received Royal Assent. One section of it abolished the death penalty for high treason and piracy, whilst the Human Rights Act, which became law a few months later abolished capital punishment under military law, thus making the United Kingdom completely abolitionist.

In the early hours of the morning of Tuesday April 7th, 1964, John West was found dead in his house at 28 King's Avenue, Seaton, Workington in Cumberland. He was a 55-year-old, who had lived with his parents all his life. His father had died many year prior, but his mother Ada, had only died in 1963. West was a laundry-driver, who had worked for the same firm Lakeland Laundry, for the last 25 years. His house was one of six houses in a quiet cul-de-sac, which bordered on a ploughed field. West had returned from work as usual on the evening of the sixth, and had been seen working on his car in the early evening. However at 3.00 a.m. in the morning his immediate neighbours were awoken by a loud thud.

John Fawcett, his next door neighbour, had been surprised earlier, when West's front-room light had been on at 10.00 p.m. West was such a person of strict routine that the when the Fawcett's return home, they were shocked. West always retired to bed at ten, and read for one hour, with a dim bedside lamp. Even when the Fawcett's retired at eleven, they noticed his full light was still on!

After the loud thud, Fawcett said, "I heard heavy thuds, as though something were hitting the foundations of the house. Then there were several shrill screams, followed by a couple of lighter thuds. Then I heard a car-engine starting up and saw a vehicle driving away". Having been aroused Fawcett noticed a dimmed light on, on West's landing. The car sped away along Coronation Avenue towards Seaton town centre. Both the Fawcetts quickly dressed, and ran into the road. Here they were met by another neighbour Walter Lister, who had been awoken by the car-engine. It was now 3.20 a.m. Fawcett knocked on West's door, but received no reply, to which Lister responded by immediately calling the police.

At 3.30 a.m. Sergeant James Park and P.C. John Rogers arrived, and Lister retrieved West's spare front-door key from his garden shed. Park wrote in his report, "I saw the body of a man lying on the floor at the foot of the stairs. The body was on its back, dressed only in a shirt and vest. The body was at an angle to the staircase. There were obvious severe head injuries. There was a large amount of blood on the floor, and the man was obviously dead. There was also quite a lot of blood on the staircase, and it appeared a struggle had taken place". By 4.00 a.m. the cul-de-sac was full of detectives, headed by D.I. John Gibson, and D.C. Fred Smith of the Cumberland and Westmoreland C.I.D., and 18 other detective constables.

Gibson noticed that the stairs were covered in blood. In the doorway to the living room, he discovered a piece of metal tube sheathed by rubber. Around it was wrapped West's pyjama bottoms.

At 6.00 a.m. the pathologist Dr J.S. Faulds arrived from Carlisle, and in the morning he carried out the post-mortem. Death had been caused by a haemorrhage in the head, and the shock of a stab wound near the heart.

In the house fingerprints were taken. Sets on the metal tube, and on the internal doors did not belong to West. However Gibson could not find the knife. At 1.30 p.m. a major piece of evidence was found. A coat in West's bedroom was not his. Inside was a key, and a medallion with the inscription: "G.O. Evans, July 1961", and also a slip of paper with the name "O'Brien" and a Liverpool address written on it. In the early evening the police visited the house. Miss O'Brien was a 17-year-old girl, who worked in a factory. She immediately identified the medallion. She had seen it around the neck of a man called Gwynne Evans, a 24-year-old, who lodged with Miss O'Brien's, sister, and brother-in-law. She had dated him a few times, and his nickname was Sandy. He lodged with a 21-year-old man Peter Allen and his young family at 2 Clarendon Street, Preston. Both were dairymen.

By the evening the police had found and traced the car that was heard speeding away. It belonged to a Mr James Cook, and had been stolen in Preston, and abandoned in Ormskirk. It was covered in Allen and Evans's fingerprints. Both men were "well-known" to the Preston police, and had criminal records.

At 6.45 p.m. Allen was interviewed at Workington police station. Two hours earlier a D.S. Hodgson had arrested Evans in Manchester. On him was James Cook's driving licence. He said he had found it in Preston, and thought it might be useful, but he was lost for words explaining, why he had watched engraved "J.A. West". Then he told D.S. Hodgson, "I bought it this morning from a man in Preston. I gave him two pounds for it, because he wanted some money for petrol". Told it belonged to a recently murdered man, Evans yielded, for he was well acquainted to West. "Jack West has been a friend of mine for about five years. He told me if I ever was short of money, he would lend me a couple of quid. I will tell you all about it", he said.

Evans described how he and Allen, accompanied by Mrs Allen and her two young children, desperate for money, had driven to Seaton, and arrived at about 3.00 a.m., and found West awake. In his statement Evans said, "I knocked at the door, and Jack came down and let me in. We were talking inside, when there was a knock at the door. Jack went to answer it, and when I followed, I saw Peter Allen hitting him in the corner by the stairs. I shouted, "For Christ's sake, stop it!", but Peter just said, "He's got the cash, and I want it". After the murder they drove to Liverpool, where Allen burned his bloodstained shirt. When the banks opened they withdrew £10 from West's account, having stolen his bankbook. Having made this "confession" in Manchester, Evans was driven to Workington, and handed over to Gibson. Both he and Allen were now in Workington, being questioned separately.

Allen was interviewed by D.C.S. Roberts, head of the Lancashire C.I.D. (1958-1965), and D.C. Watson. The latter never spoke, merely writing as Allen spoke. This was admitted as evidence at the trial in June and was not challenged by Allen's defence. Roberts first asked Allen, when he had last worked. He replied, "I've not worked for about a week. Last Saturday was the last time".

Roberts :" Where were you yesterday, Tuesday ?"

Allen:" Liverpool"

Roberts:" Just describe your movements."

Allen:" We left Preston at about 8.00 a.m., and went by train to Liverpool-Me, the wife, two children, and my mate Sandy Evans, who lives with us".

Roberts:" Why did you go?"

Allen:" We went to look at empty houses, because we've had notice to quit. We are about ten or fifteen pounds behind with the rent-the wife can tell you".

Roberts:" Doesn't Sandy give you something?"

Allen:" Sandy hasn't been working ".

Roberts: " You have been brought here because I want to ask you some questions about a man called West, who was killed at 28 King's Avenue, during the early hours of Tuesday morning".

Allen: " You don't mean that man that was murdered? Listen, you can get a stack of bibles in here and I'll stand on them and swear I know nothing about "

Roberts: " Have you been to Workington before today?"

Allen: " No."

Roberts: "Weren't you in Workington about six weeks ago?"

Allen: "Yes, I'd forgotten. Sandy brought me and the wife and youngsters up".

Roberts: " Where did you go after leaving Liverpool?"

Allen: " To New Brighton and Seacombe. We couldn't find any houses so we went down Faulkland Road-that's the place for flats-but they are all coming down. We left about 4.30 p.m. and got back to Preston between 6.30 p.m. and 6.45 p.m."

Roberts: " Where did you get the money to go with?"

Allen: " Sandy got his National Assistance "

Roberts: " Where were you on Monday night?"

Allen : " All Monday night I stayed in-me, the wife, two babies and Sandy. We went to bed about 9.30 p.m. to ten."

Roberts: " Did Sandy knock about with anyone else besides you and your wife?"

Allen: " He didn't knock about with my wife"

Roberts: " You have been telling me how he went out with you and your wife-did he go out with anyone else?"

Allen: " I don't know. I don't think so "

Roberts: " Would it surprise you to know they were together in Manchester, when the police traced them?"

Allen: " It would, very much"

Roberts: " Well, they were. They are on their way here now. How long have you been wearing those clothes?"

Allen: " Two days"

Roberts: " Were you wearing them on Monday night?"

Allen: " Yes"

Roberts: " Can you drive?"

Allen: " No. I have no licence and can't drive anyway"

Roberts: " So if you go out in a car Sandy drives?"

Allen: " Yes"

Roberts: " Did Sandy have a car on Monday night?"

Allen: " Not to my knowledge"

Roberts: " You weren't in a car on Monday night?"

Allen: " No, I wasn't "

Roberts: " Whether you are involved in this business or not I do not know, but further inquiries will be made, and I'm going to question your wife and Evans, when they arrive".

Allen who was now visibly sweating struck the desk with his fist and buried his head in his arm. He then destroyed the notepapers with his previous statement on. He said it was all lies, and then said he would tell the complete truth. Roberts then cautioned him, and Allen began his new statement.

"I'll tell you what happened. It started as an innocent robbery. All right-Monday night at about 9.30 a.m. we went to a garage in Preston and pinched a car. I picked up the wife and babies up but she didn't know what was going on. We came up here, and when we got here Sandy went in. We got here at 1.10 a.m. This bloke knew Sandy and Sandy said he had money lying around. We parked the car in front of the road works. He went in and he came out for me about ten to three and I went in. Sandy told him he wanted some fresh air and let me in without the chap knowing, but when he came down the stairs he saw me so I hit him. Sandy had the bar and gave it to me. Sandy put the light out and I was hitting out blindly. I only had my fists until Sandy gave me the bar. I only hit him twice with it, and then gave it back to Sandy.

I went upstairs to see if there was any loose cash, but there wasn't. There was a bunch of letters and two bankbooks in the drawer and I just grabbed the lot. The wife and children were asleep in the car. We went straight down the road towards Cockermouth. I threw my gloves out of the window. When we got to Windermere we ran out of petrol, but Sandy got some. We went to Kendal and the wife cashed her family allowance and we went straight to Liverpool to see my mum. On the way back we left the car in a yard, a builder's yard, near the bus depot. We got a bus back. Yesterday Sandy got two five-pound notes from a bank in Liverpool. The wife went to the door with him.

When we got back I scrubbed my jeans and burned the letters. Sandy took the chap's watch and jacket and I left his own coat in the house. I'll you this-I'm glad you've found me. Sandy said it was an easy touch. Who am I to take a human life in my hands? All I wanted was a hundred pounds for a deposit on a house. "

Allen then told Roberts about the clothing he wore on Monday night. The shirt had been burnt. He had washed his jeans, and his wife had taken his jacket to Manchester. He was still wearing his shoes though.

Roberts then explained to Allen, that he could make a written statement, which Allen did. It actually follows his oral statement, apart from one vital part. Allen then said, after he had hit West, he "remembers seeing Gwynne hit him with a rubber pipe". West then fell down the stairs.

Interestingly Allen does not mention the stab wound, and neither had Roberts. Now Roberts decided to interview Gwynne Evans. It transpired that Gwynne Evans was an adopted name, and that he had born in Innsbruck, Austria of German parentage. When cautioned Evans informed Roberts, that he would tell everything he knew.

"Right, sir. We set out to see my father by car at 10.30 p.m. on Monday night I decided to steal a car and take Peter, his wife and children with me. My mother has a wristwatch belonging to me, which I could sell for money. I've known Mr West for some time, and he said that if I ever was in

Workington and required money to see him. I was going to ask him for the loan of a hundred pounds. we got there at about 2.00 a.m. I knocked on the door and he said, "I didn't expect to see you tonight". I told him I was up to see my mother. he asked me where I was staying and I said I had a friend with me in the car. He asked me to go to bed with him. I don't know whether anyone knows it or not, but West was a homosexual.

A knock came to the door and West said, "Who can that be?" I said I didn't know. He went to the door and Peter rushed in and said, "I want some bloody money". I said, "We'll leave him alone, he hasn't got anything". When I went up to the bedroom, Jack said he wanted something from the airing cupboard and I put my coat on the chair, then he said it didn't matter. I don't know anything about a knife. I don't have to use a knife to kill a man-I'm an expert at Judo and Karate-It was Peter that did all the hitting.

Me and Peter got the bankbooks from a cupboard in the kitchen and I picked the watch up from the kitchen table. I got a jacket from the kitchen as well because Peter said he wanted one. Mary knew I was going to borrow money, but she must have known what had happened, because Peter was covered in blood and not on me-I was wearing these clothes. We set off in the car and Peter threw a pair of gloves and some other object out of the window. I think we were just outside Windemere. We stopped at Kendal to get Mary's family allowance. Then we went to Liverpool and I got ten pounds on the bankbooks. Peter told me to do it and he said he would go into another bank to get another ten pounds, but we didn't. We went to Wallasay and New Brighton. Then back through Ormskirk, where we left the car at about 7.30 p.m. and got a bus back to Preston. At Clarendon Street, Peter burned his shirt and tore the bankbooks up and burned them. He also burned some letters.

This morning Mary and I went to see Mary's mother in Manchester, but more than anything else to borrow a hundred pounds to put down on a house. I went to see my girl in Manchester and then I went to collect Mary at her mother's. The police picked me up there. They told me to empty my pockets and they searched me and found Jack West's watch in my pocket. Peter told his wife to take his jacket to Manchester and lose it.

She said, "Burn it", but he said, "No, take it in to Manchester and get rid of it". Peter washed his jeans and tried to wash the bloodstains from his jacket.

Jack West was like my own father."

The crucial piece of evidence against Evans was in his statement. He mentioned the use of the knife, where neither the police nor Allen had previously done so. Even at the Coroner's Inquest before the trial in June it was only stated West only had been killed by a battering with a blunt instrument. Evans then made a formal written statement.

He explained he had known West for about five years, and had been drinking with him in the Lake District. He said that he declined West's homosexual advances, but that West invited him to come upstairs to the airing cupboard, when Allen knocked on the door. He said it was Allen, who hit West with the tube, but that he told Mary that he had done it to impress her ! He said that he had discussed robbing West, but that no violence would be needed, as West did not have much cash in the house. He believed West would loan him the £100 by writing a cheque. In conclusion he said he never intended robbing or killing, and that was "all Peter's fault. I never hit him once". He had invited Allen along for moral support, and the hope it might pursued West to be generous.

It seems likely that Allen knocked at the door at a pre-arranged time, after Evans had discussed with West the loan. Evans told West he was going outside for some fresh air. It is probable he told Allen to hit West, but that in the panic Evans hit him the tube, and then stabbed him. Evans said Allen knocked at the door unexpectedly, whereas Allen said his entrance was planned (by Evans).

Following their statement Allen and Evans were both charged with capital murder, in the course or furtherance of theft, and at Workington Magistrates Court they were remanded in custody until they appeared at Manchester Crown Court June 30th. The original trial had been set for May 28th, at the Lancashire Assizes in Lancaster, but the defence successfully applied for it to be put back. They were both taken to Durham Prison on remand awaiting trial.

The pair appeared before Mr Justice John Ashworth. Allen was represented by Mr F.J. Nance Q.C., and Mr R.G. Hamilton, Evans by Mr Morris Jones Q.C., and Mr G.W. Guthrie-Jones Q.C. The jury included three women. Mr J.D. Cantley, Q.C., represented the Crown. Dr John Faulds, who performed the post-mortem on Mr West said he had received a three and half inch deep wound on the left side of his chest, which had clipped one of his lungs, but penetrated his heart. There was a fracture from his right eye to his chin.

Allen was called by his counsel Mr Nance, Q.C. He said he had known Evans since November 1963. He said Evans told him, "We were to break in. I made the point clear to Evans there was to be no violence and he said, "All right". Having parked the car outside West's, at 2.55 a.m. Evans beckoned him in. Allen said he climbed the stairs, and was surprised by West, and hit him. Then the lights went out, and Evans began hitting him, but Allen admitted being given the bar and hitting West "once or twice". Then Allen explained, "Evans came out of a room nearly opposite the stairs. He put his hand somewhere inside his coat and pulled out a knife and stuck in West". Evans had allegedly done this because West knew him.

Allen's wife Mary gave evidence next. She said she deeply hated Evans now, although she had visited Evans home and implied to people she was his wife, and they had shared the same bed, but denied they were lovers. Mary was cross-examined by Evans's council Mr Morris-Jones, Q.C., who insisted they were lovers. She denied this and said in that letters to her husband and Evans in prison she said she blamed everything on Evans, and that she was, ".... with Peter all the way".

In the witness box Evans admitted the iron-pipe used to kill John West was from Allen's house, but denied any knowledge of the knife. He maintained that Allen knocked at the door without him prompting him, and that after Allen had been let Allen he starting hitting West, who fled up the stairs, followed by Allen. Evans said he did not intervene because he panicked. He admitted stealing West's watch, but he believed West was still alive, when the pair fled. On the question of the knife, he denied disposing it in Windemere, but said he had seen Allen with a sheath some five to six weeks prior.

In his closing speech for the Crown, Mr Cantley, Q.C., said the fact West had been murdered by a brutal attack was not in dispute, and that theft had taken place, therefore it was legally capital murder. However under the terms of the Homicide Act (1957) it was only capital murder in respect of any person who *actually* killed or inflicted grievous bodily harm or tried to kill or do the former by his own hands. If the jury believed either Allen or Evans were merely bystanders, then that man would be guilty of non-capital murder. Similarly if it could not proved, who actually killed or struck West, then both men should be guilty only of non-capital murder.*(See Henry Mitchell and George Jones, 1959)*

Allen's counsel Mr Nance Q.C. submitted to the jury that his defendant's statement was the truthful one, and that if Allen did strike West it was not to kill or cause grievous bodily harm, and he did not know Evans would kill or cause grievous bodily harm to West, so the most Allen could be guilty of was manslaughter. Evans's counsel naturally switched the argument around in his client's favour.

After six days on Tuesday July 7th the trial concluded. Mr Justice Ashworth summed up. He told the jury that both men need not be guilty of capital or even plain murder, and that evidence given by each man to the police was not evidence against the other unless corroborated. He also caste doubt on the motives of Mary Allen, and suggested she had an obvious motive in making Evans the guilty man. The judge described Allen as slow and not very bright, who answered all his questions in a dull manner, but that Evans was boastful and quick to answer. But was Evans, the judge asked, truthful?

At 1.53 p.m. the jury, which included three women, retired, but were absent until 2.38 p.m., just 45 minutes! The foreman of the jury stated both men were guilty of capital murder. Both men declined to answer why the sentence according to the law should not be passed, then the judge told, "The law provides only one penalty for the crime of which, in my judgement, you have been rightly convicted. The sentence of the court is that you suffer death in the manner authorised by law. May the Lord have mercy on your soul".

In a tradition that dated back to the Middle Ages, the Under Sheriff of the county where the murder took place had to organise the execution. Mr Lionel Lightfoot held such a post in Cumberland. Since that county no longer had a prison equipped with a gallows, and since the Homicide Act (1957) "suggested" double hangings should be exacted in different prisons, the Under-Sheriff requested Harry Allen the "number one" to execute Gwynne Evans at Strangeways Prison, Manchester, and his usual assistant Les Stewart to hang Peter Allen at Walton Prison, Liverpool. Since verdicts involving death sentences for murder were automatically appealed, no exact date was fixed. On Monday July 20th the Court of Criminal Appeal in London consisting of the Lord Chief Justice, Lord Parker, and Lord Justices Winn and Widgery sat. Lord Parker in dismissing the appeal said, "A more brutal murder it would be difficult to imagine. The court is unable to find any substance in the criticisms on behalf of these two appellants. "

Although no one knew it would be the last hanging in the British Isles, it was to be the first since December 1963, and the lack of public and private protest is remarkable. No questions were asked in Parliament, no petitions nation-wide or local, so an event of subsequent historic magnitude passed by almost unnoticed. Even the *Daily Mirror*, the only national newspaper in 1964, to oppose the death penalty recorded the whole event in nine lines. It stated that Gwynne Evans was hanged (by Harry Allen) at Strangeways Prison at 8.00 a.m., and that there were no demonstrations. At Walton Prison, there was an all night vigil by two known abolitionists Mr Robert Burt of Portishead, Somerset, and Mr Roger Moody of Bristol. In Bristol a crowd gathered bare headed outside the cathedral in silence awaiting the dread hour.

On Wednesday August 12th, the day before the hanging **[Thursday, August 13th, 1964]**, Mary Allen visited her husband for the very last time, with her two children. The decision of the Home Secretary, Henry Brooke not to order a reprieve was already known. Allen went berserk. He threw himself against the bulletproof glass breaking his wrist in the process. A number of warders had to drag him back to the death-cell. Earlier in the day the mothers of both men sent telegrams to the Queen, who was at Balmoral, asking for mercy on the grounds of their age and mental state.

At Walton demonstrators passed out leaflets stating that had both men not stolen anything, then they could not have been sentenced to death. At 8.00 a.m., forty people bowed, as the prison clock chimed. Allen's executioner Robert Stewart noted in his diary that Allen had, ".....smashed his head against a wall during his last visit and broke a finger. As I was strapping his wrist in the morning, he shouted, "Jesus". That was it. Not another word".

On Friday October 16th, 1964, after 13 years of continuous Tory government the Labour Party were elected with a working majority of just five! The arch-abolitionist Sidney Silverman, M.P., assured by the new Labour administration, that there would never be another hanging under a Labour government launched his final successful Murder (Abolition of the Death Penalty) Bill. The bill passed its first reading on Monday December 21st, and the new Home Secretary, Frank Soskice, "let it be known" publicly through the media, that all murderers, who had been sentenced to death, would be reprieved. However "officially" since the bill did not became law until November 1965, it was only a "factor" in deciding whether to commute the death sentence to life imprisonment.

Royal Assent was given to the act on Tuesday, November 9th, 1965. Between October 1964 and this date, 17 men were convicted of capital murder, and formally sentenced to death, and equally formally reprieved[i]. In 2004 the UK brought into force Protocol 13 of the European Convention on Human Rights which bans member states from restoring capital punishment under any circumstances ....

MATTHEW SPICER

MAY 2024

i   The seventeen men who were convicted of murder after October 1964 and sentenced to death were:

1) Ronald Cooper – Casino-worker shot dead with a revolver a businessman in a bungled payroll robbery at the victim's home in East London. Instead of the rope at Pentonville Prison he served nearly 15 years .... Cooper would soon know *officially* he wouldn't hang – exactly a week after he was told he would "suffer death in the manner authorised by law" the House of Commons voted overwhelmingly to abolish the death penalty for murder ....

2) Peter Dunford – A prisoner at HMP Wakefield he was party to a "gangland" murder, where a fellow prisoner was beaten to death with an iron-bar – he was sentenced to hang as he was already serving an indefinite sentence for another "gangland" murder committed in Sussex in 1963, when he was aged 17. He served just over 20 years ....

3) Glyndwr Evans – Driven by jealousy he blasted to death with a shotgun his pretty 18-year-old girlfriend at her place of work in South Wales – He was the last person to be under sentence of death in Wales – in Cardiff Prison - and he served nearly 11 years ....

4) Laurence Dean – Convicted of the murder by beating and kicking to death of a baby daughter and son in separate incidents when he lost his temper – the second was at the Gatehouse to Wadhurst Castle in Sussex .... he served just over 13 years ....

5) Joseph Lawrence – A Jamaican, who with a fellow countryman attacked and robbed an Indian clothes salesman, in his van in Wolverhampton. Lawrence who strangled the victim with his bare hands was sentenced to death and served 11 ½ years: the accomplice was given a life-sentence for murder; but on appeal this was reduced to a 7-year sentence for 'assisting an offender'

6) Ralph Robinson – A retired ex-soldier who driven with passion and jealousy shot dead with a rifle his girlfriend and her husband at their home in Bedford .... served just under 9 years ....

7-9) William Dunning, Michael Odam and John Simpson – Three burglars who in the course of robbing a gay police civilian worker in his home in West London beat him to death ..... They all served between 11 and 12 years ....

10) Richard Latham – Shot dead his married girlfriend with a revolver at her home in Leeds, where she had moved in with another man – motive jealousy .... served 14 years ....

11) Michael Copeland – Serial killer – killed a teenage boy whilst in the Army in Germany and two gay men in Derbyshire, all of whom were stabbed in 1960 and 1961 .... Served nearly 34 years .... He was recalled to prison in 2009 and died in custody in November 2013 ....

12) John Stoneley – With an iron-bar beat to death during a robbery a taxi-driver in Hampshire .... Served just under 10 years: an accomplice was convicted of murder and served 7 years of a life-sentence ....

      13) Frank Pockett – Killed a scrap-dealer and ex-employer in Derbyshire with blows from a hammer whilst robbing his house from where he ran his business – served just under 10 years .... [He was sentenced to death on his 28th birthday]

      14) Frederick Williams – Shot dead with a shotgun his ex-girlfriend's mother-in-law at her home thinking his ex-girlfriend's new *husband* would have opened the door .... Served just over 12 years ....

      15) Henry Burgess – Married serving Police-Officer he shot dead with a revolver his girlfriend, a nurse, nearly 20 years his junior, at her home in East London when she said she no longer wanted to see him .... Served just over 12 years ....

      16) David Wardley – A Borstal Youth who had absconded and returned to his home town of Wolverhampton, where he stabbed to death a detective-sergeant who'd tried to arrest him outside a shop. He remains in custody having served nearly 60 years and is one of Britain's longest serving killers ....

      17) David Chapman – Along with an accomplice, who was convicted of a lesser crime, Chapman broke into a swimming pool in Scarborough to rob it, when they were disturbed by a night-watchman whom Chapman drowned. The last person in Britain to be told he would die on the gallows, Chapman served just over 13 ½ years ....

      Thirty-three years later in 1998 the UK government abolished the death penalty for high treason and under military law

Printed in Great Britain
by Amazon

50904698R00178